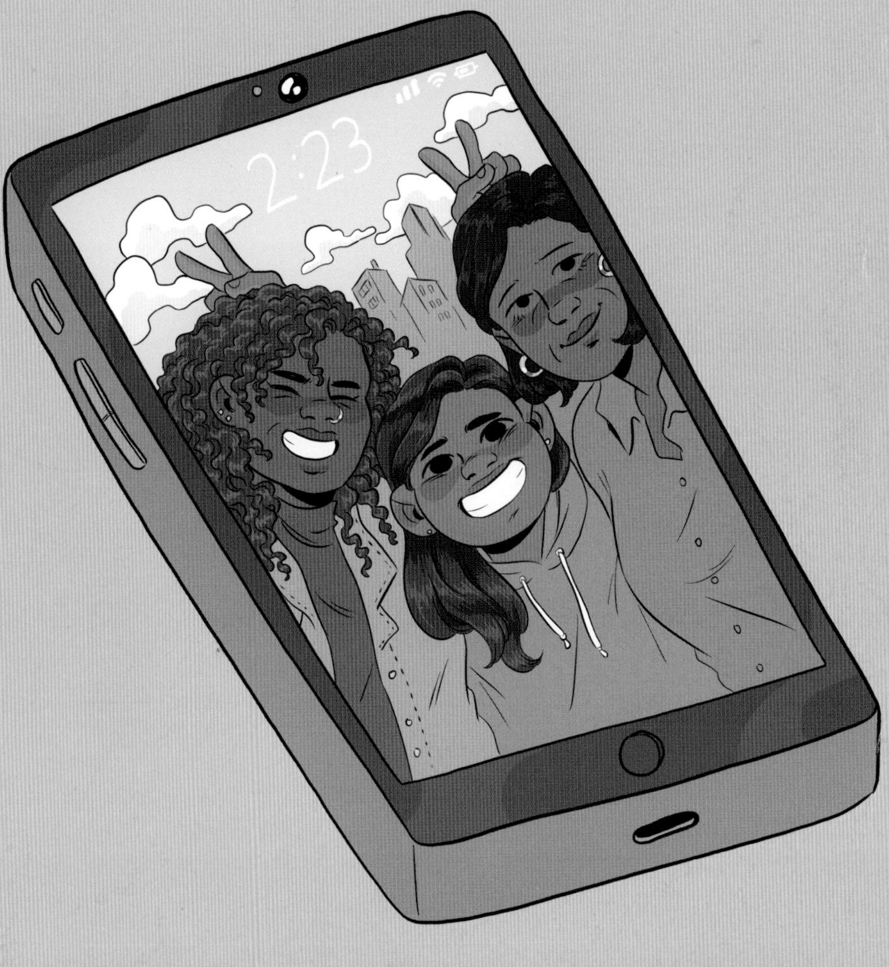
2:23

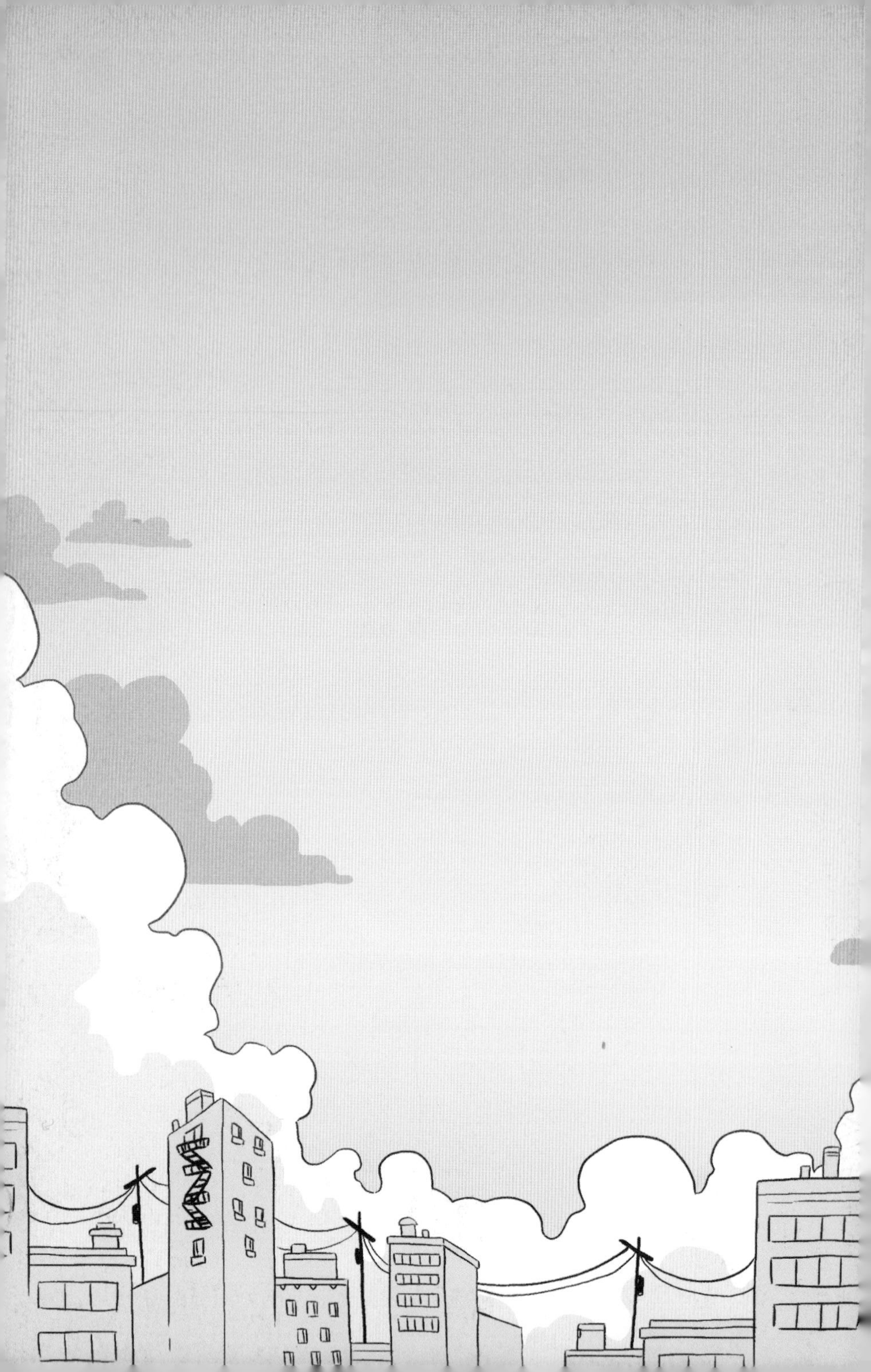

FRIZZY

written by
CLARIBEL A. ORTEGA

art by
ROSE BOUSAMRA

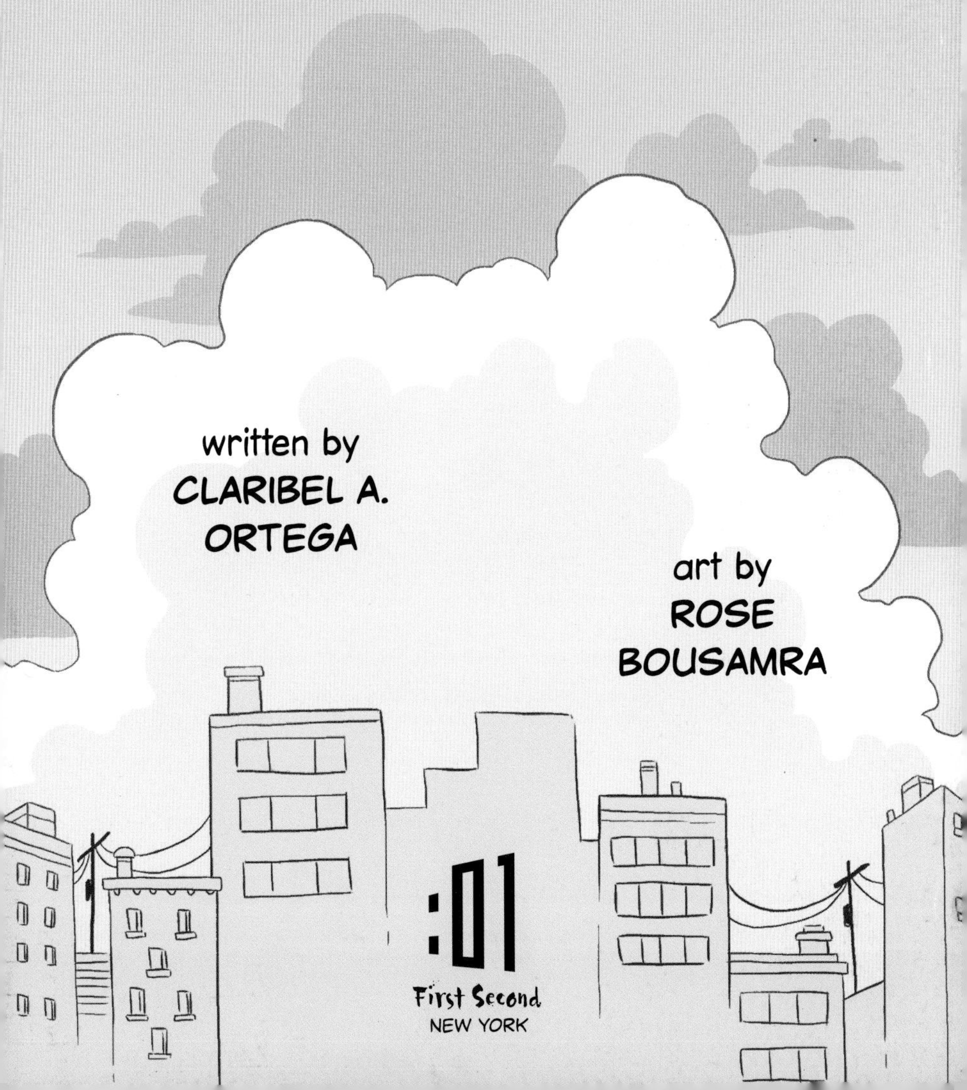

:01
First Second
NEW YORK

Published by First Second
First Second is an imprint of Roaring Brook Press,
a division of Holtzbrinck Publishing Holdings Limited Partnership
120 Broadway, New York, NY 10271
firstsecondbooks.com
mackids.com

Library of Congress Cataloging-in-Publication Data is available.

Our books may be purchased in bulk for promotional, educational,
or business use. Please contact your local bookseller or the Macmillan
Corporate and Premium Sales Department at (800) 221-7945 ext. 5442
or by email at MacmillanSpecialMarkets@macmillan.com.

First edition, 2022
Edited by Kiara Valdez
Cover design by Kirk Benshoff
Interior book design by Sunny Lee and Yan Moy

Penciled digitally with Clip Studio Paint. Inked with a
G-pen style digital nib and colored digitally with Clip Studio Paint.

Printed in October 2022 in China by 1010
Printing International Limited, Kwun Tong, Hong Kong

ISBN 978-1-250-25963-9 (paperback)
1 3 5 7 9 10 8 6 4 2

ISBN 978-1-250-25962-2 (hardcover)
1 3 5 7 9 10 8 6 4 2

Don't miss your next favorite book from First Second! For the latest
updates go to firstsecondnewsletter.com and sign up for our enewsletter.

For Gigi, Josh, Evan, Samantha & Maia.
You're perfect, however you choose to be.

—Claribel

For my sisters, Brittany and Cece.
It was your boundless love and support
that made this book what it is today.

—Rose

EL SALON

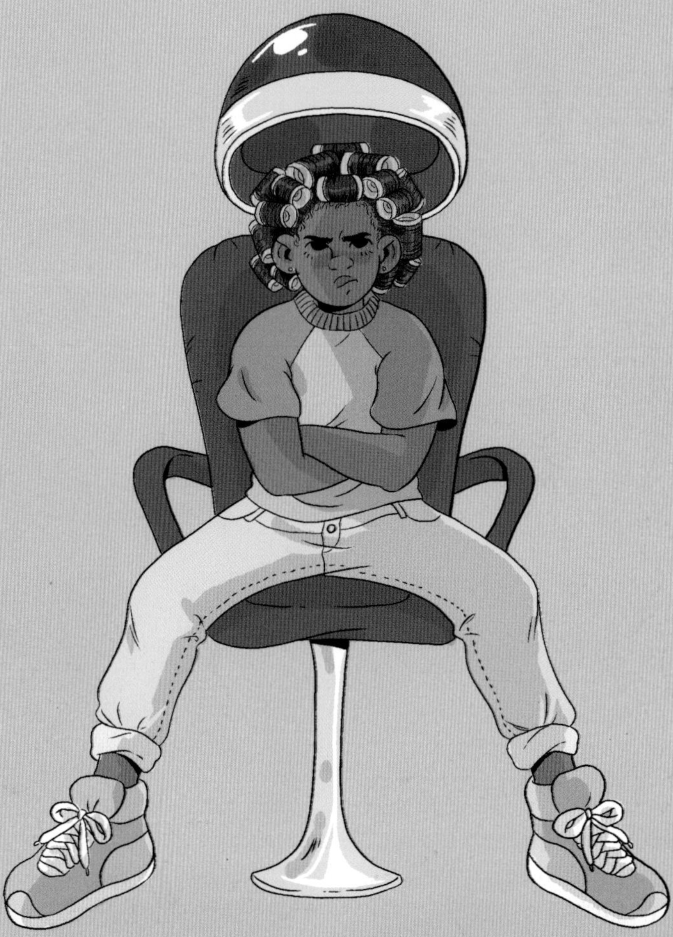

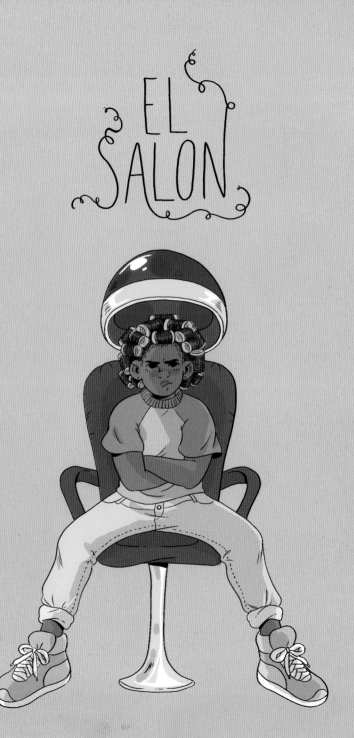

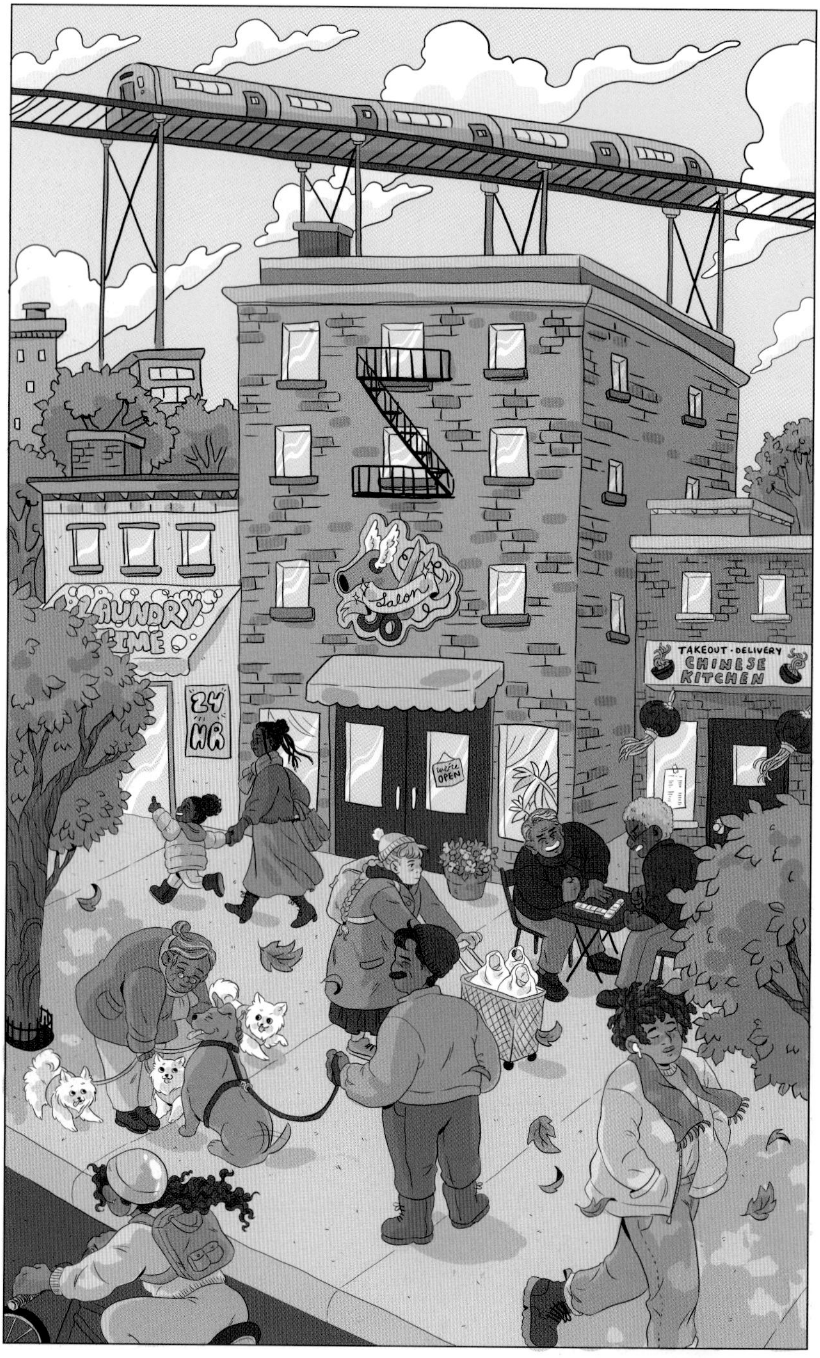
LAUNDRY TIME
24 HR
Salon
we're OPEN
TAKEOUT · DELIVERY
CHINESE KITCHEN

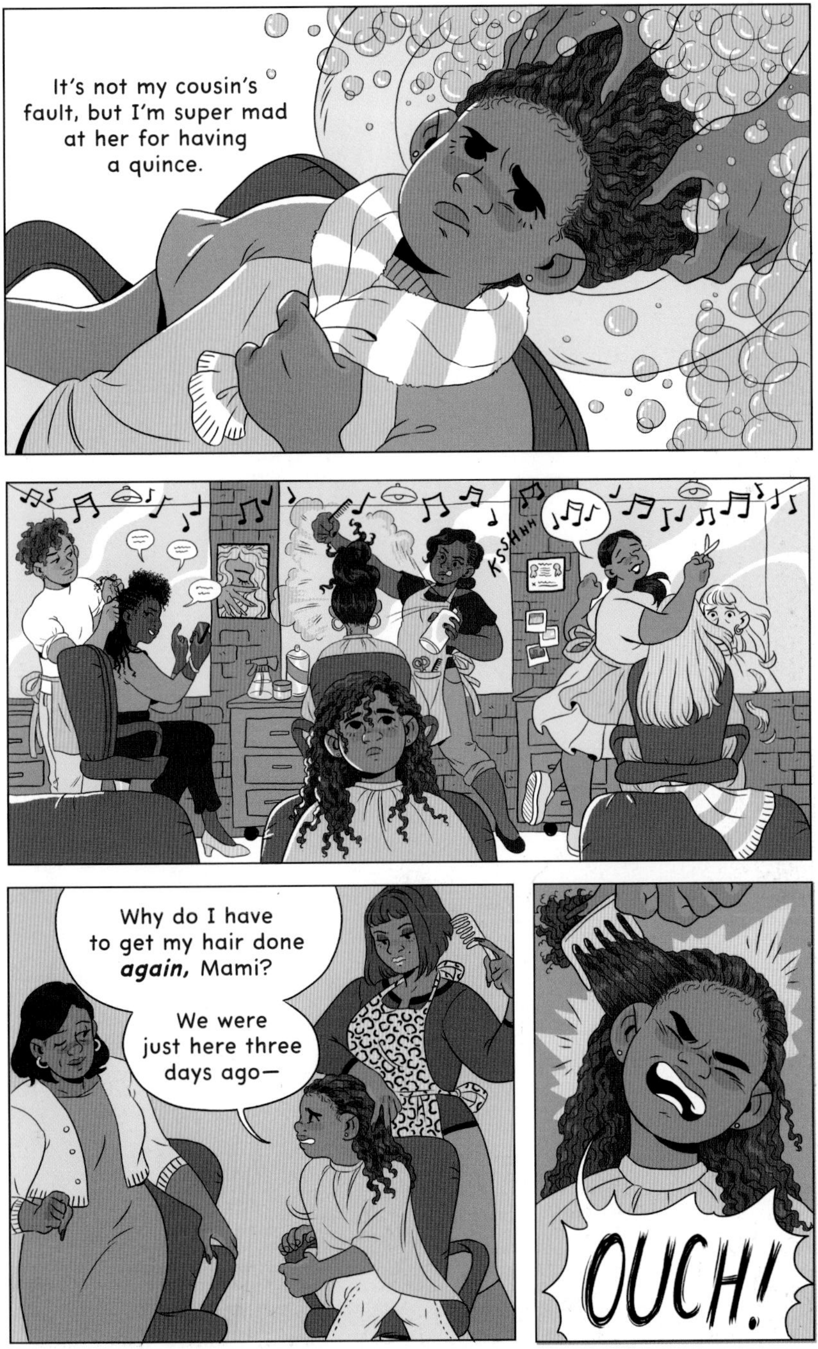
It's not my cousin's fault, but I'm super mad at her for having a quince.
KSSHHH
Why do I have to get my hair done *again*, Mami?
We were just here three days ago—
OUCH!

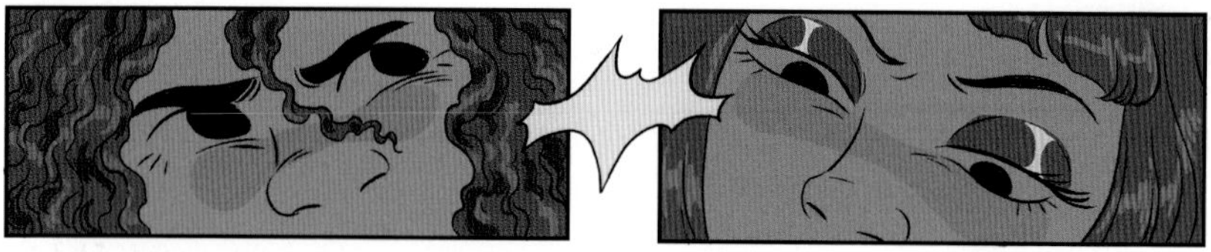

Gleny always made me feel like I was getting in trouble when she did my hair. As if my hair being curly and hard to detangle was ***my fault.***

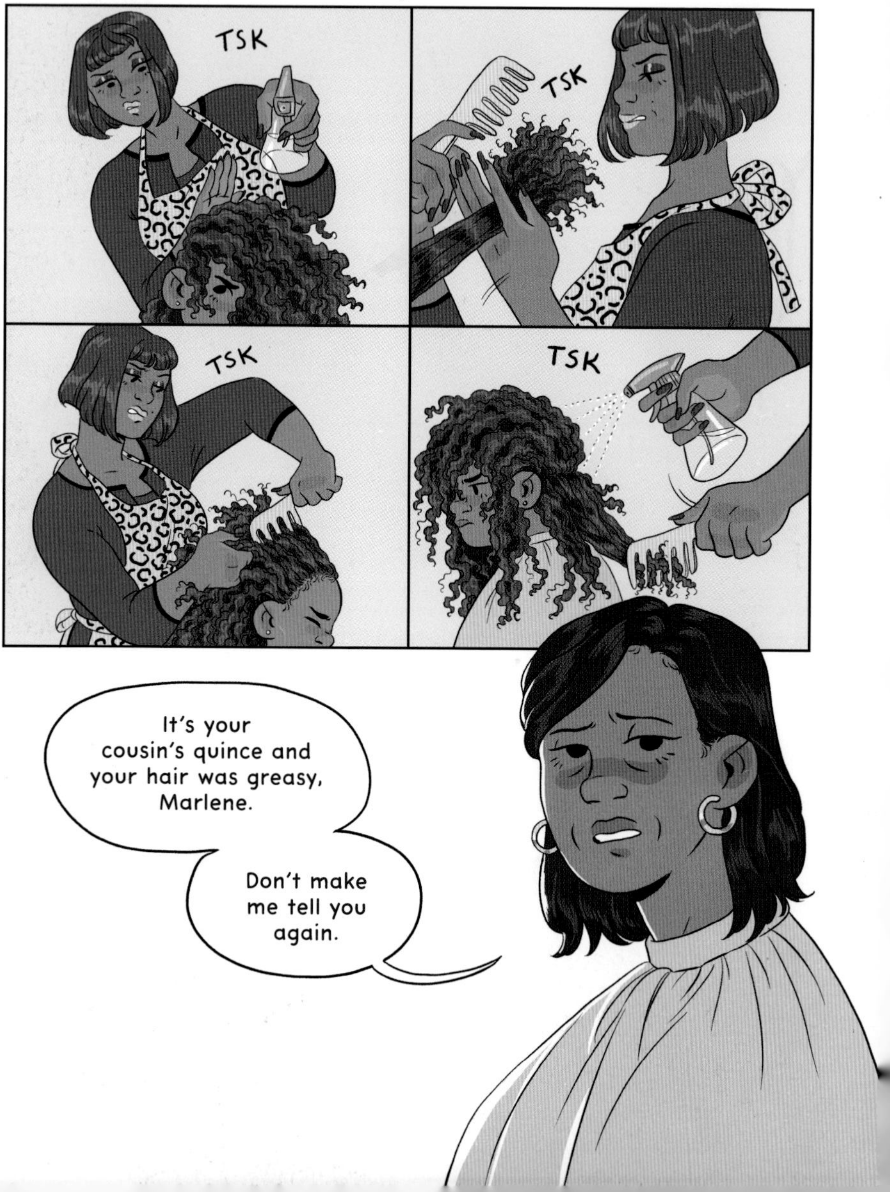
TSK
TSK
TSK
TSK
It's your cousin's quince and your hair was greasy, Marlene.
Don't make me tell you again.

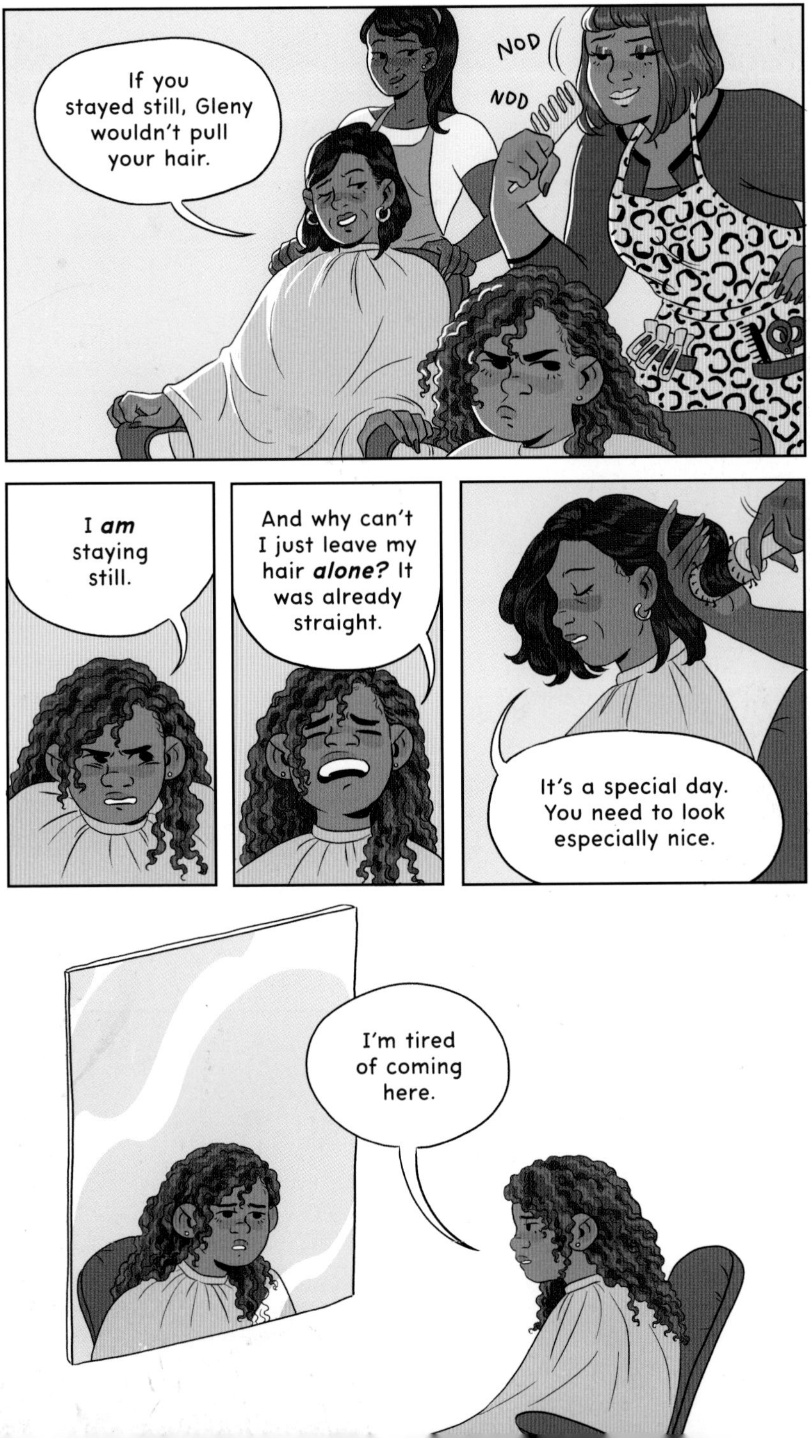
If you stayed still, Gleny wouldn't pull your hair.
NOD
NOD
I *am* staying still.
And why can't I just leave my hair *alone?* It was already straight.
It's a special day. You need to look especially nice.
I'm tired of coming here.

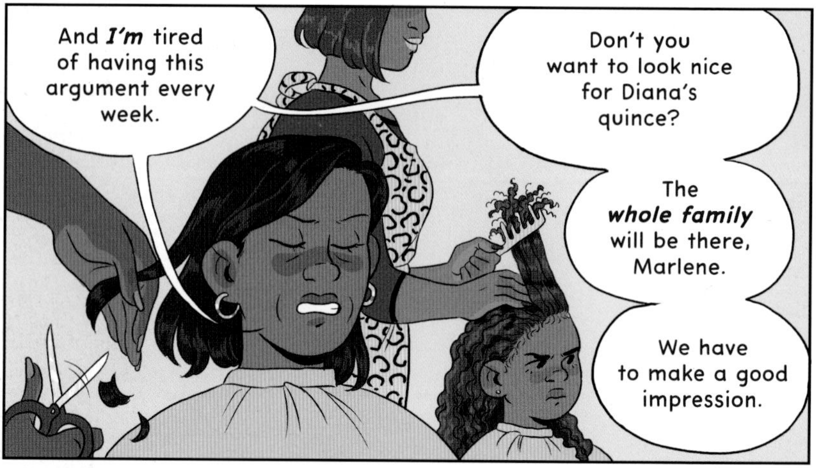
And *I'm* tired of having this argument every week.
Don't you want to look nice for Diana's quince?
The *whole family* will be there, Marlene.
We have to make a good impression.

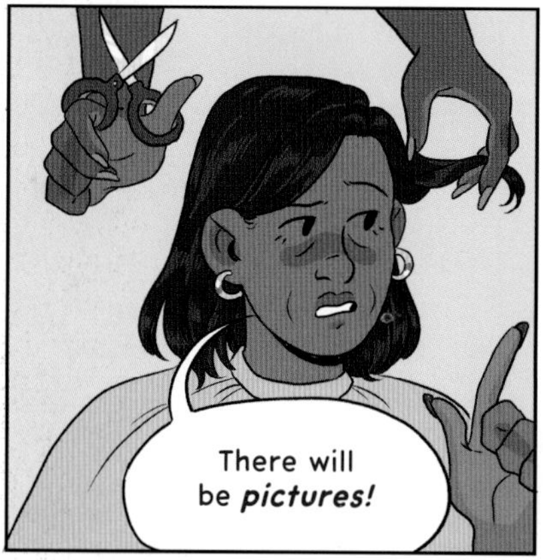
There will be *pictures!*

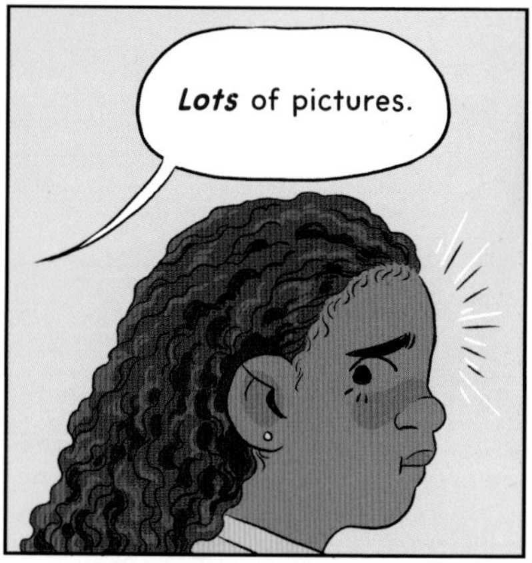
Lots of pictures.

I tried to focus on something else. ***Anything*** but how much my scalp already hurt and we hadn't even put the rollers in.

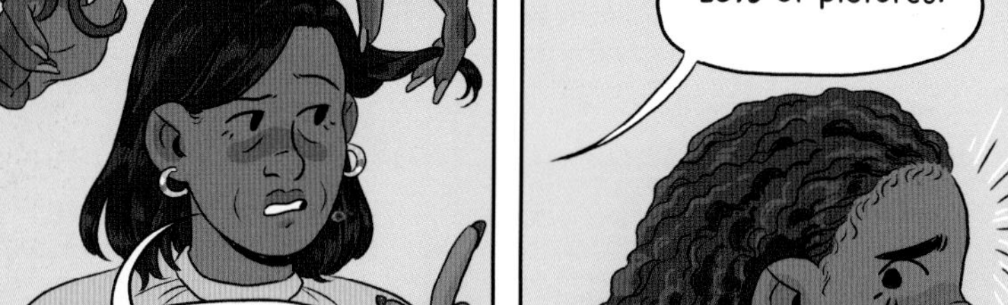

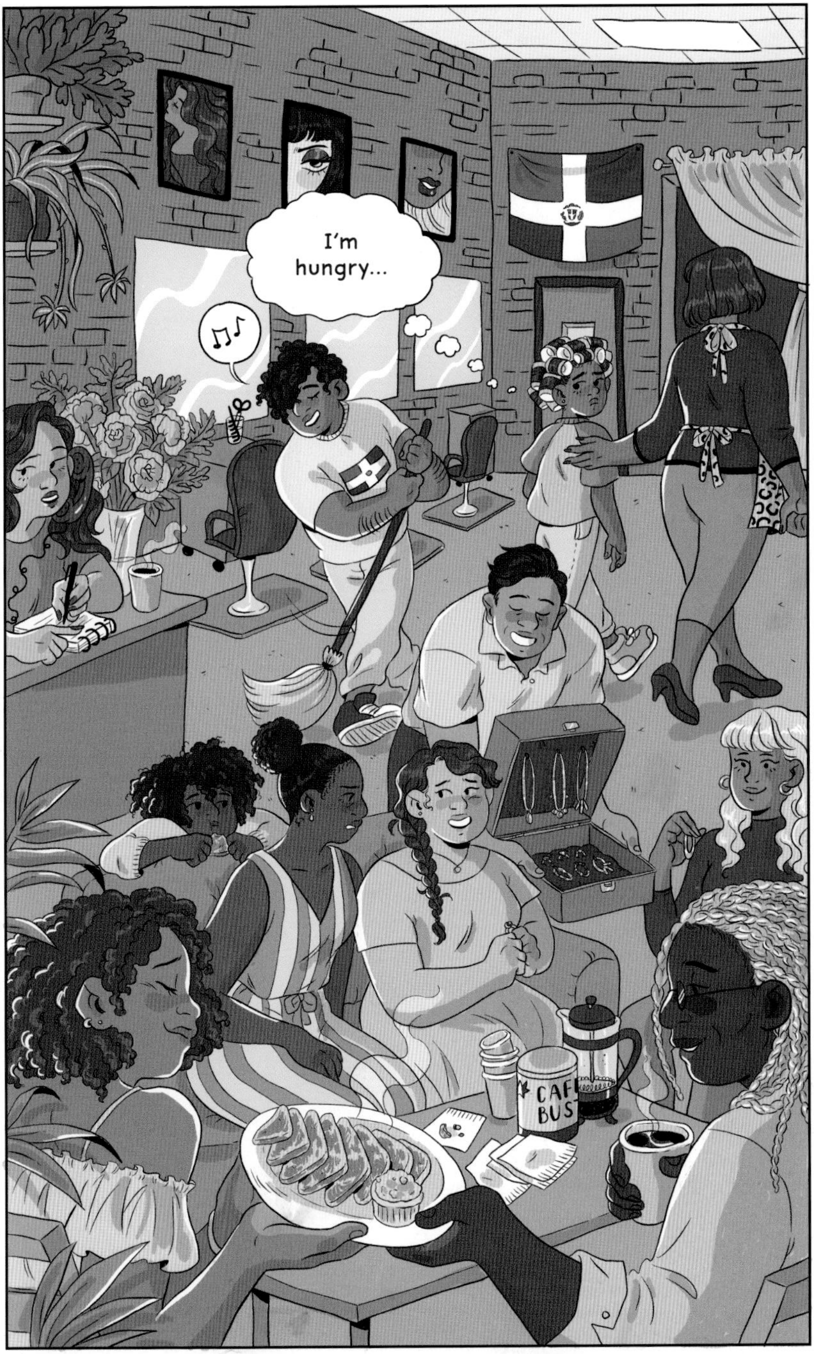
I'm hungry...
CAFE BUS

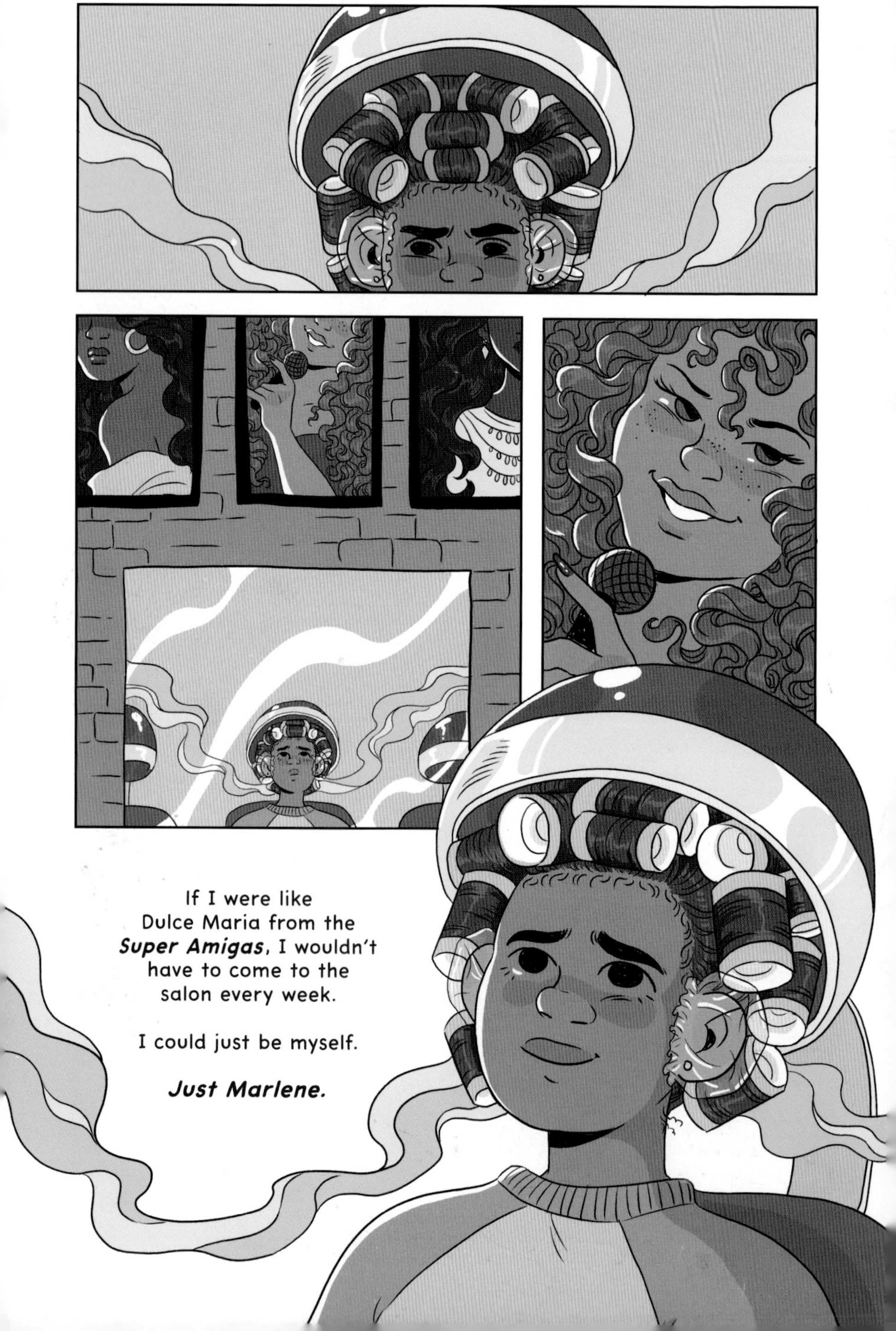
If I were like Dulce Maria from the *Super Amigas*, I wouldn't have to come to the salon every week.
I could just be myself.
Just Marlene.

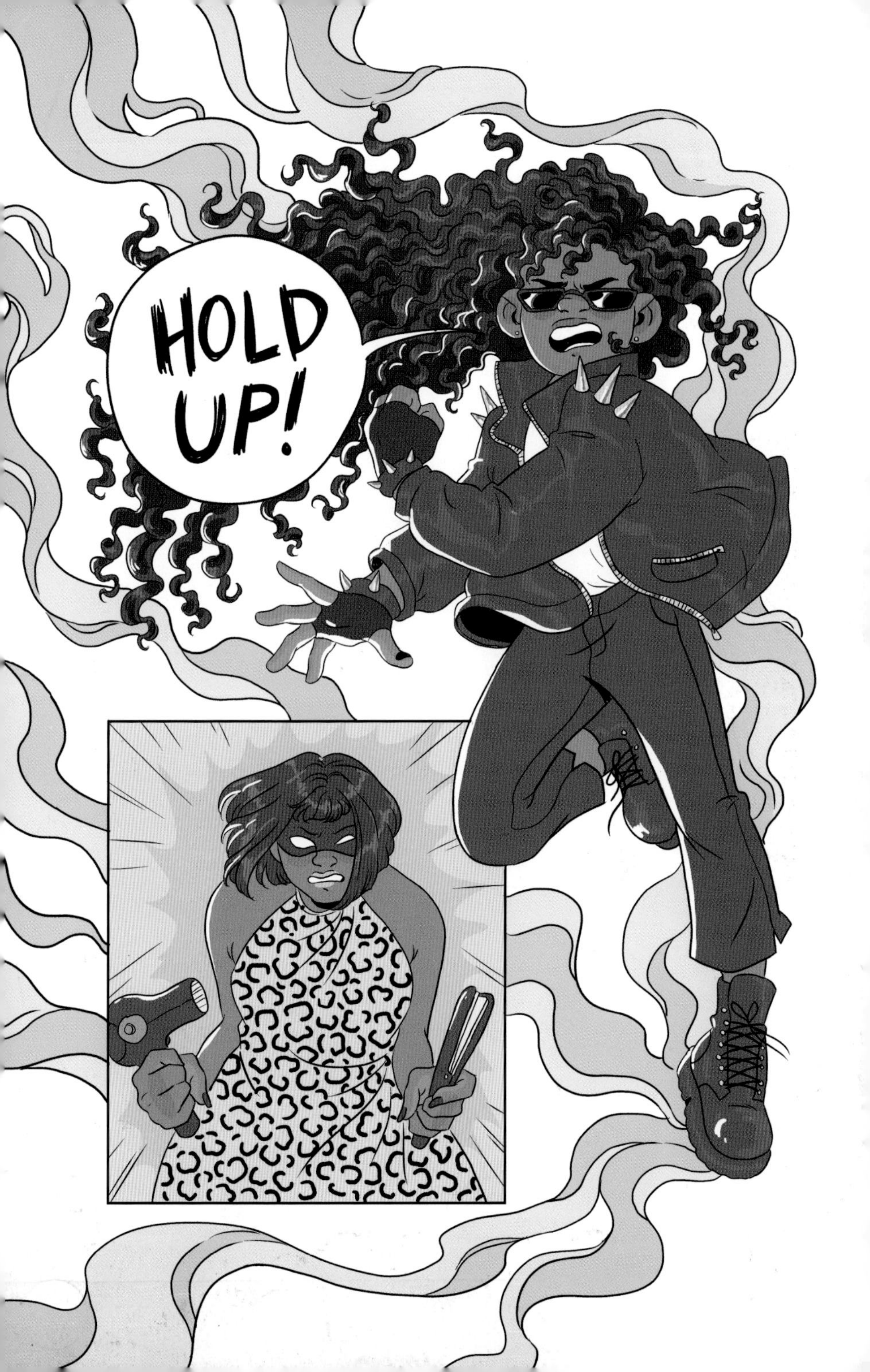
HOLD UP!

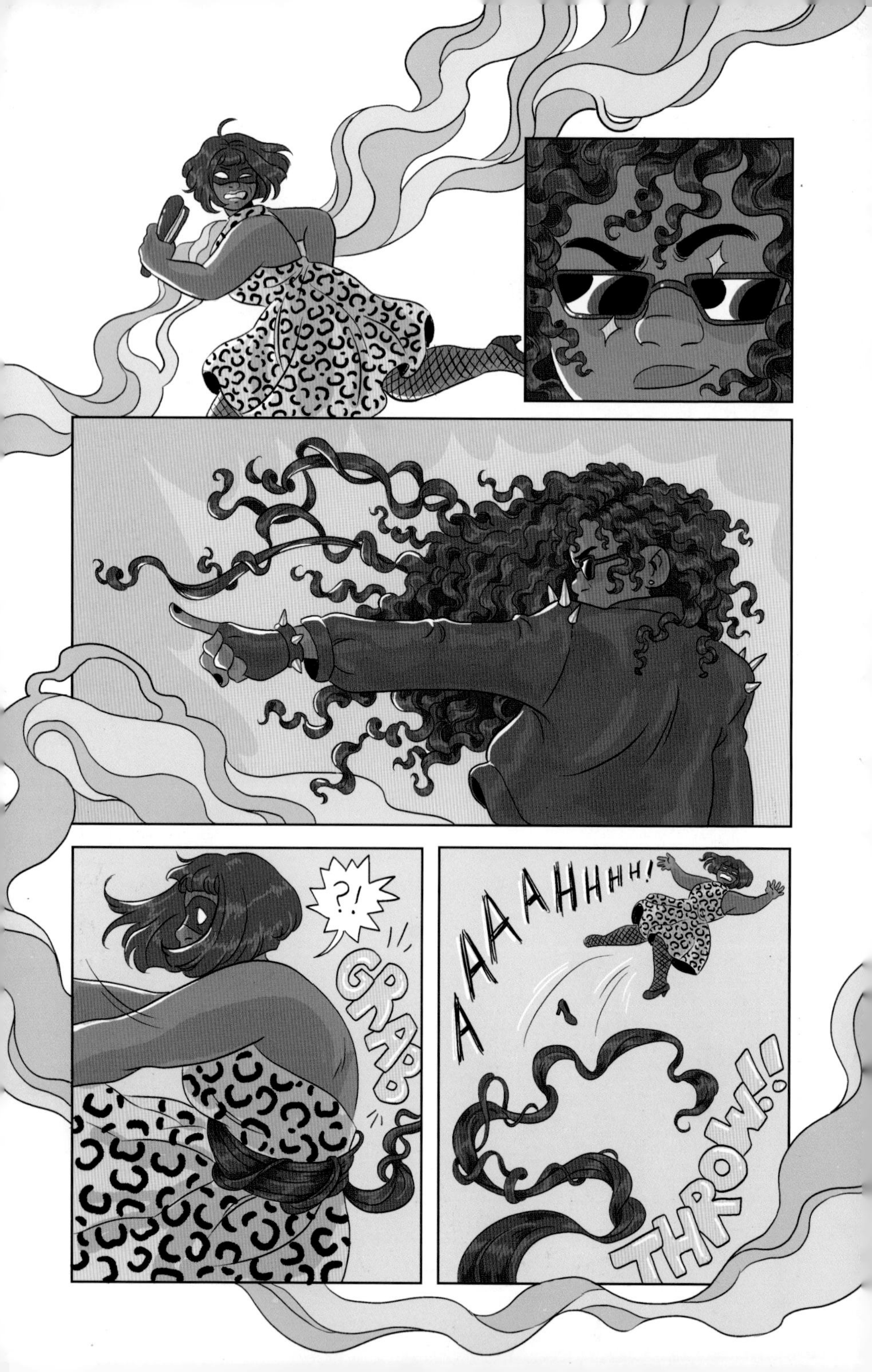
?!
GRAB
AAAAHHHH!
THROW!!

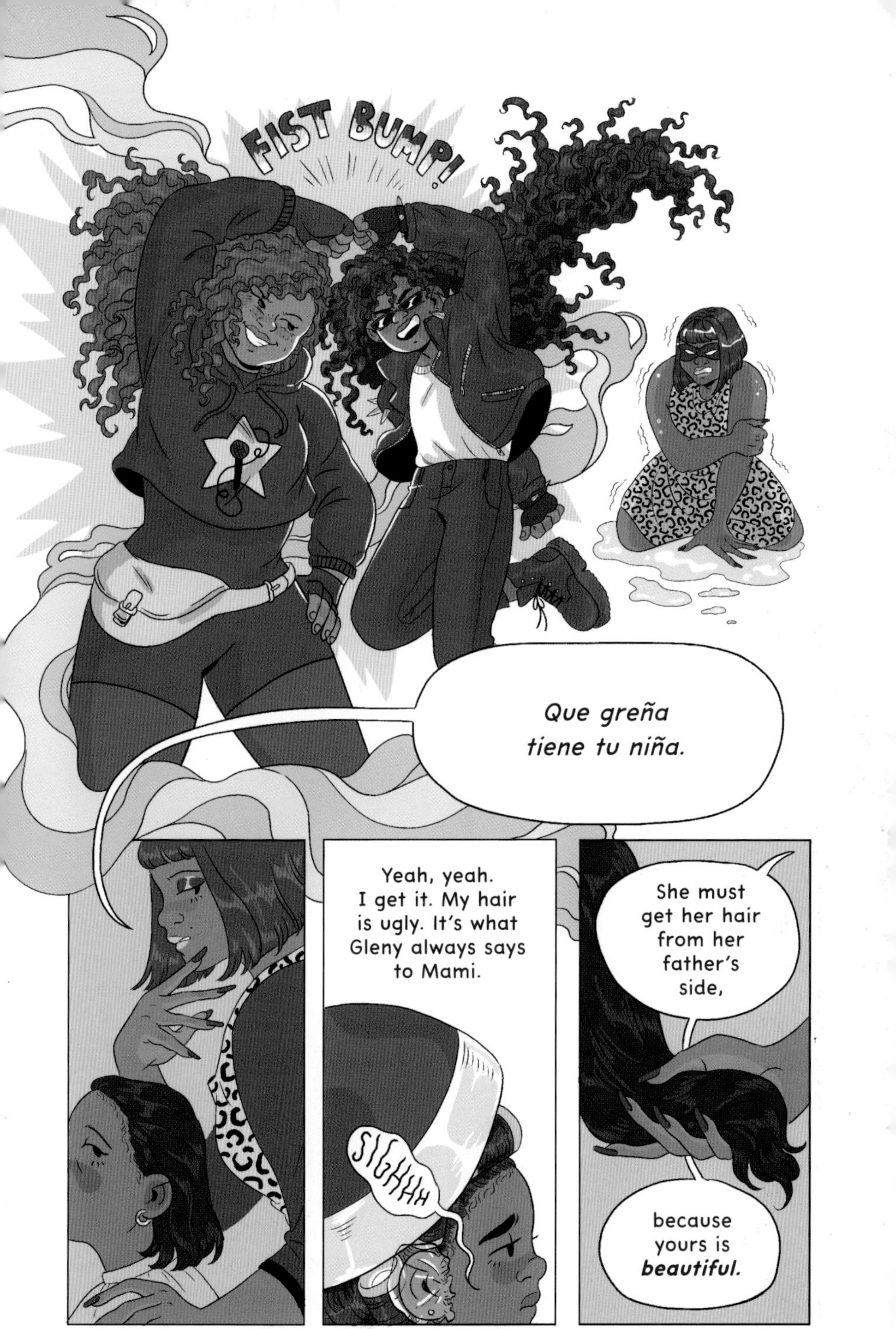
FIST BUMP!
Que greña tiene tu niña.
Yeah, yeah. I get it. My hair is ugly. It's what Gleny always says to Mami.
SIGHHH
She must get her hair from her father's side,
because yours is ***beautiful.***

It's taken a long time to get my hair under control.

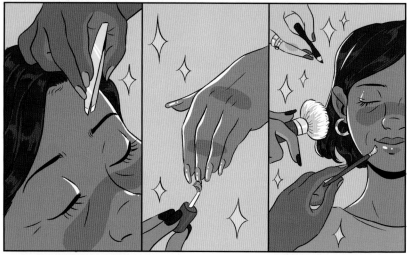

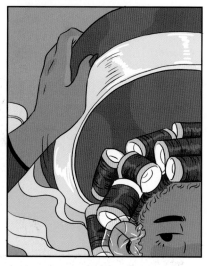

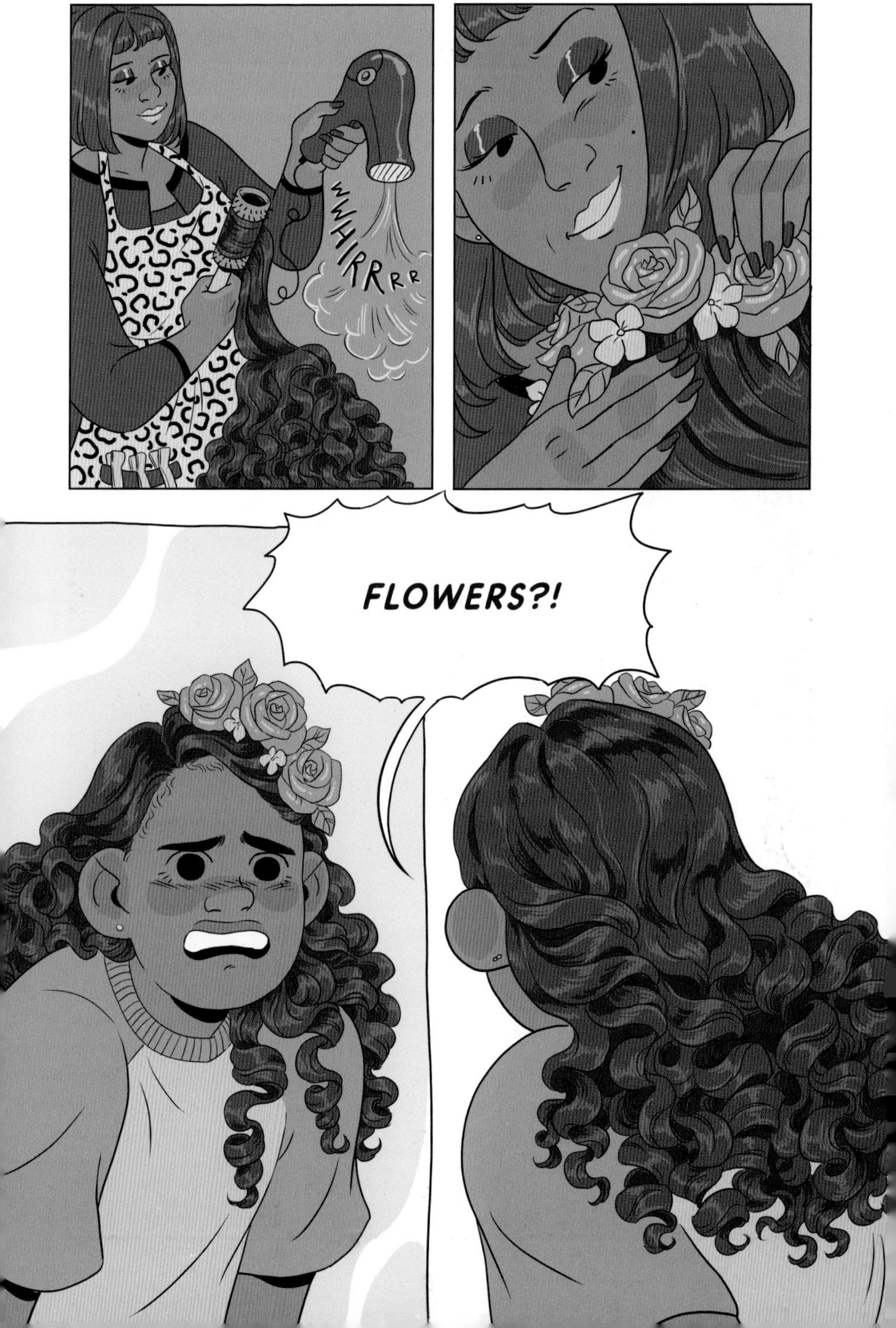
WWHIRRRrr
FLOWERS?!

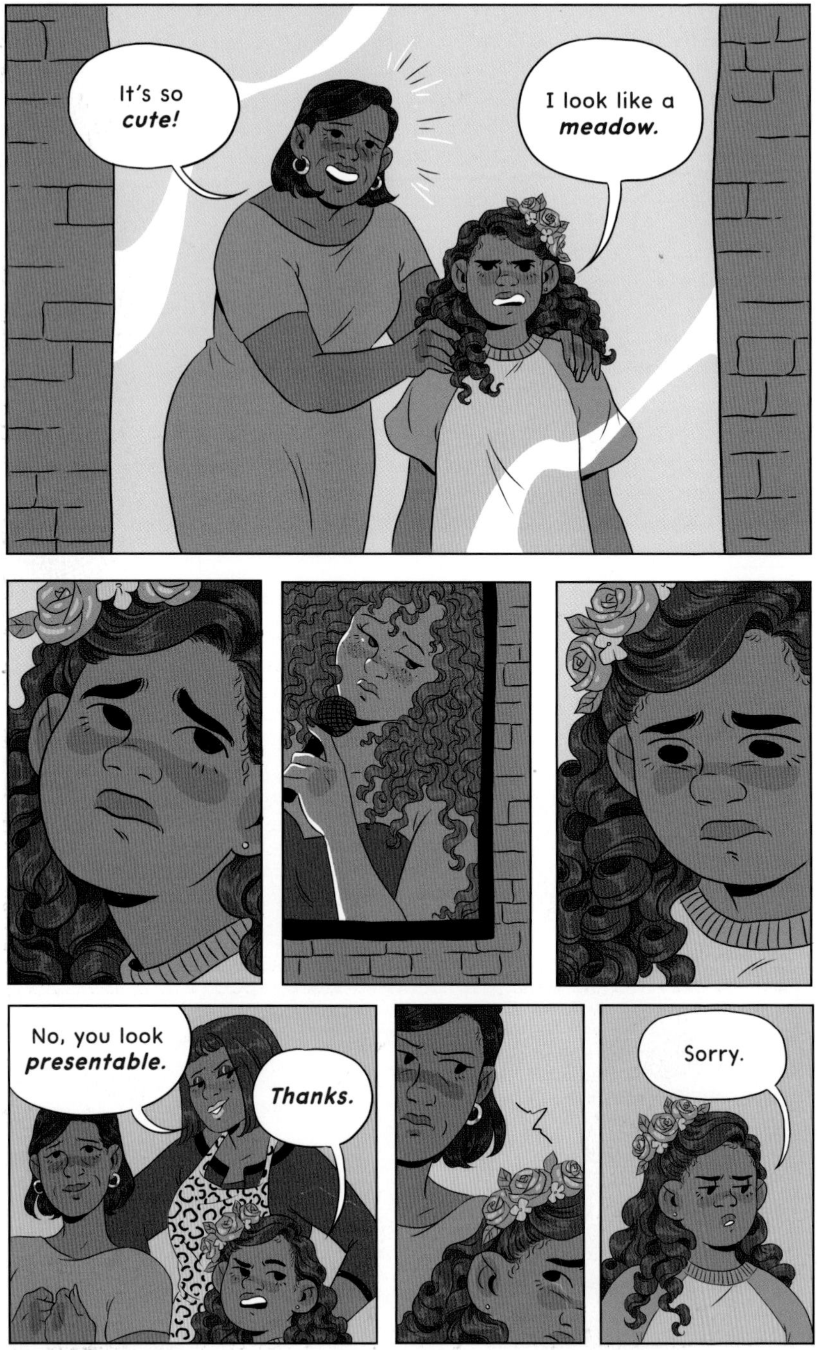
It's so *cute!*
I look like a *meadow.*
No, you look *presentable.*
Thanks.
Sorry.

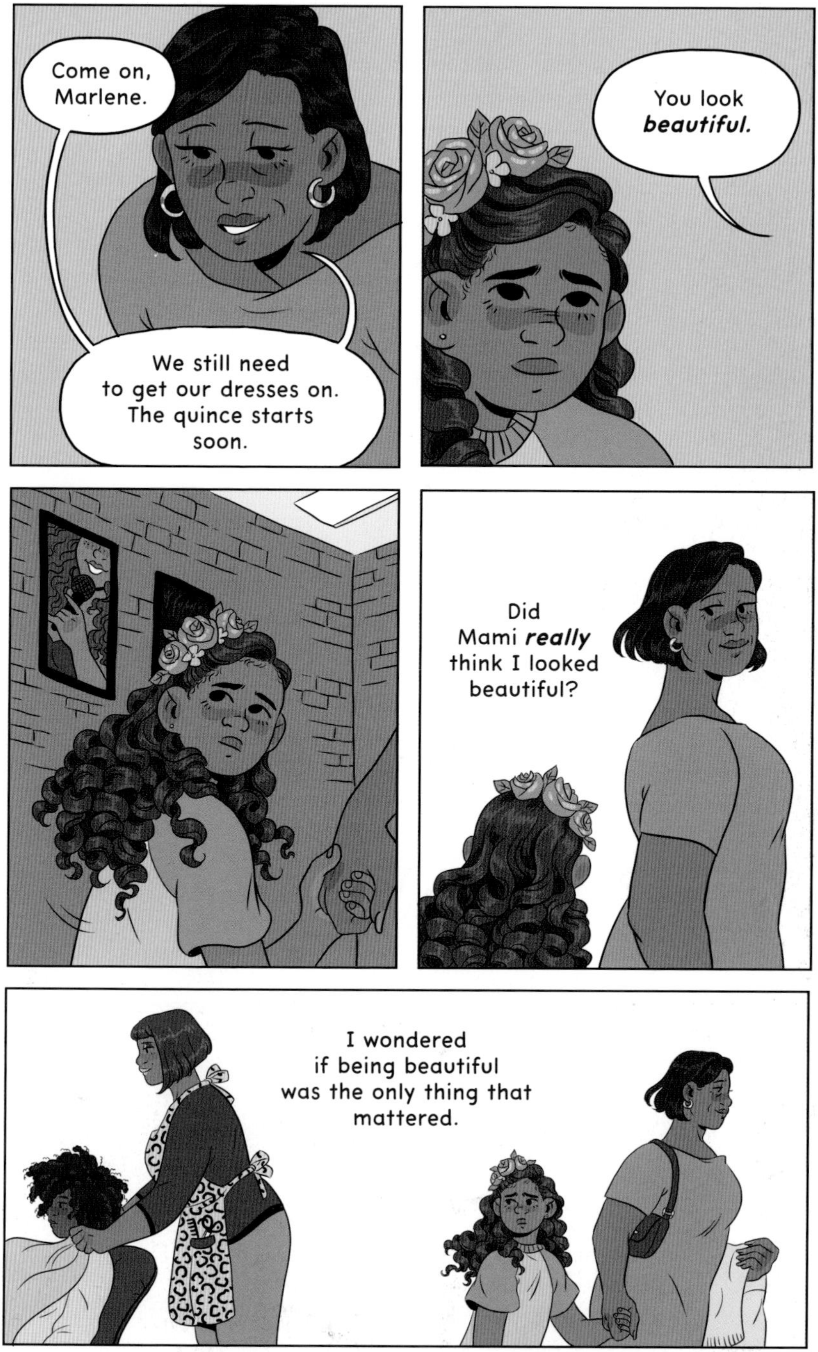
Come on, Marlene.
We still need to get our dresses on. The quince starts soon.
You look ***beautiful.***
Did Mami ***really*** think I looked beautiful?
I wondered if being beautiful was the only thing that mattered.

I had been to the salon a billion times before.
The salon was a Sunday tradition.

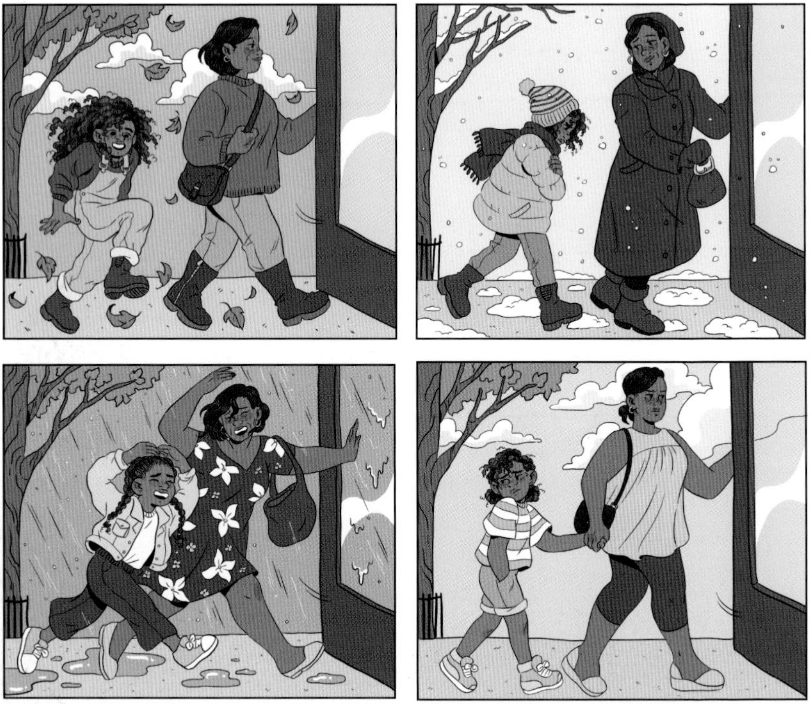

Every week without fail, we'd get on the subway, then the bus, then spend hours in the salon. Sometimes until the sun went down.

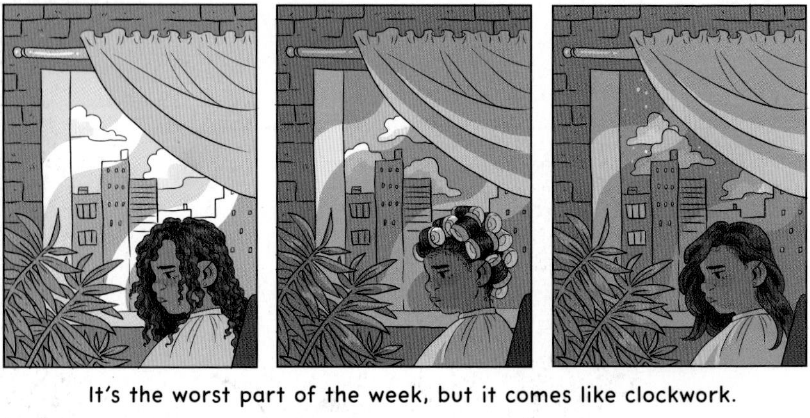

It's the worst part of the week, but it comes like clockwork.

At least it makes my mami happy.

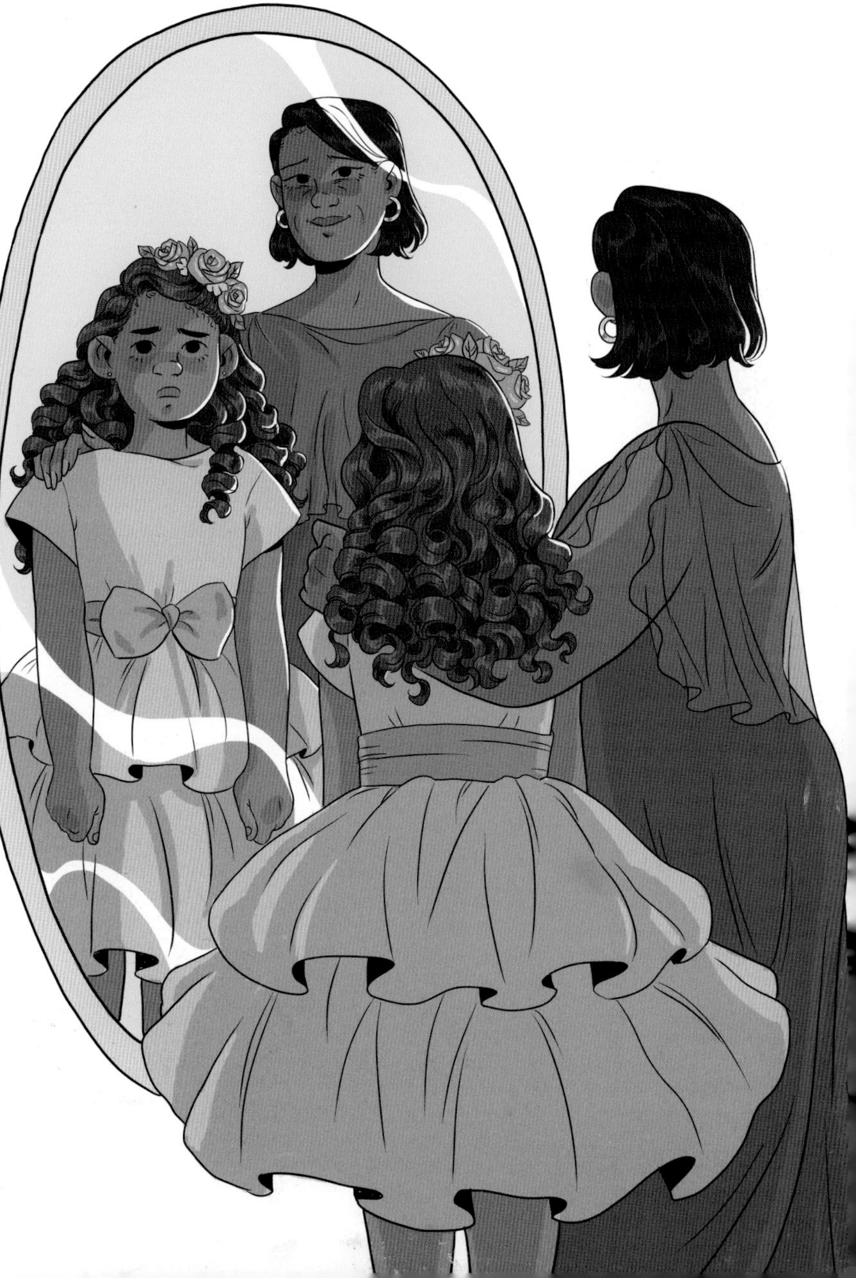

¡QUINCE!

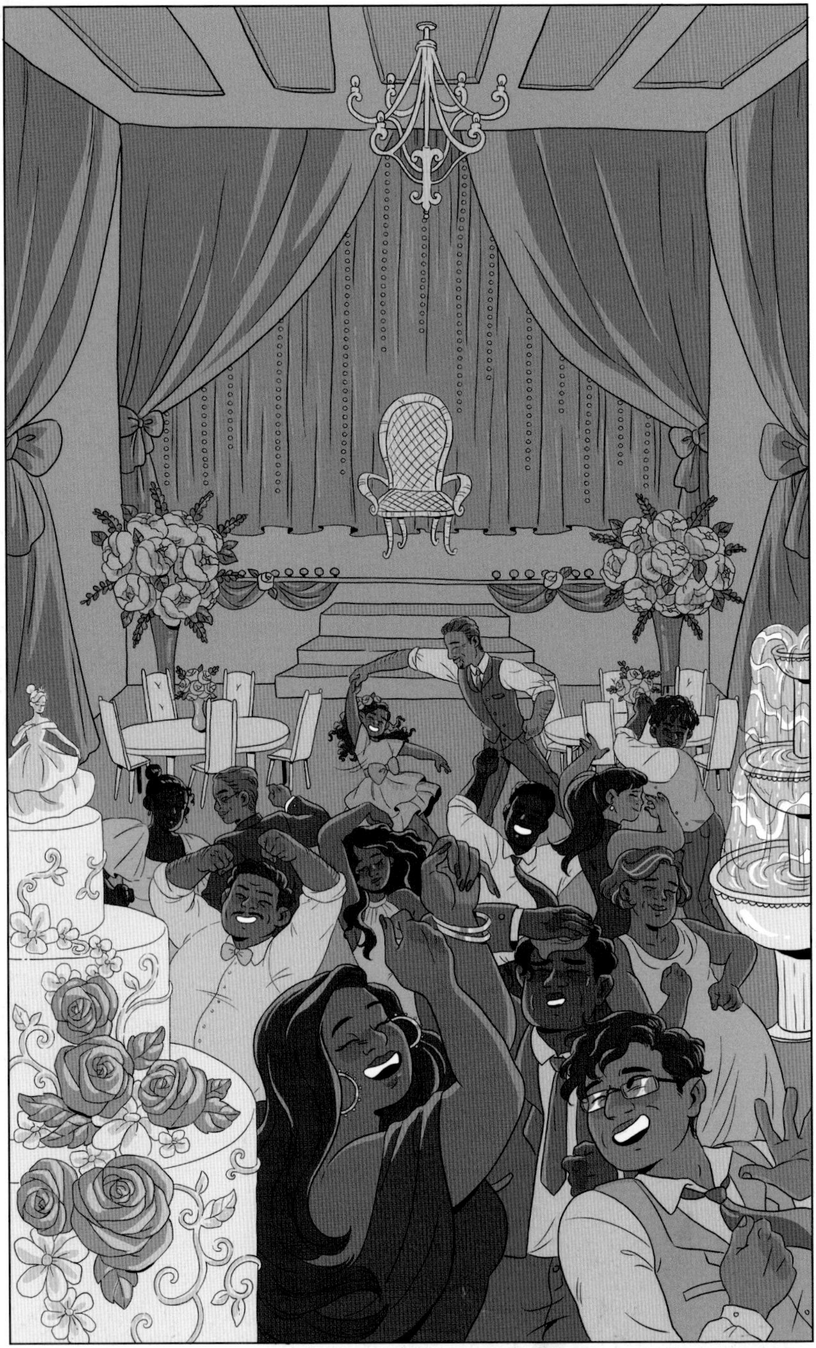

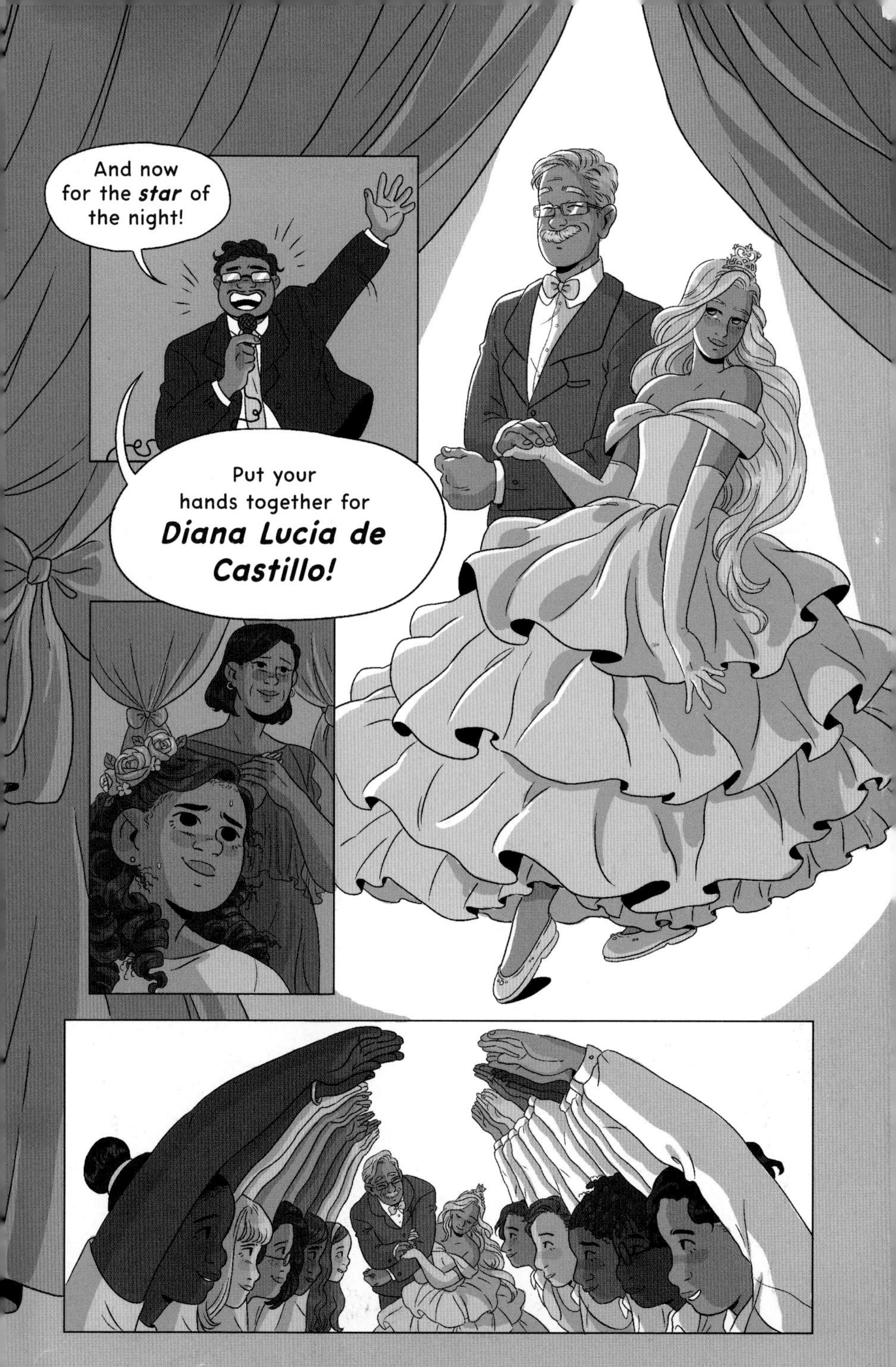
And now for the *star* of the night!
Put your hands together for ***Diana Lucia de Castillo!***

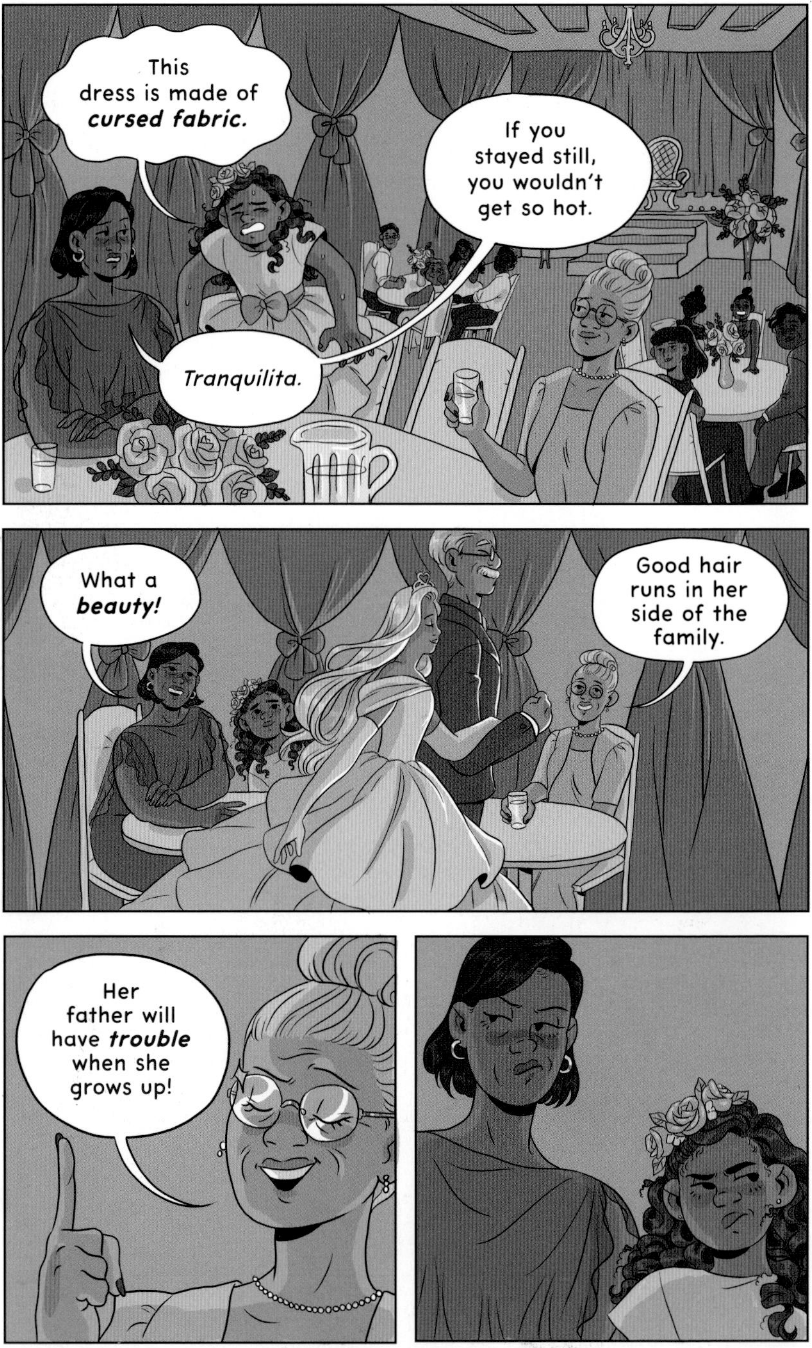
This dress is made of ***cursed fabric.***
If you stayed still, you wouldn't get so hot.
Tranquilita.
What a ***beauty!***
Good hair runs in her side of the family.
Her father will have ***trouble*** when she grows up!

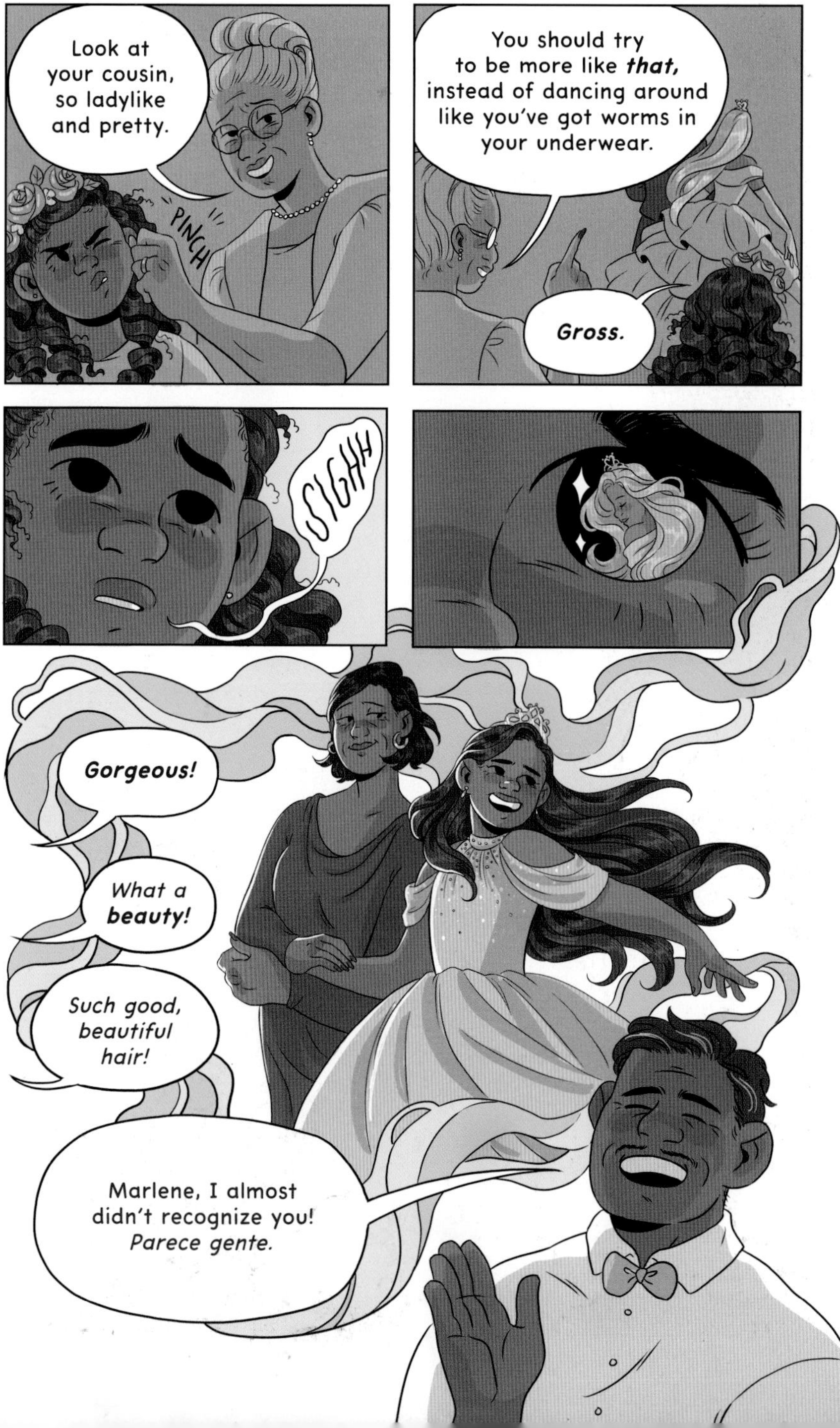
Look at your cousin, so ladylike and pretty.
PINCH
You should try to be more like ***that,*** instead of dancing around like you've got worms in your underwear.
Gross.
SIGHH
Gorgeous!
*What a **beauty!***
Such good, beautiful hair!
Marlene, I almost didn't recognize you! *Parece gente.*

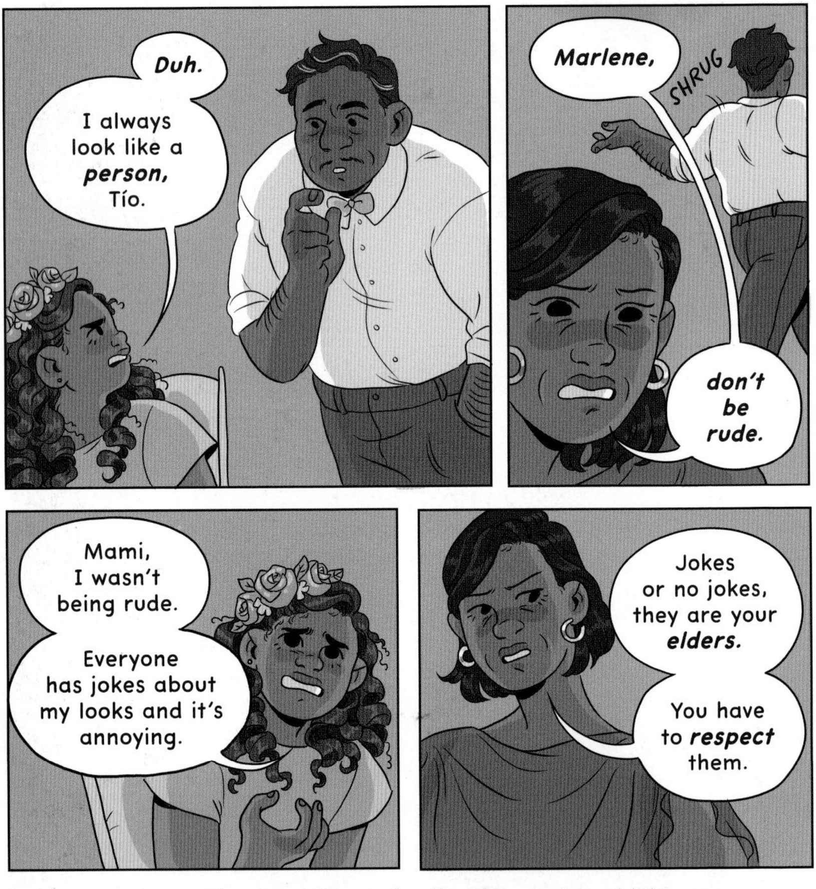
Duh.
I always look like a *person,* Tío.
Marlene,
SHRUG
don't be rude.
Mami, I wasn't being rude.
Everyone has jokes about my looks and it's annoying.
Jokes or no jokes, they are your *elders.*
You have to *respect* them.

It's always like this with my family. They make a billion mean or judgy comments and the moment I say one little thing, *I* get in trouble.

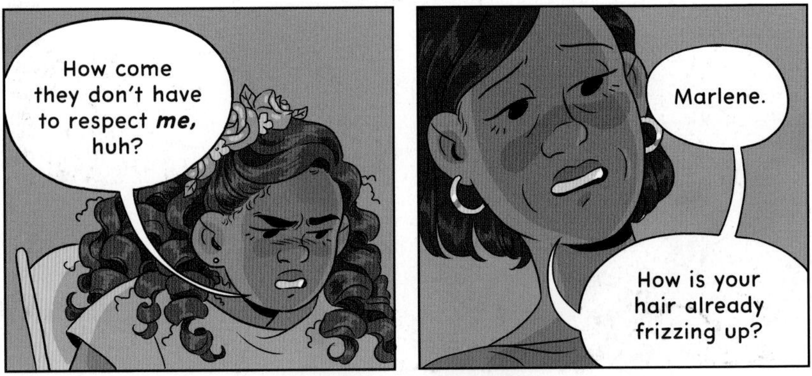
How come they don't have to respect *me,* huh?
Marlene.
How is your hair already frizzing up?

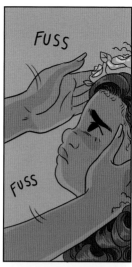

FUSS

FUSS

MWAH!

'Ción, Tía.

MWAH!

On a scale from one to ten, how *annoying* is everyone being tonight?

Oh you know. About a *twenty-seven.*

25

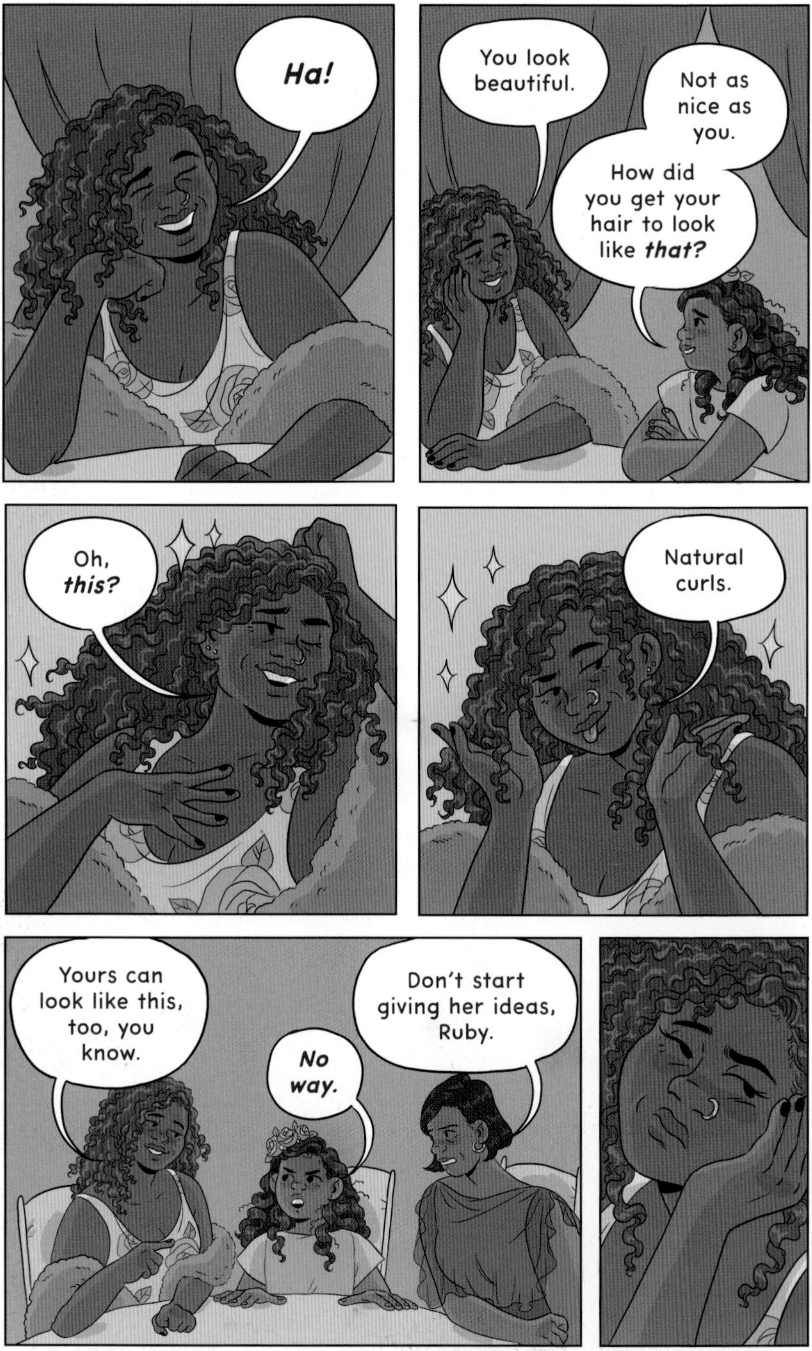
Ha!
You look beautiful.
Not as nice as you.
How did you get your hair to look like *that?*
Oh, *this?*
Natural curls.
Yours can look like this, too, you know.
No way.
Don't start giving her ideas, Ruby.

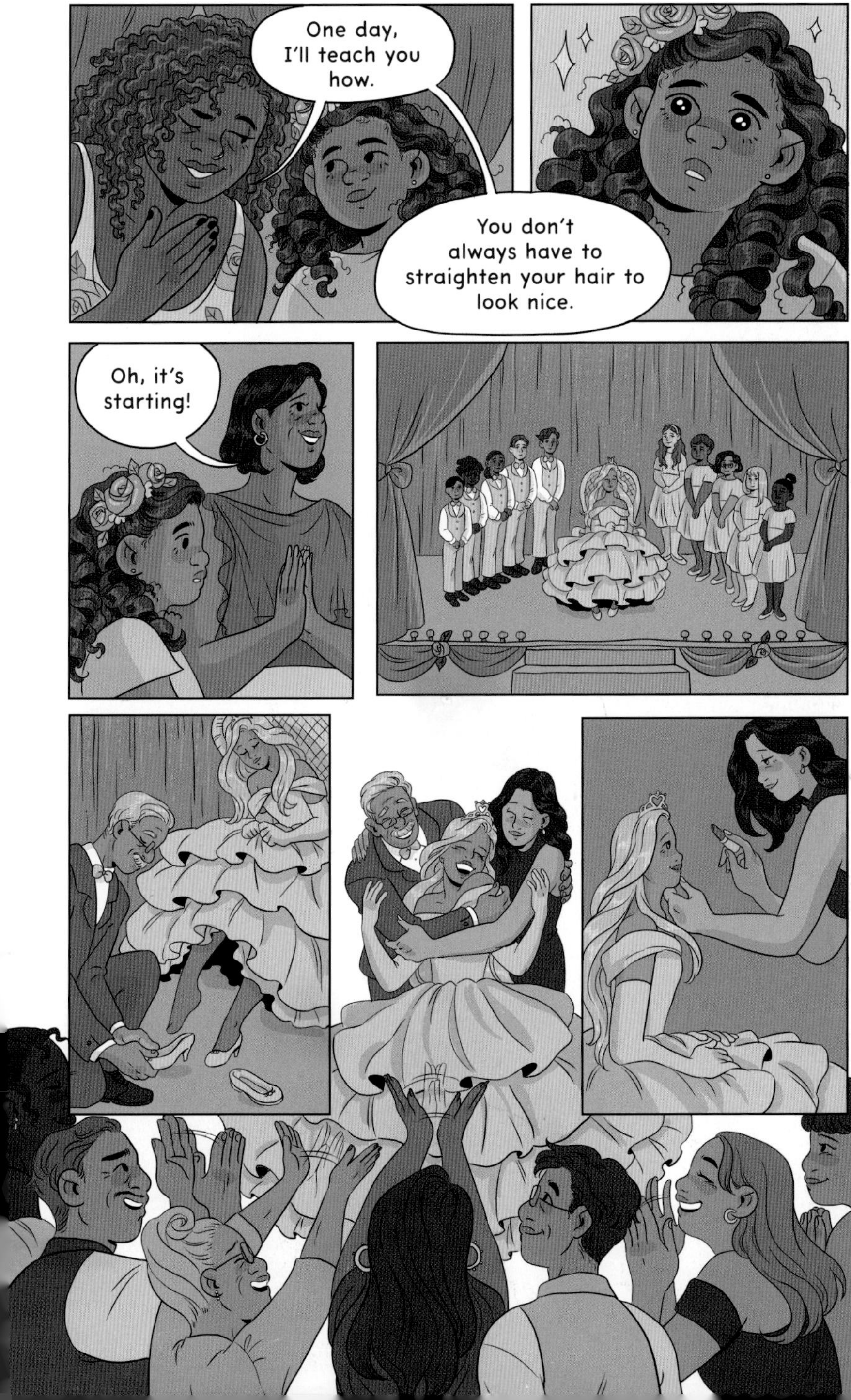
One day, I'll teach you how.
You don't always have to straighten your hair to look nice.
Oh, it's starting!

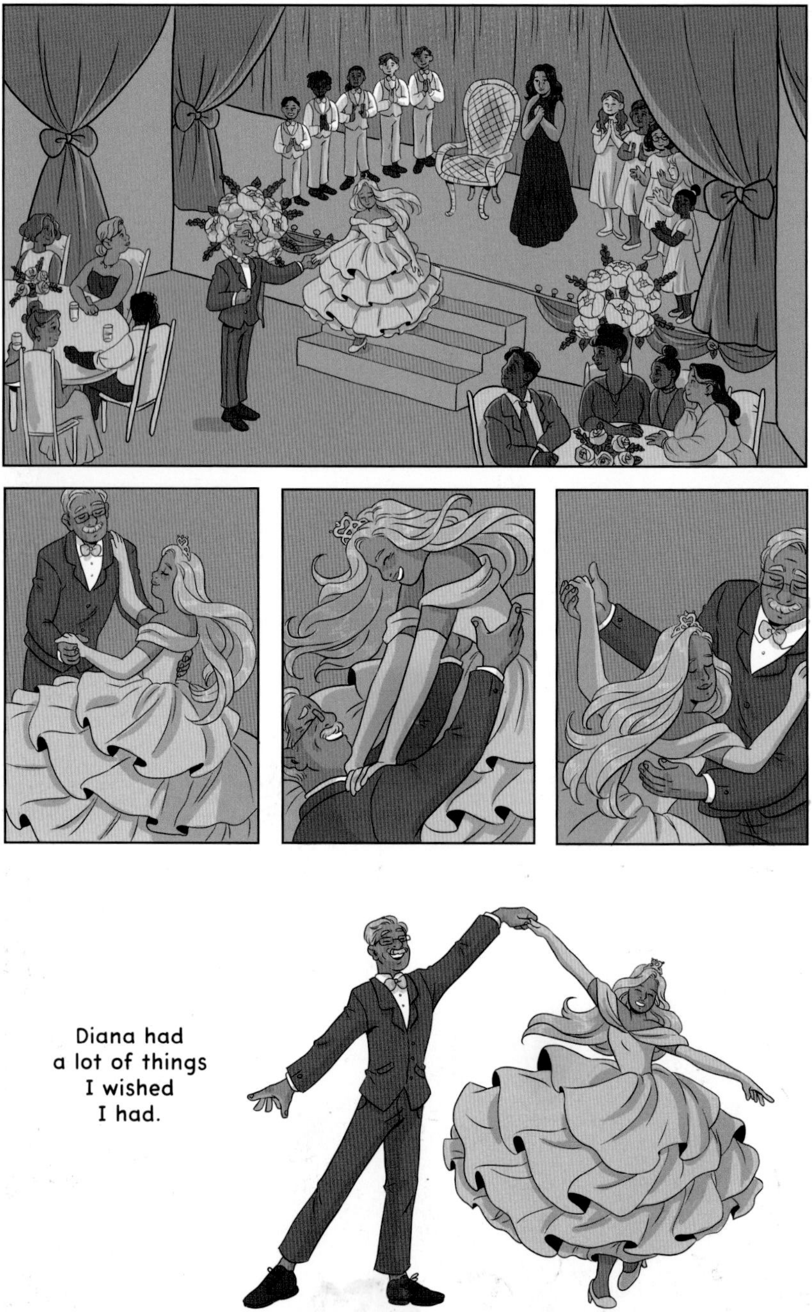
Diana had
a lot of things
I wished
I had.

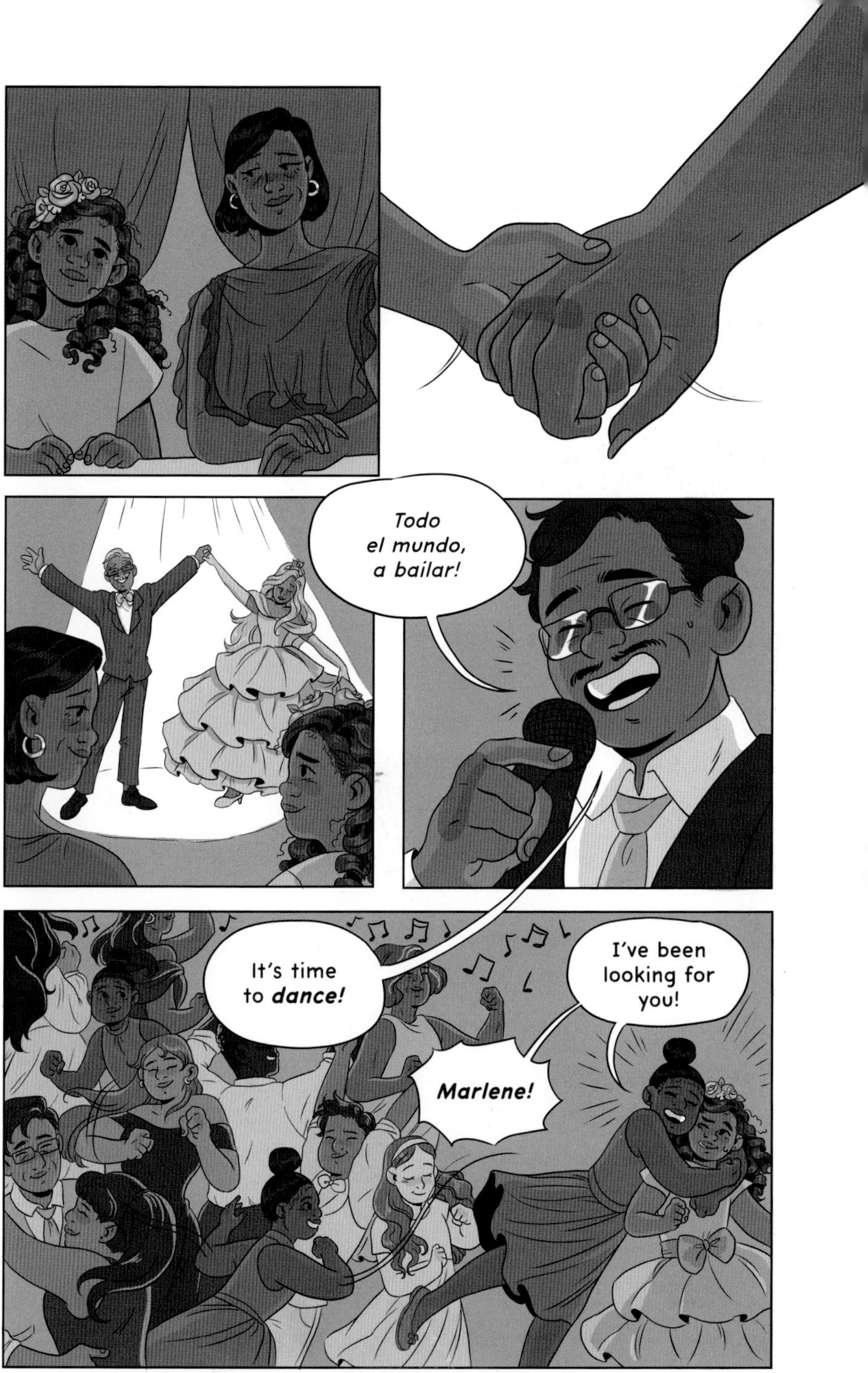
Todo el mundo, a bailar!
It's time to *dance!*
I've been looking for you!
Marlene!

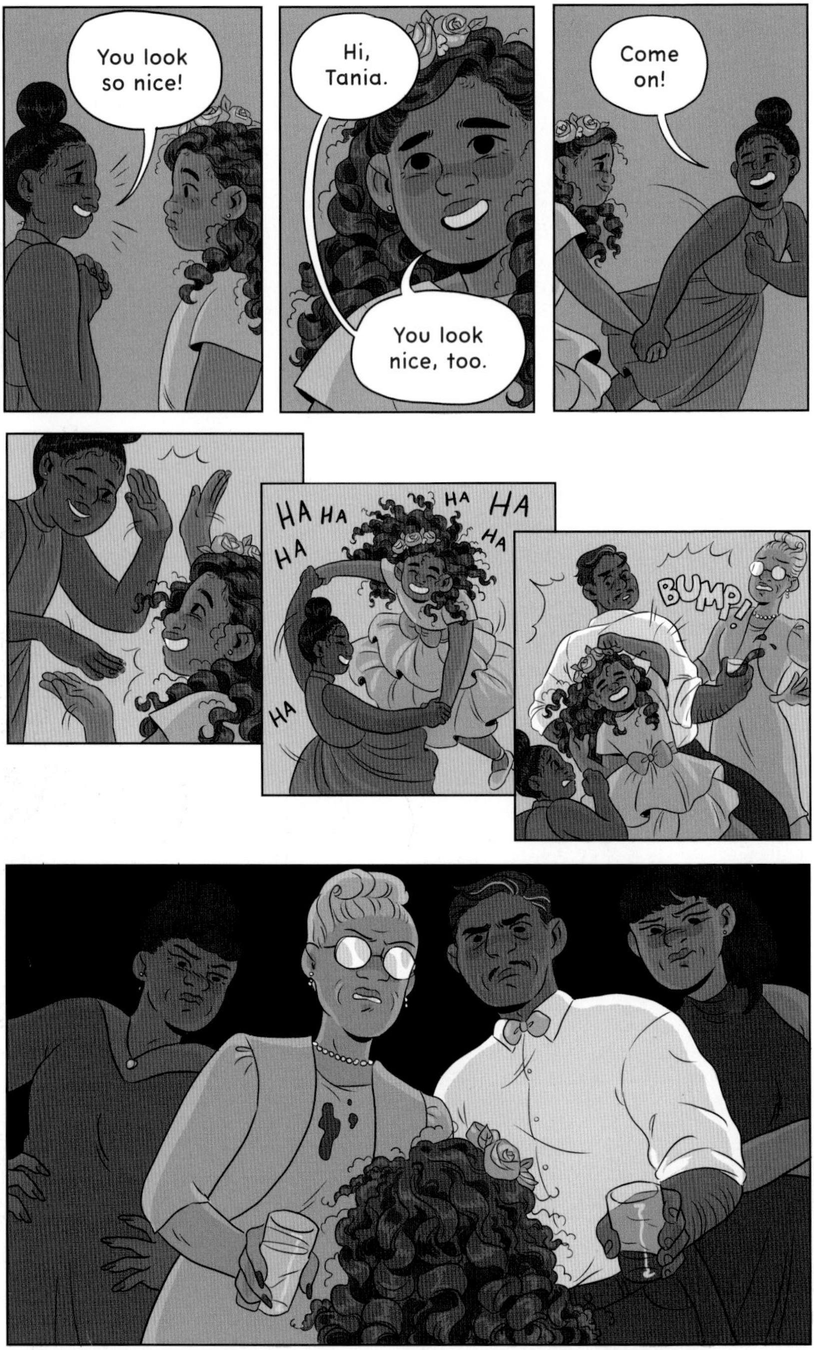
You look so nice!
Hi, Tania.
You look nice, too.
Come on!
HA HA HA HA HA HA HA
BUMP!

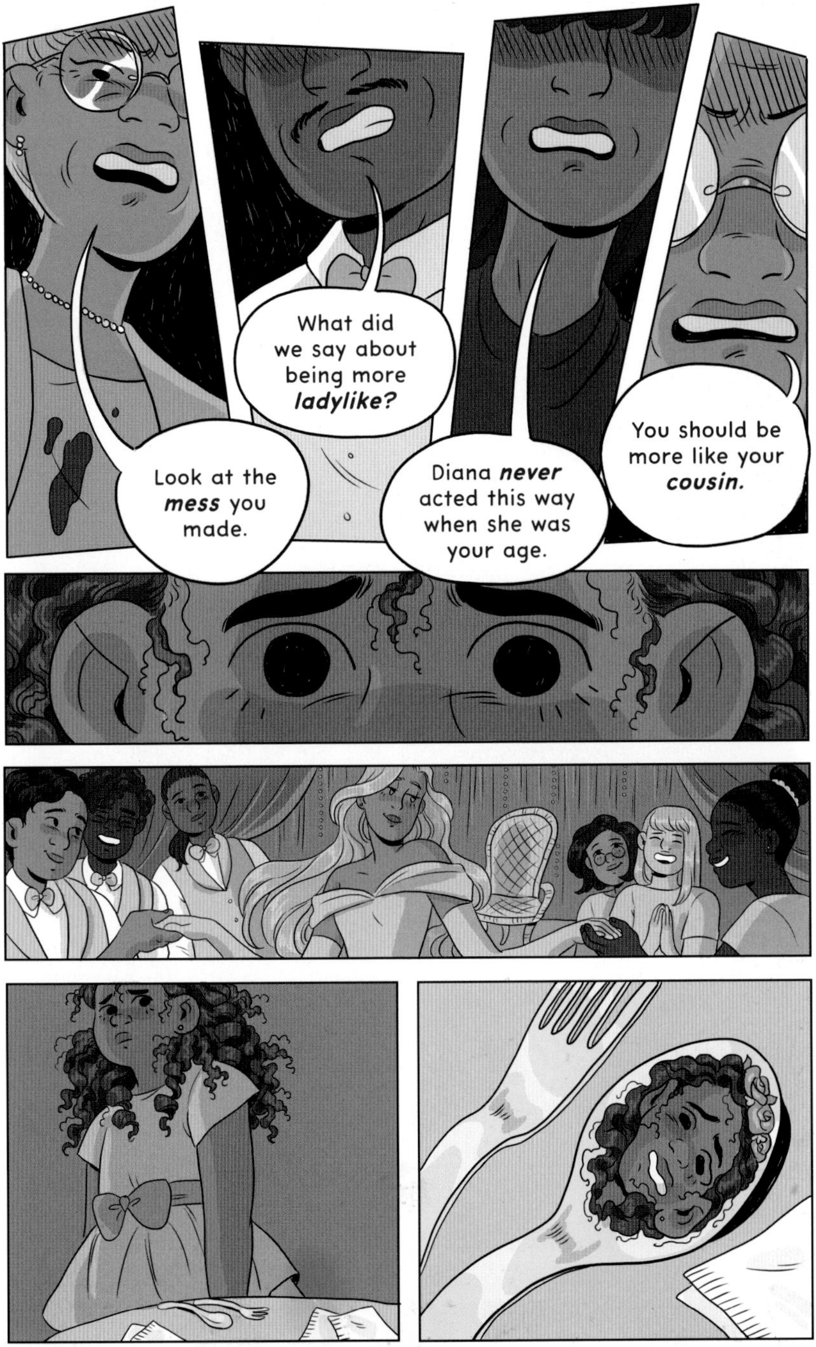
What did we say about being more *ladylike?*
Look at the *mess* you made.
Diana *never* acted this way when she was your age.
You should be more like your *cousin.*

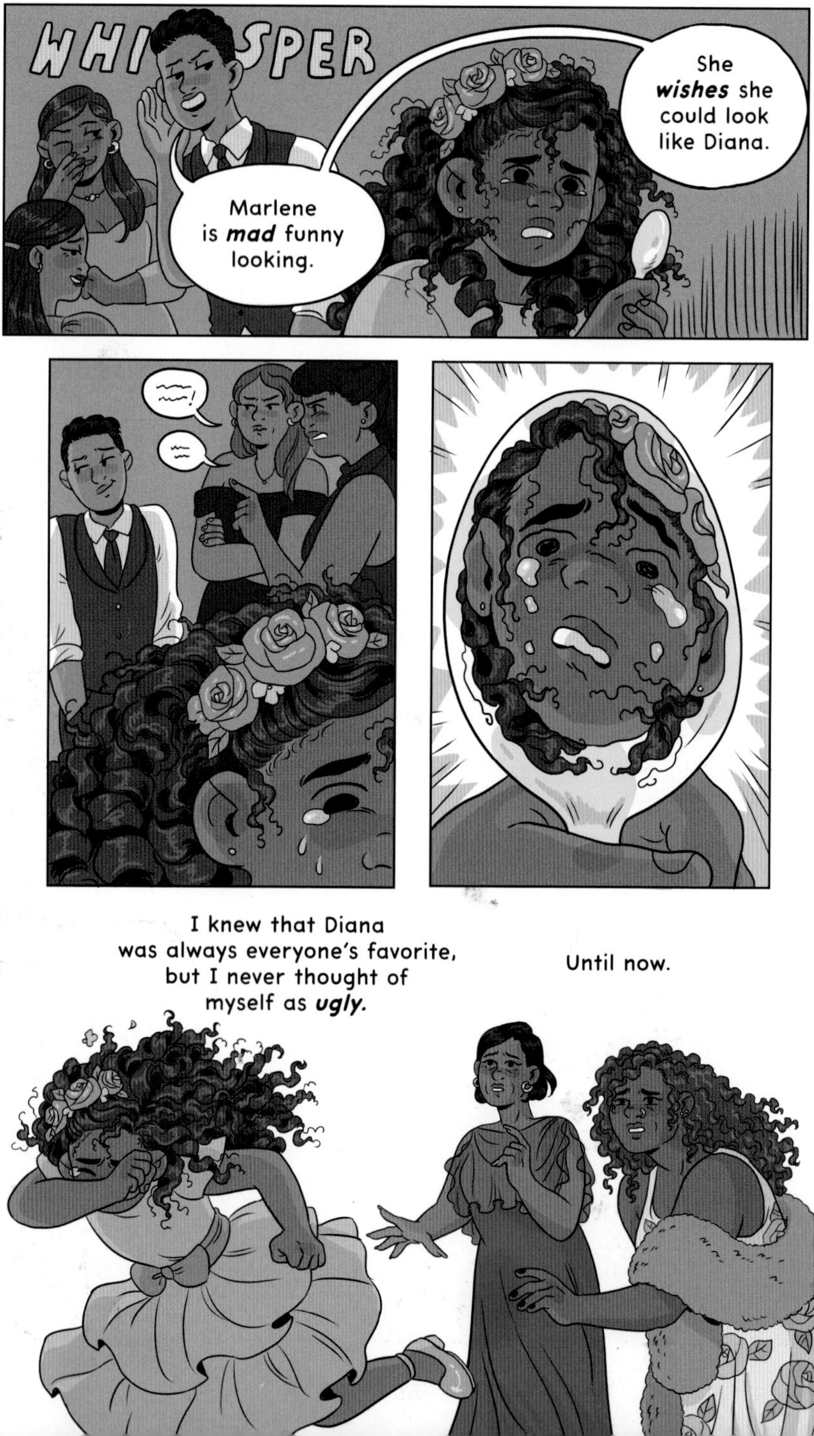
WHISPER
Marlene is *mad* funny looking.
She *wishes* she could look like Diana.
I knew that Diana was always everyone's favorite, but I never thought of myself as *ugly.*
Until now.

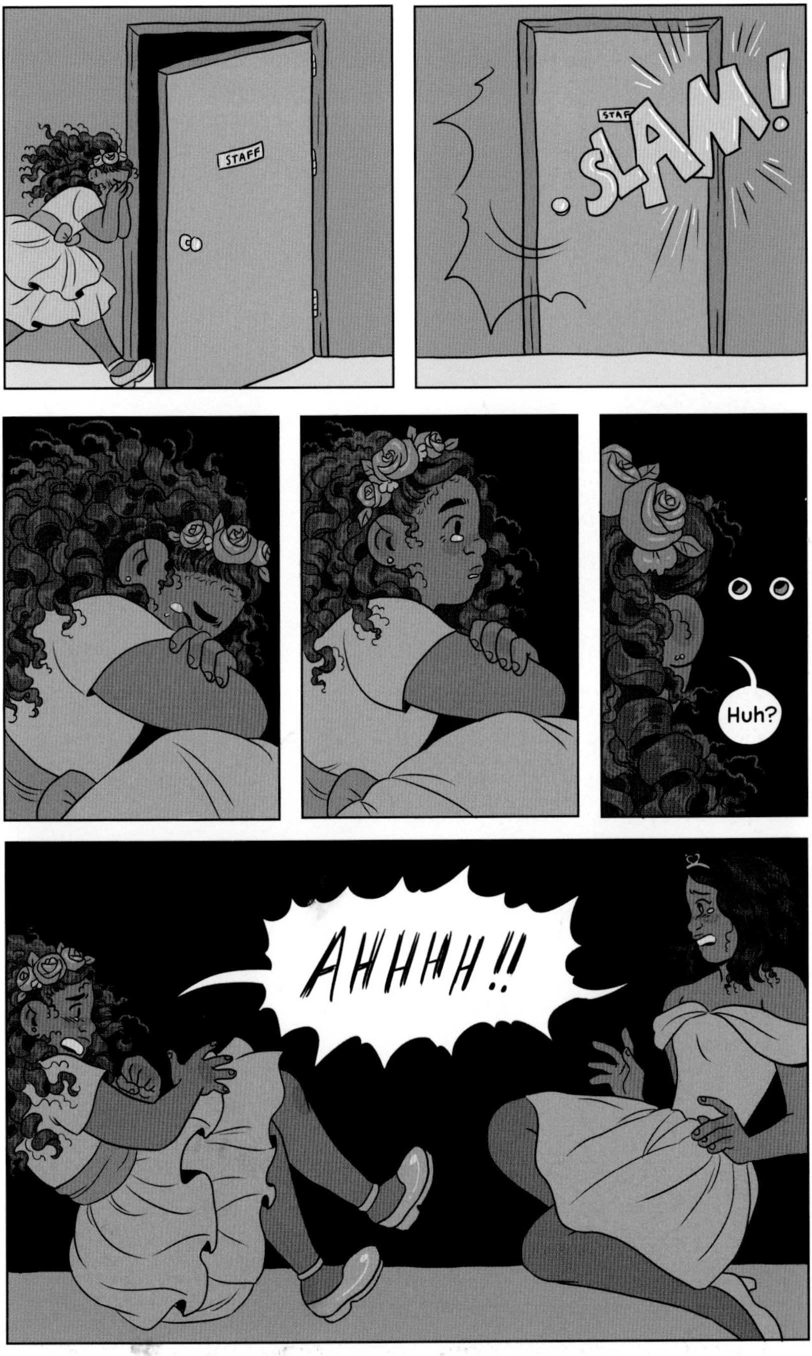
STAFF
STAFF
SLAM!
Huh?
AHHHH!!

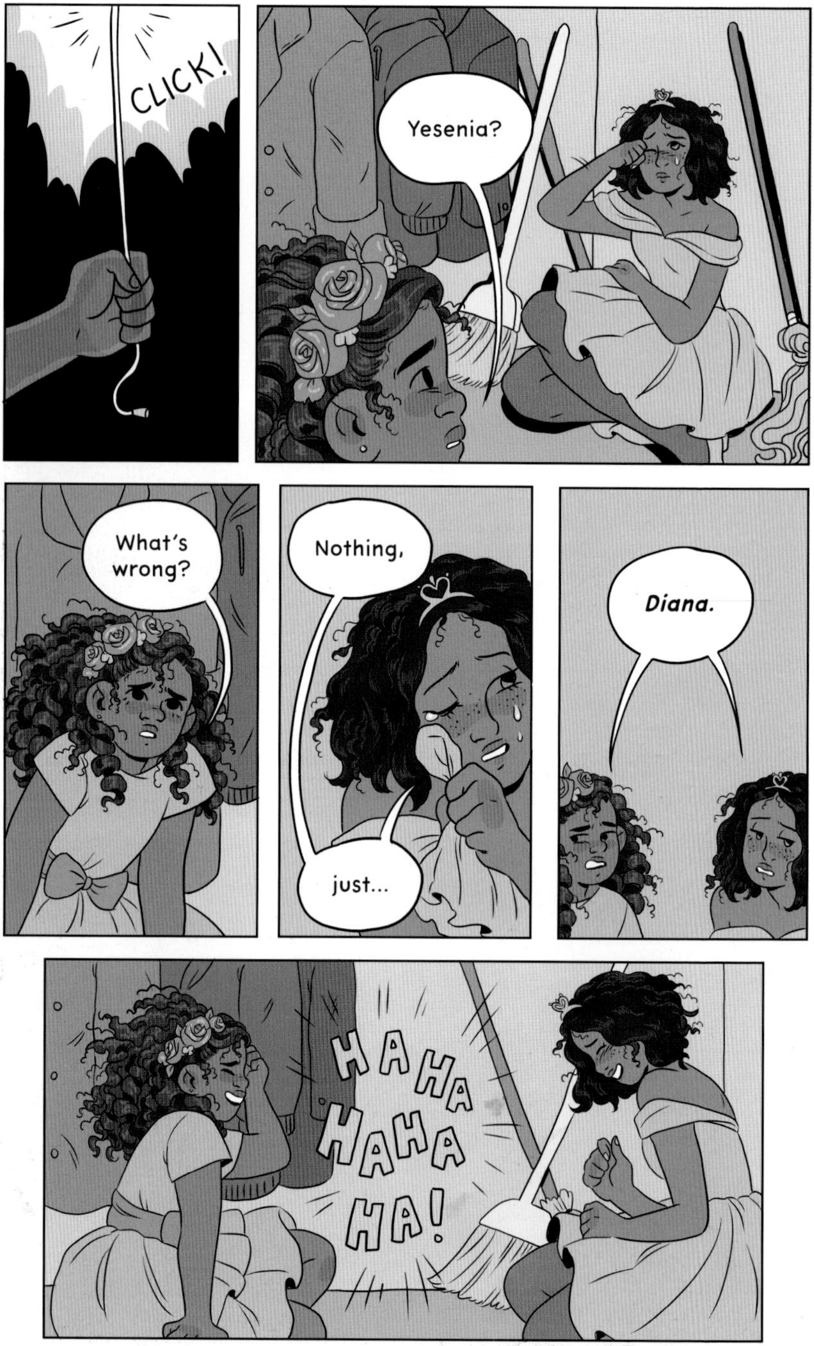
CLICK!
Yesenia?
What's wrong?
Nothing,
just...
Diana.
HAHA HAHA HA!

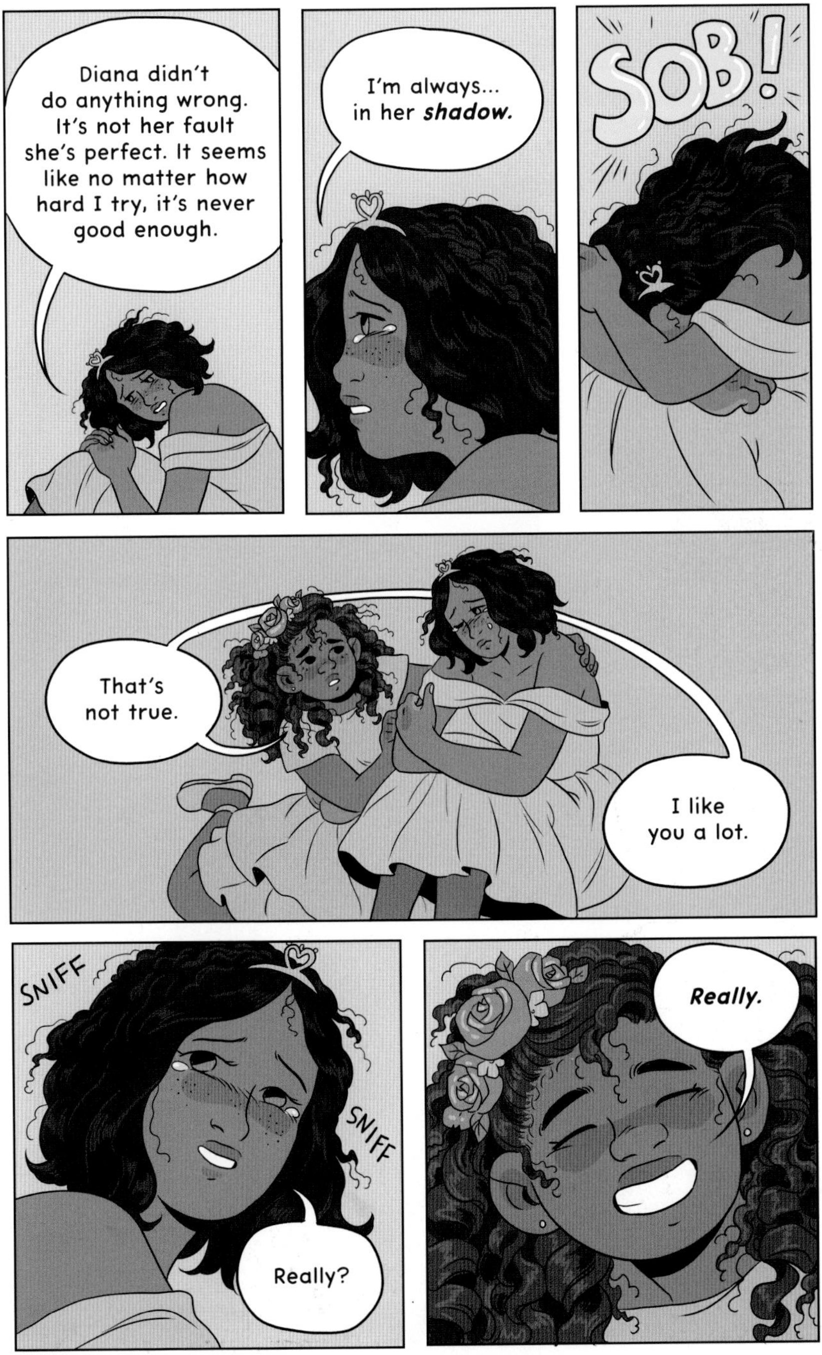
Diana didn't do anything wrong. It's not her fault she's perfect. It seems like no matter how hard I try, it's never good enough.
I'm always... in her *shadow.*
SOB!
That's not true.
I like you a lot.
SNIFF
SNIFF
Really?
Really.

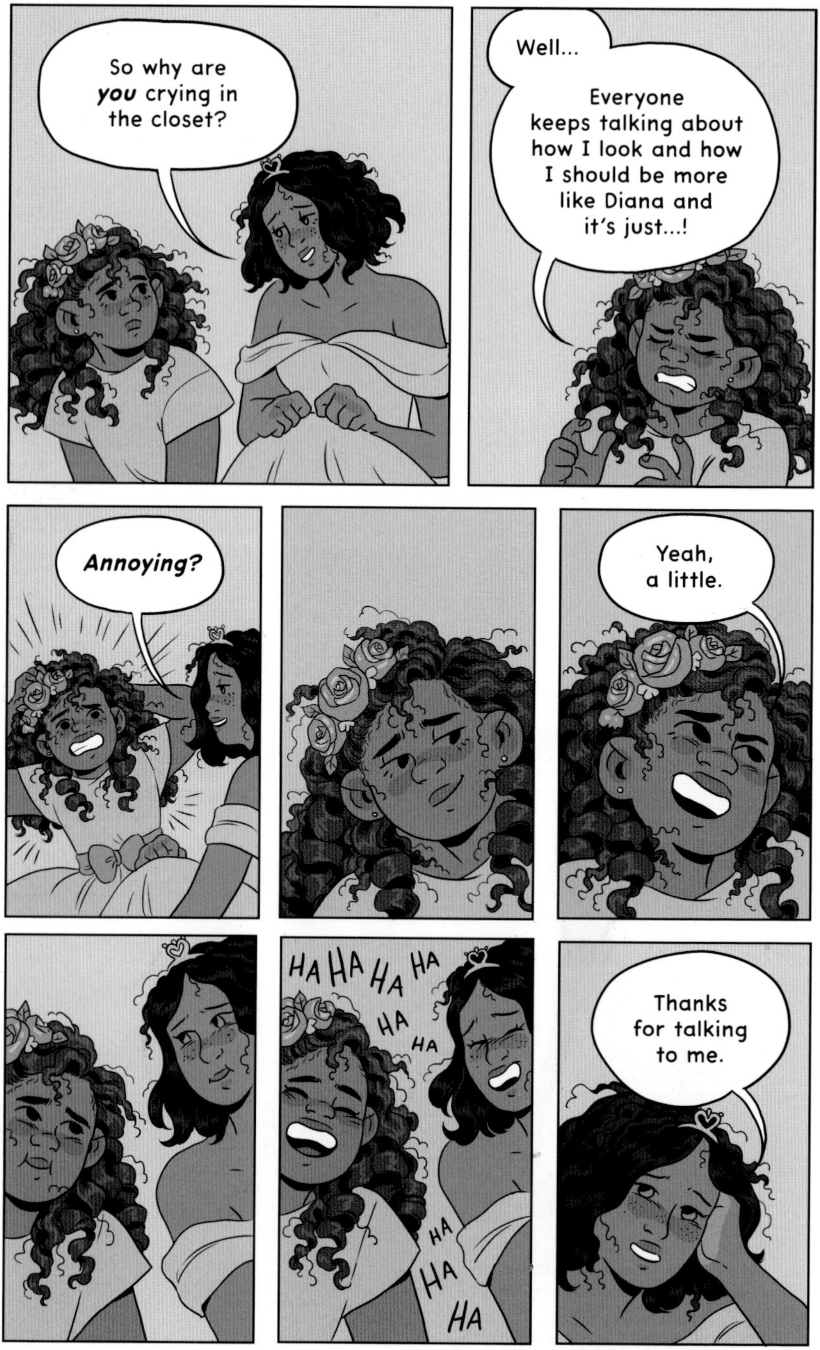
So why are ***you*** crying in the closet?
Well...
Everyone keeps talking about how I look and how I should be more like Diana and it's just...!
Annoying?
Yeah, a little.
HA HA HA HA HA HA
HA HA
HA HA HA
Thanks for talking to me.

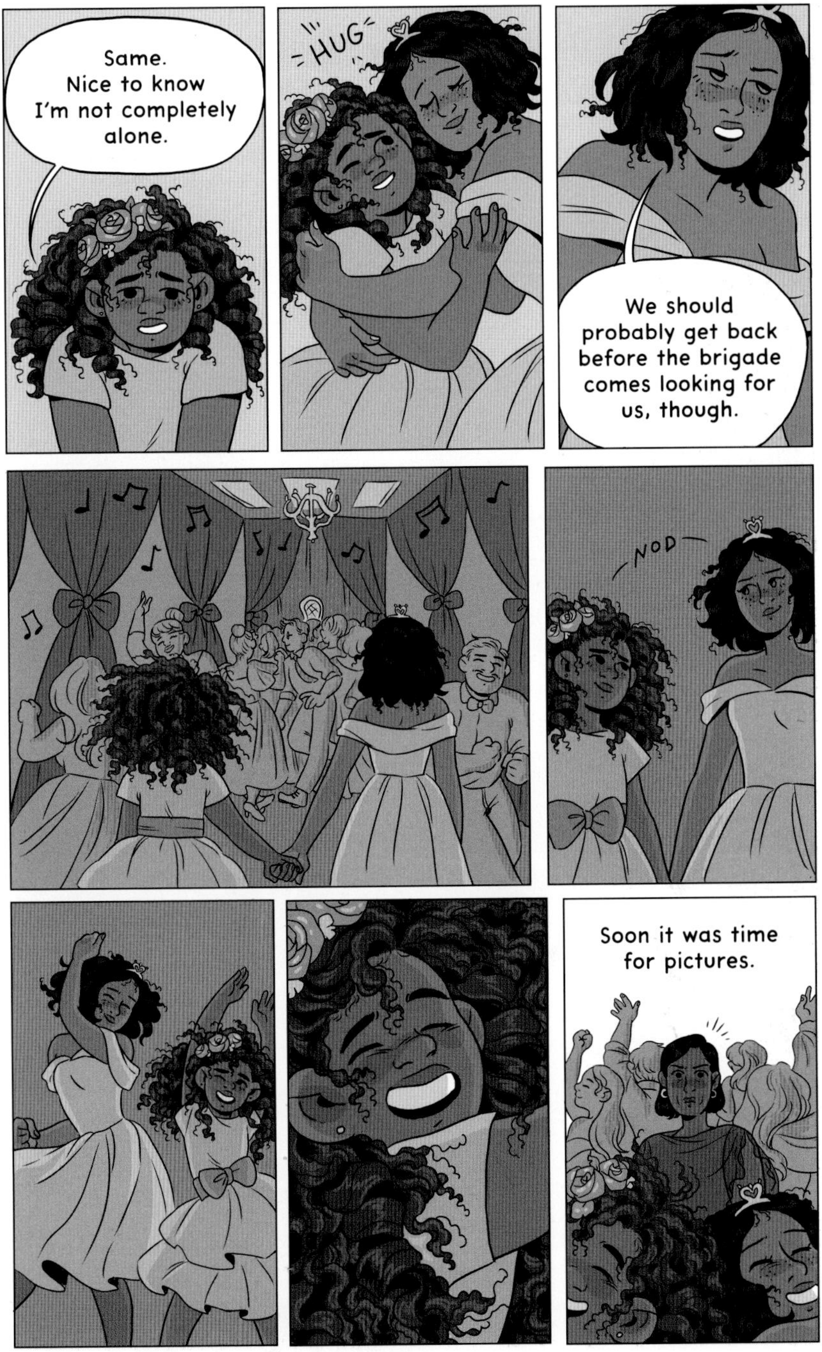
Same.
Nice to know
I'm not completely
alone.
HUG
We should probably get back before the brigade comes looking for us, though.
NOD
Soon it was time for pictures.

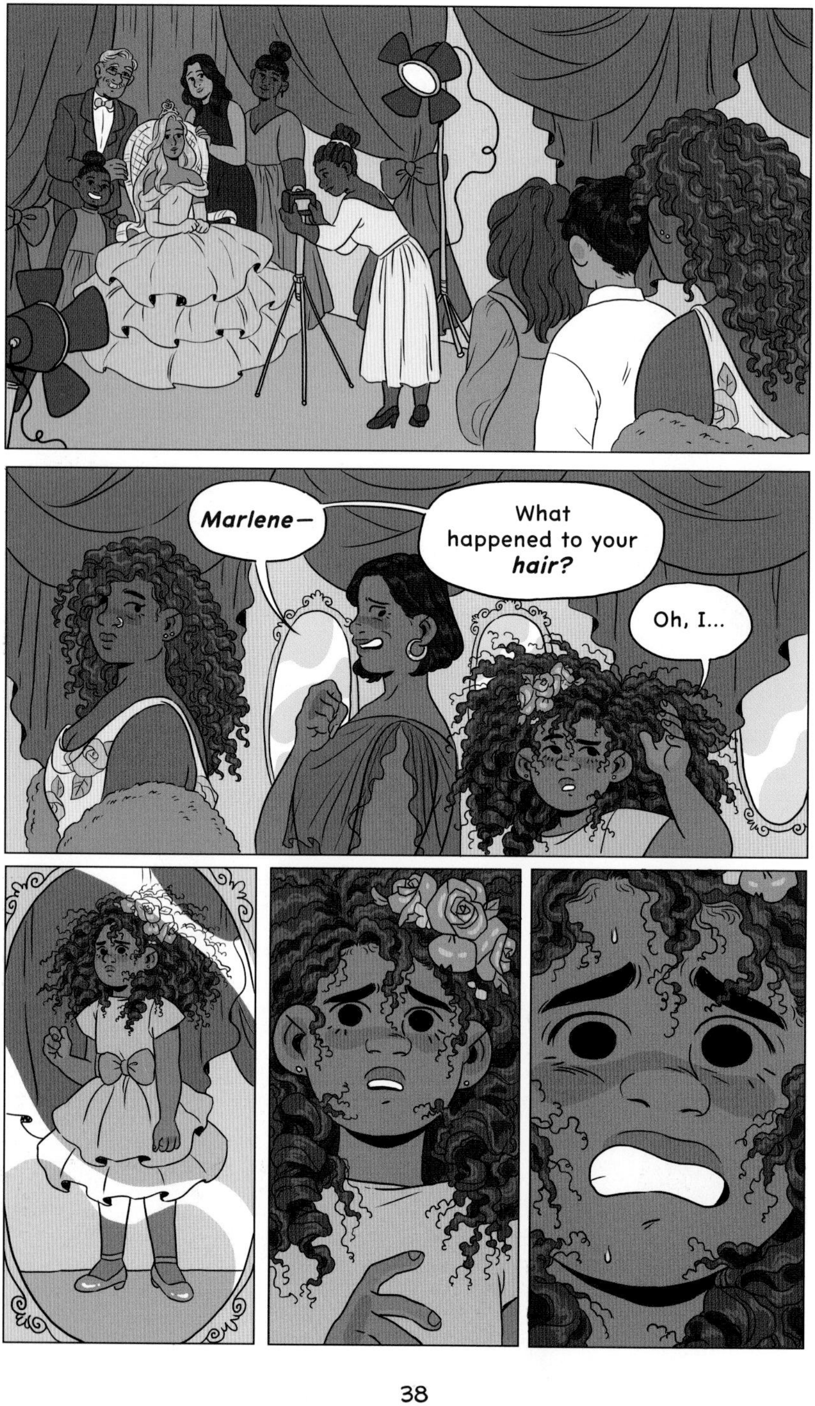
Marlene—
What happened to your hair?
Oh, I...

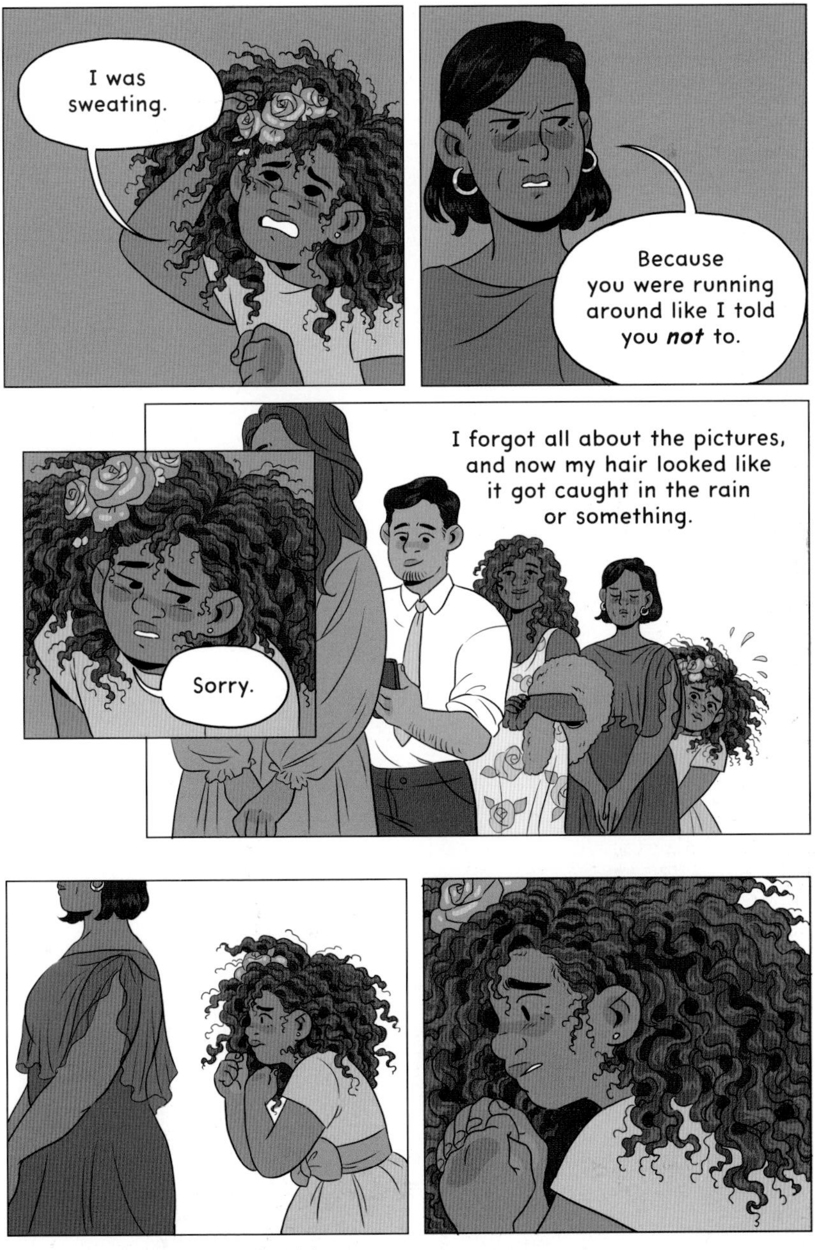
I was sweating.
Because you were running around like I told you *not* to.
I forgot all about the pictures, and now my hair looked like it got caught in the rain or something.
Sorry.

These pictures would be ***everywhere.*** Online, in family albums...

I would never, ever live it down.

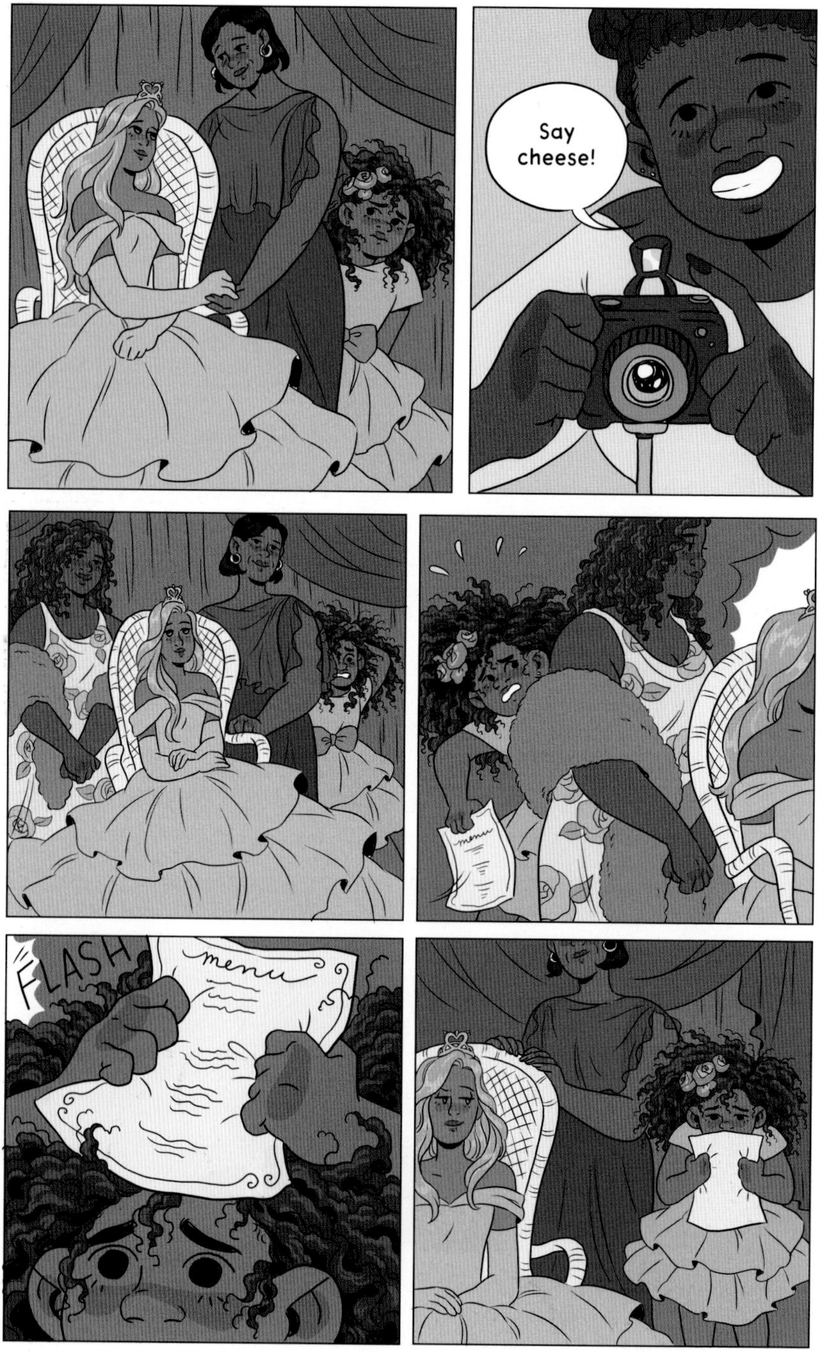
Say cheese!
menu
FLASH
menu

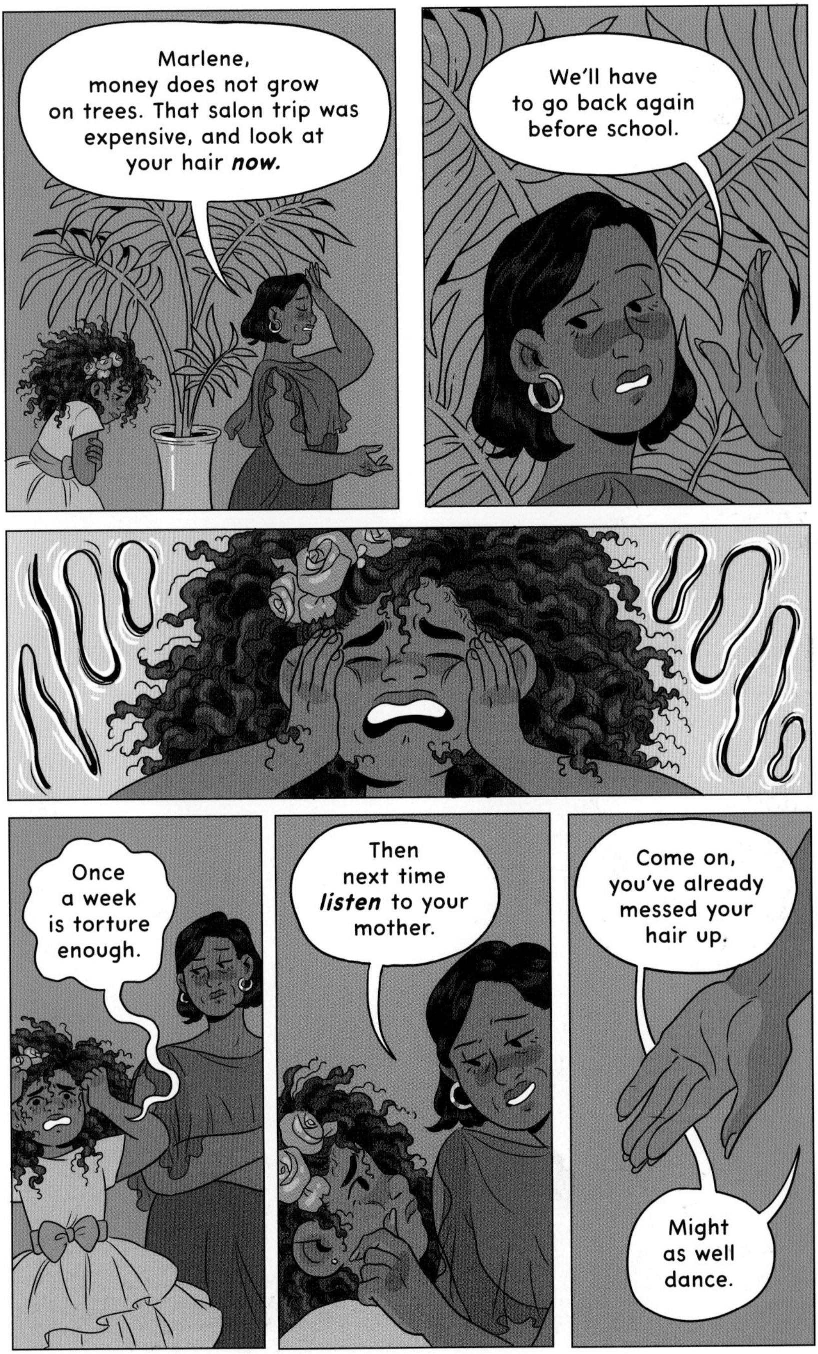
Marlene, money does not grow on trees. That salon trip was expensive, and look at your hair *now.*
We'll have to go back again before school.
Once a week is torture enough.
Then next time *listen* to your mother.
Come on, you've already messed your hair up.
Might as well dance.

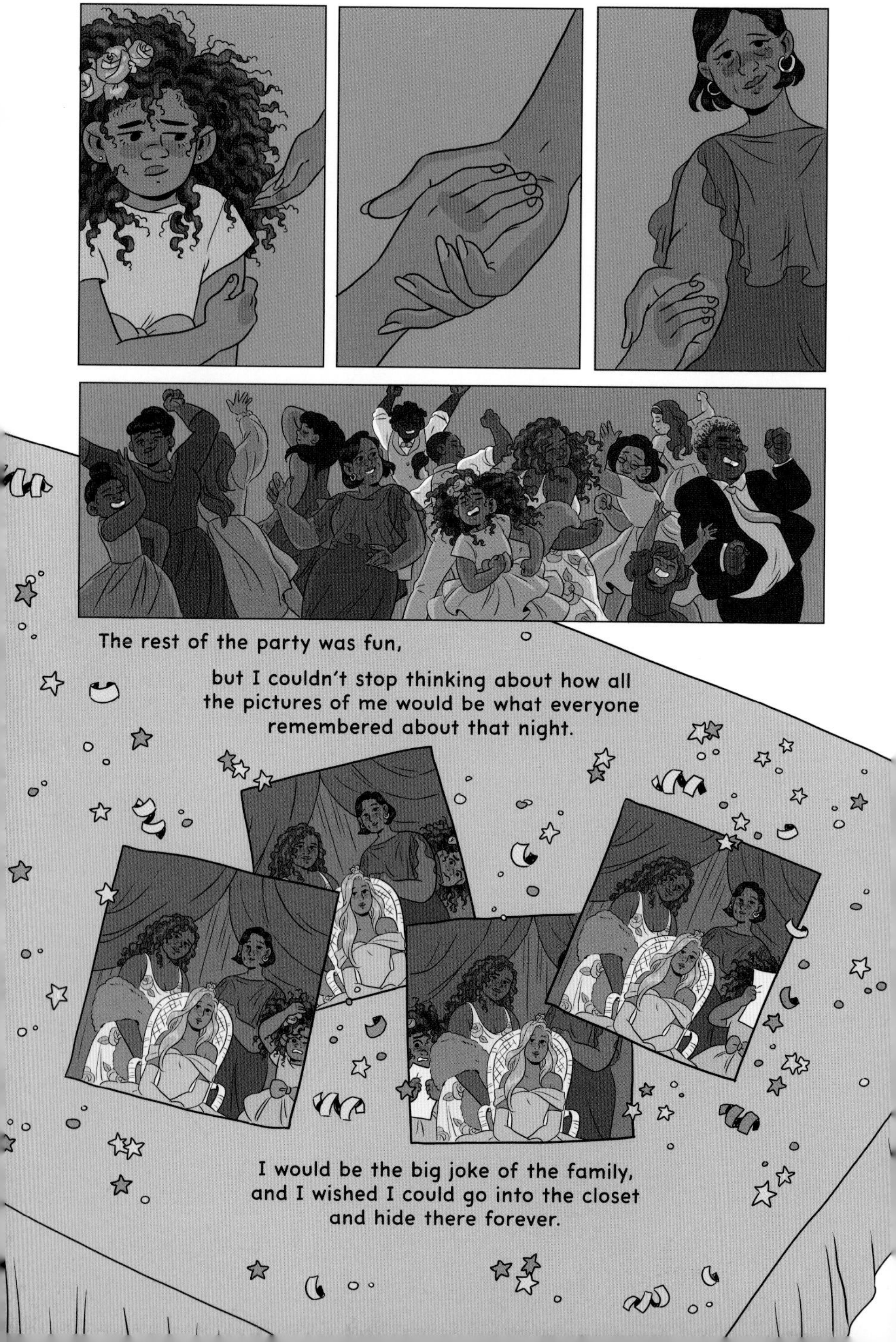

The rest of the party was fun,
but I couldn't stop thinking about how all the pictures of me would be what everyone remembered about that night.
I would be the big joke of the family, and I wished I could go into the closet and hide there forever.

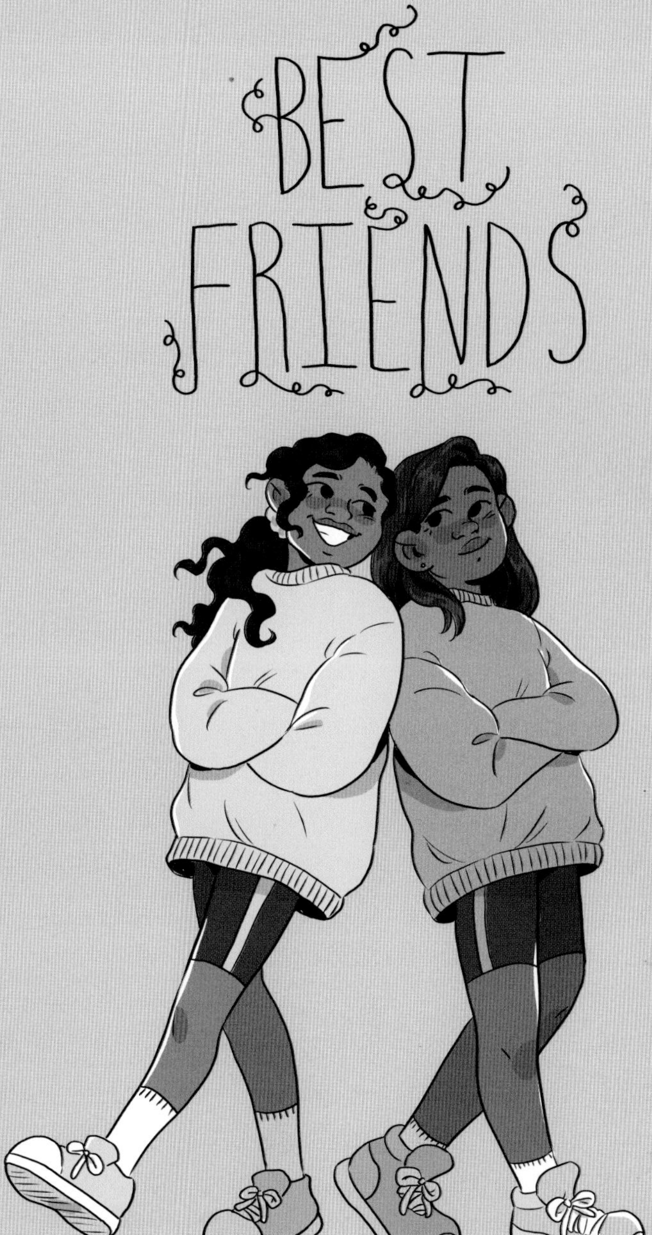
BEST
FRIENDS

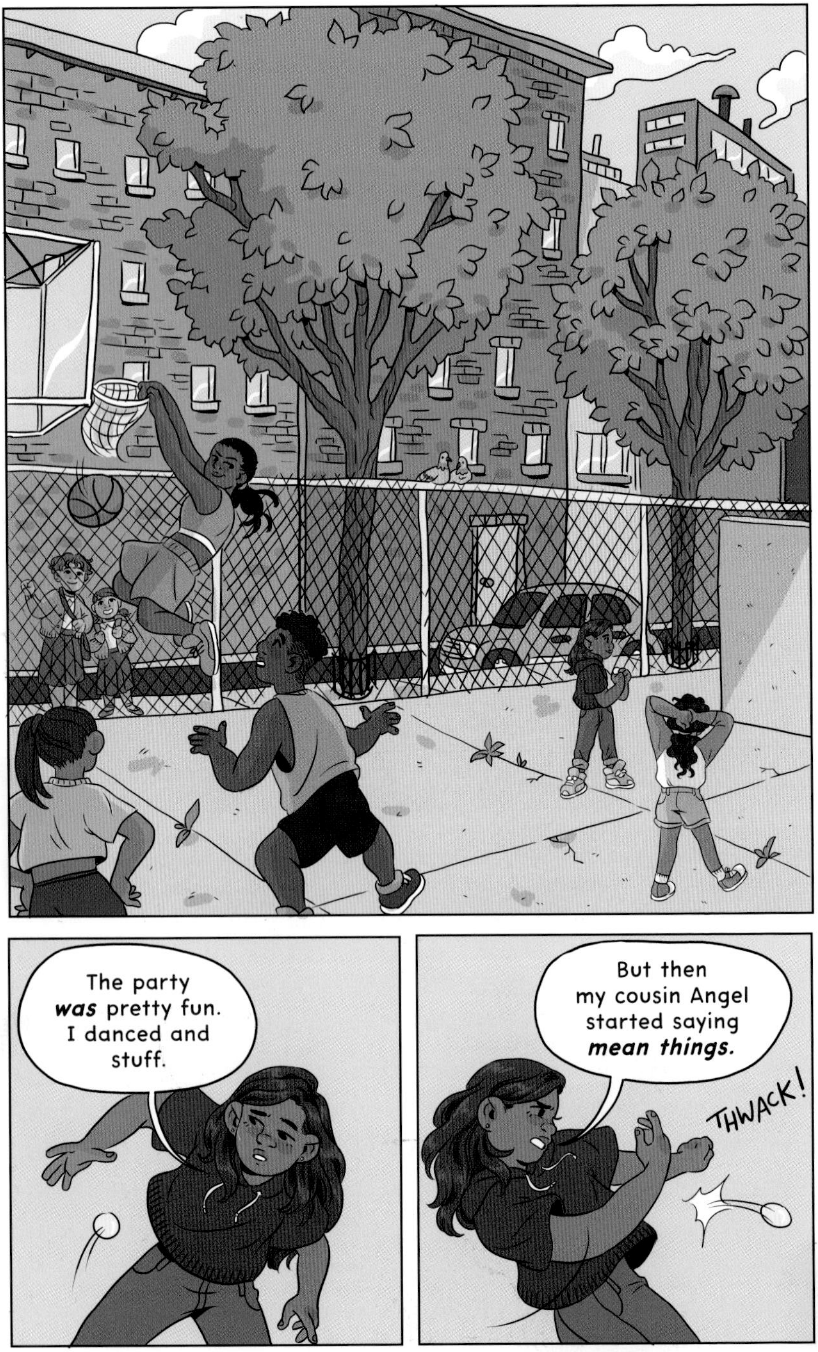
The party *was* pretty fun. I danced and stuff.
But then my cousin Angel started saying *mean things.*
THWACK!

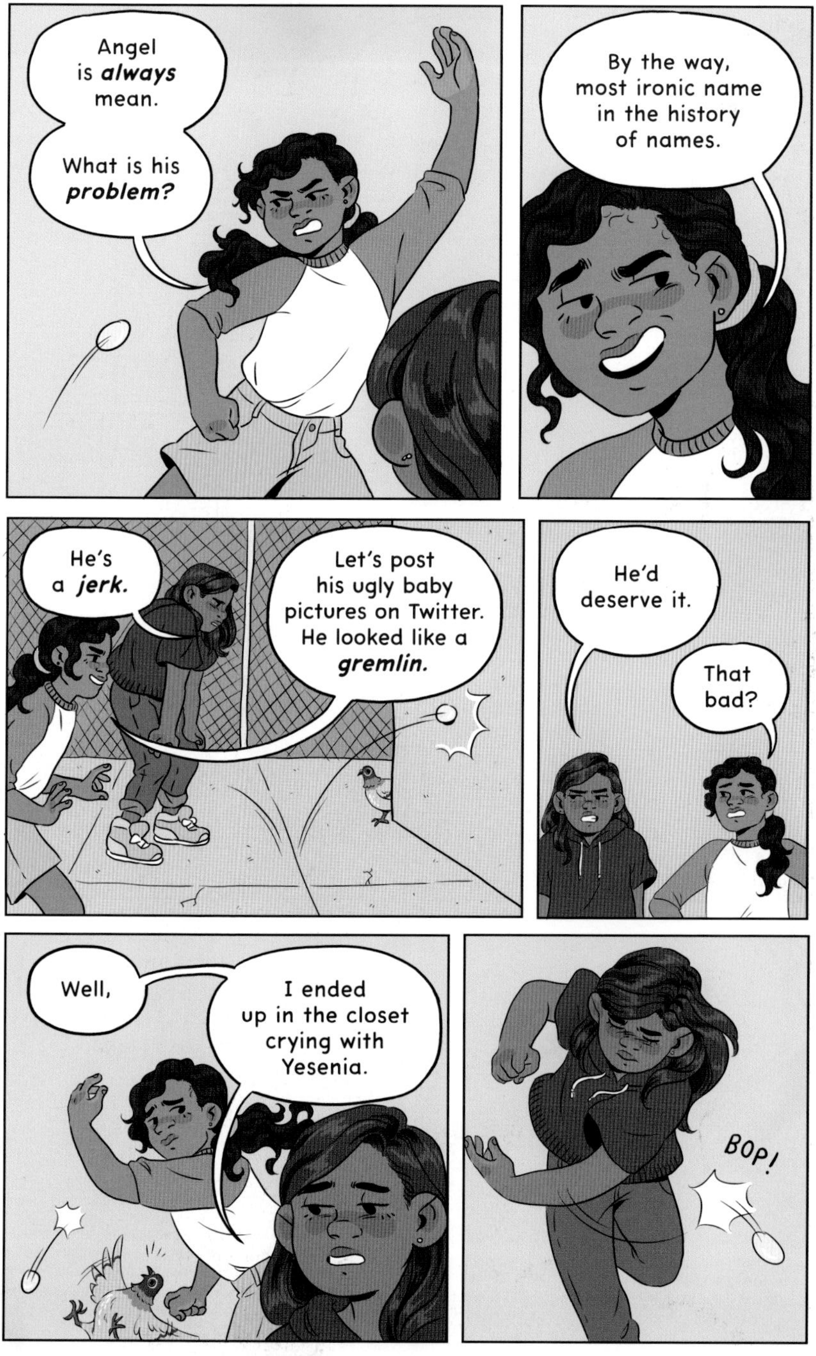
Angel is ***always*** mean.
What is his ***problem?***
By the way, most ironic name in the history of names.
He's a ***jerk.***
Let's post his ugly baby pictures on Twitter. He looked like a ***gremlin.***
He'd deserve it.
That bad?
Well,
I ended up in the closet crying with Yesenia.
BOP!

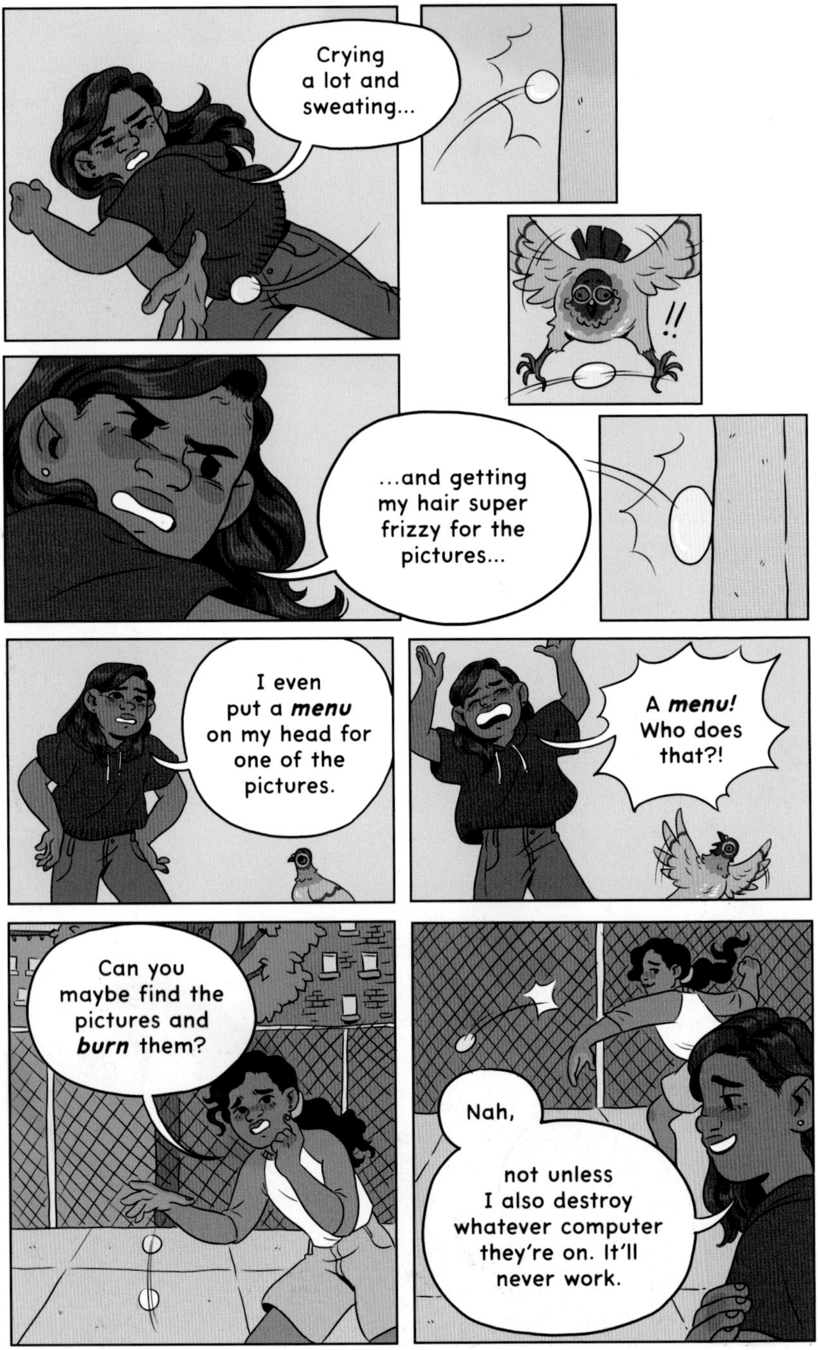
Crying a lot and sweating...
...and getting my hair super frizzy for the pictures...
!!
I even put a *menu* on my head for one of the pictures.
A *menu!* Who does that?!
Can you maybe find the pictures and *burn* them?
Nah,
not unless I also destroy whatever computer they're on. It'll never work.

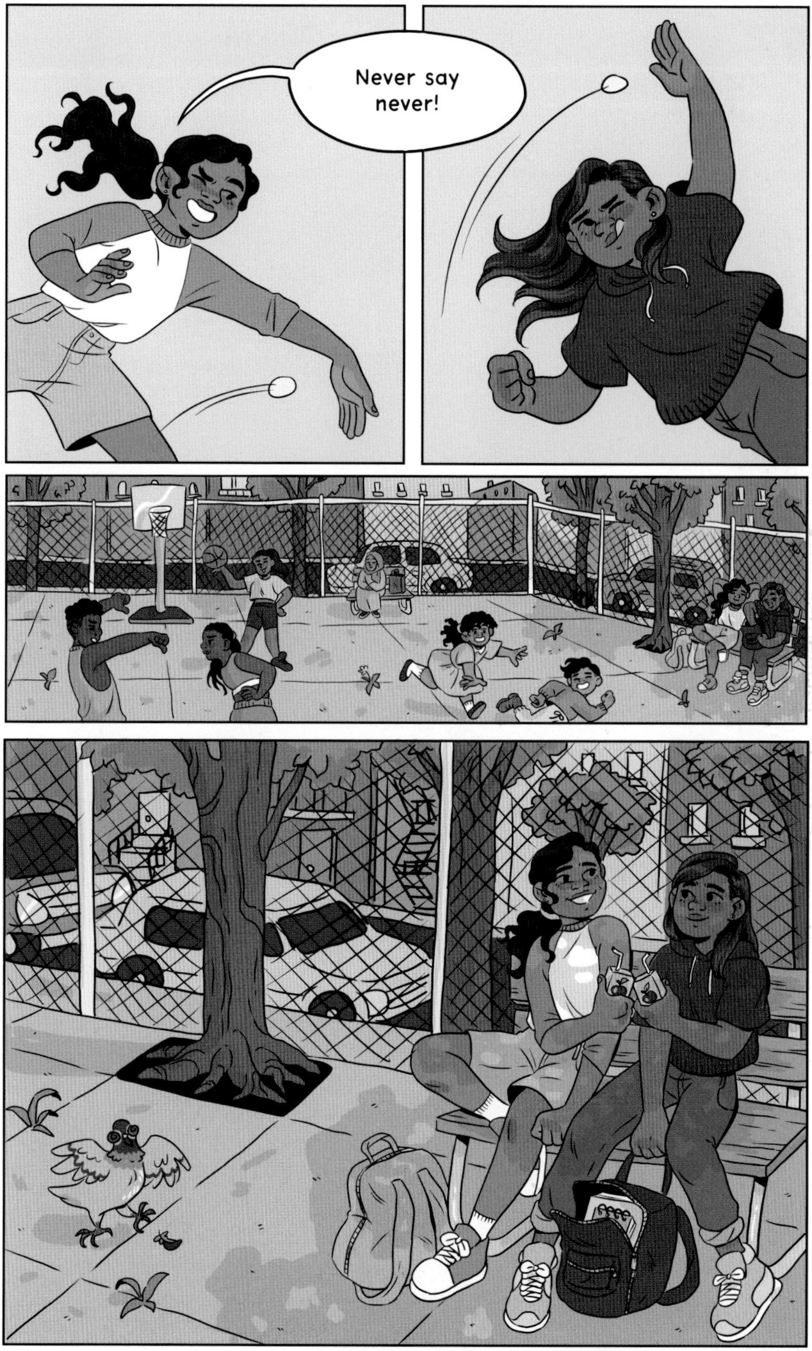
Never say never!

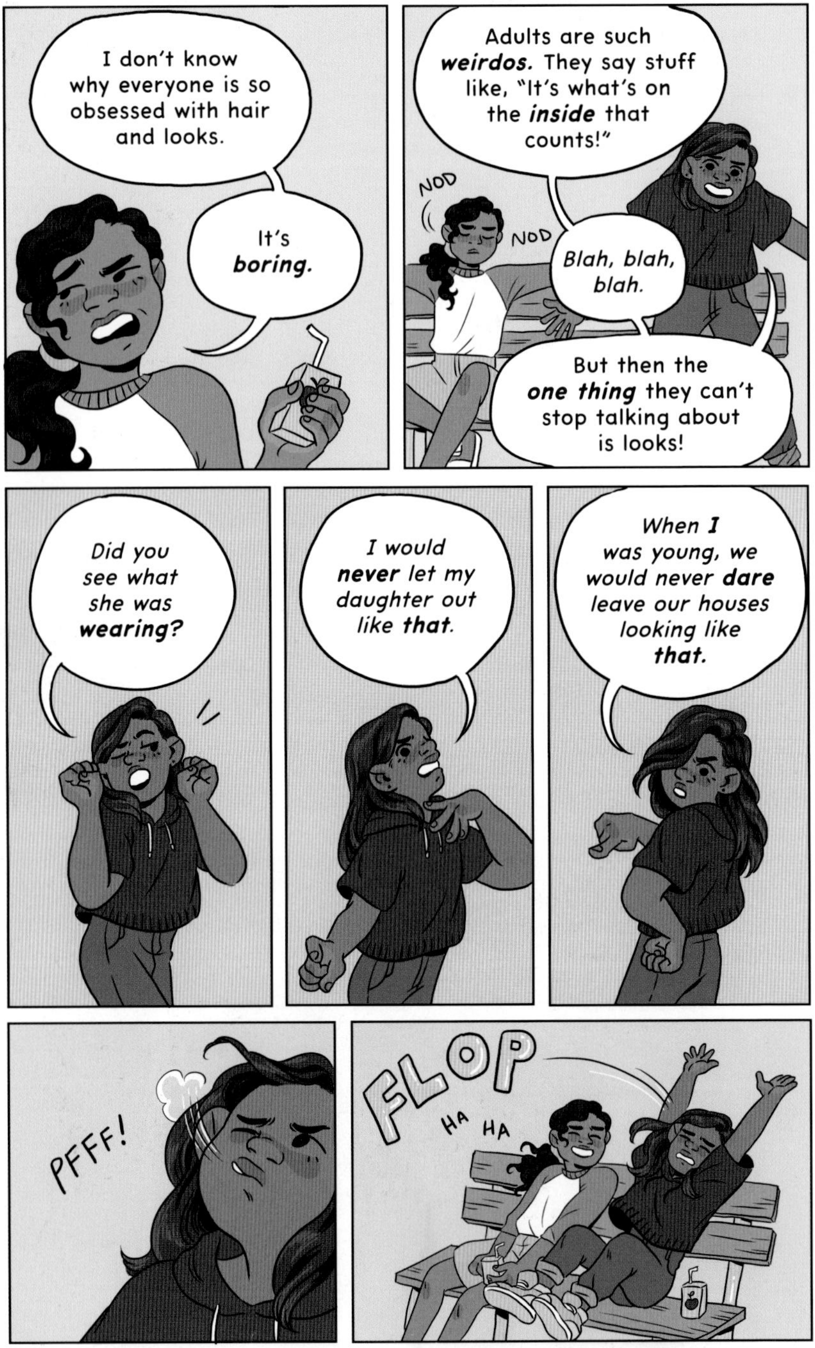
I don't know why everyone is so obsessed with hair and looks.
It's **boring.**
Adults are such ***weirdos.*** They say stuff like, "It's what's on the ***inside*** that counts!"
NOD
NOD
Blah, blah, blah.
But then the ***one thing*** they can't stop talking about is looks!
Did you see what she was ***wearing?***
I would ***never*** *let my daughter out like* ***that.***
When ***I*** *was young, we would never* ***dare*** *leave our houses looking like* ***that.***
PFFF!
FLOP
HA HA

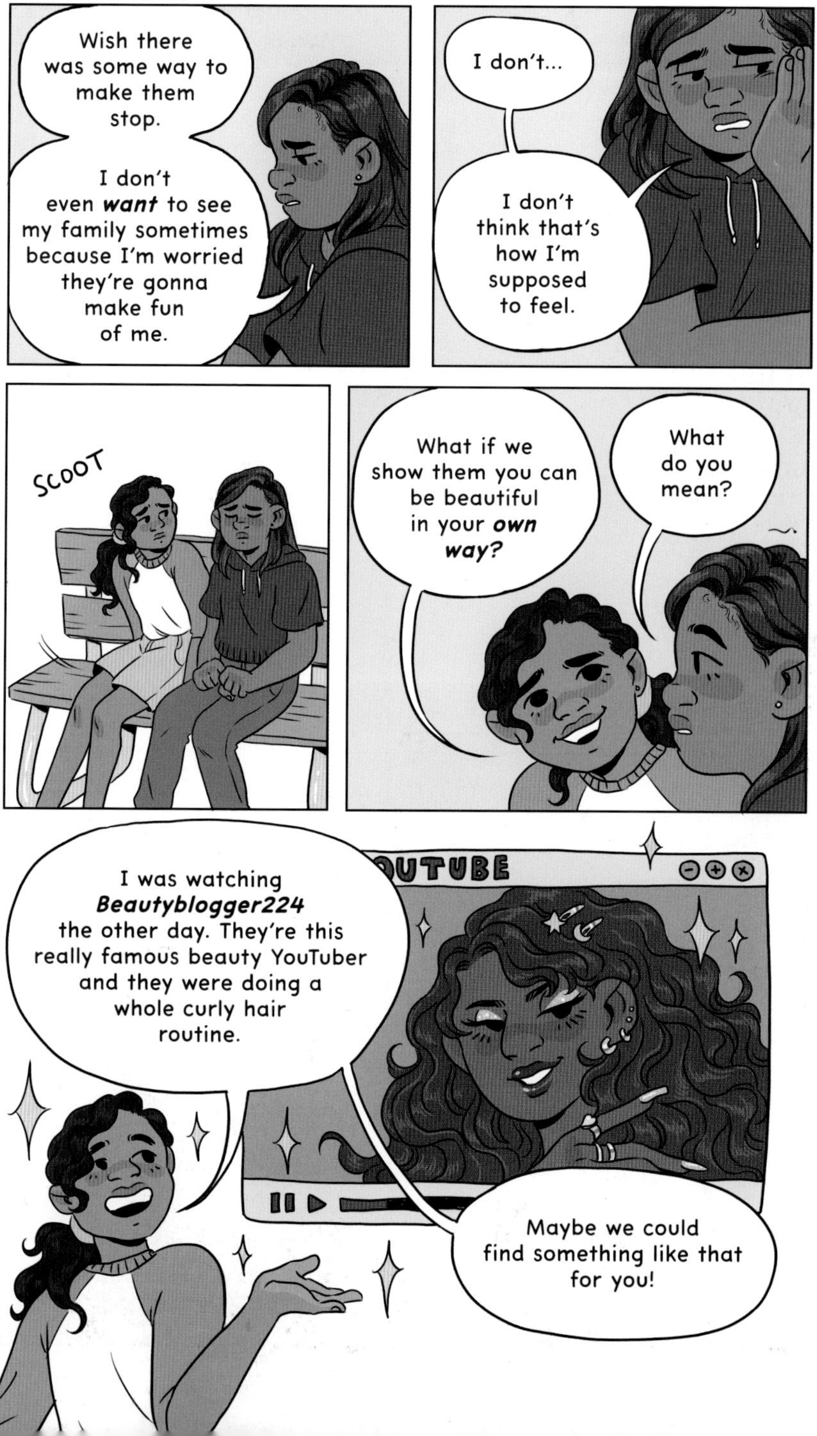
Wish there was some way to make them stop.
I don't even *want* to see my family sometimes because I'm worried they're gonna make fun of me.
I don't...
I don't think that's how I'm supposed to feel.
SCOOT
What if we show them you can be beautiful in your ***own way?***
What do you mean?
I was watching ***Beautyblogger224*** the other day. They're this really famous beauty YouTuber and they were doing a whole curly hair routine.
OUTUBE
Maybe we could find something like that for you!

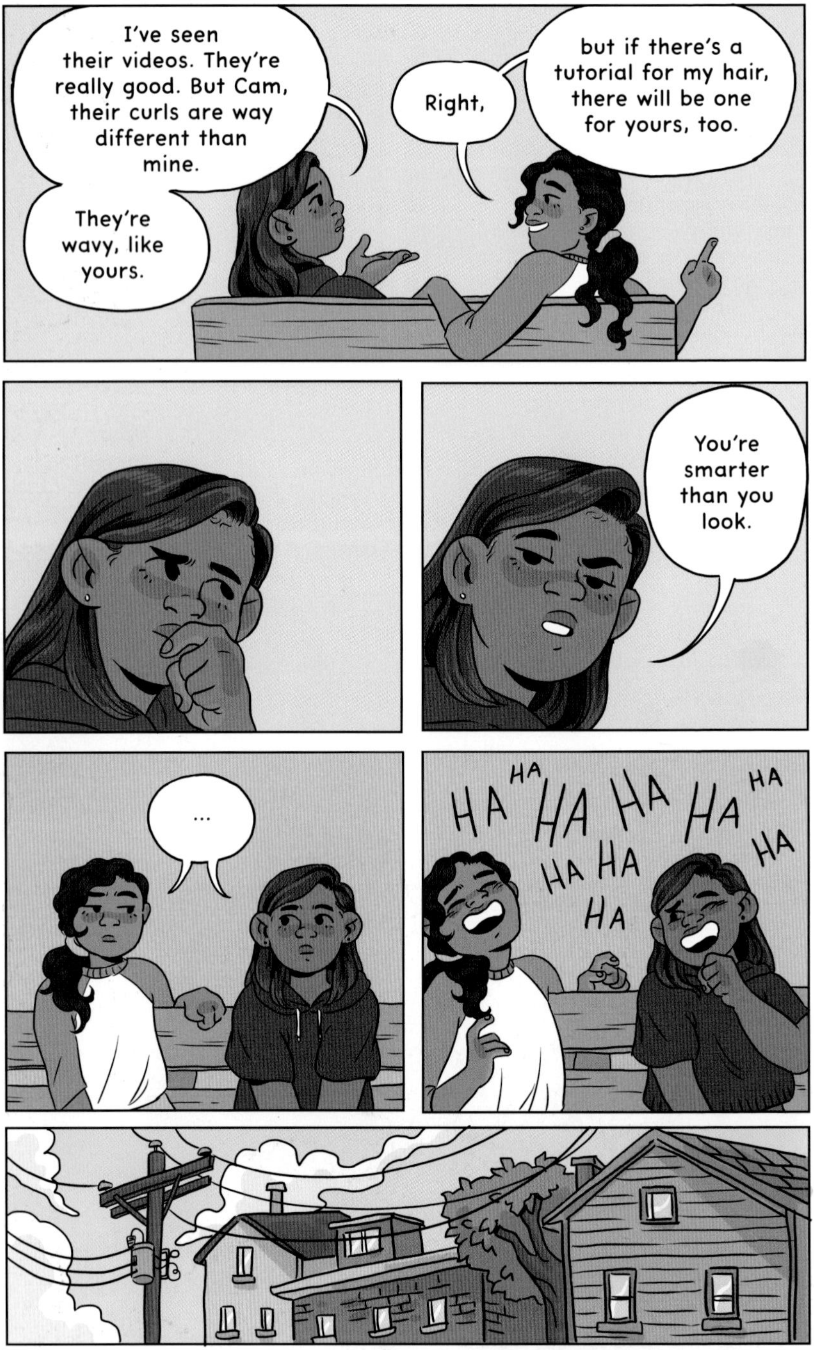
I've seen their videos. They're really good. But Cam, their curls are way different than mine.
They're wavy, like yours.
Right,
but if there's a tutorial for my hair, there will be one for yours, too.
You're smarter than you look.
...
HA HA HA HA HA HA HA HA HA HA HA HA

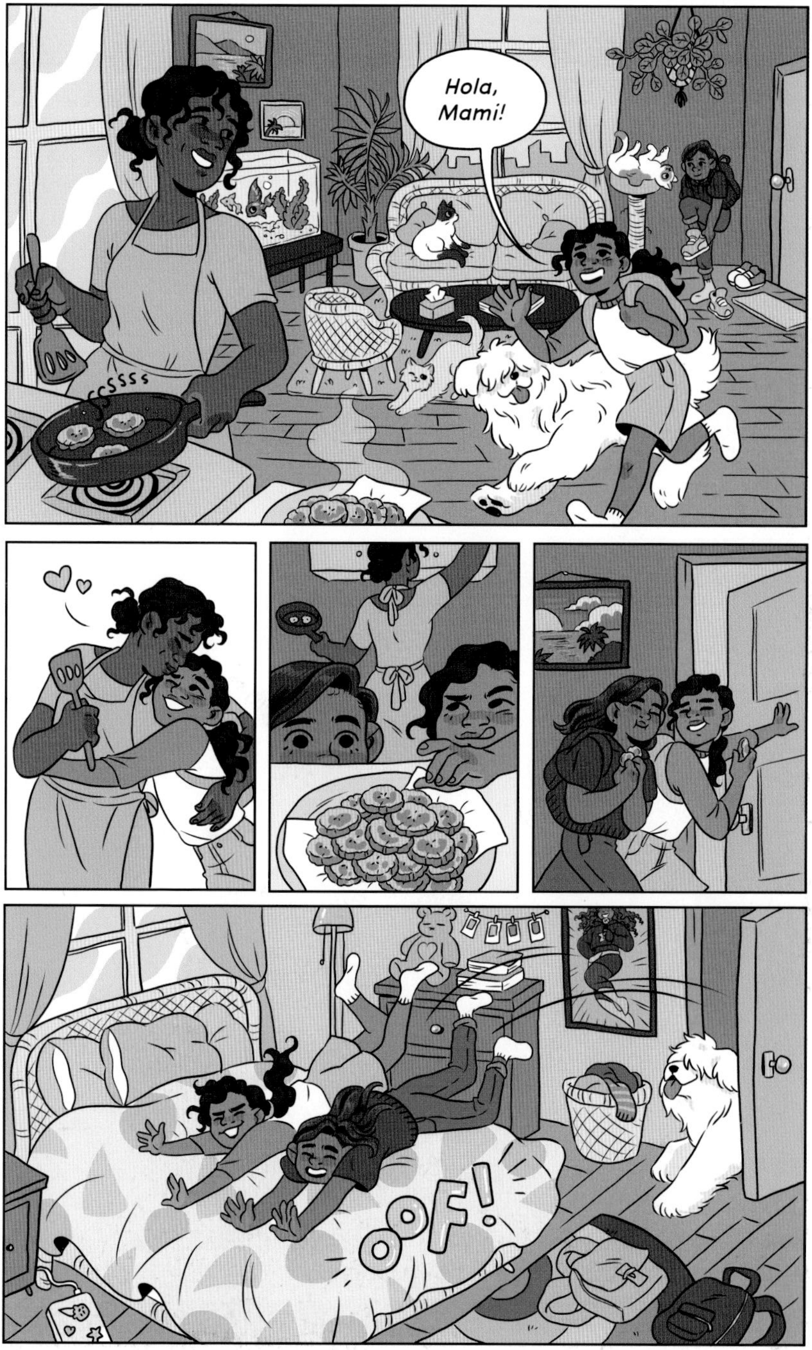
Hola, Mami!
CCSSSS
OOF!

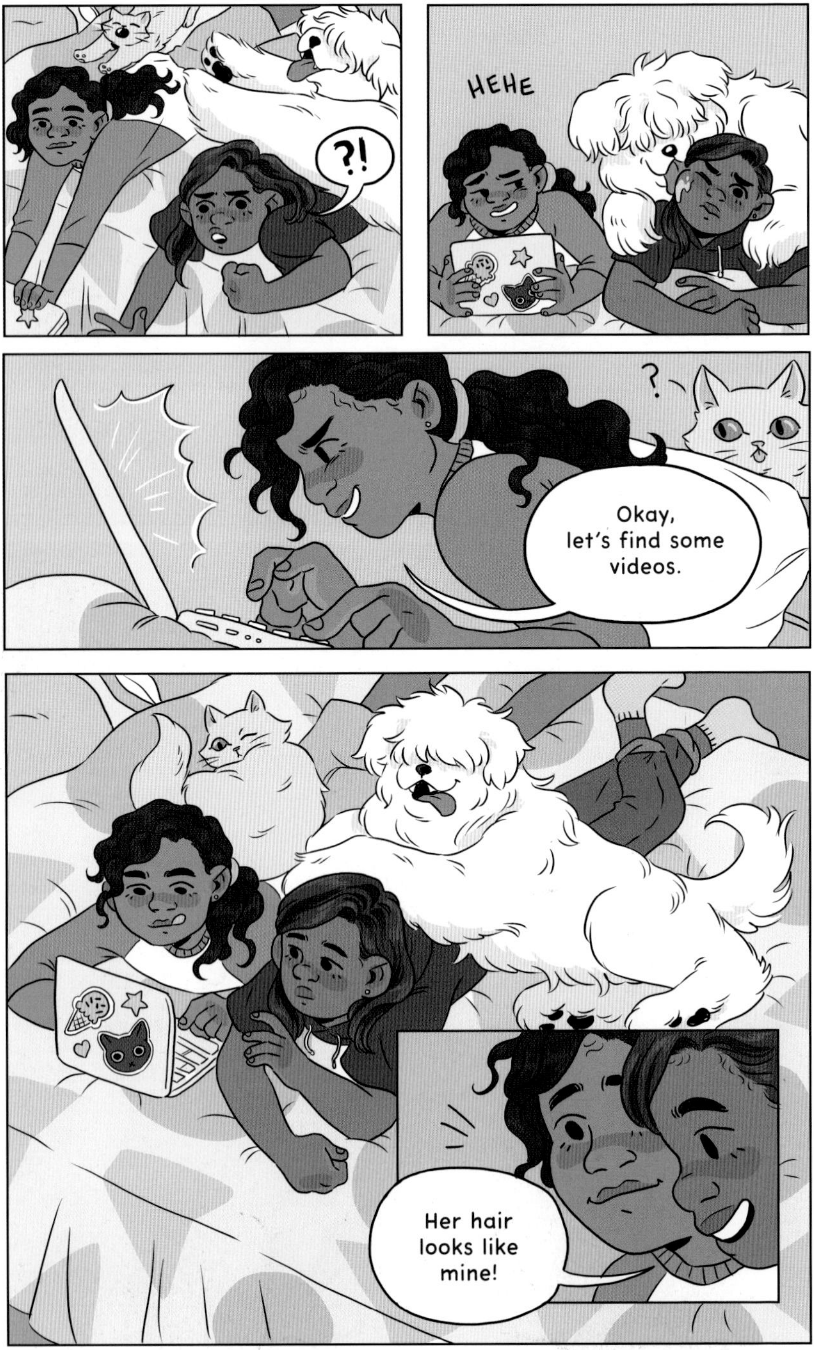
?!
HEHE
?
Okay, let's find some videos.
Her hair looks like mine!

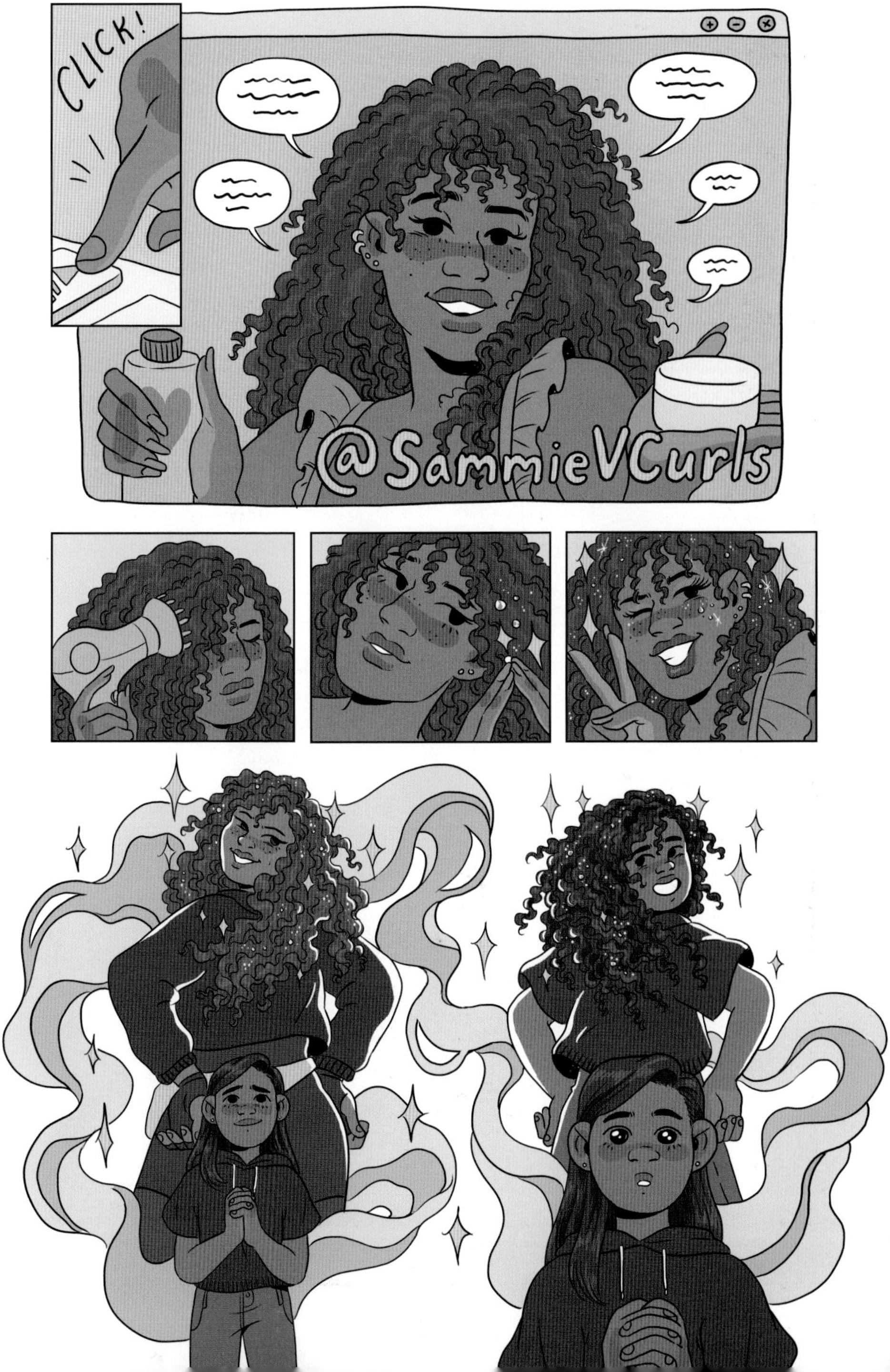
CLICK!
@SammieVCurls

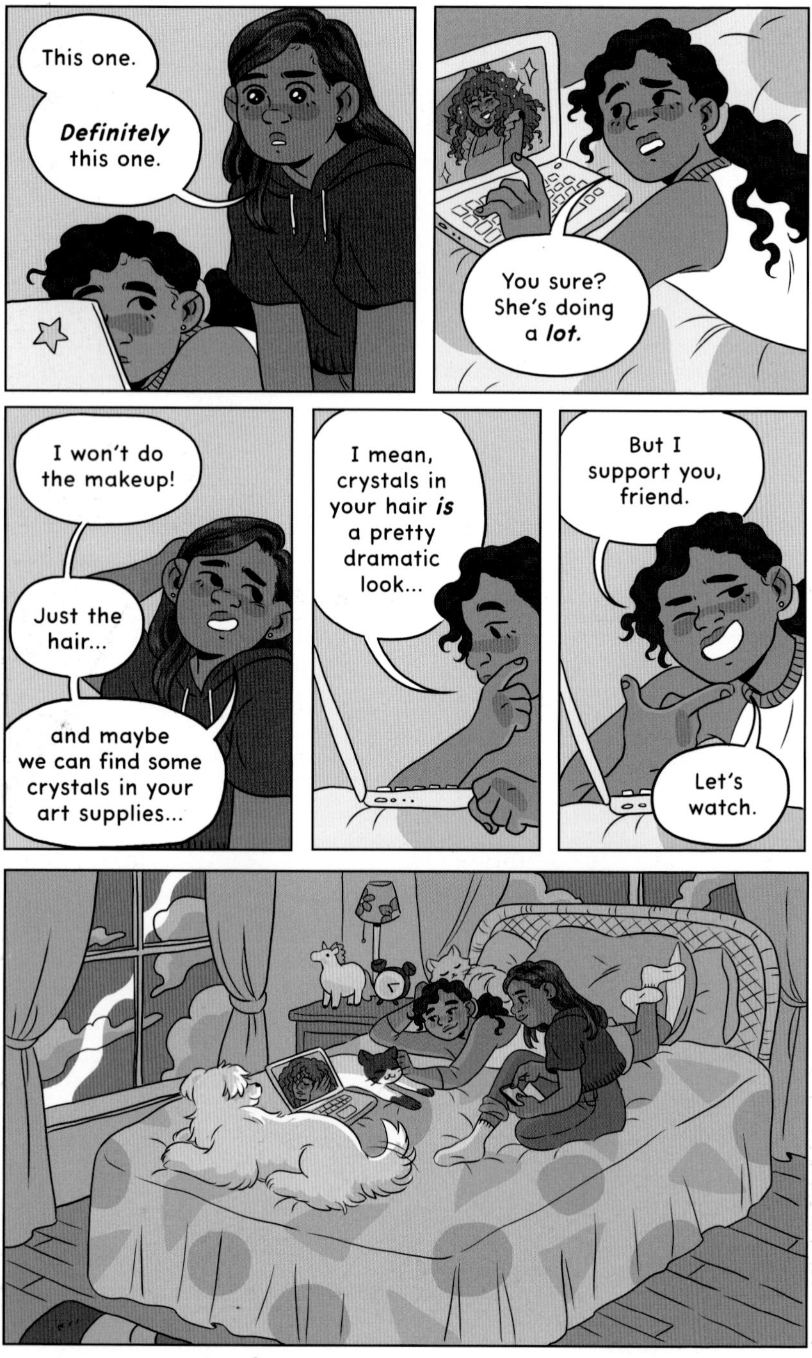
This one.
Definitely this one.
You sure? She's doing a ***lot.***
I won't do the makeup!
Just the hair...
and maybe we can find some crystals in your art supplies...
I mean, crystals in your hair ***is*** a pretty dramatic look...
But I support you, friend.
Let's watch.

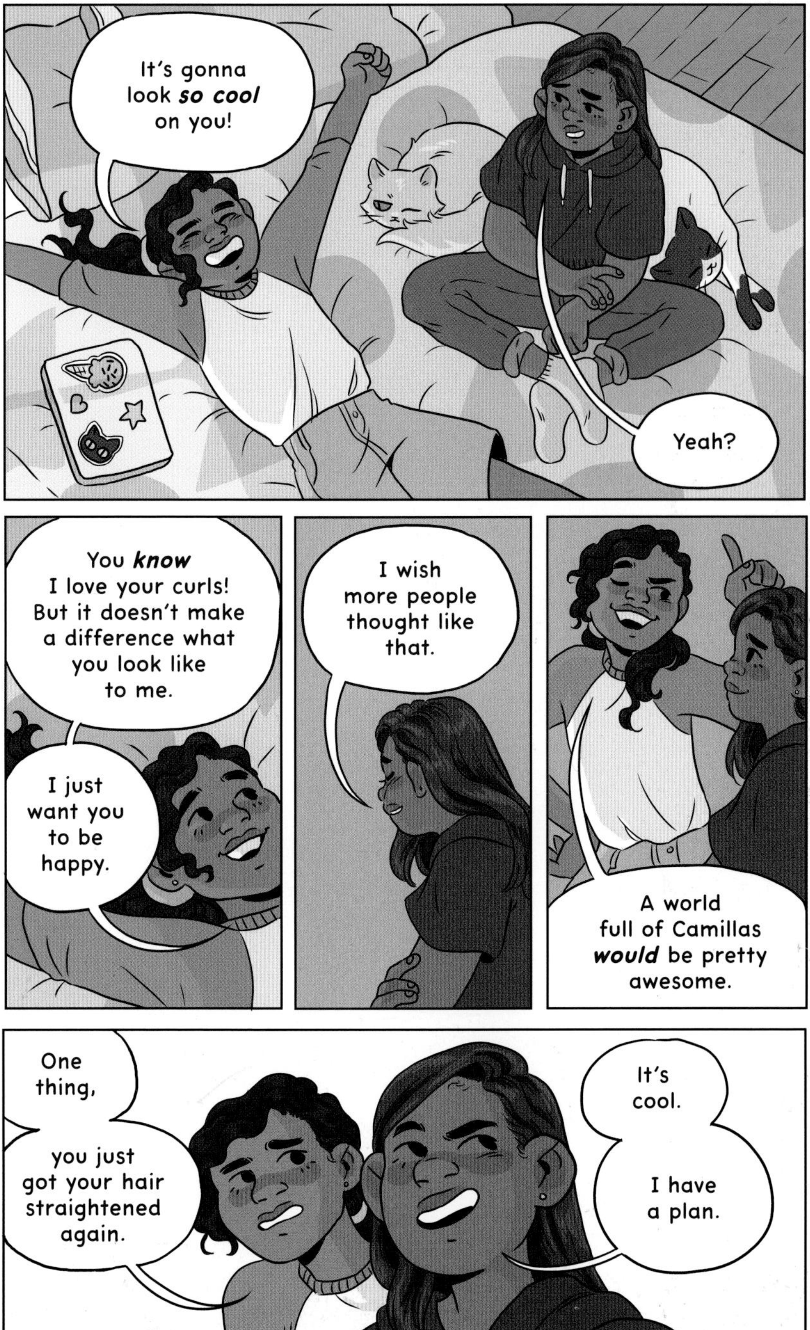
It's gonna look ***so cool*** on you!
Yeah?
You ***know*** I love your curls! But it doesn't make a difference what you look like to me.
I just want you to be happy.
I wish more people thought like that.
A world full of Camillas ***would*** be pretty awesome.
One thing,
you just got your hair straightened again.
It's cool.
I have a plan.

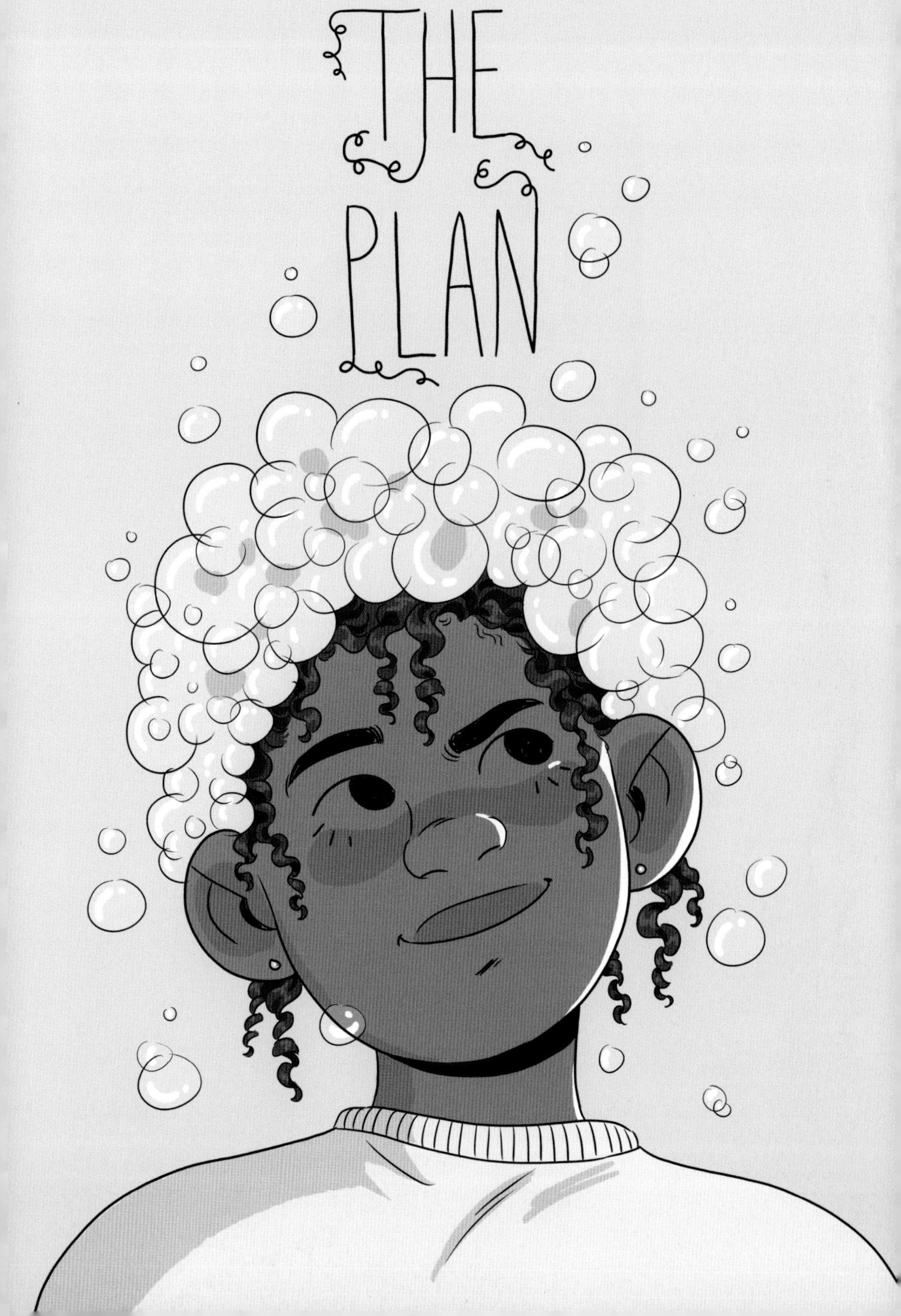
THE
PLAN

It's not like I had never gotten in trouble or broken a rule,

but something about messing up my straight hair felt more important.

It felt *scarier.*

Maybe because I hadn't always thought about it so much.

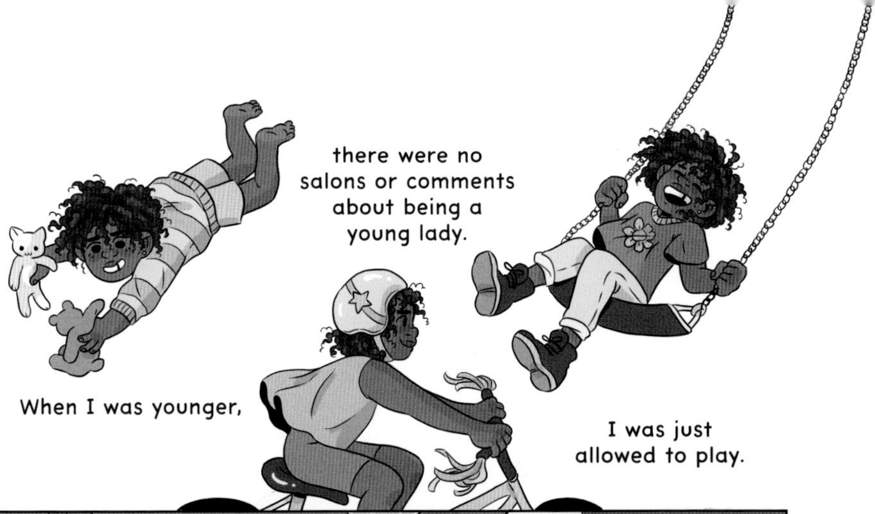
When I was younger,
there were no salons or comments about being a young lady.
I was just allowed to play.

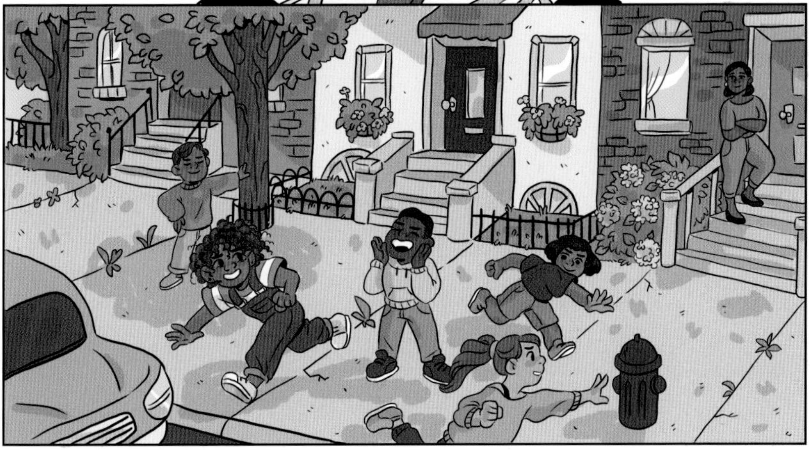

I could get sweaty and dirty, and the only thing I worried about was the sun going down and having to go inside.

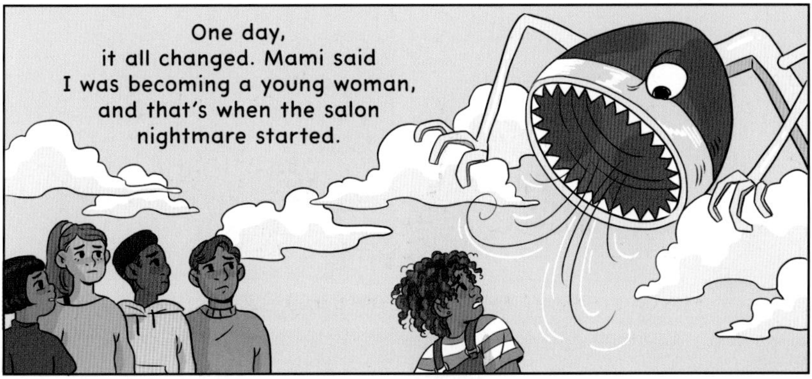
One day, it all changed. Mami said I was becoming a young woman, and that's when the salon nightmare started.

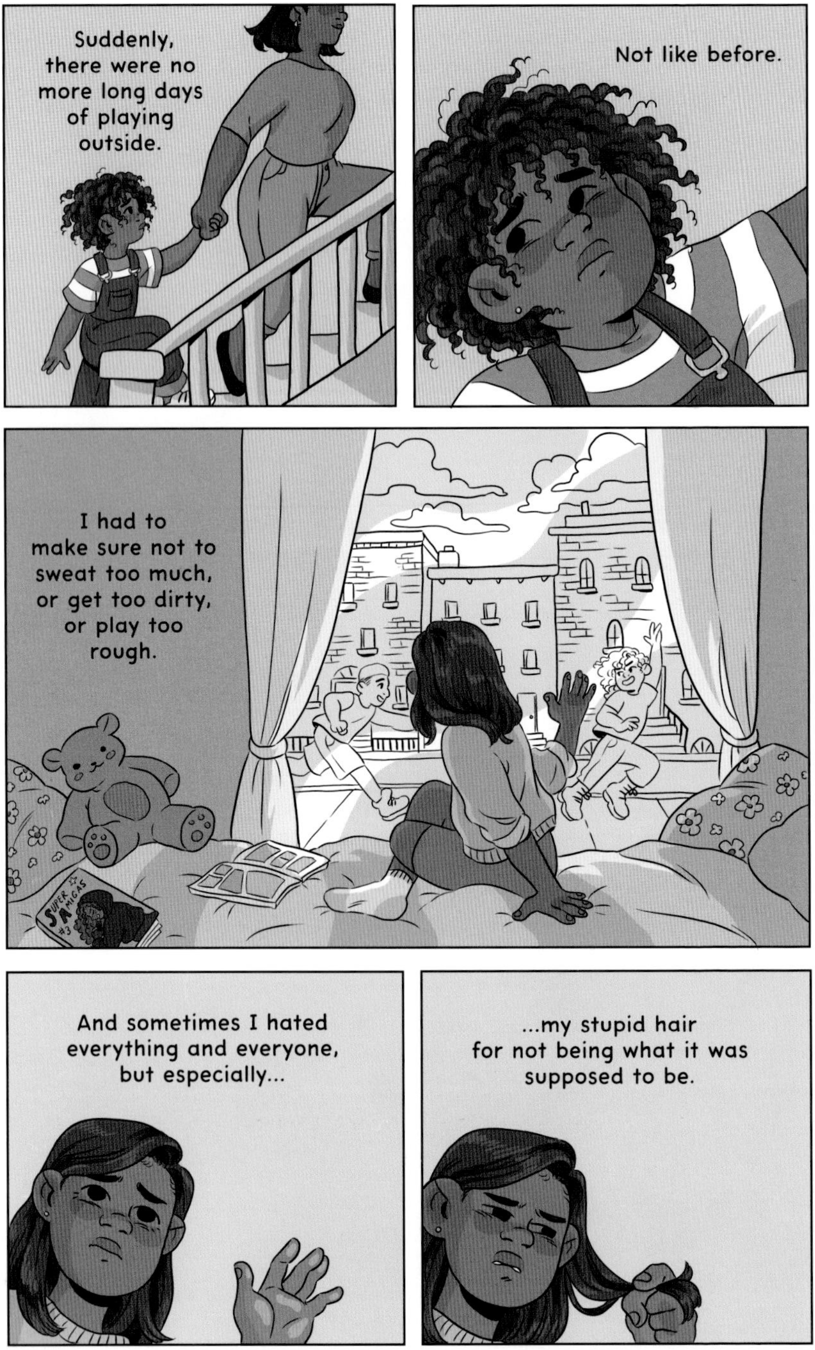
Suddenly, there were no more long days of playing outside.
Not like before.
I had to make sure not to sweat too much, or get too dirty, or play too rough.
SUPER AMIGAS #3
And sometimes I hated everything and everyone, but especially...
...my stupid hair for not being what it was supposed to be.

Maybe if it was,

people would just let me be me.

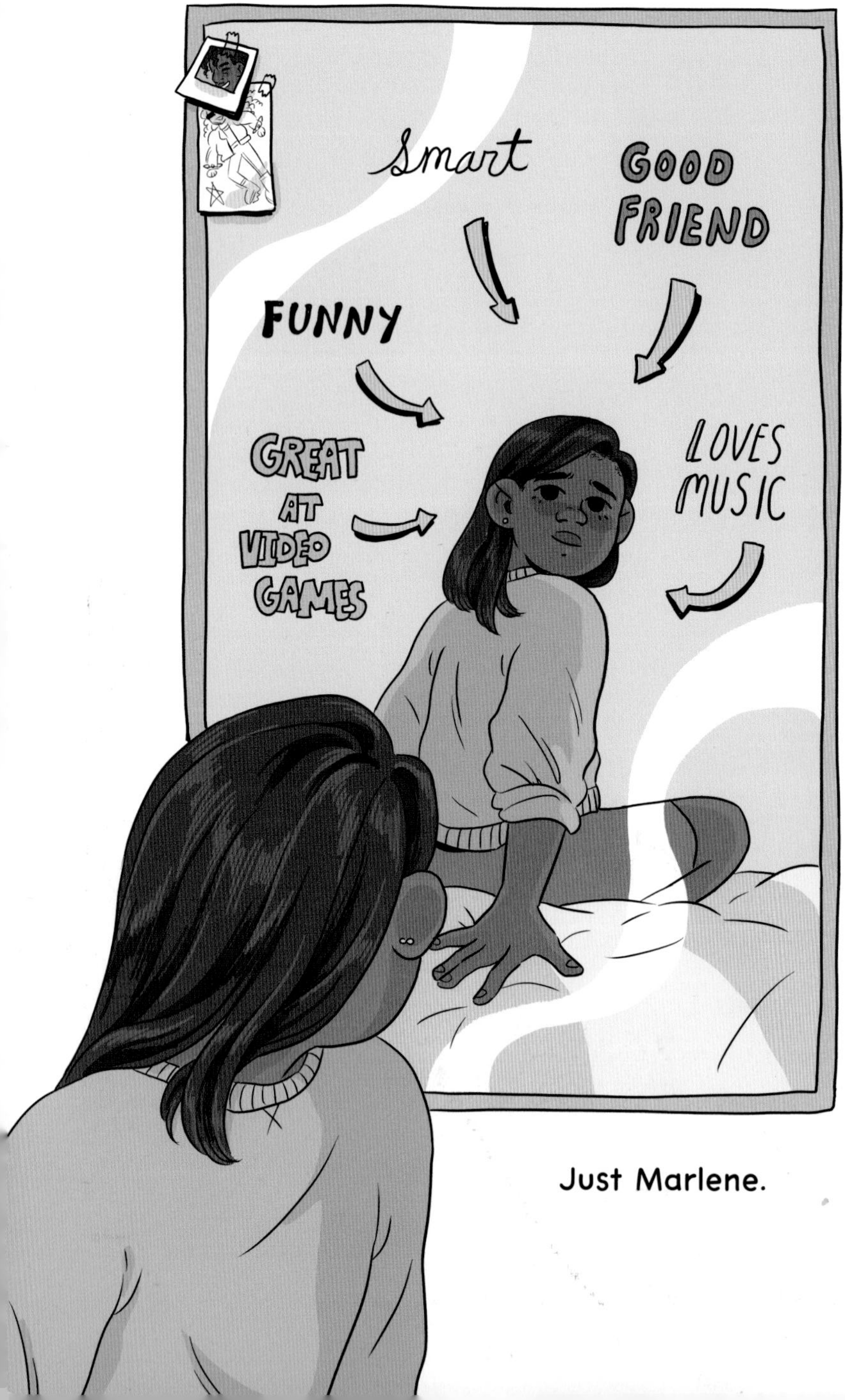
Smart
GOOD FRIEND
FUNNY
GREAT AT VIDEO GAMES
LOVES MUSIC

Just Marlene.

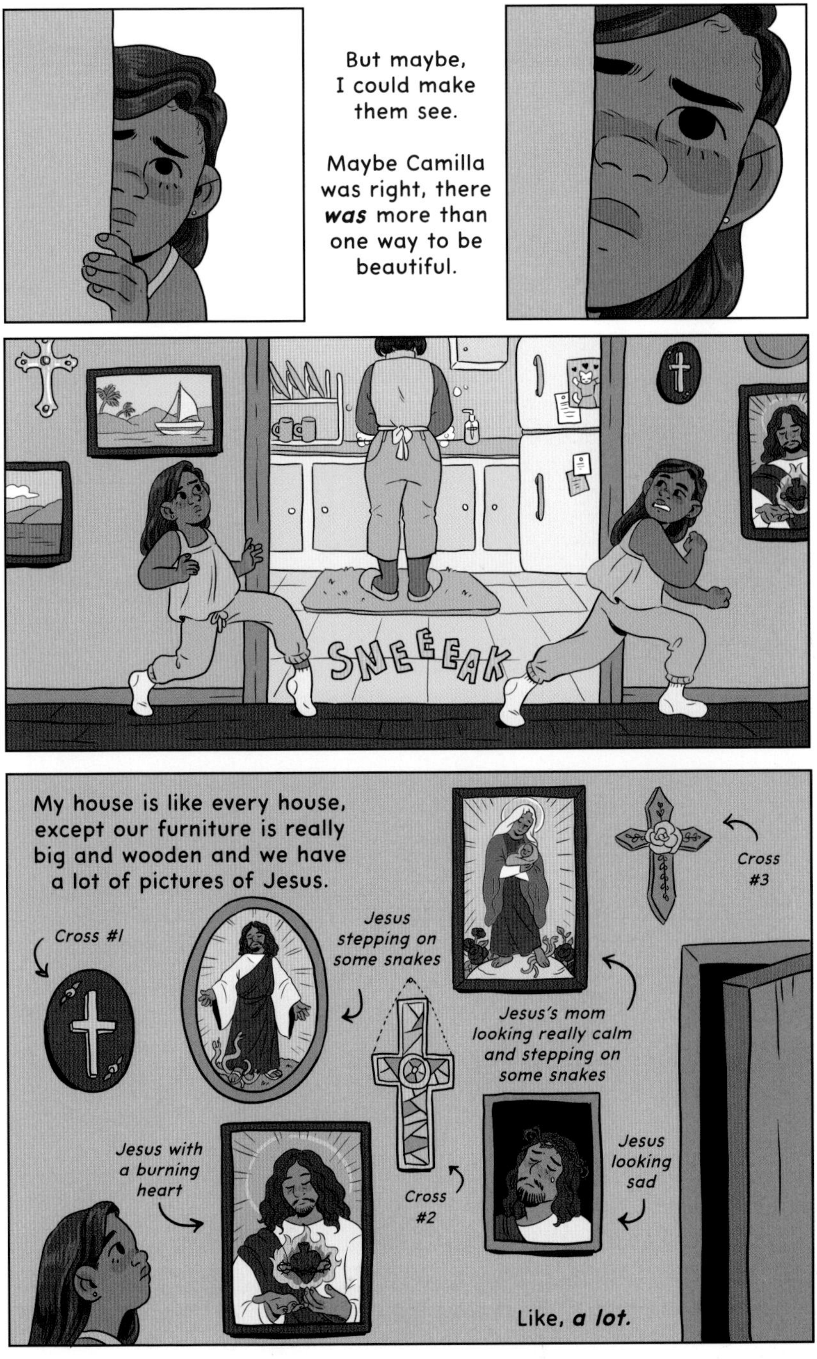
But maybe, I could make them see.
Maybe Camilla was right, there ***was*** more than one way to be beautiful.
SNEEEAK
My house is like every house, except our furniture is really big and wooden and we have a lot of pictures of Jesus.
Cross #1
Jesus stepping on some snakes
Jesus's mom looking really calm and stepping on some snakes
Cross #3
Jesus with a burning heart
Cross #2
Jesus looking sad
Like, ***a lot.***

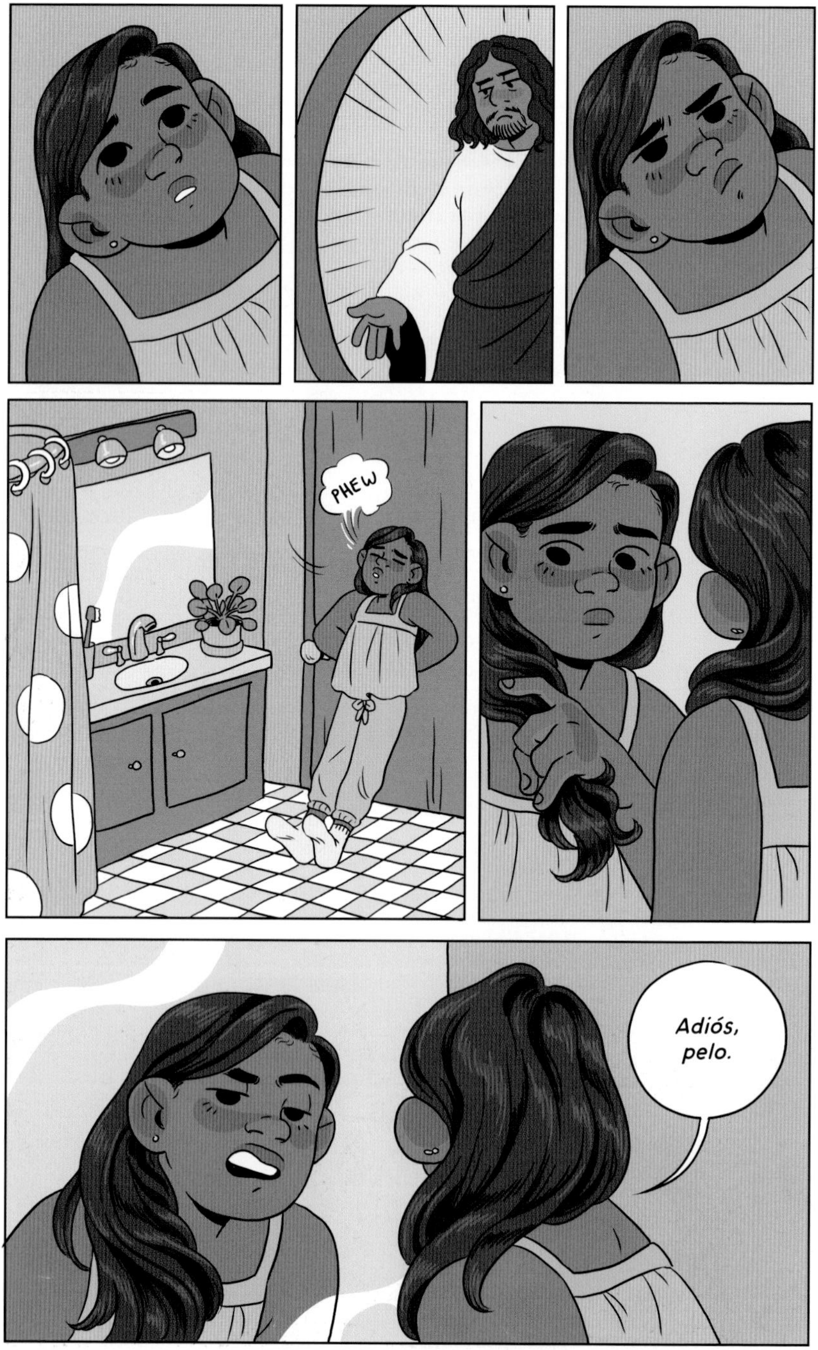
PHEW
Adiós, pelo.

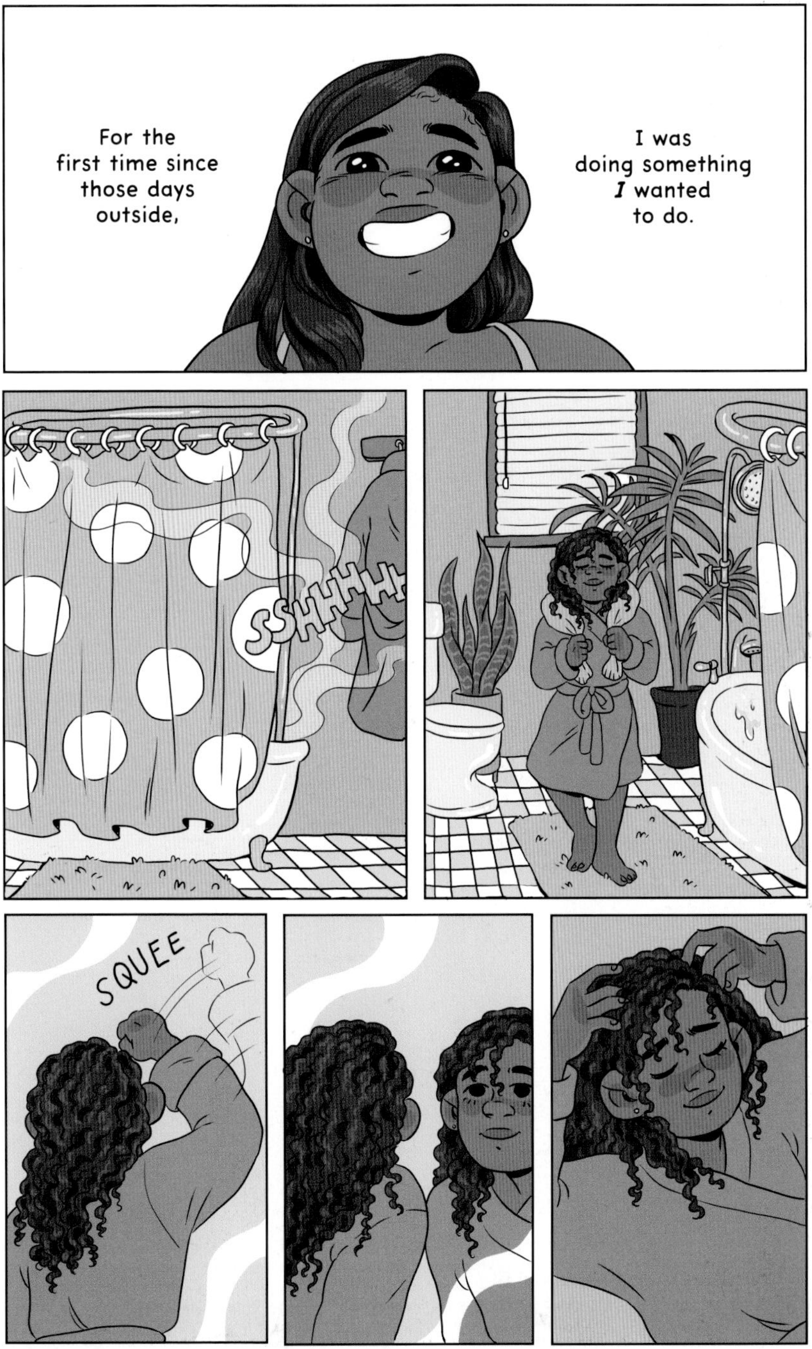
For the first time since those days outside,
I was doing something *I* wanted to do.
SSHHHH
SQUEE

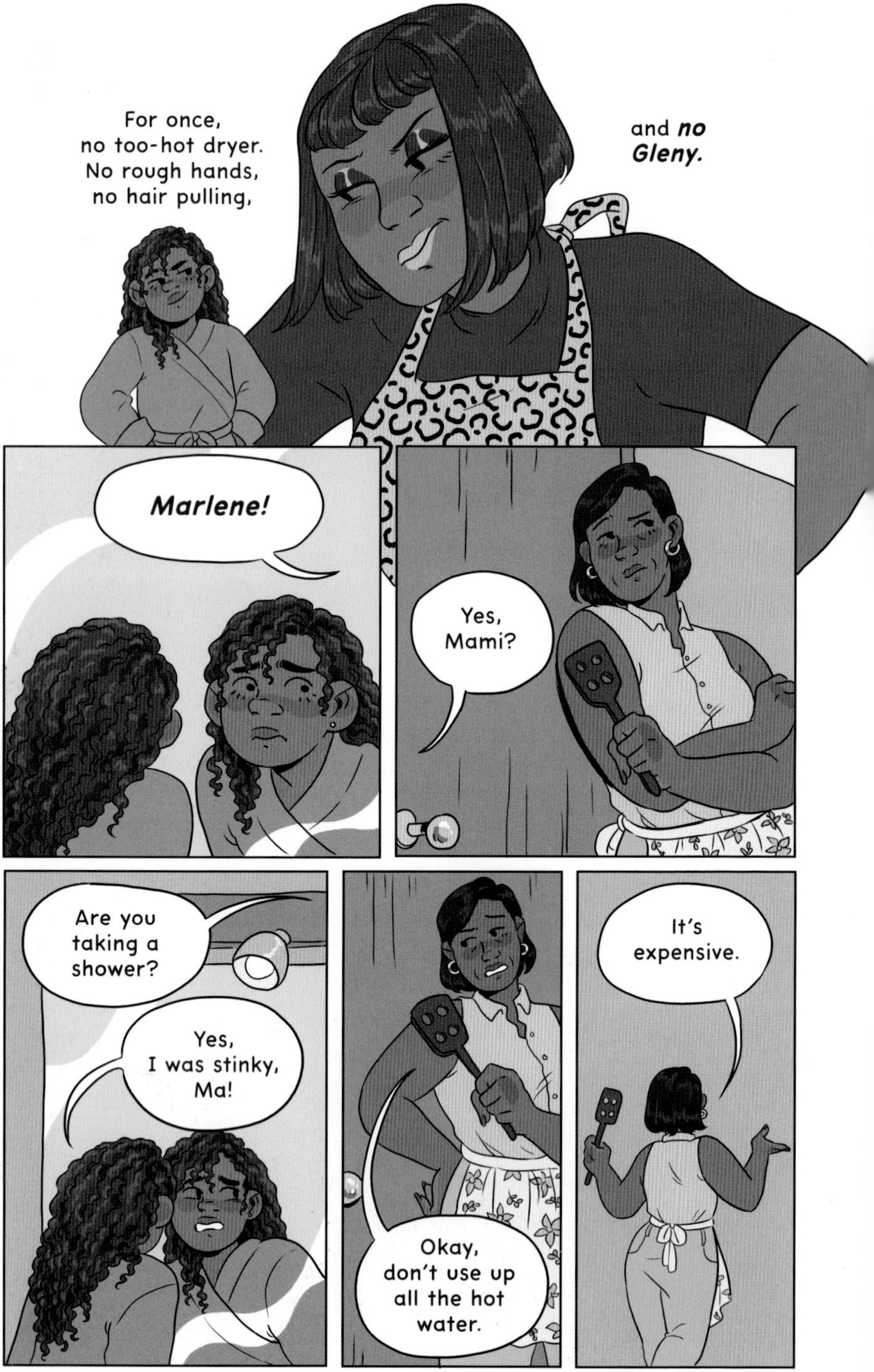
For once, no too-hot dryer. No rough hands, no hair pulling,
and *no Gleny.*
Marlene!
Yes, Mami?
Are you taking a shower?
Yes, I was stinky, Ma!
Okay, don't use up all the hot water.
It's expensive.

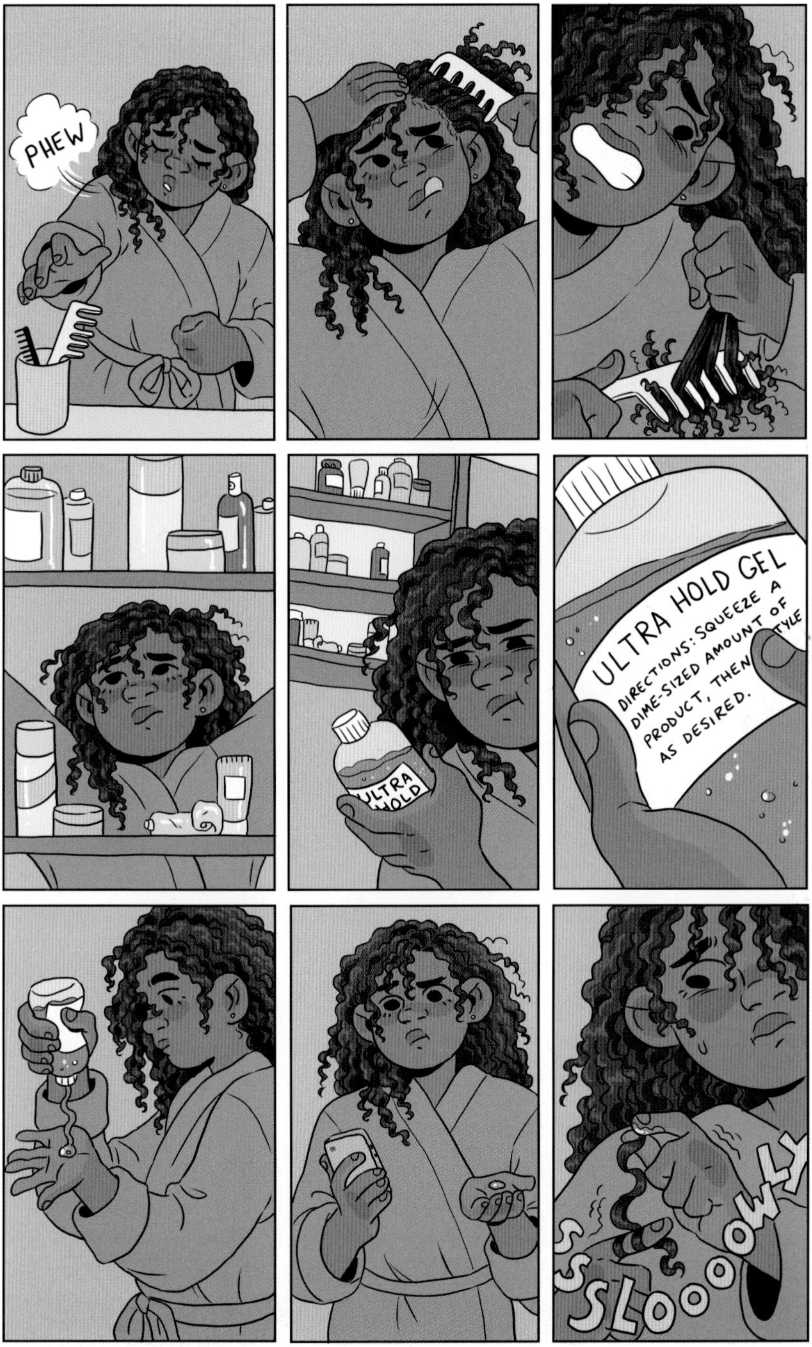
PHEW
ULTRA HOLD
ULTRA HOLD GEL
DIRECTIONS: SQUEEZE A DIME-SIZED AMOUNT OF PRODUCT, THEN STYLE AS DESIRED.
SSLOOOOWLY

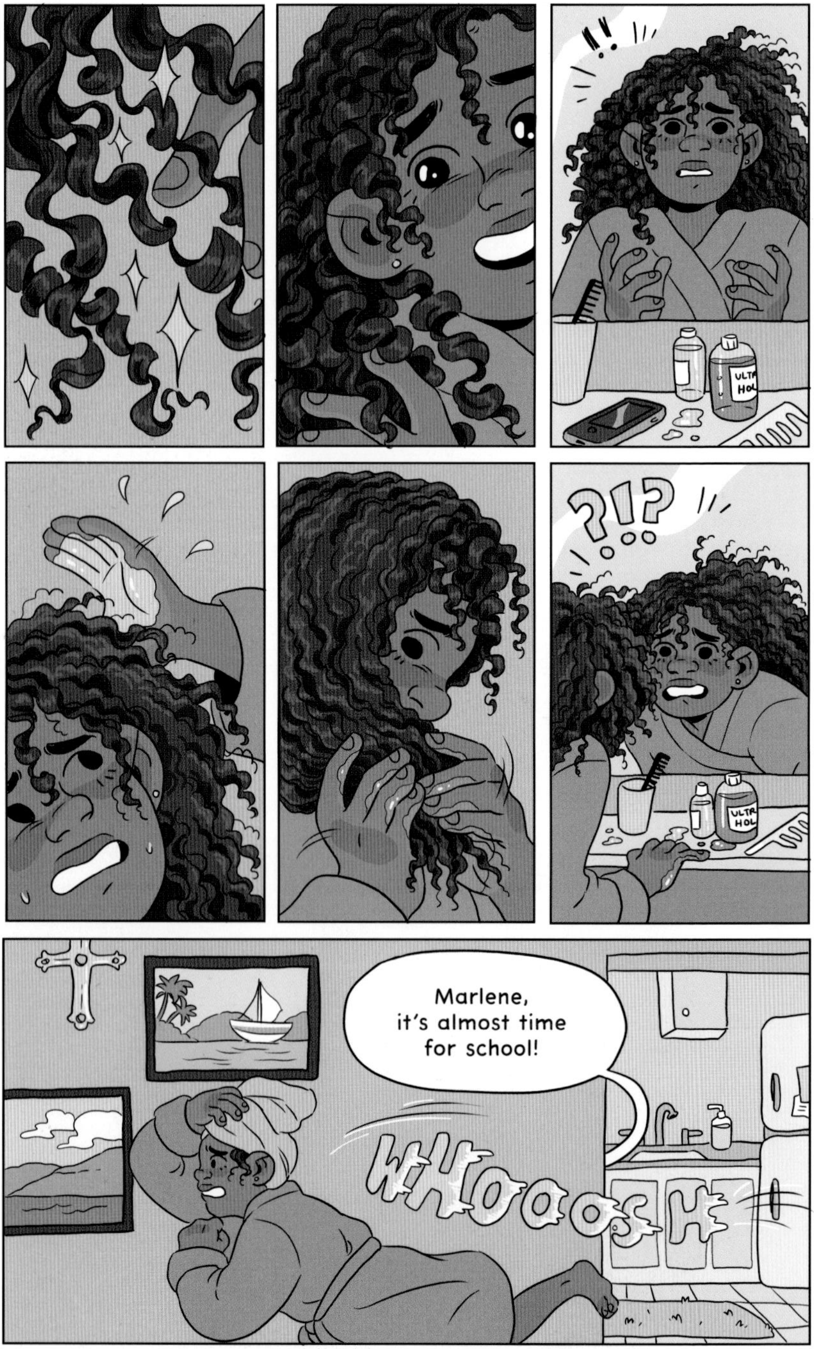
!!
?!?
Marlene,
it's almost time
for school!
WHOOOSH

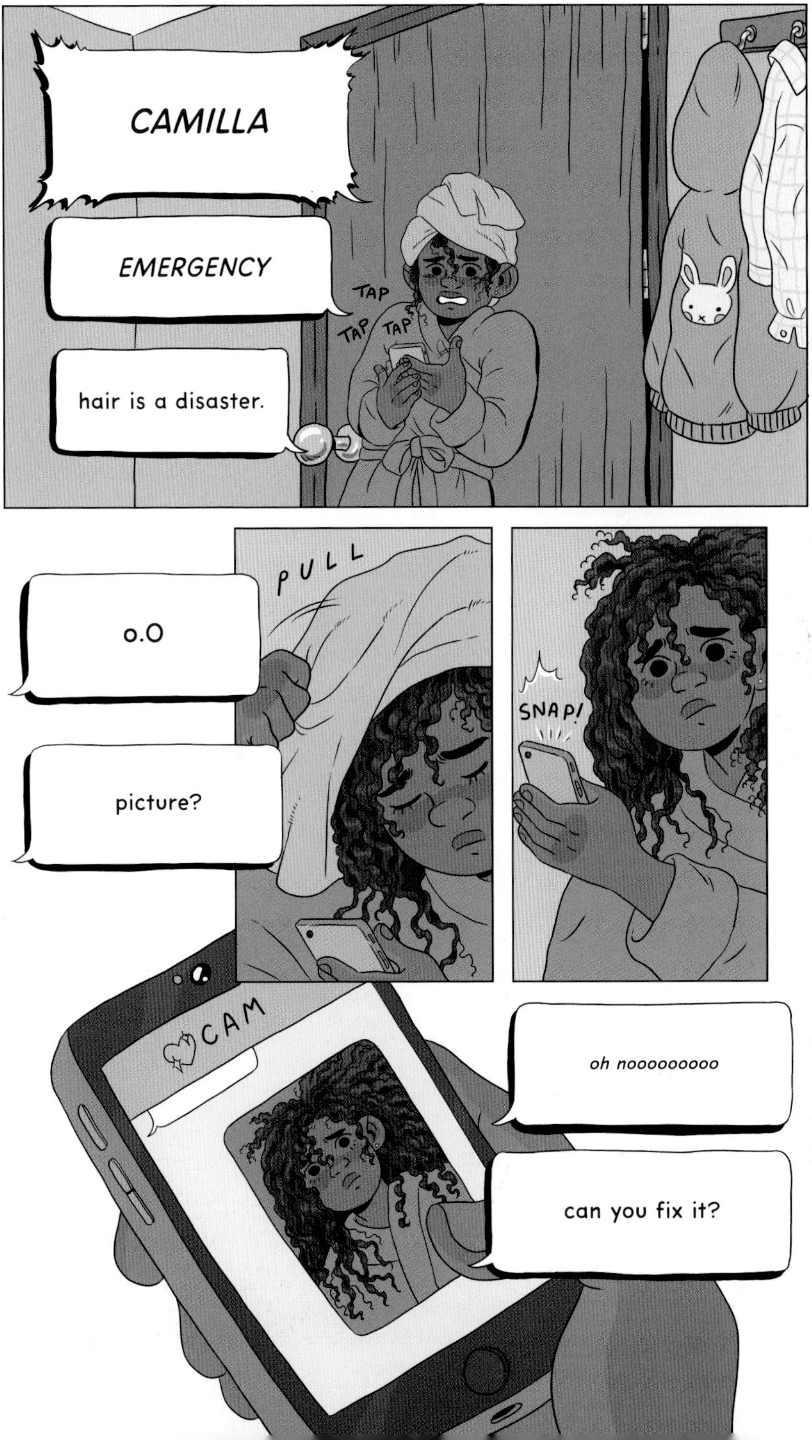
CAMILLA
EMERGENCY
hair is a disaster.
TAP
TAP TAP
PULL
o.O
picture?
SNAP!
CAM
oh noooooooo
can you fix it?

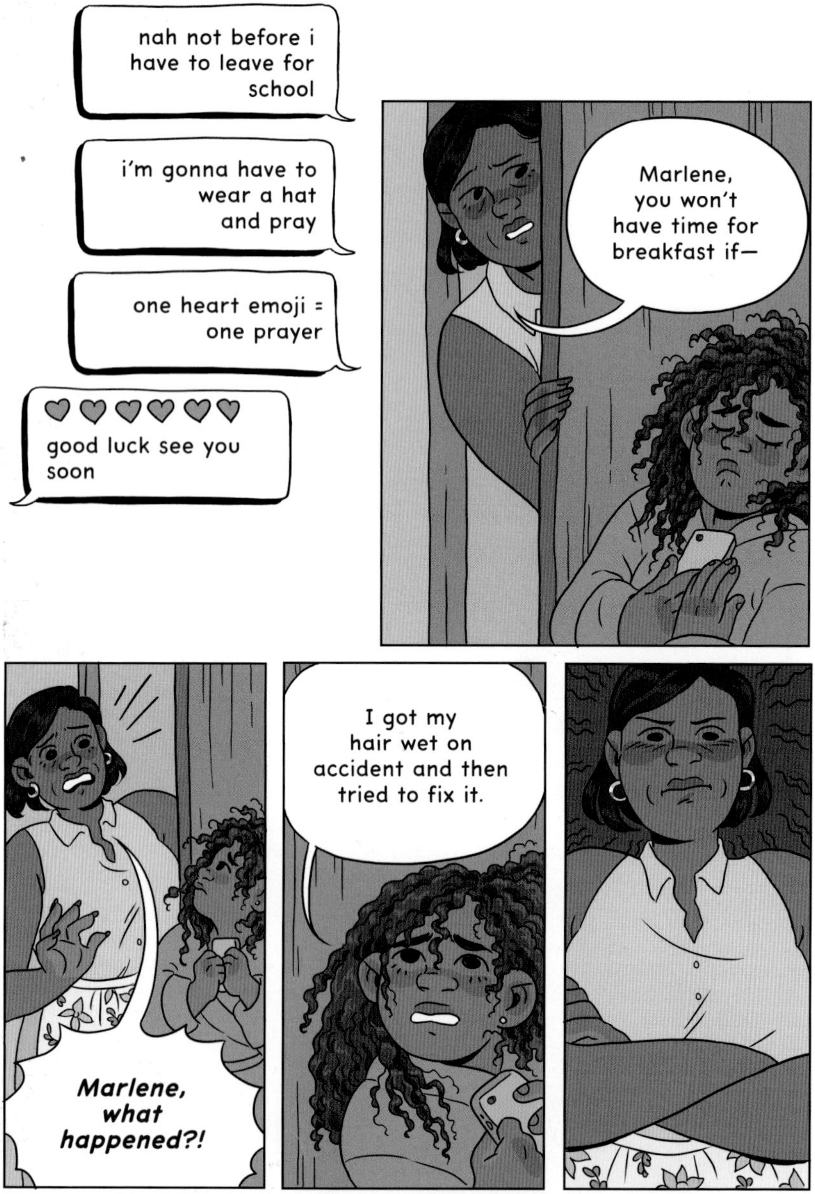
nah not before i have to leave for school
i'm gonna have to wear a hat and pray
one heart emoji = one prayer
good luck see you soon
Marlene, you won't have time for breakfast if—
Marlene, what happened?!
I got my hair wet on accident and then tried to fix it.

I knew I shouldn't lie, but it just slipped. Plus, if I told her about the plan, she'd only be angrier.

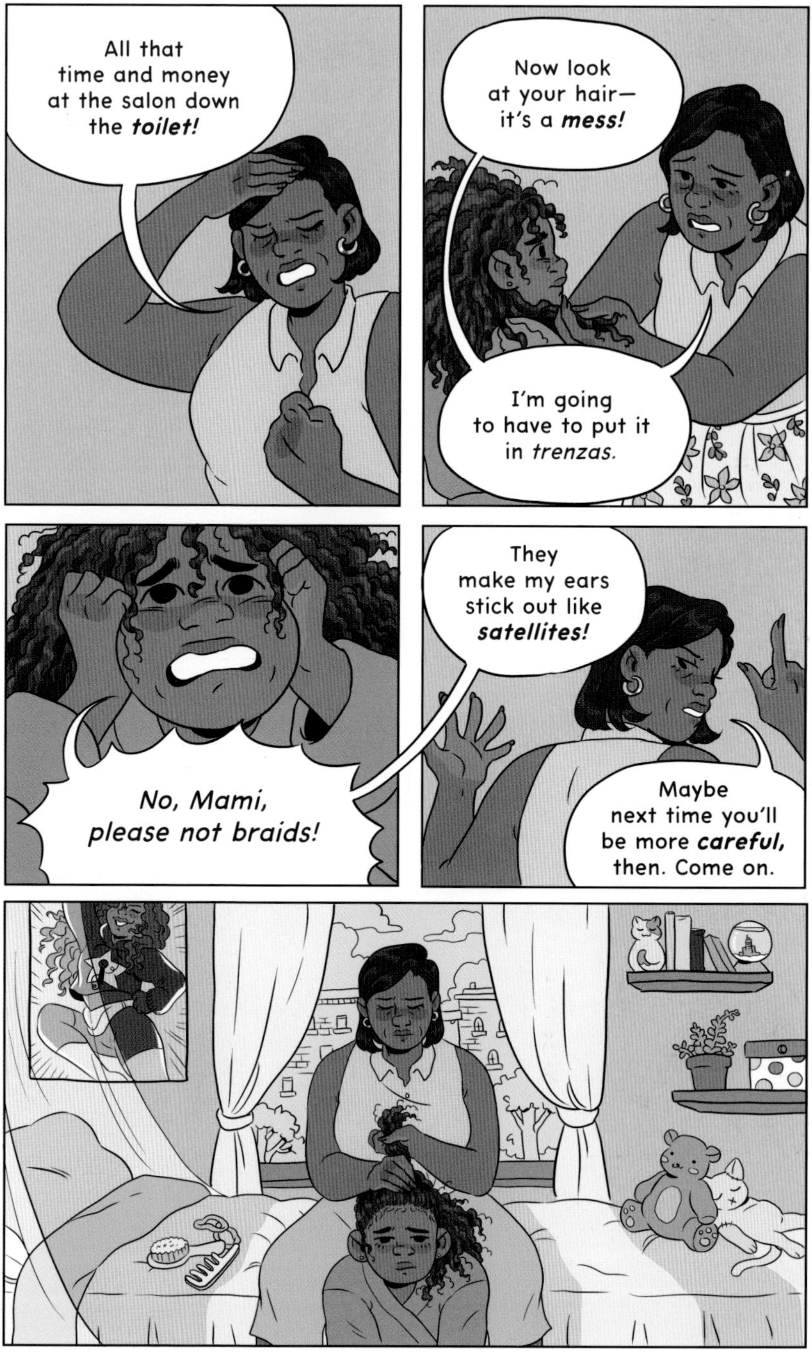
All that time and money at the salon down the *toilet!*
Now look at your hair— it's a *mess!*
I'm going to have to put it in *trenzas.*
No, Mami, please not braids!
They make my ears stick out like *satellites!*
Maybe next time you'll be more *careful,* then. Come on.

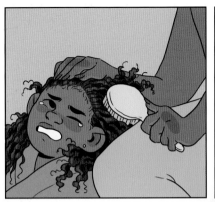

This plan was a bad idea. Now my mom was mad, my hair was a mess, and I was in trouble.

The only thing I wanted to do was make people see me how I saw myself in my head.

Why was that so hard?

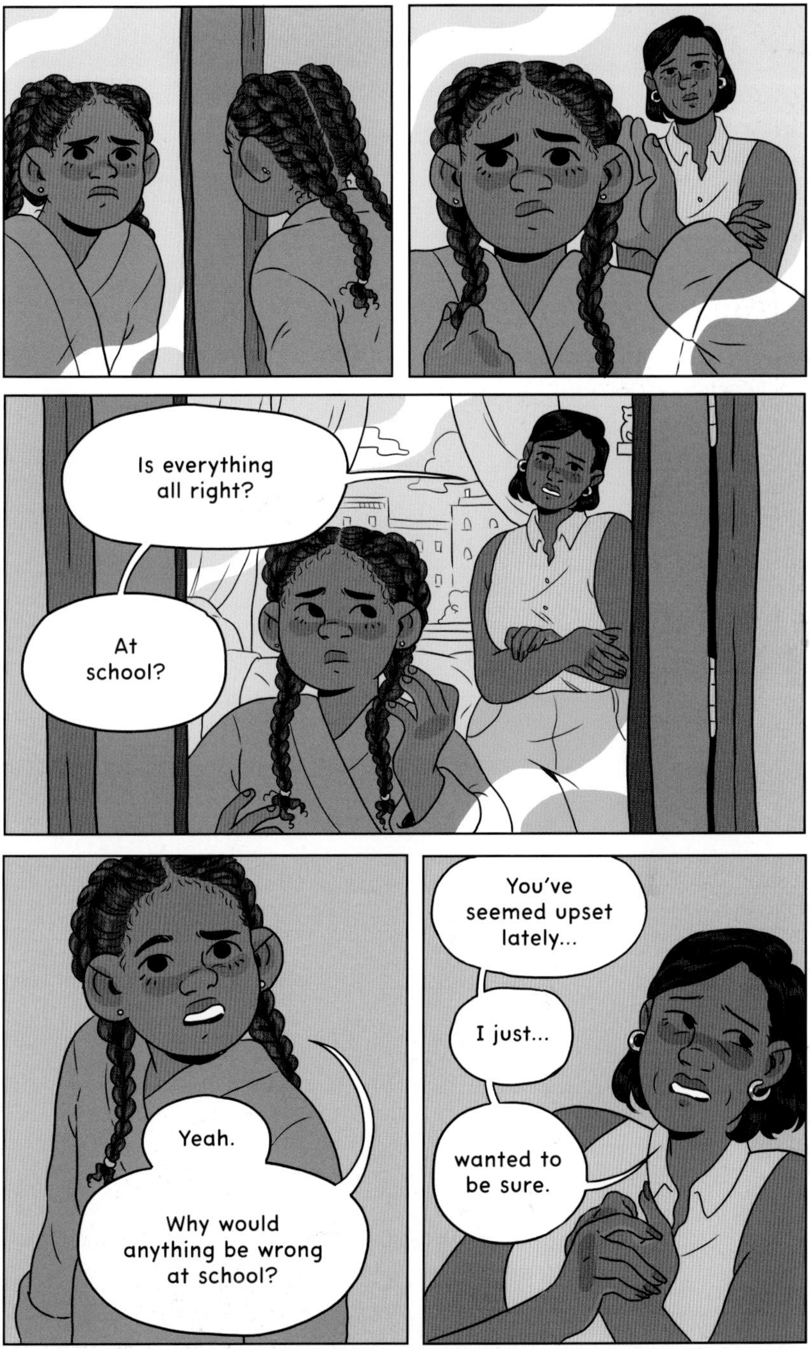
Is everything all right?
At school?
Yeah.
Why would anything be wrong at school?
You've seemed upset lately...
I just...
wanted to be sure.

How could I tell her
the thing we did every Sunday
that seemed so important to her
was making me sad?

I didn't want to lie again,
but making her even more upset
would be worse.

Right?

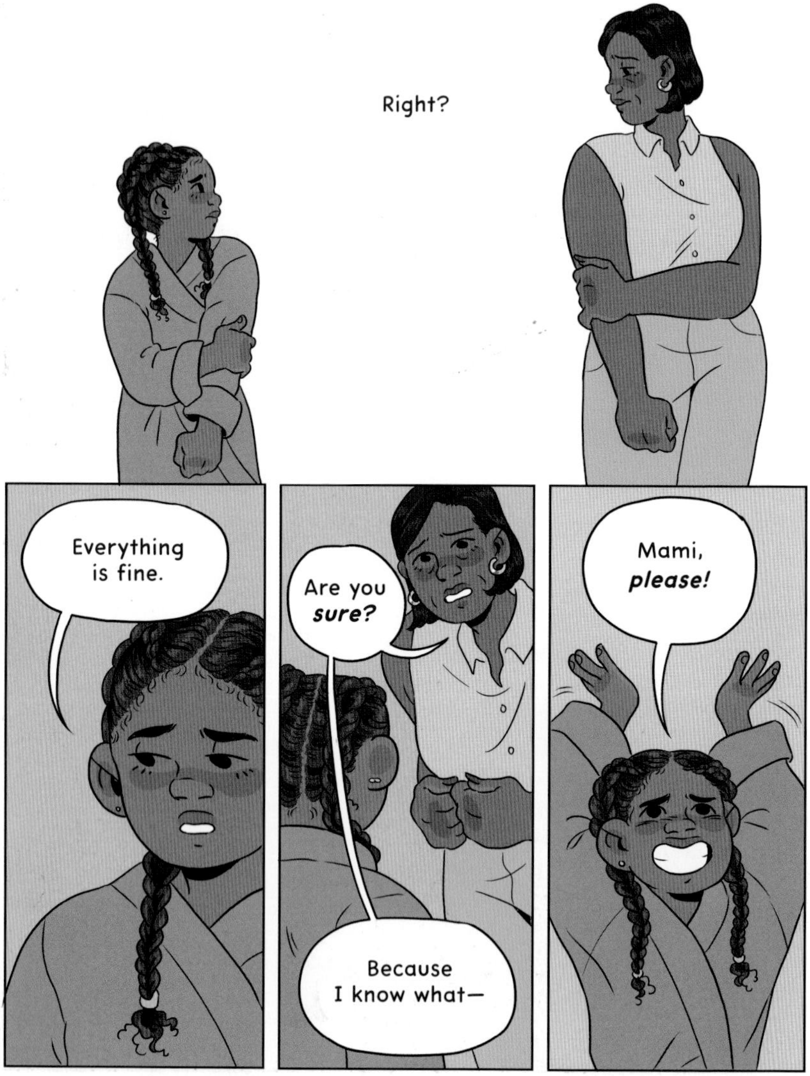
Everything is fine.
Are you *sure?*
Because I know what—
Mami, *please!*

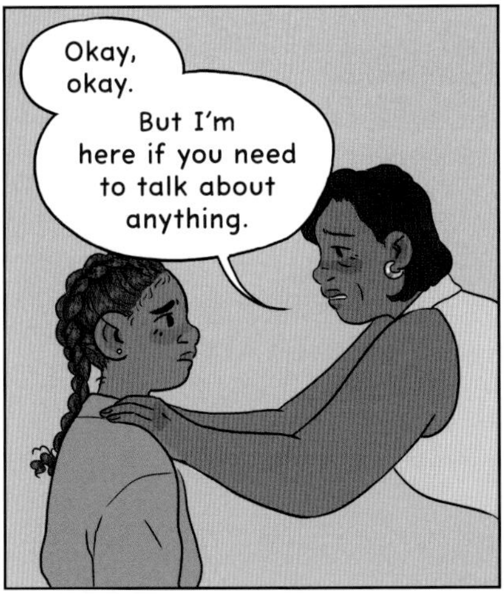
Okay, okay. But I'm here if you need to talk about anything.

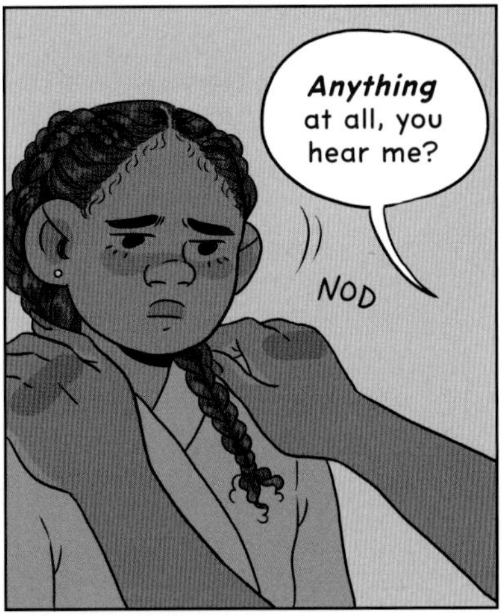
Anything at all, you hear me?
NOD

It wasn't even eight in the morning and the day was already ***awful.***
And now it was about to get worse.

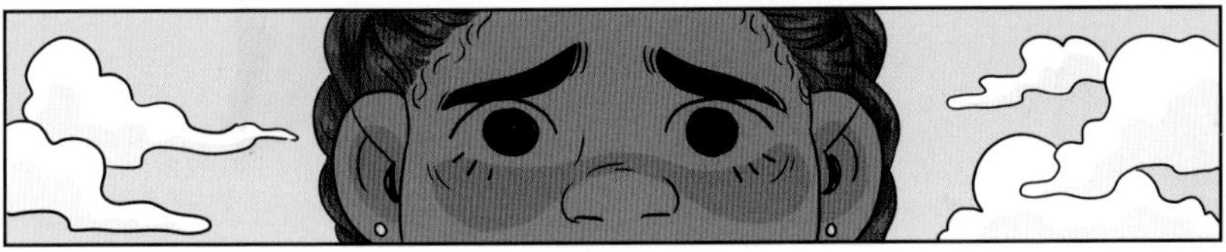

I had to go to school.

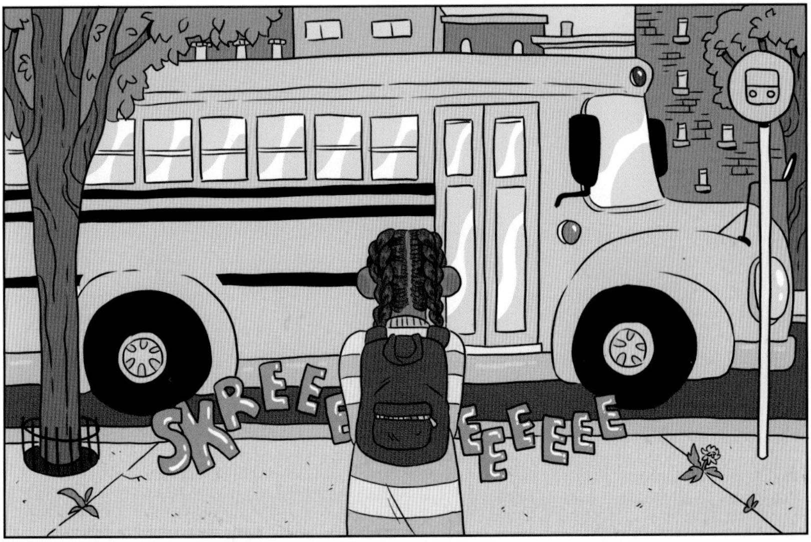
SKREEEE EEEEEE

The bus is the ***worst.***

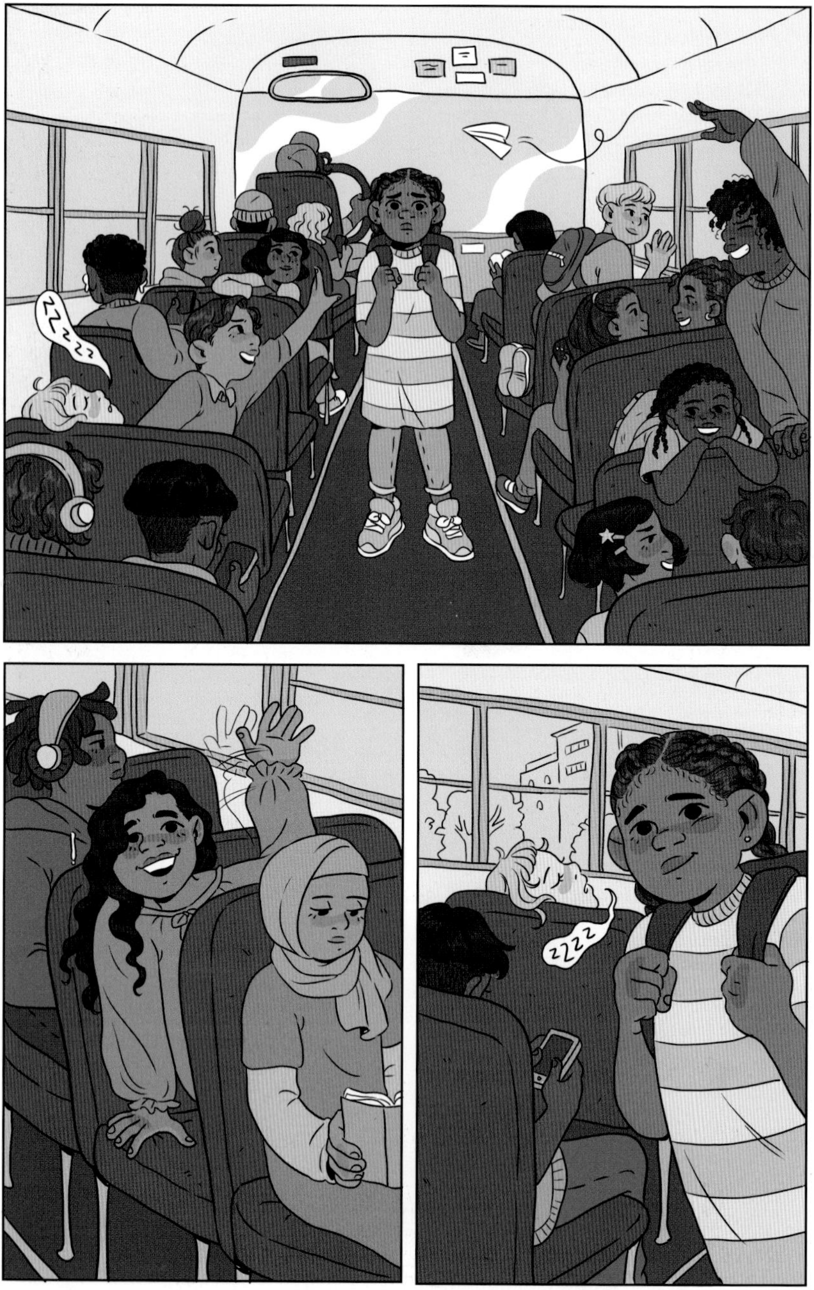
ZZZZ
ZZZZ

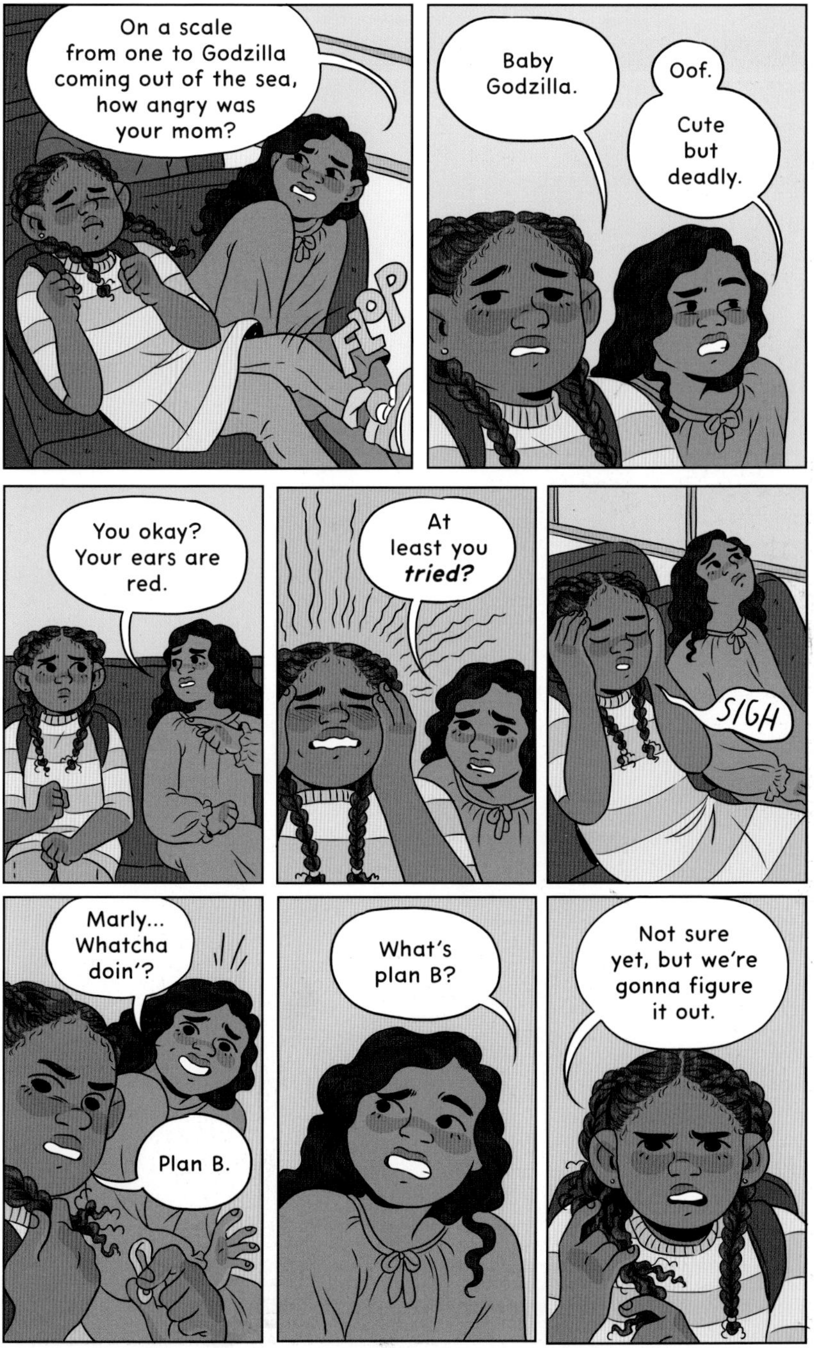
On a scale from one to Godzilla coming out of the sea, how angry was your mom?
FLOP
Baby Godzilla.
Oof.
Cute but deadly.
You okay? Your ears are red.
At least you *tried?*
SIGH
Marly... Whatcha doin'?
Plan B.
What's plan B?
Not sure yet, but we're gonna figure it out.

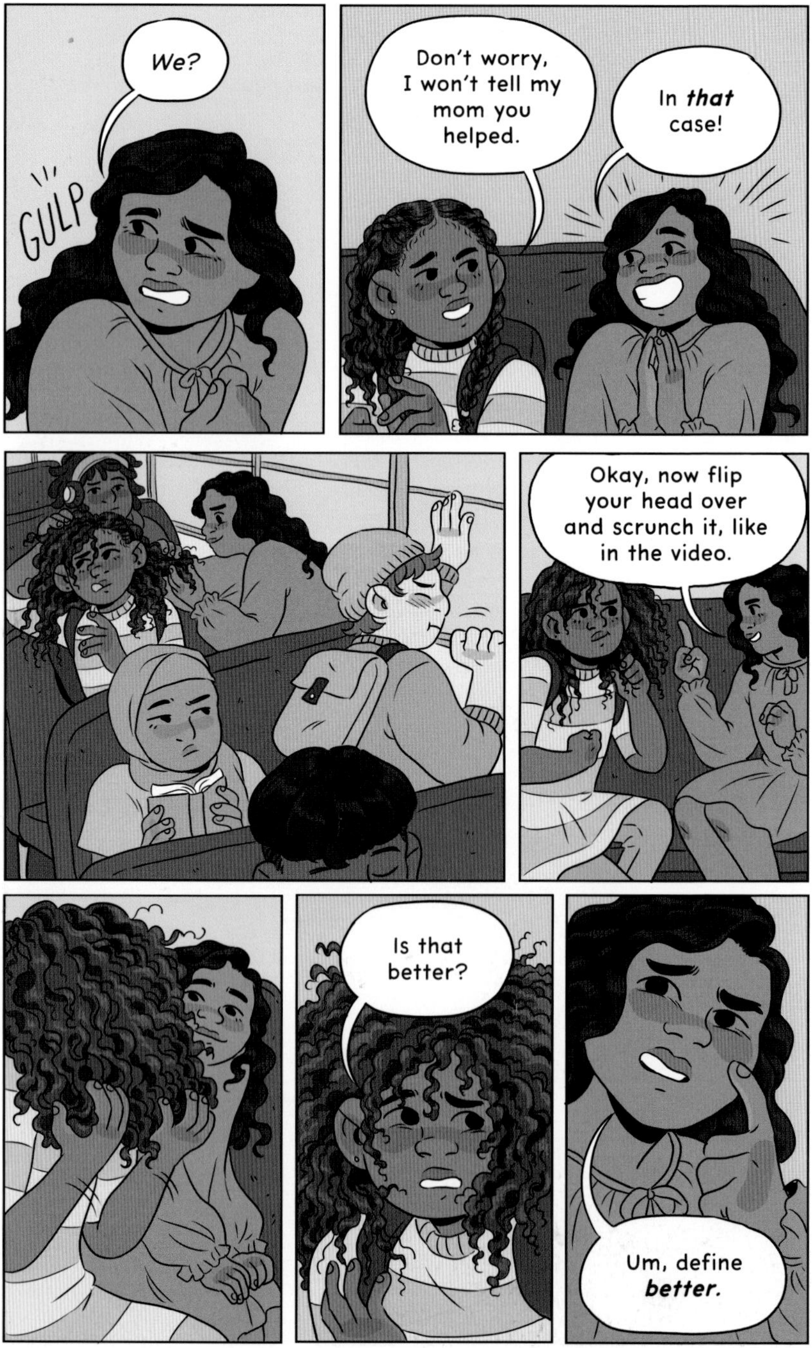
We?
GULP
Don't worry, I won't tell my mom you helped.
In *that* case!
Okay, now flip your head over and scrunch it, like in the video.
Is that better?
Um, define *better.*

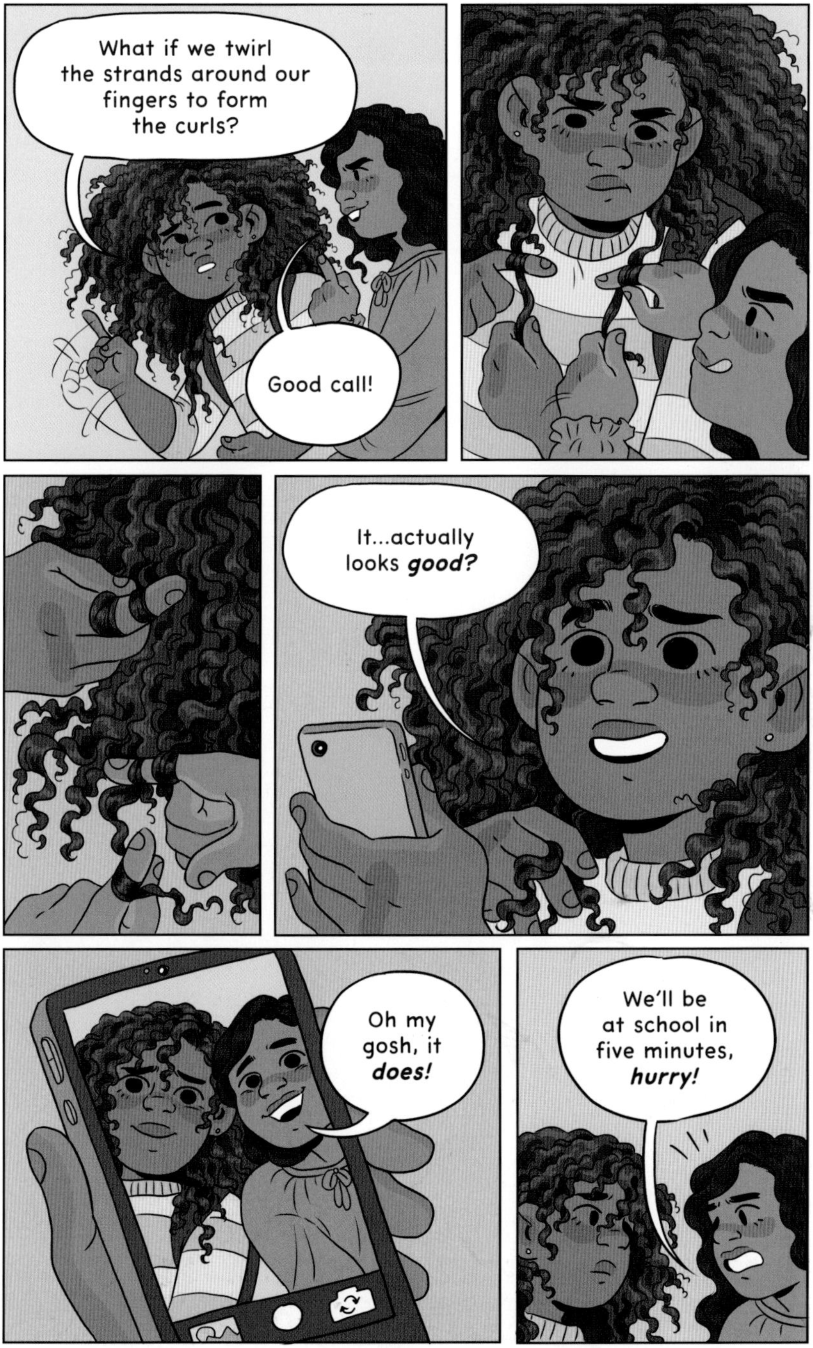
What if we twirl the strands around our fingers to form the curls?
Good call!
It...actually looks ***good?***
Oh my gosh, it ***does!***
We'll be at school in five minutes, ***hurry!***

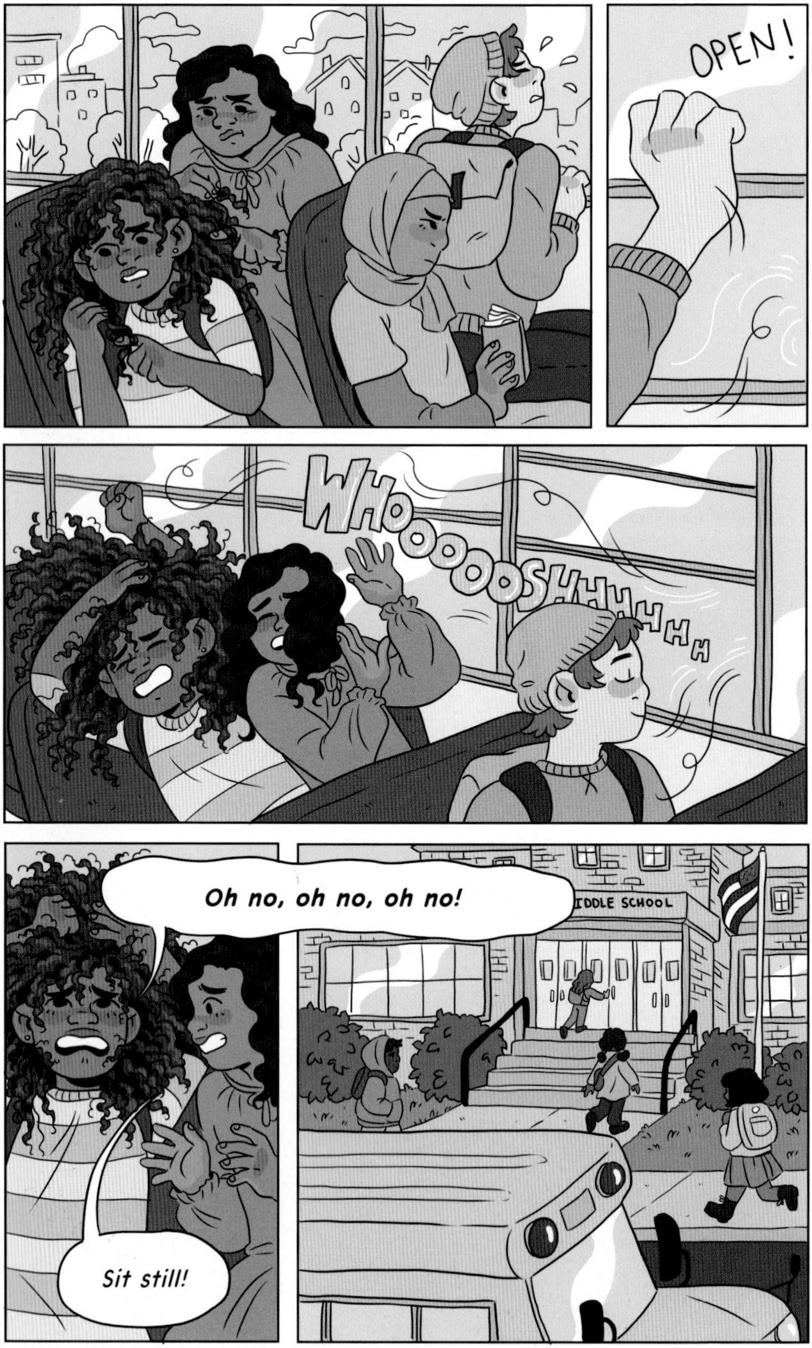
OPEN!
WHOOOOOOSHHHHHHH
Oh no, oh no, oh no!
Sit still!
IDDLE SCHOOL

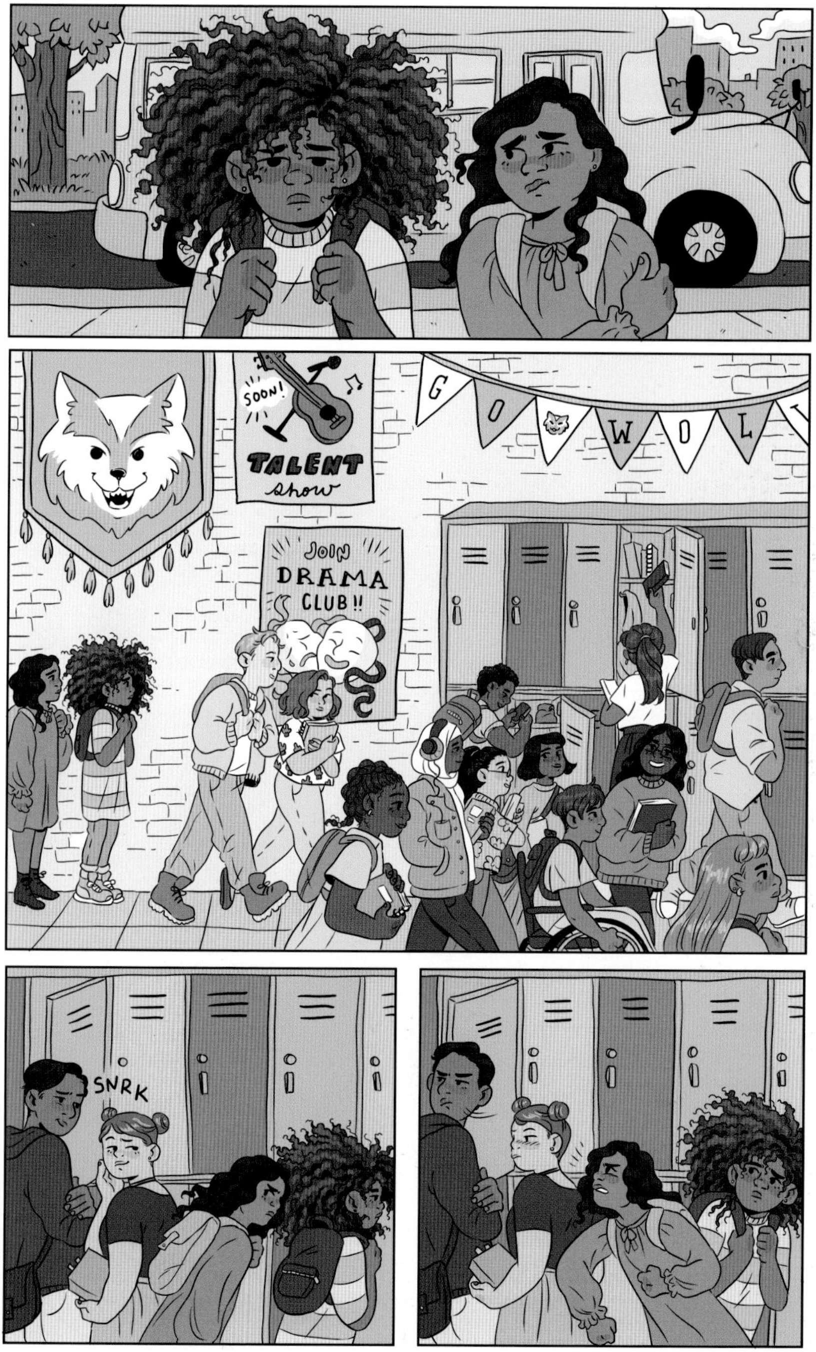
SOON!
TALENT show
G O WOL
JOIN DRAMA CLUB!!
SNRK

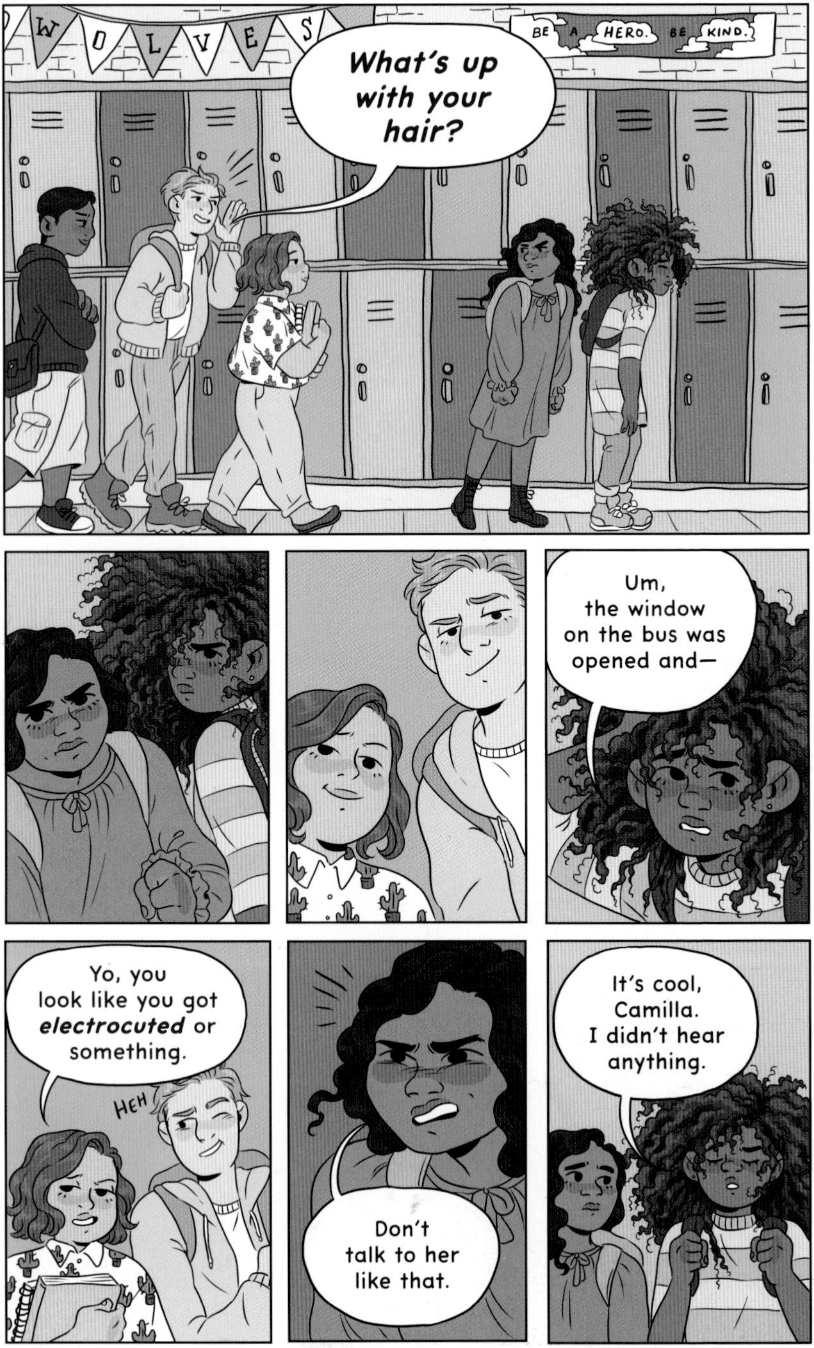
WOLVES
BE A HERO. BE KIND.
What's up with your hair?
Um, the window on the bus was opened and—
Yo, you look like you got *electrocuted* or something.
HEH
Don't talk to her like that.
It's cool, Camilla. I didn't hear anything.

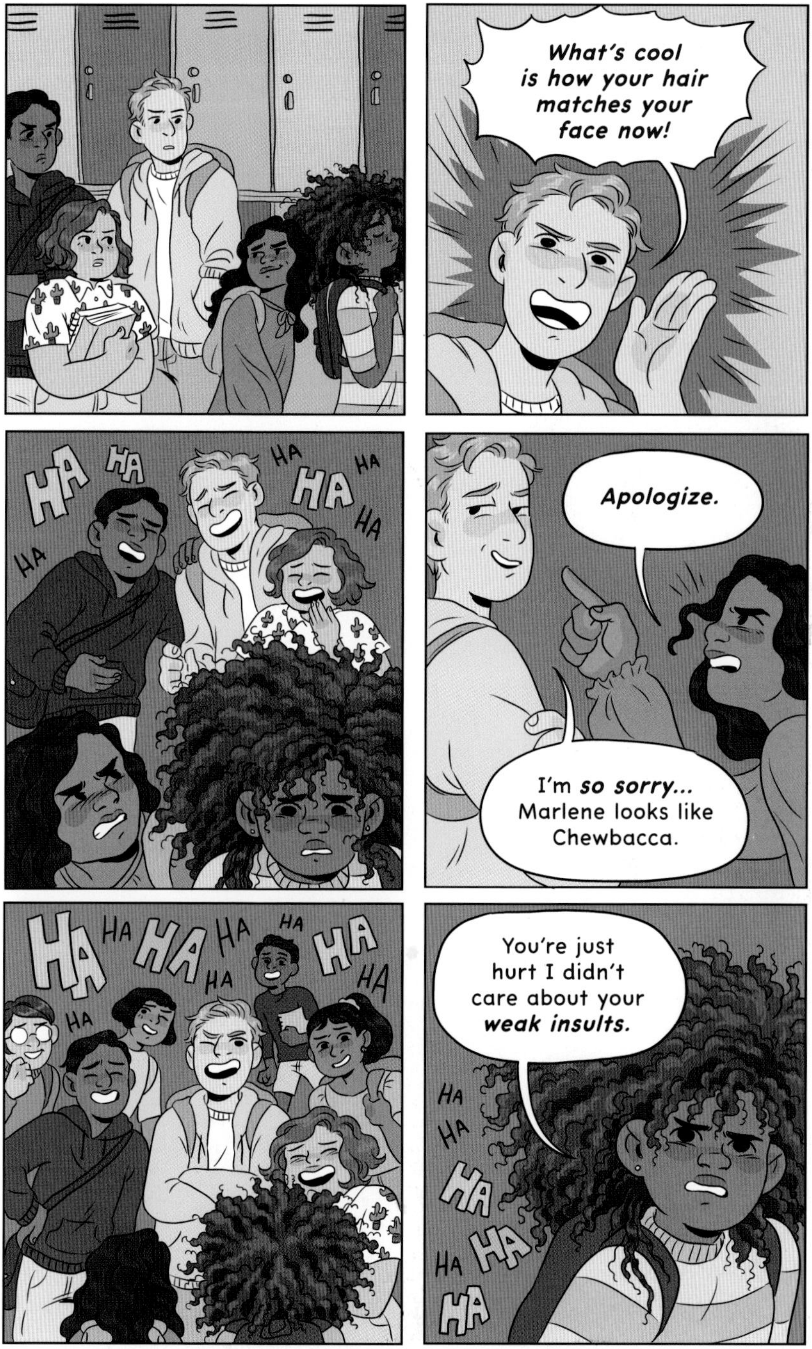
What's cool is how your hair matches your face now!
HA HA HA HA HA HA HA HA
Apologize.
I'm ***so sorry...*** Marlene looks like Chewbacca.
HA HA HA HA HA HA HA HA HA HA HA
You're just hurt I didn't care about your ***weak insults.***
HA HA HA HA HA HA

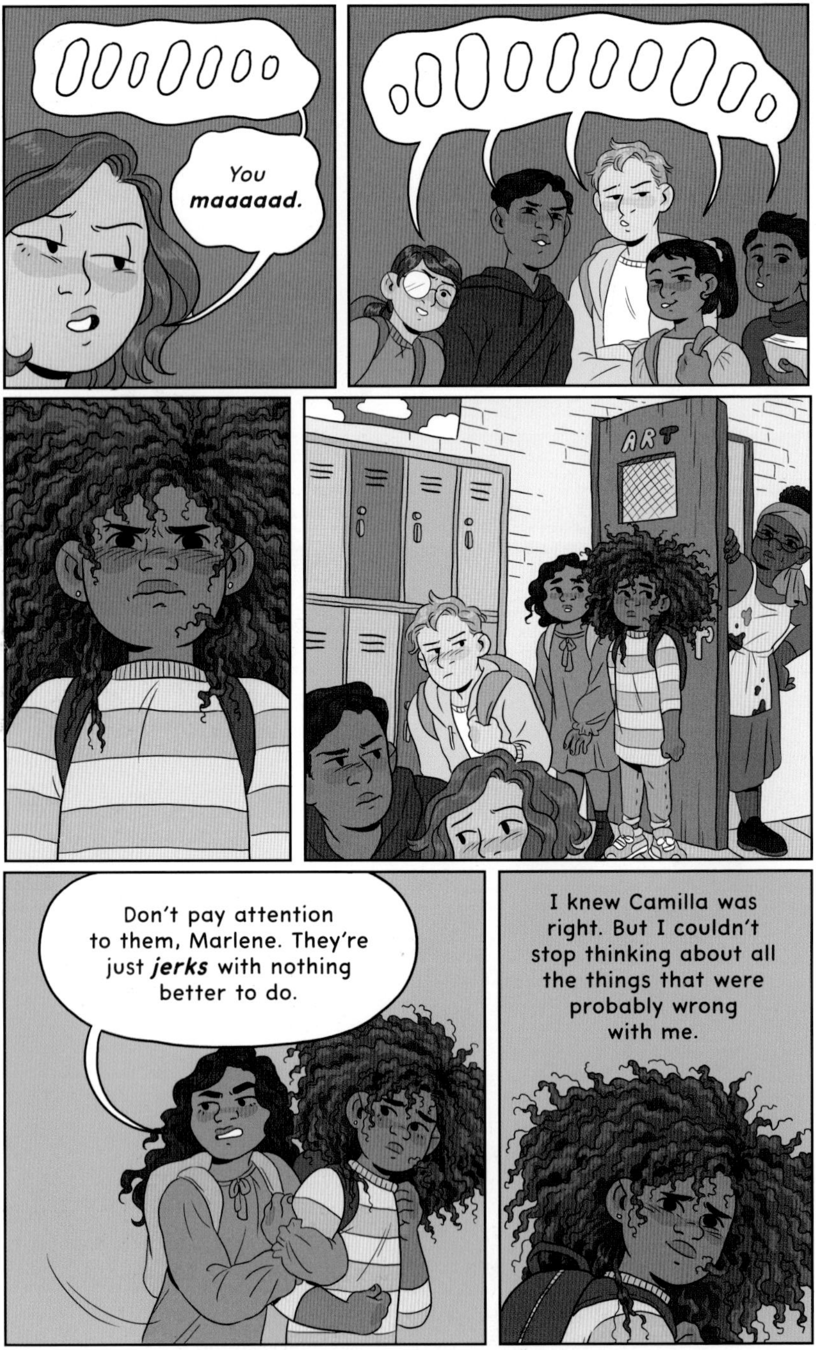
OOOOOOOO
You maaaaad.
OOOOOOOOOOOOO
ART
Don't pay attention to them, Marlene. They're just jerks with nothing better to do.
I knew Camilla was right. But I couldn't stop thinking about all the things that were probably wrong with me.

Nobody else bothered me that morning. Probably because they were too scared of Camilla. And then it was time for my favorite class.

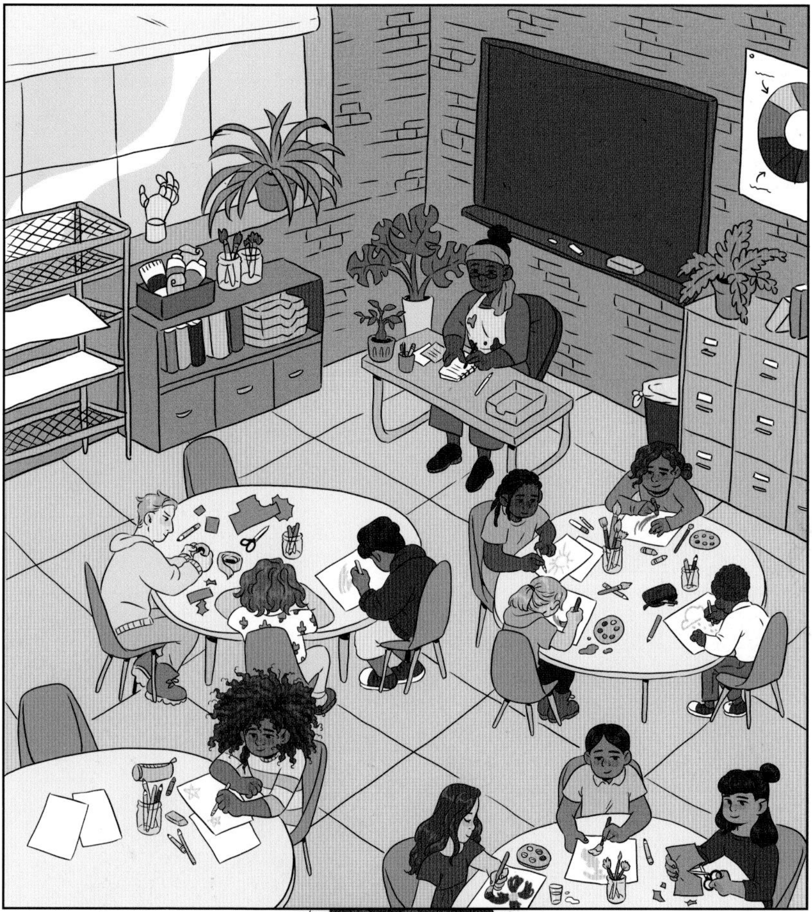

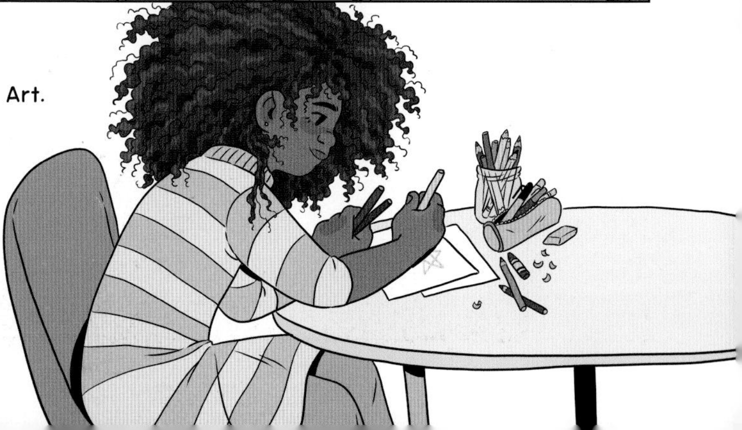
Art.

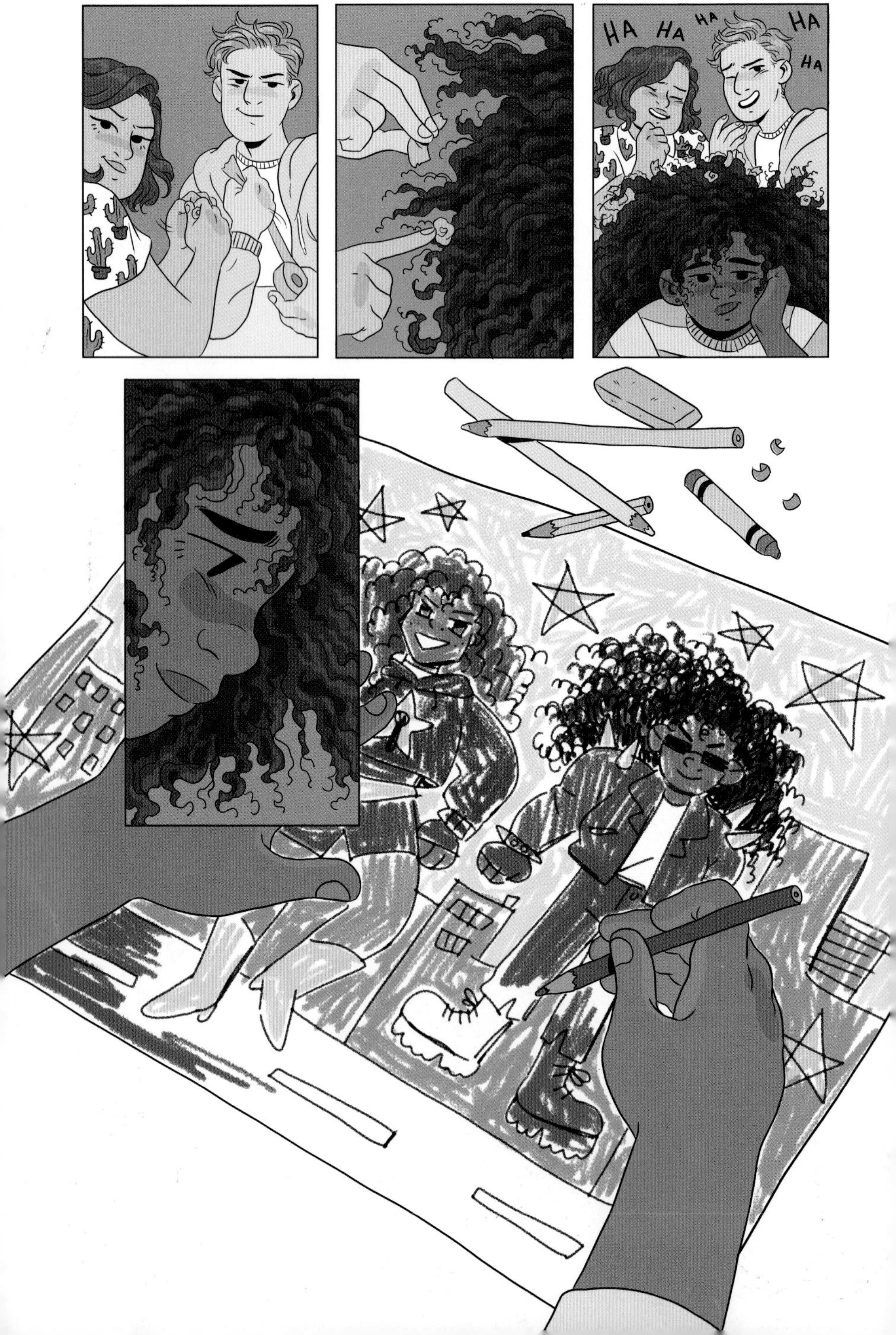
HA HA HA HA HA

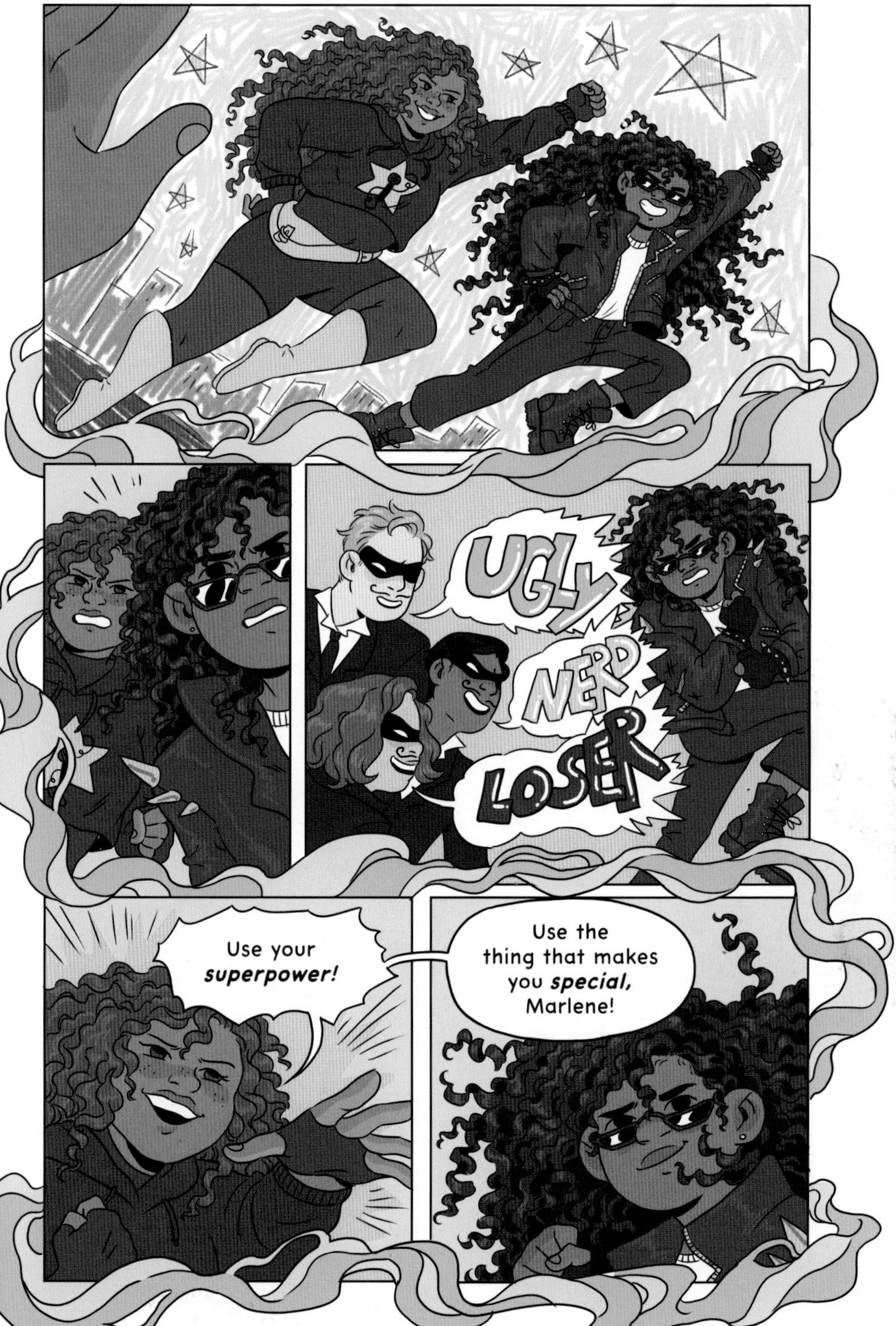
UGLY
NERD
LOSER
Use your *superpower!*
Use the thing that makes you *special,* Marlene!

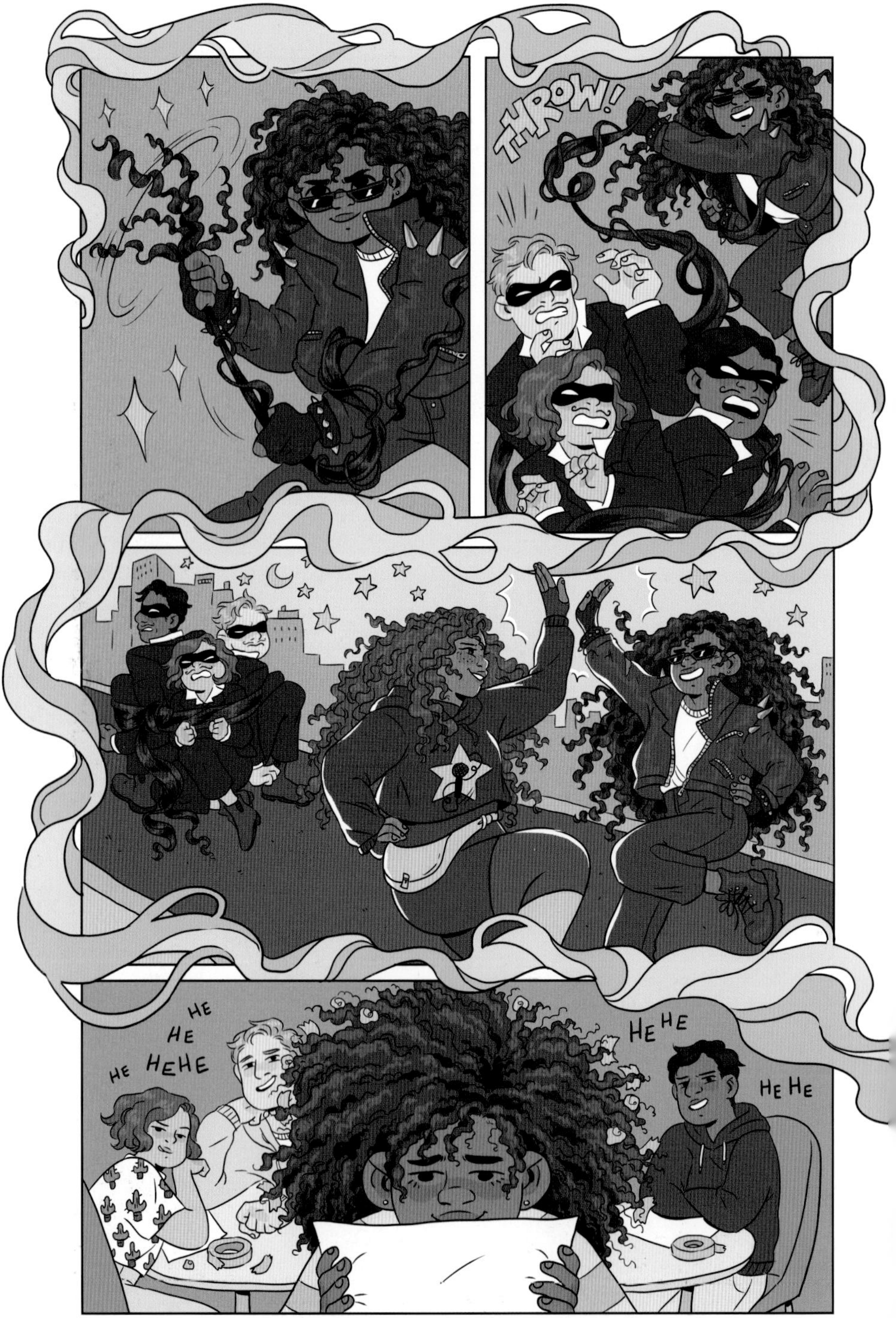
THROW!
HE
HE
HE HEHE
HEHE
HEHE

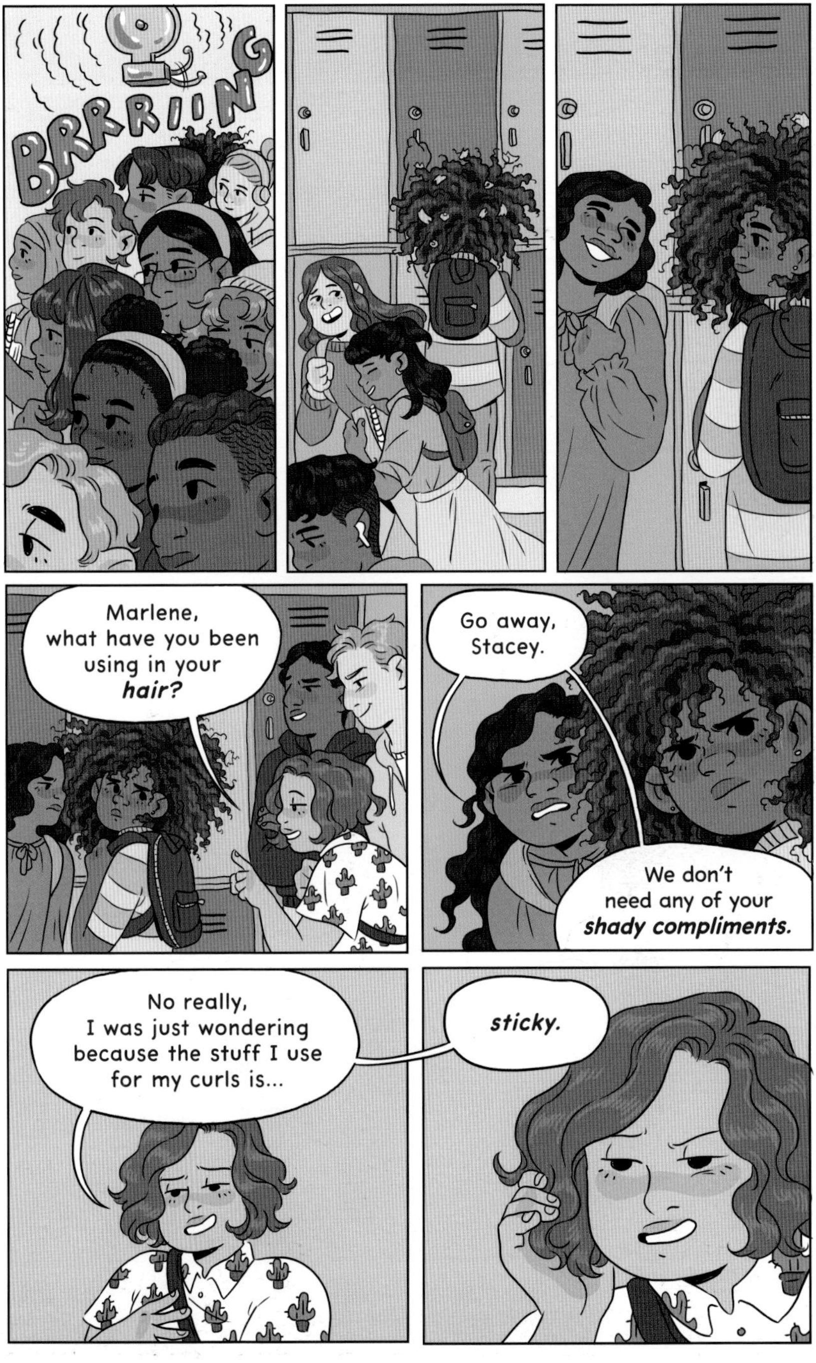
BRRRIING
Marlene, what have you been using in your ***hair?***
Go away, Stacey.
We don't need any of your ***shady compliments.***
No really, I was just wondering because the stuff I use for my curls is...
sticky.

What is your **problem?**

HA HA

No problem, just—

wondering how you're gonna get all that **mess** out of your hair.

Get what...

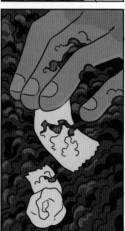

What did you do?

We didn't do anything.

I **know** it was you. Why don't you just **leave me alone?**

I've never done **anything** to you and you're always trying to make me mad.

Stop it, just **stop it!**

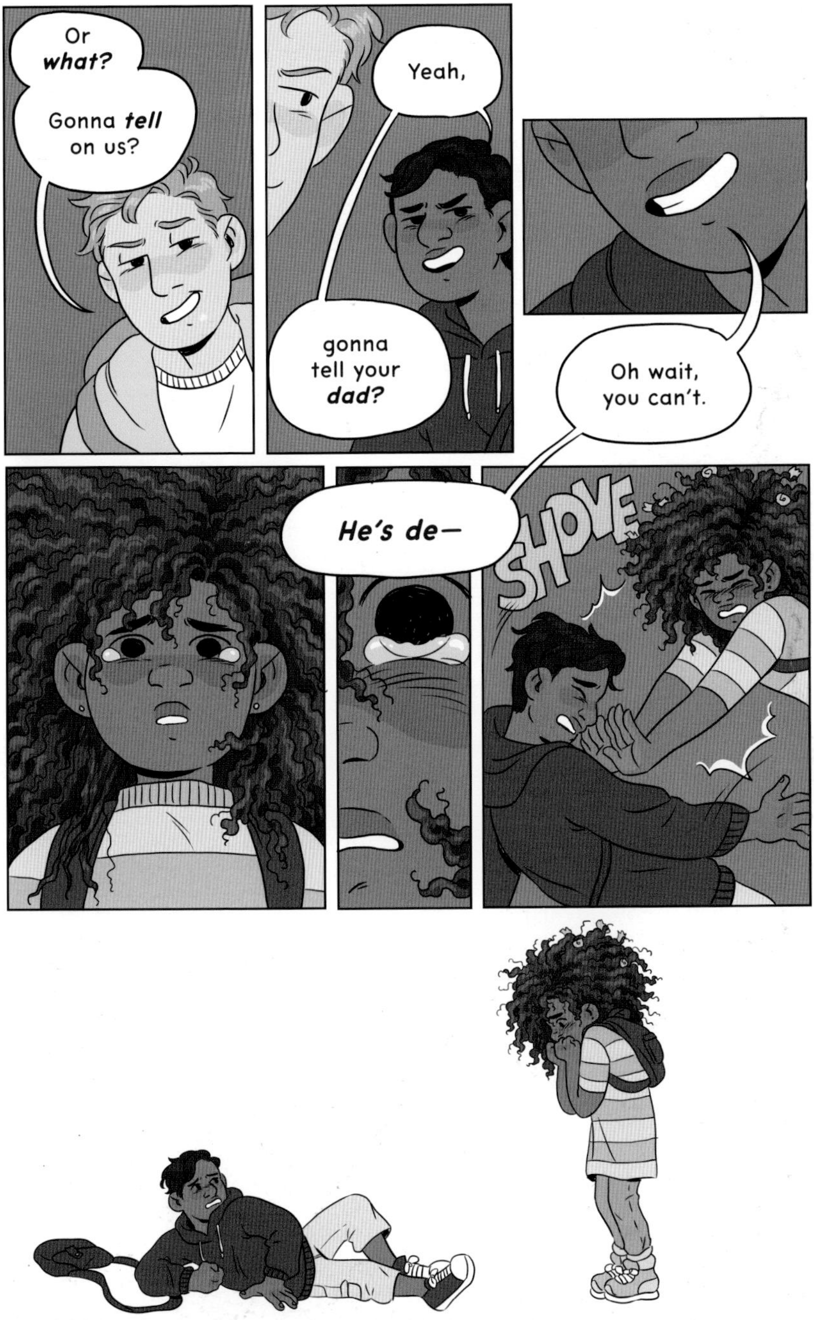
Or *what?*
Gonna *tell* on us?
Yeah,
gonna tell your *dad?*
Oh wait, you can't.
He's de—
SHOVE

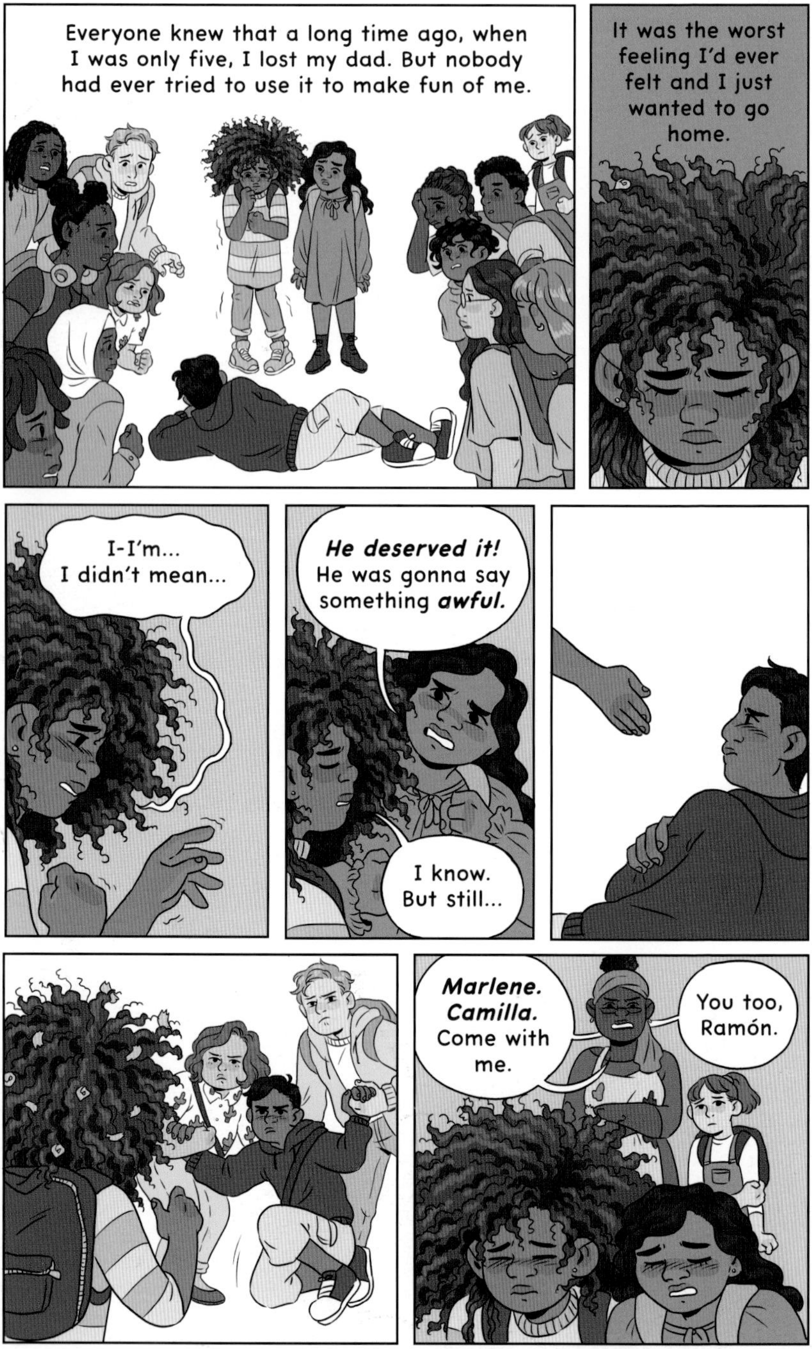
Everyone knew that a long time ago, when I was only five, I lost my dad. But nobody had ever tried to use it to make fun of me.
It was the worst feeling I'd ever felt and I just wanted to go home.
I-I'm... I didn't mean...
He deserved it! He was gonna say something *awful.*
I know. But still...
Marlene. Camilla. Come with me.
You too, Ramón.

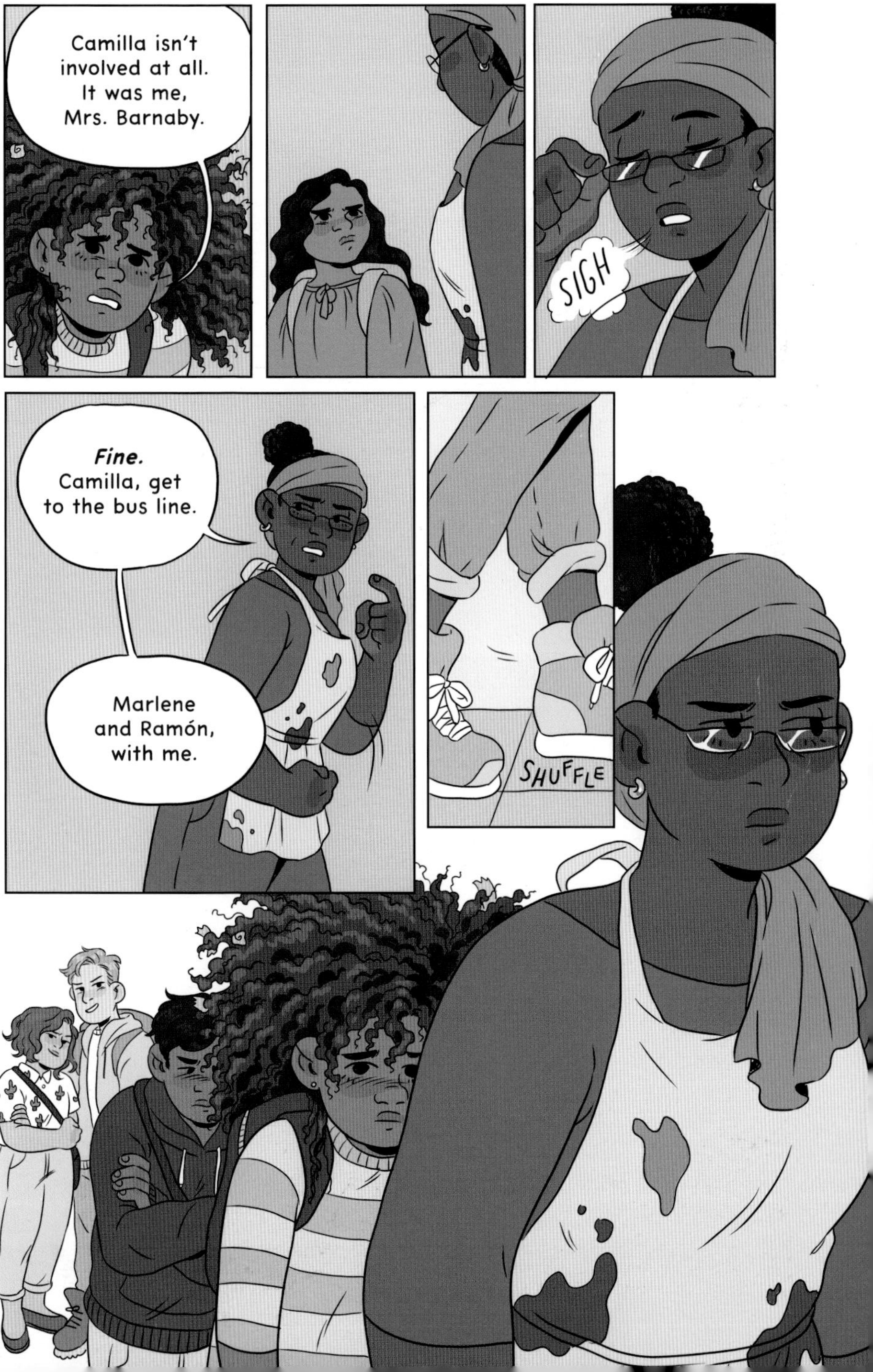
Camilla isn't involved at all. It was me, Mrs. Barnaby.
SIGH
Fine. Camilla, get to the bus line.
Marlene and Ramón, with me.
SHUFFLE

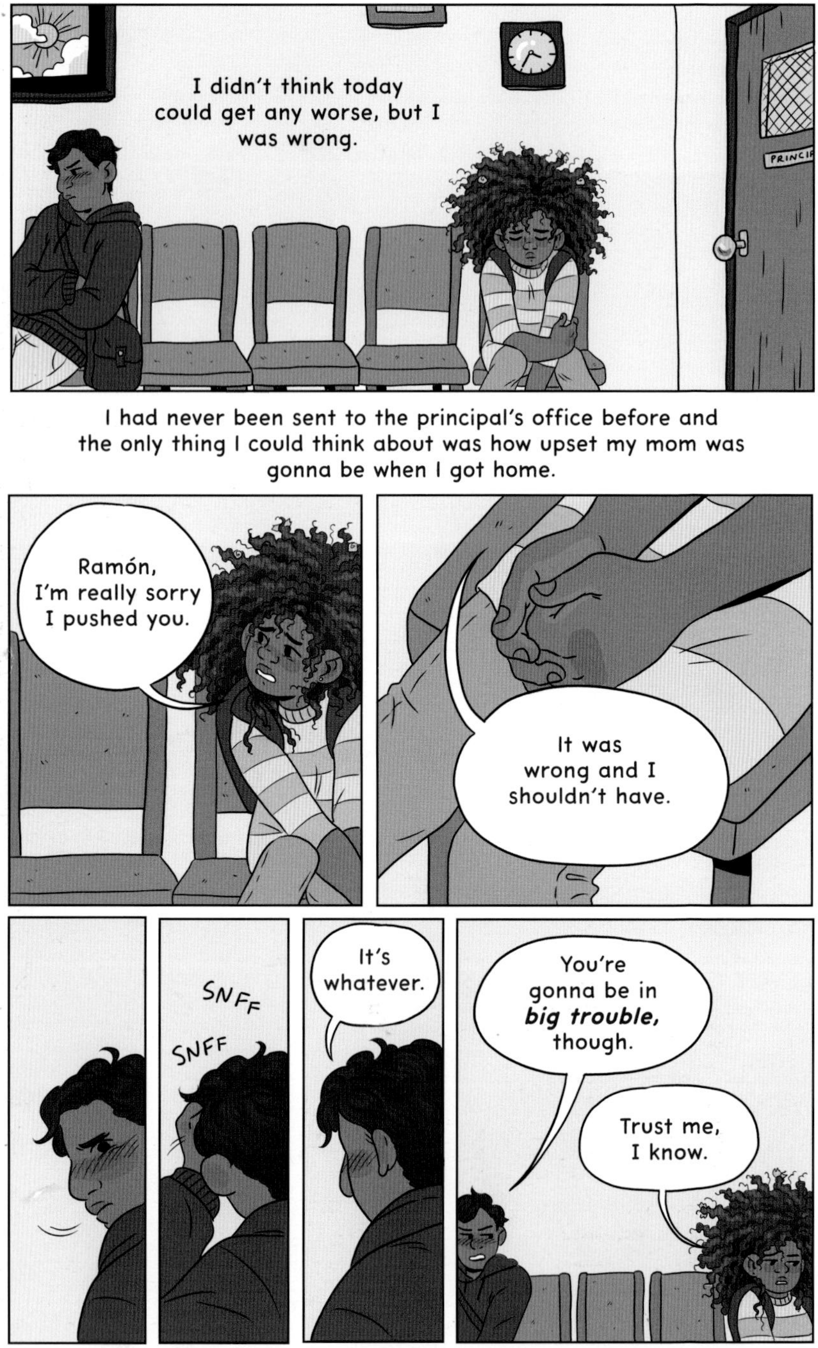
I didn't think today could get any worse, but I was wrong.
I had never been sent to the principal's office before and the only thing I could think about was how upset my mom was gonna be when I got home.
Ramón, I'm really sorry I pushed you.
It was wrong and I shouldn't have.
SNFF
SNFF
It's whatever.
You're gonna be in ***big trouble,*** though.
Trust me, I know.

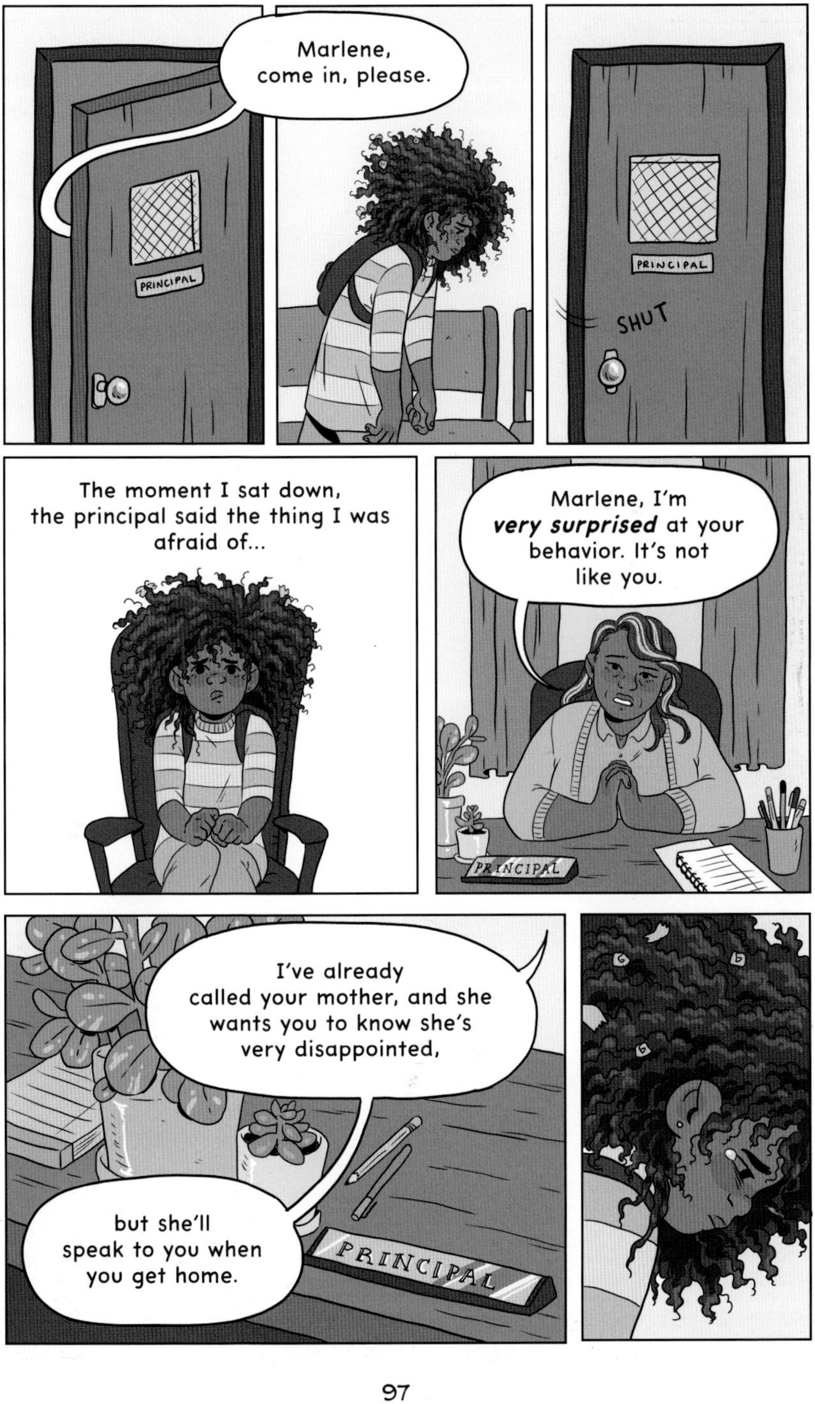
Marlene, come in, please.
PRINCIPAL
PRINCIPAL
SHUT
The moment I sat down, the principal said the thing I was afraid of...
Marlene, I'm ***very surprised*** at your behavior. It's not like you.
PRINCIPAL
I've already called your mother, and she wants you to know she's very disappointed,
but she'll speak to you when you get home.
PRINCIPAL

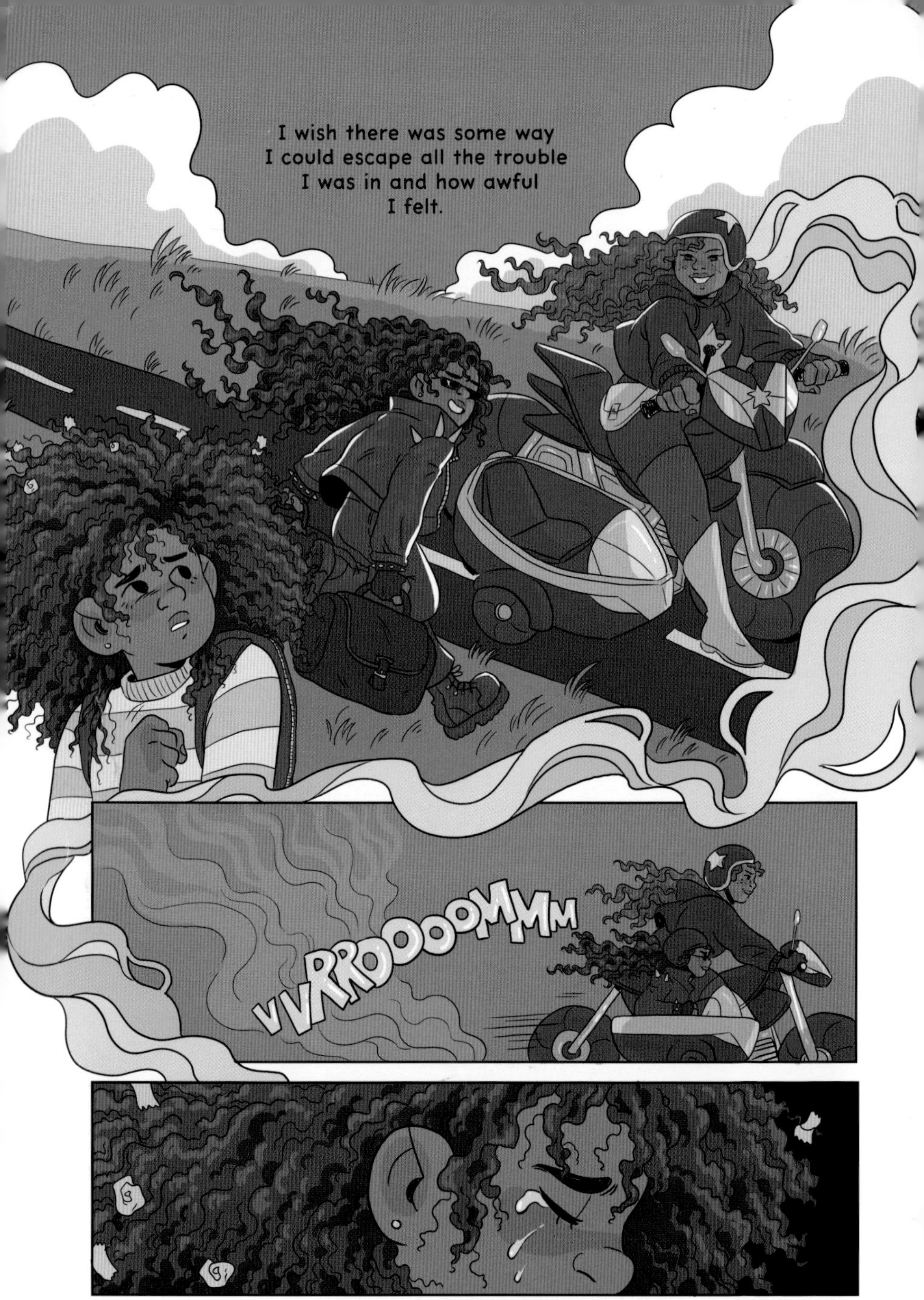
I wish there was some way I could escape all the trouble I was in and how awful I felt.
VVRROOOOMMMM

I wish I could just go far away and never come back.

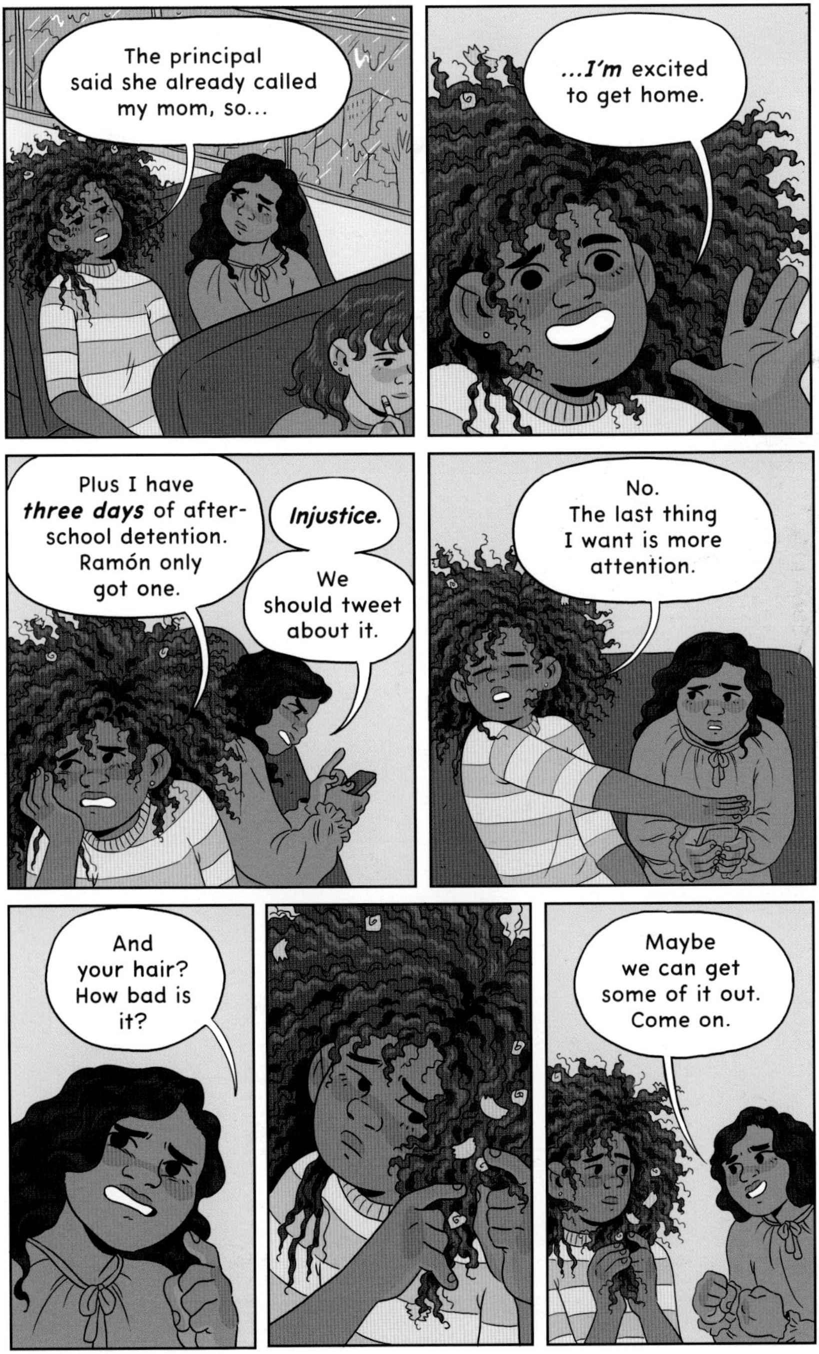
The principal said she already called my mom, so...
...*I'm* excited to get home.
Plus I have ***three days*** of after-school detention. Ramón only got one.
Injustice.
We should tweet about it.
No. The last thing I want is more attention.
And your hair? How bad is it?
Maybe we can get some of it out. Come on.

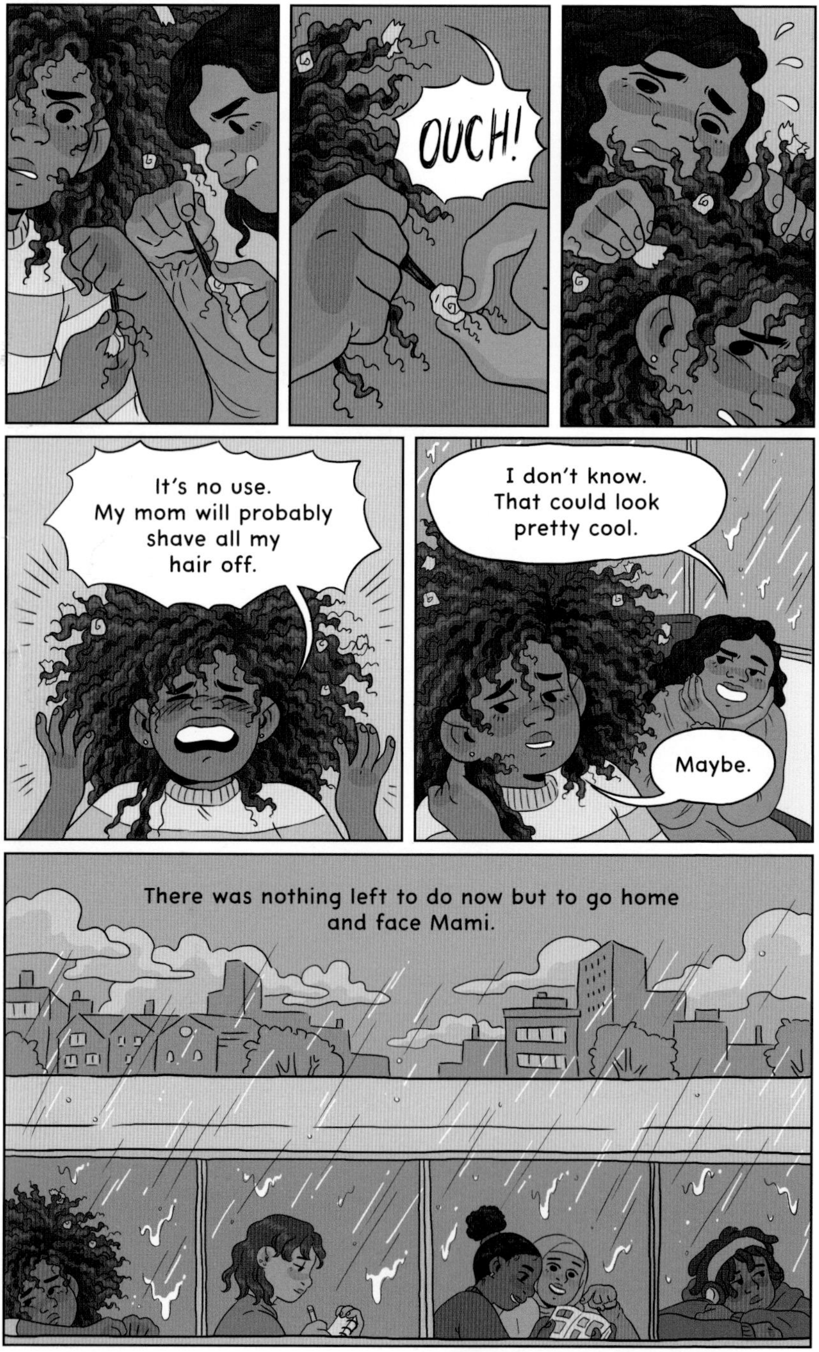
OUCH!
It's no use. My mom will probably shave all my hair off.
I don't know. That could look pretty cool.
Maybe.
There was nothing left to do now but to go home and face Mami.

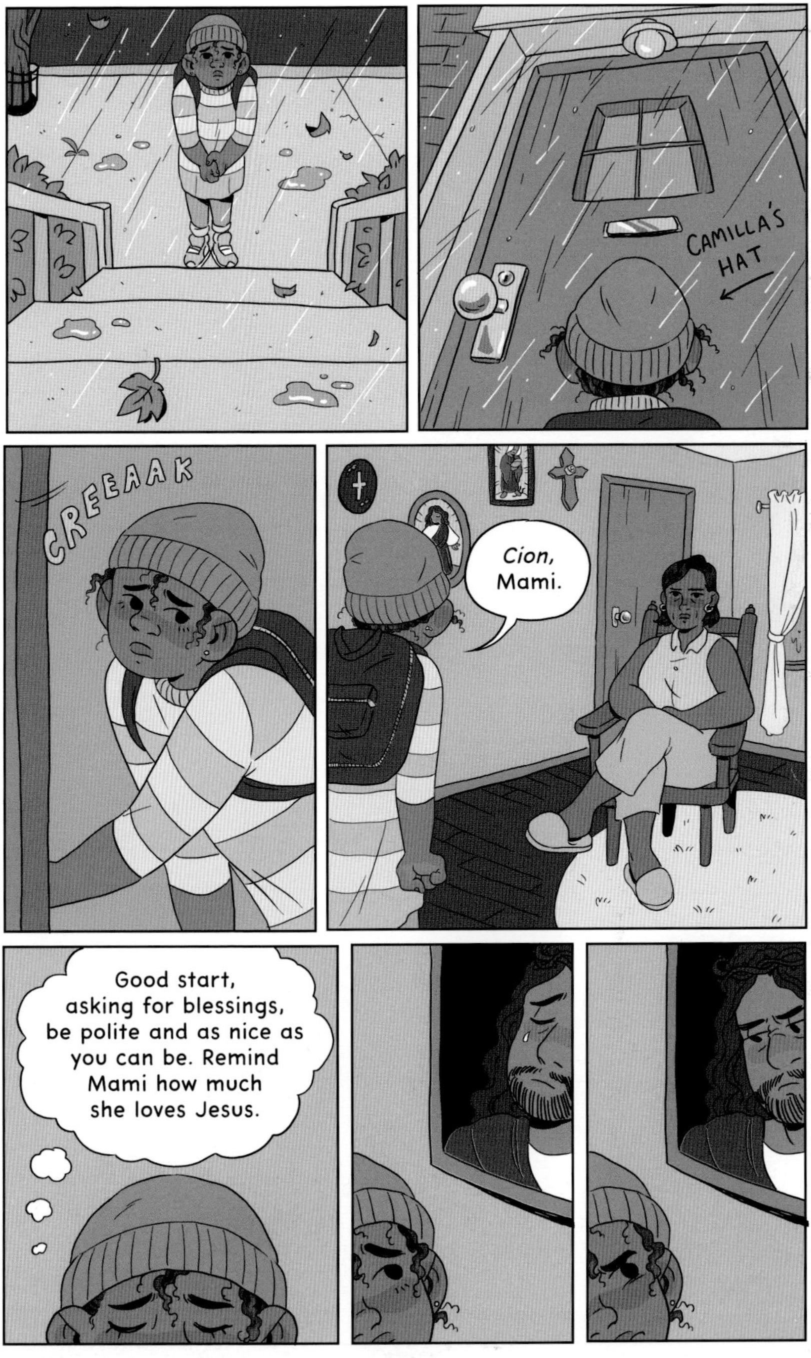
CAMILLA'S HAT
CREEEAAAK
Cion, Mami.
Good start, asking for blessings, be polite and as nice as you can be. Remind Mami how much she loves Jesus.

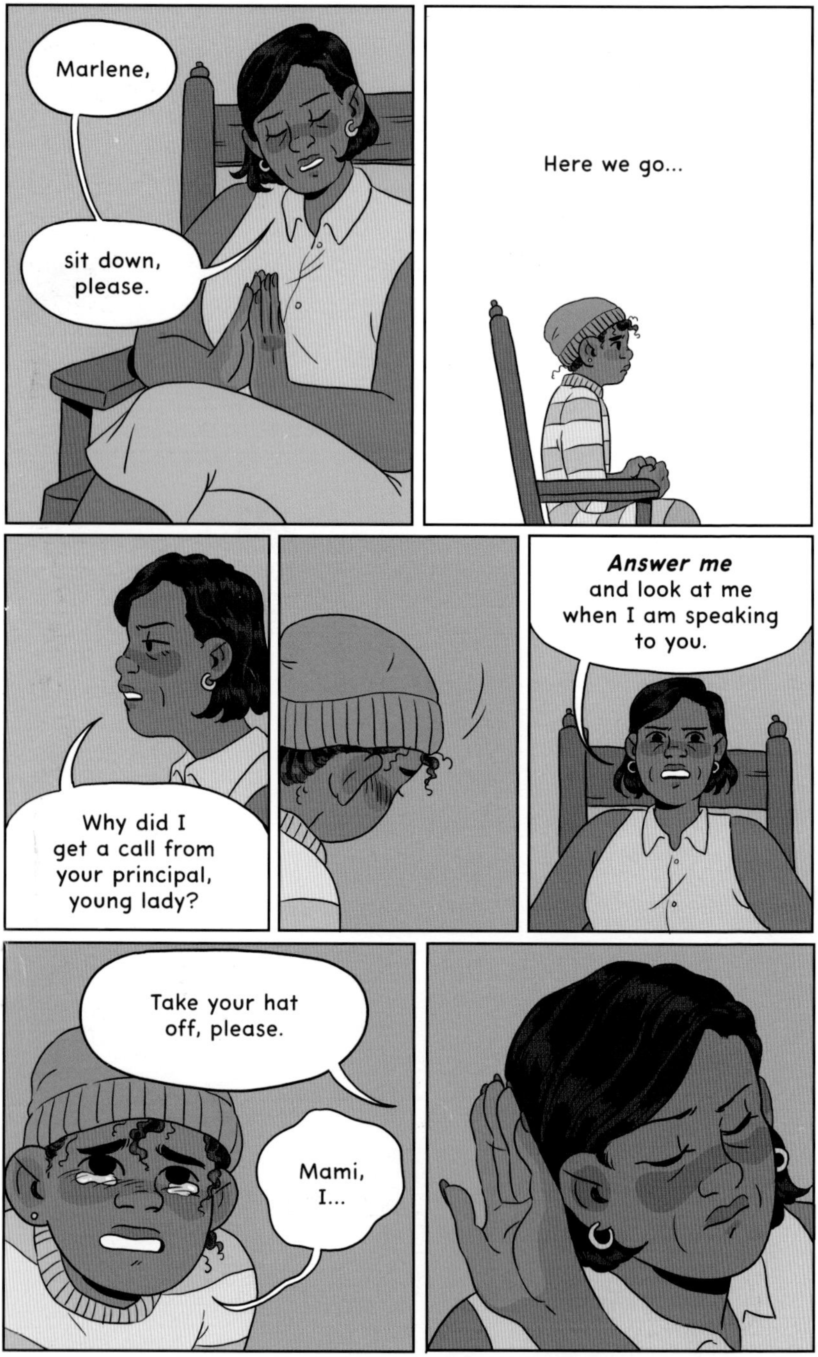
Marlene,
sit down, please.
Here we go...
Why did I get a call from your principal, young lady?
Answer me and look at me when I am speaking to you.
Take your hat off, please.
Mami, I...

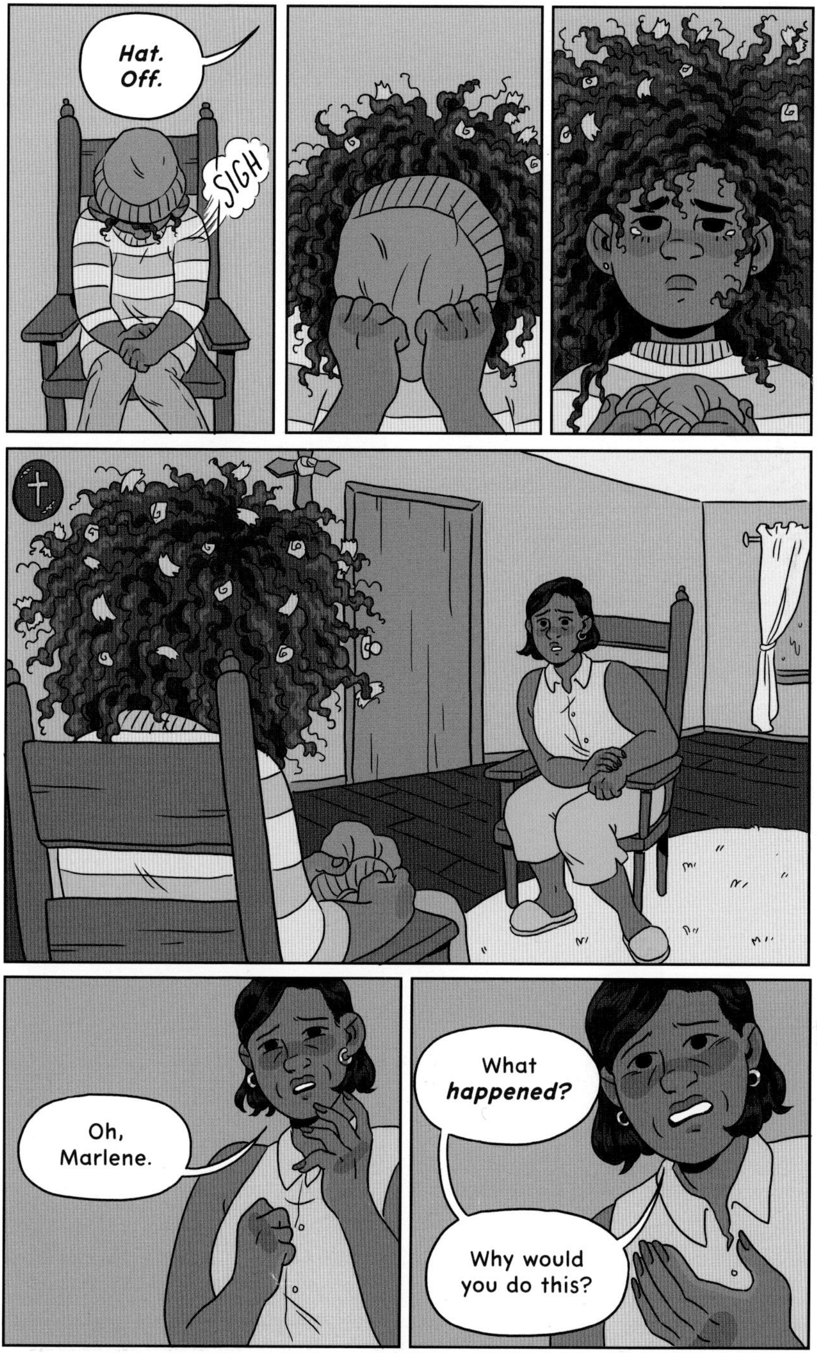
Hat. Off.
SIGH
Oh, Marlene.
What *happened?*
Why would you do this?

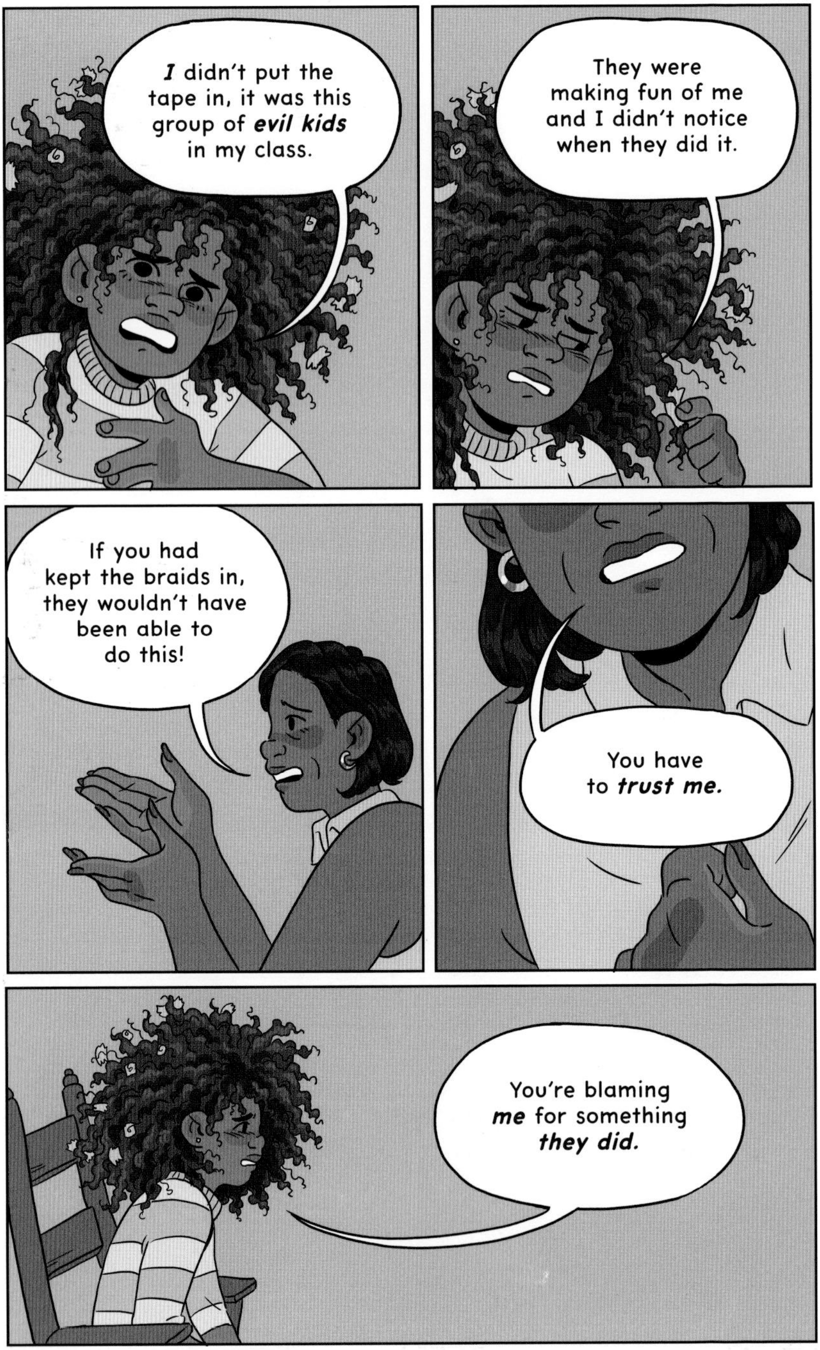
I didn't put the tape in, it was this group of ***evil kids*** in my class.
They were making fun of me and I didn't notice when they did it.
If you had kept the braids in, they wouldn't have been able to do this!
You have to ***trust me.***
You're blaming ***me*** for something ***they did.***

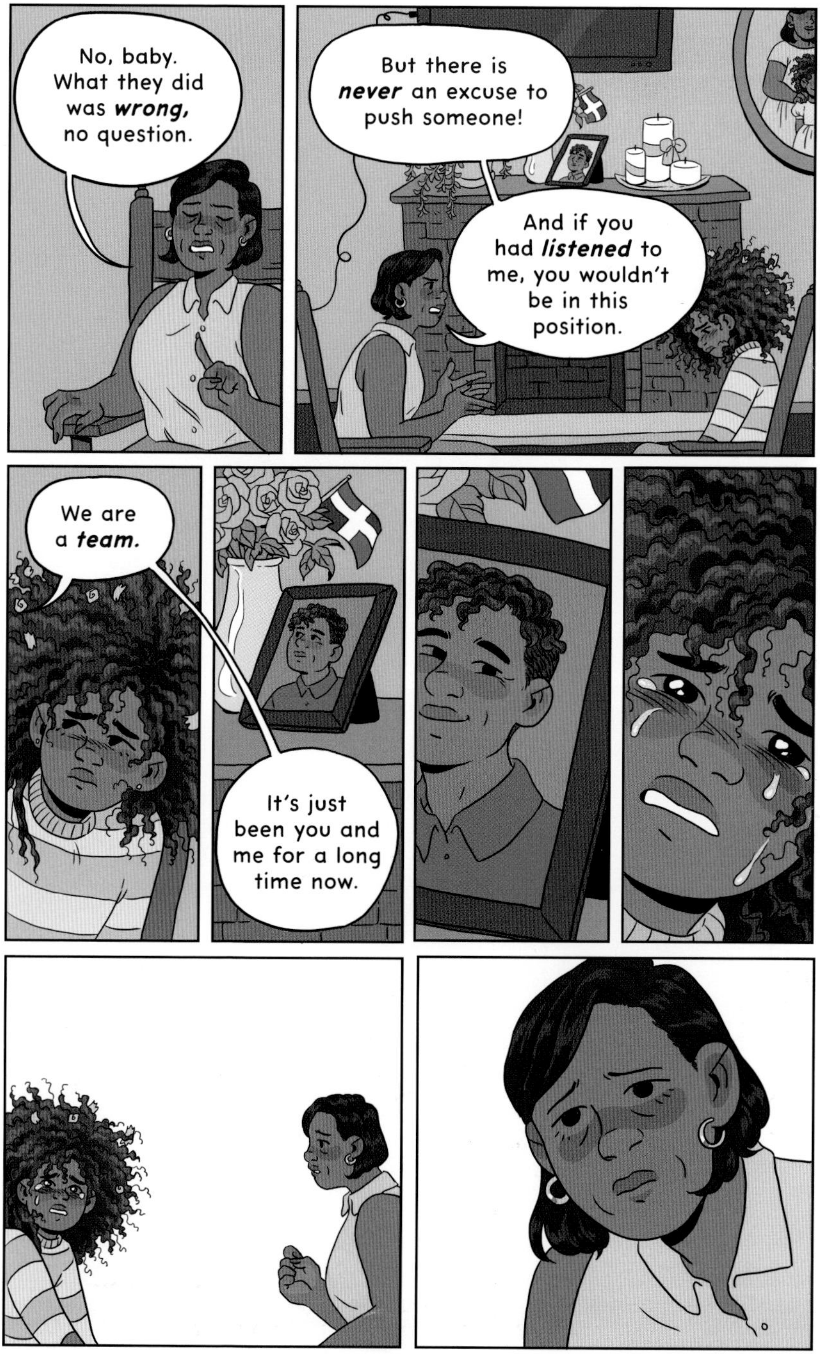
No, baby. What they did was ***wrong,*** no question.
But there is ***never*** an excuse to push someone!
And if you had ***listened*** to me, you wouldn't be in this position.
We are a ***team.***
It's just been you and me for a long time now.

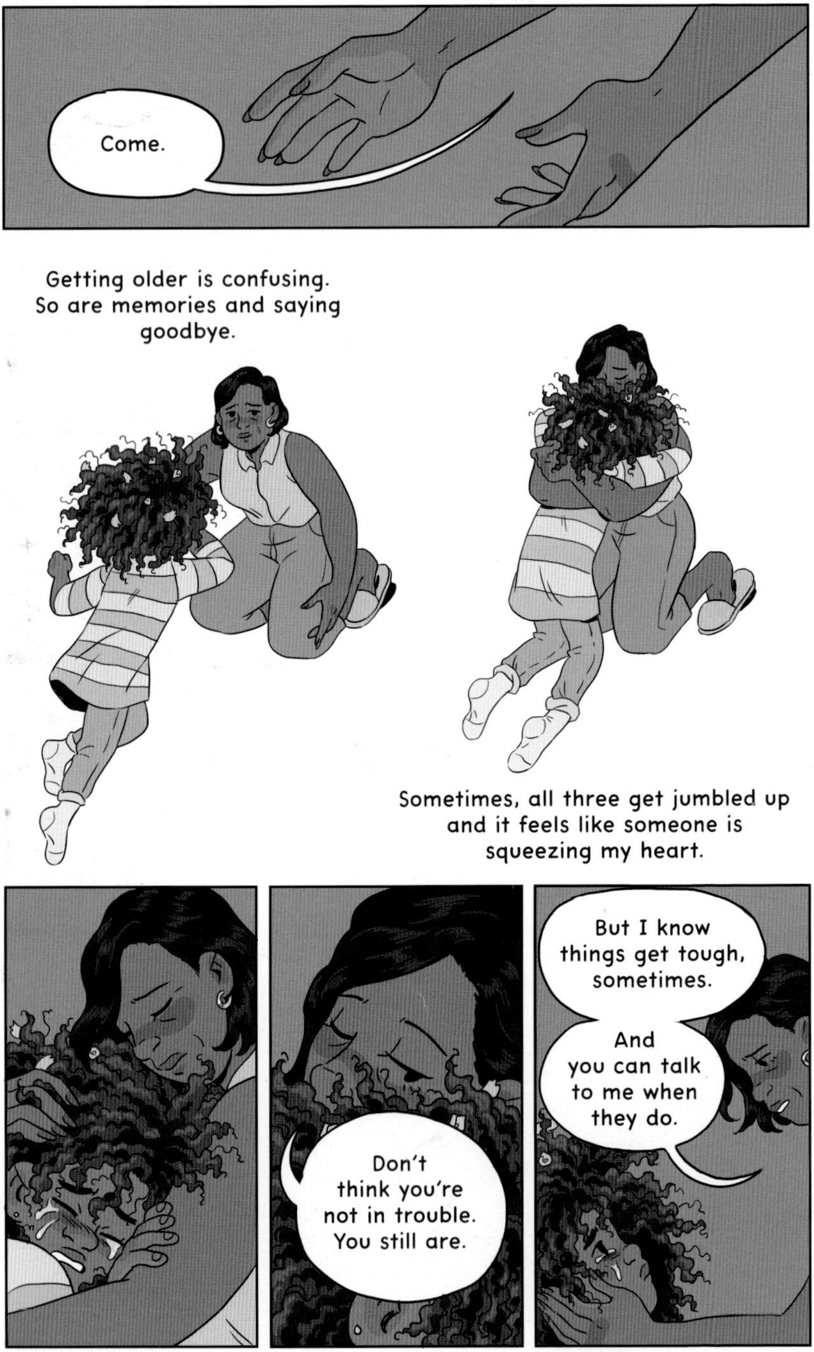
Come.
Getting older is confusing. So are memories and saying goodbye.
Sometimes, all three get jumbled up and it feels like someone is squeezing my heart.
Don't think you're not in trouble. You still are.
But I know things get tough, sometimes.
And you can talk to me when they do.

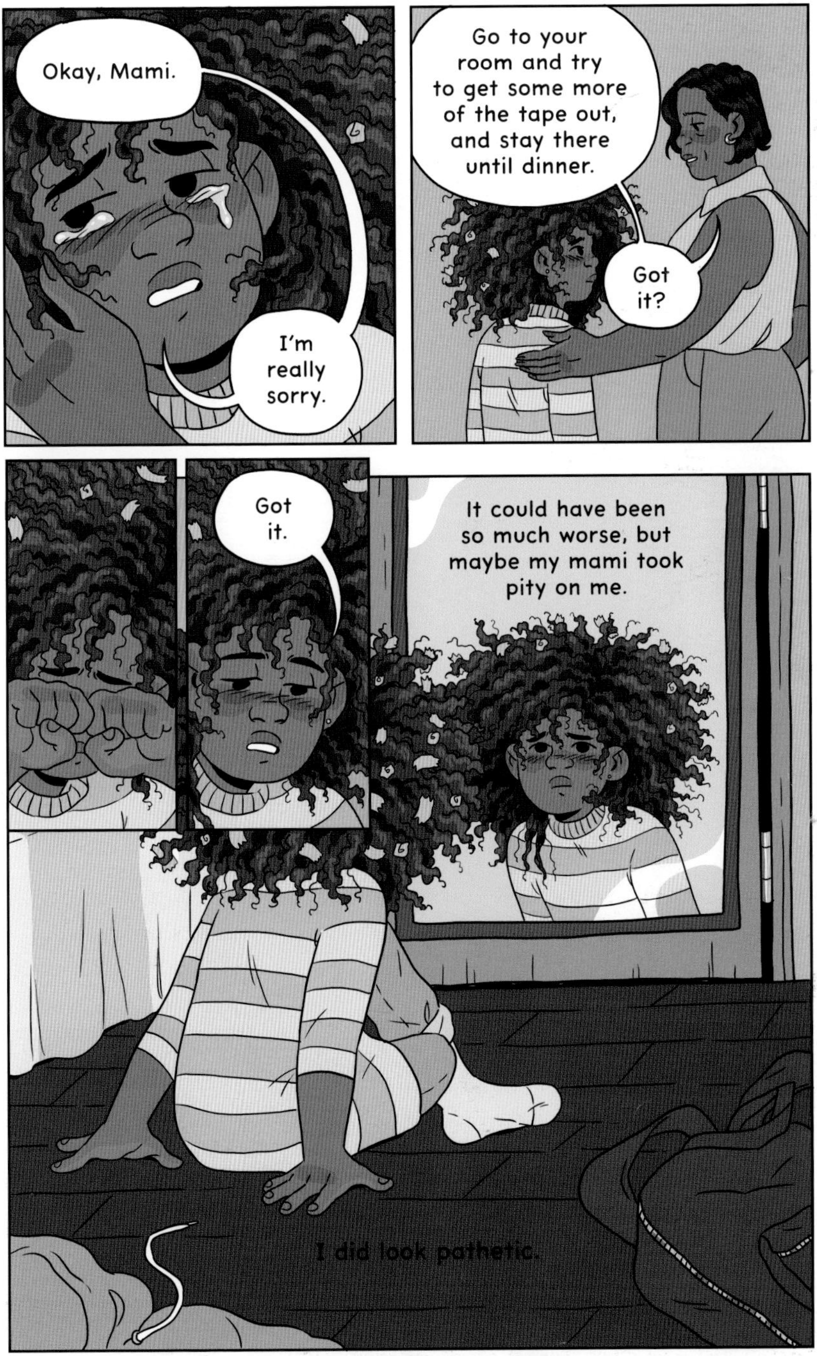
Okay, Mami.
I'm really sorry.
Go to your room and try to get some more of the tape out, and stay there until dinner.
Got it?
Got it.
It could have been so much worse, but maybe my mami took pity on me.
I did look pathetic.

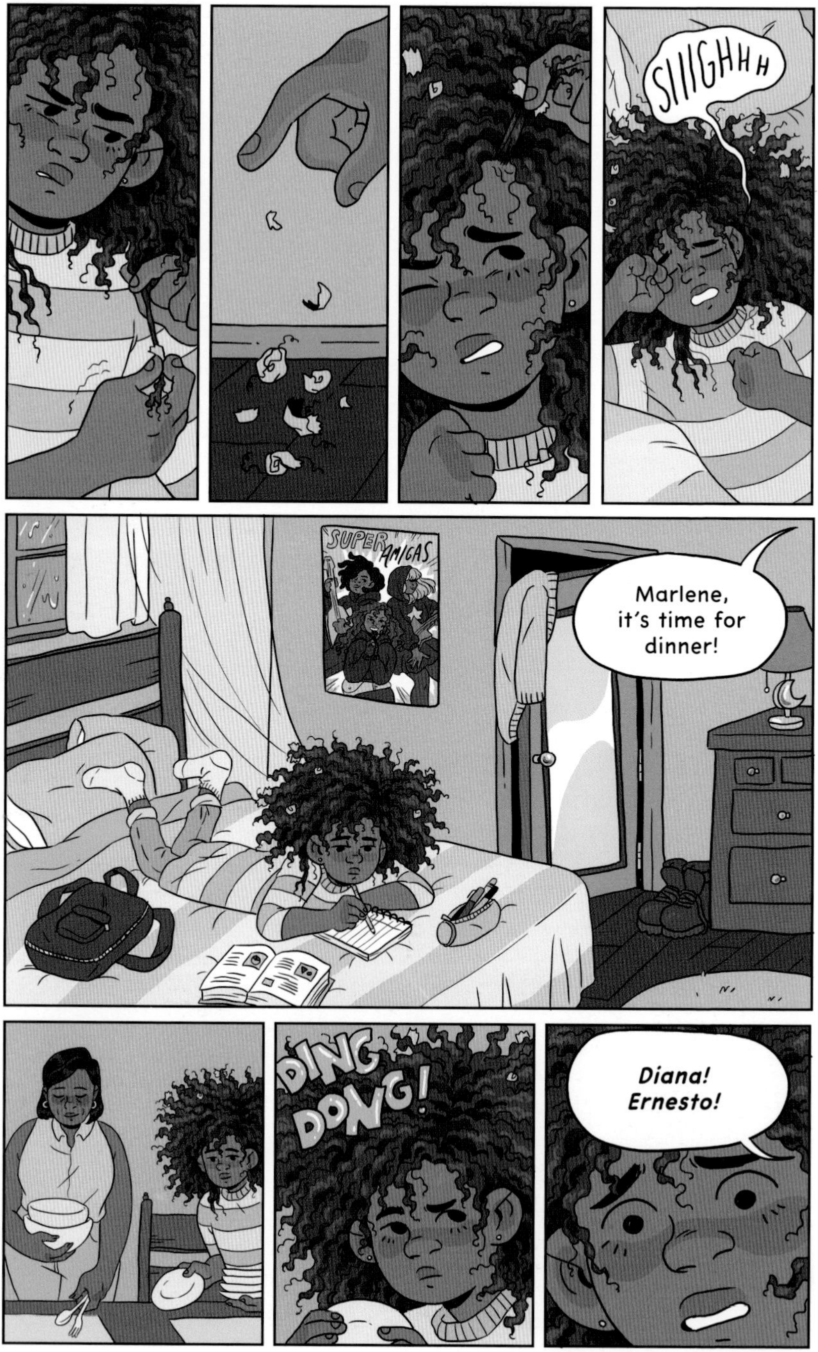
SIIIGHHH
SUPER AMIGAS
Marlene, it's time for dinner!
DING DONG!
Diana! Ernesto!

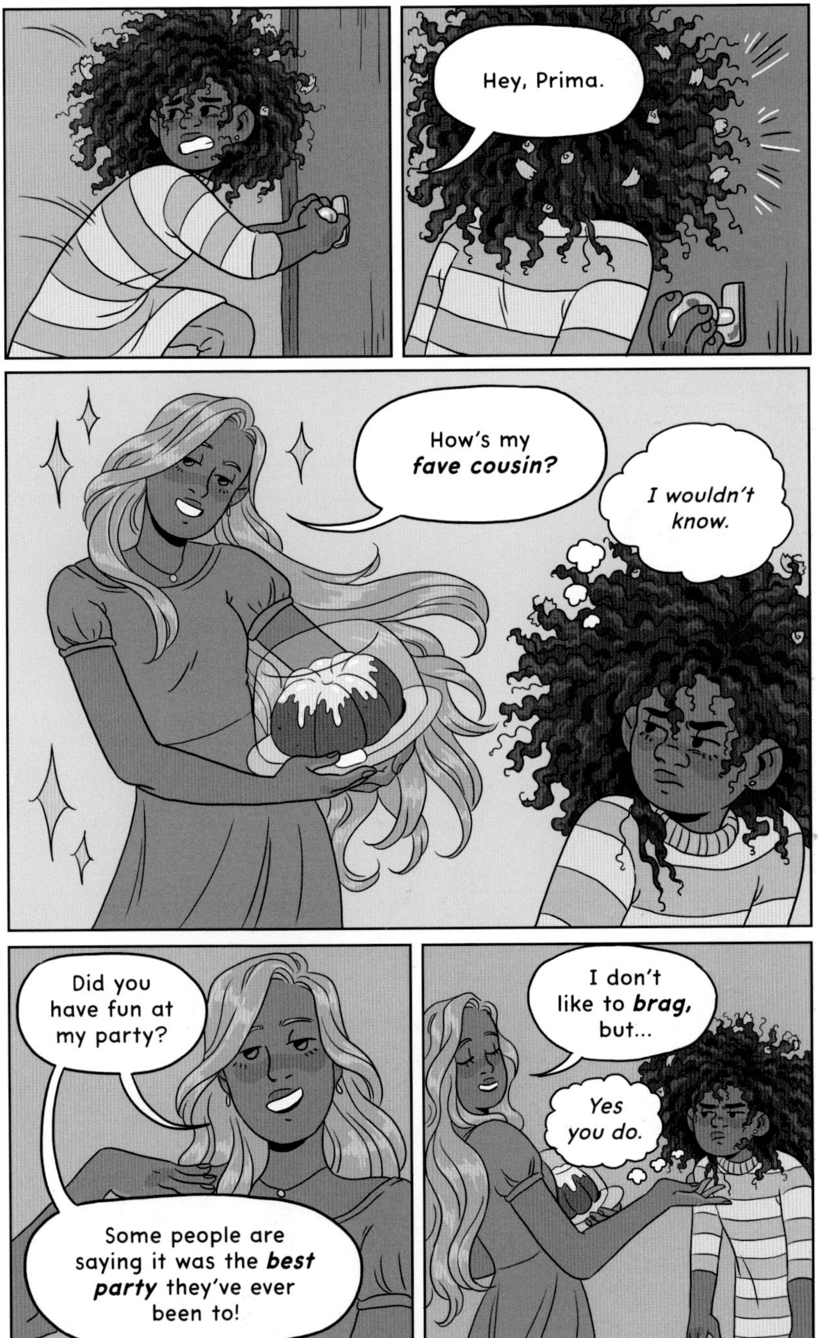
Hey, Prima.
How's my *fave cousin?*
I wouldn't know.
Did you have fun at my party?
Some people are saying it was the ***best party*** they've ever been to!
I don't like to ***brag,*** but...
Yes you do.

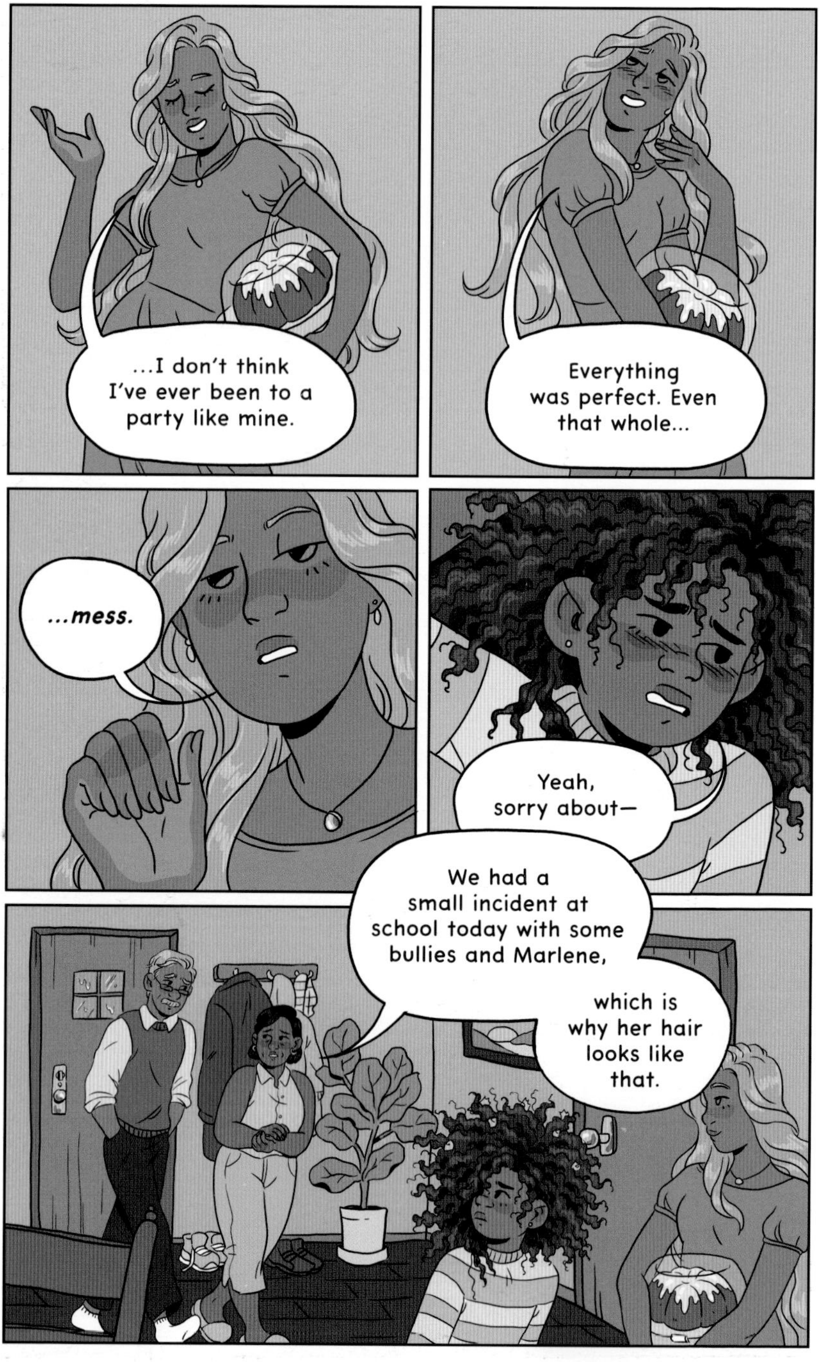

...I don't think I've ever been to a party like mine.
Everything was perfect. Even that whole...
...mess.
Yeah, sorry about—
We had a small incident at school today with some bullies and Marlene,
which is why her hair looks like that.

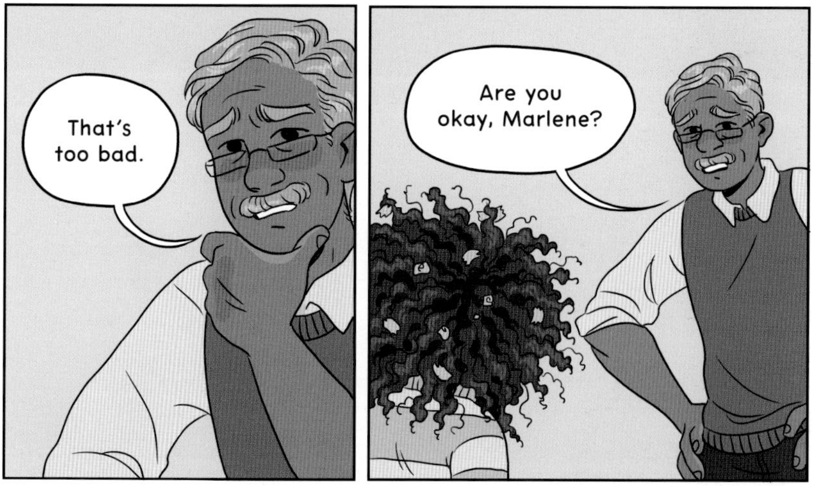
That's too bad.
Are you okay, Marlene?

Tío Ernesto was always so nice, and I sometimes wondered where Diana got her mean streak from. Her mom, Tía Lucia, was nice too, and her sister Yesenia was the best.

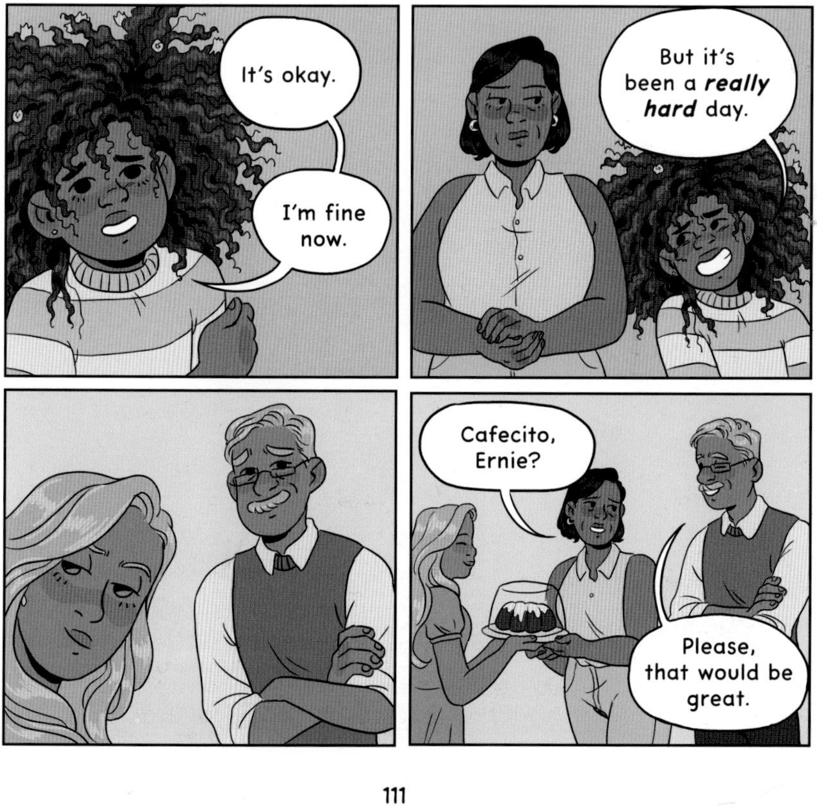
It's okay.
I'm fine now.
But it's been a ***really hard*** day.
Cafecito, Ernie?
Please, that would be great.

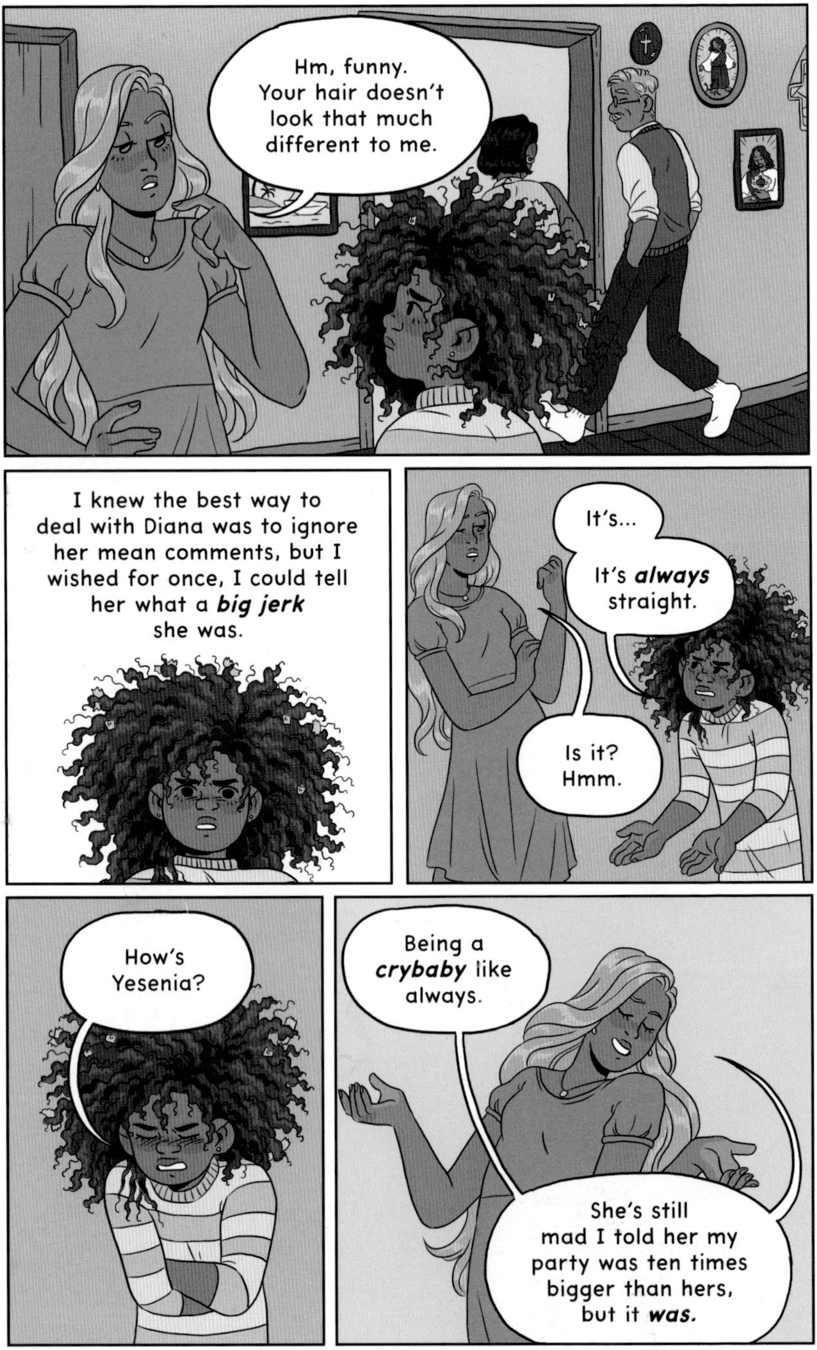
Hm, funny. Your hair doesn't look that much different to me.
I knew the best way to deal with Diana was to ignore her mean comments, but I wished for once, I could tell her what a ***big jerk*** she was.
It's...
It's ***always*** straight.
Is it? Hmm.
How's Yesenia?
Being a ***crybaby*** like always.
She's still mad I told her my party was ten times bigger than hers, but it ***was.***

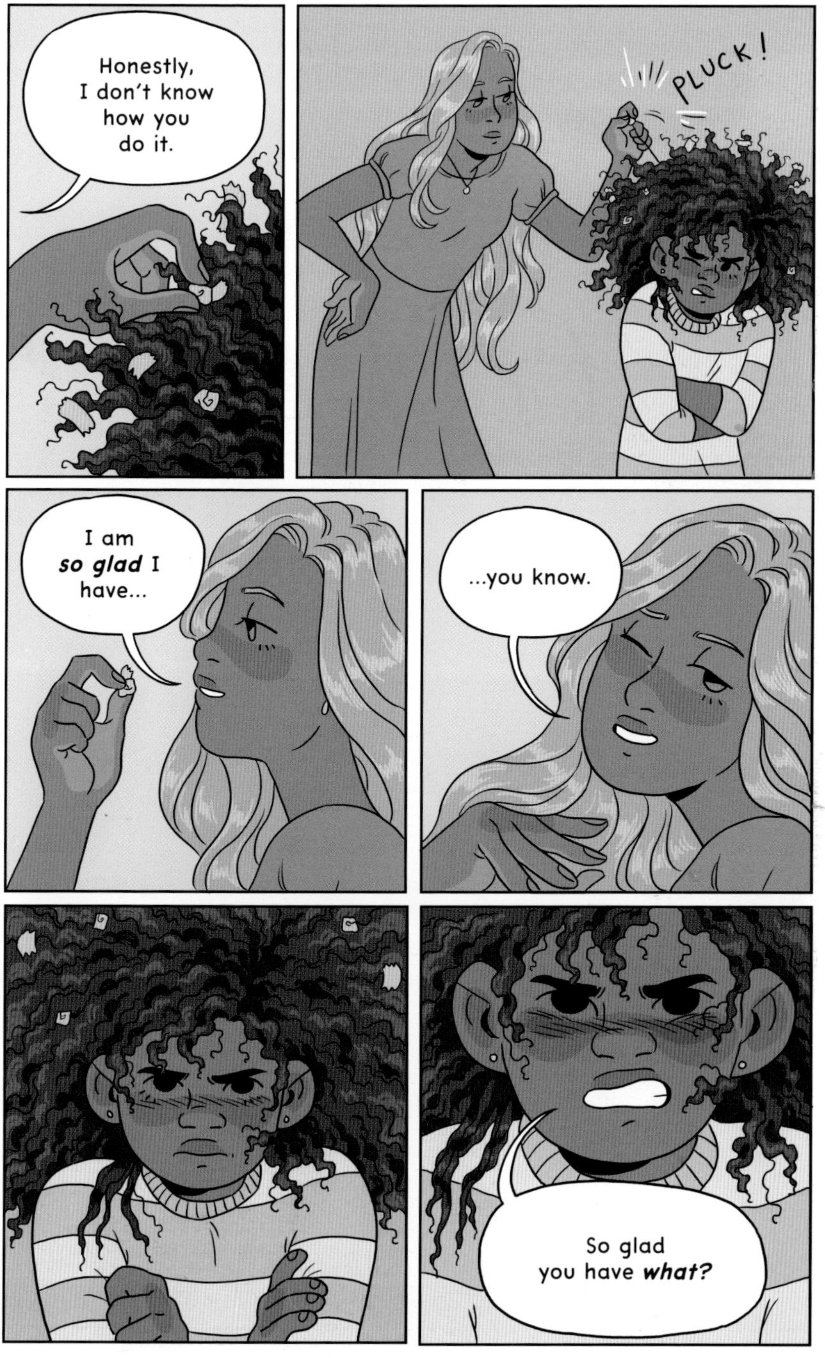
Honestly, I don't know how you do it.
PLUCK!
I am **so glad** I have...
...you know.
So glad you have ***what?***

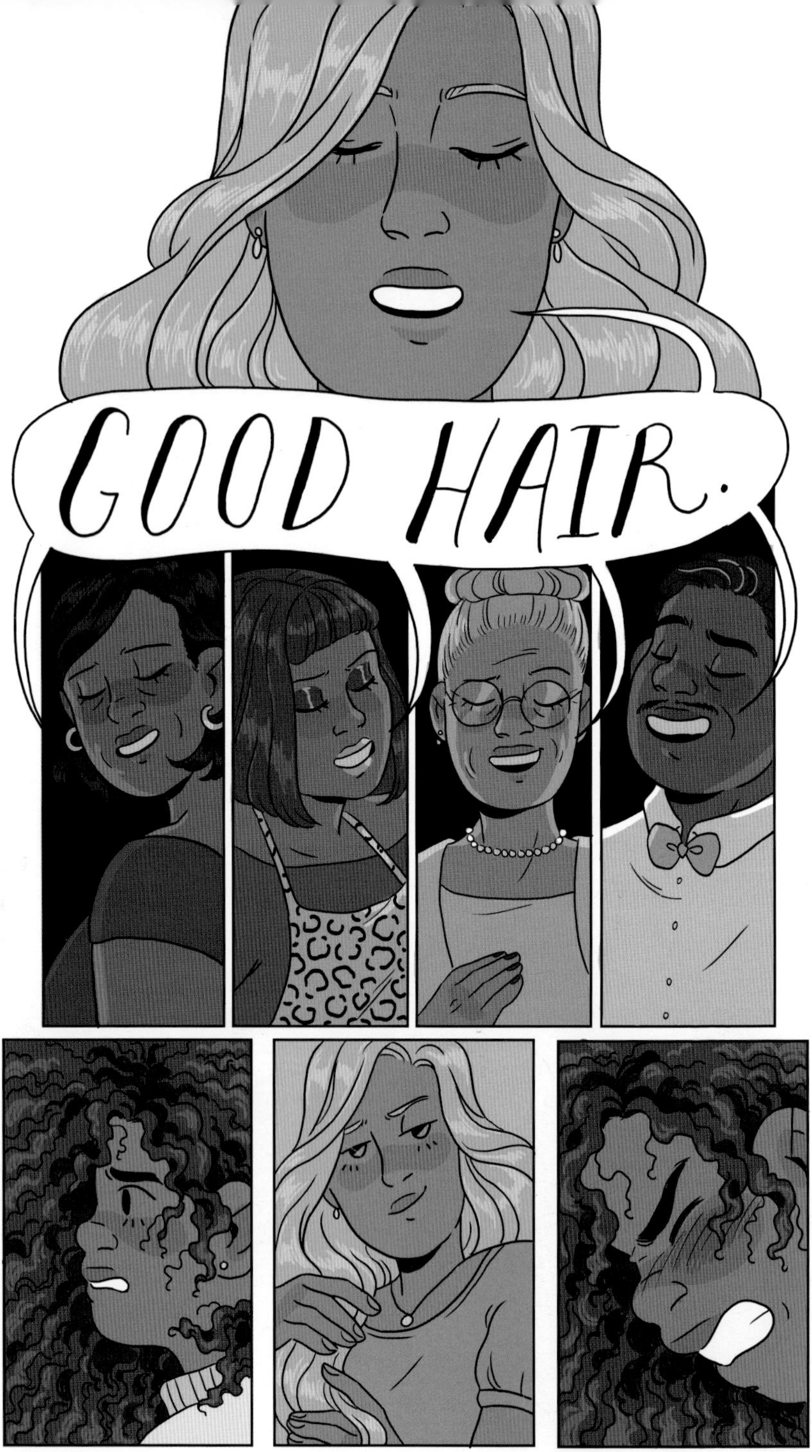
GOOD HAIR.

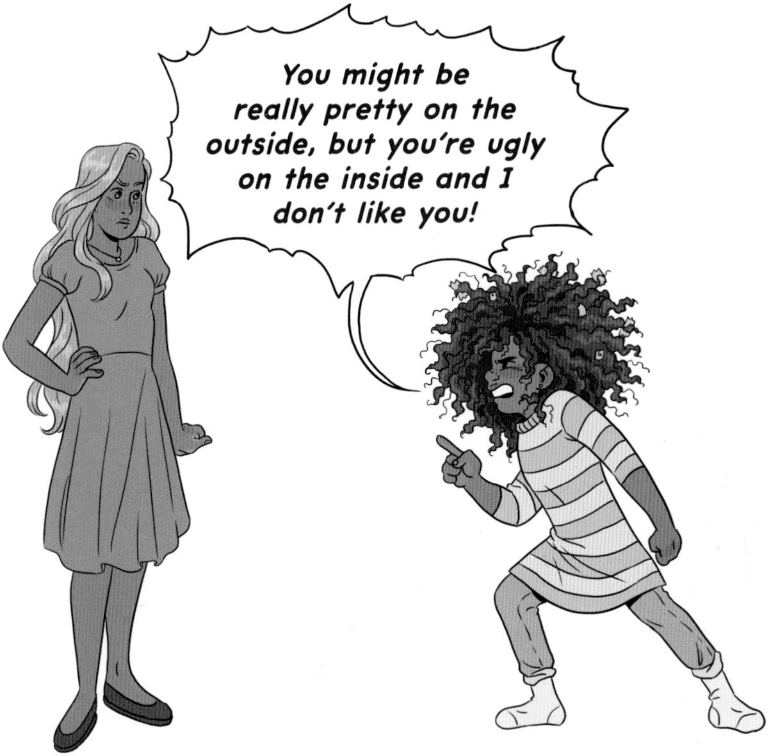
You might be really pretty on the outside, but you're ugly on the inside and I don't like you!

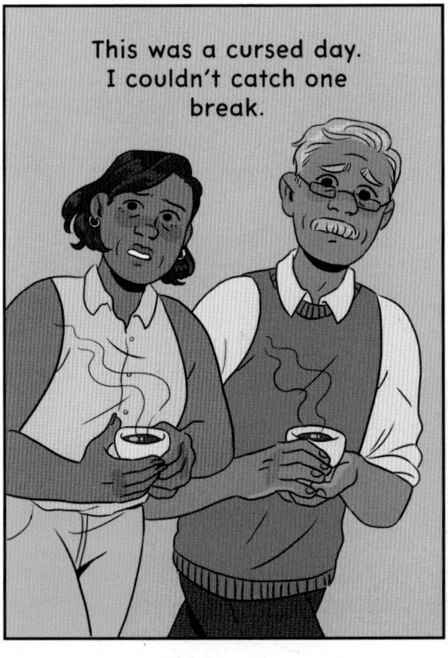
This was a cursed day. I couldn't catch one break.

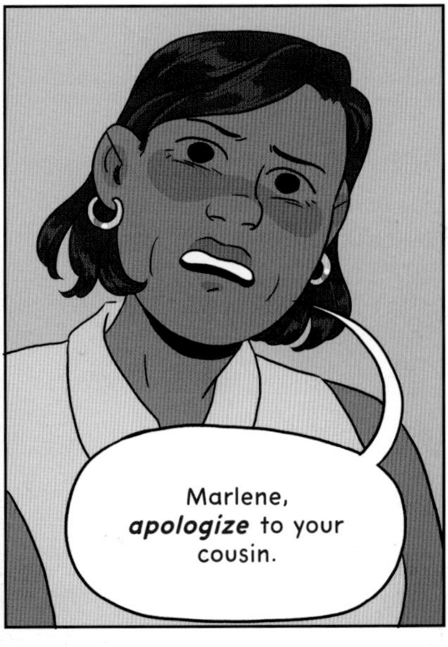
Marlene, apologize to your cousin.

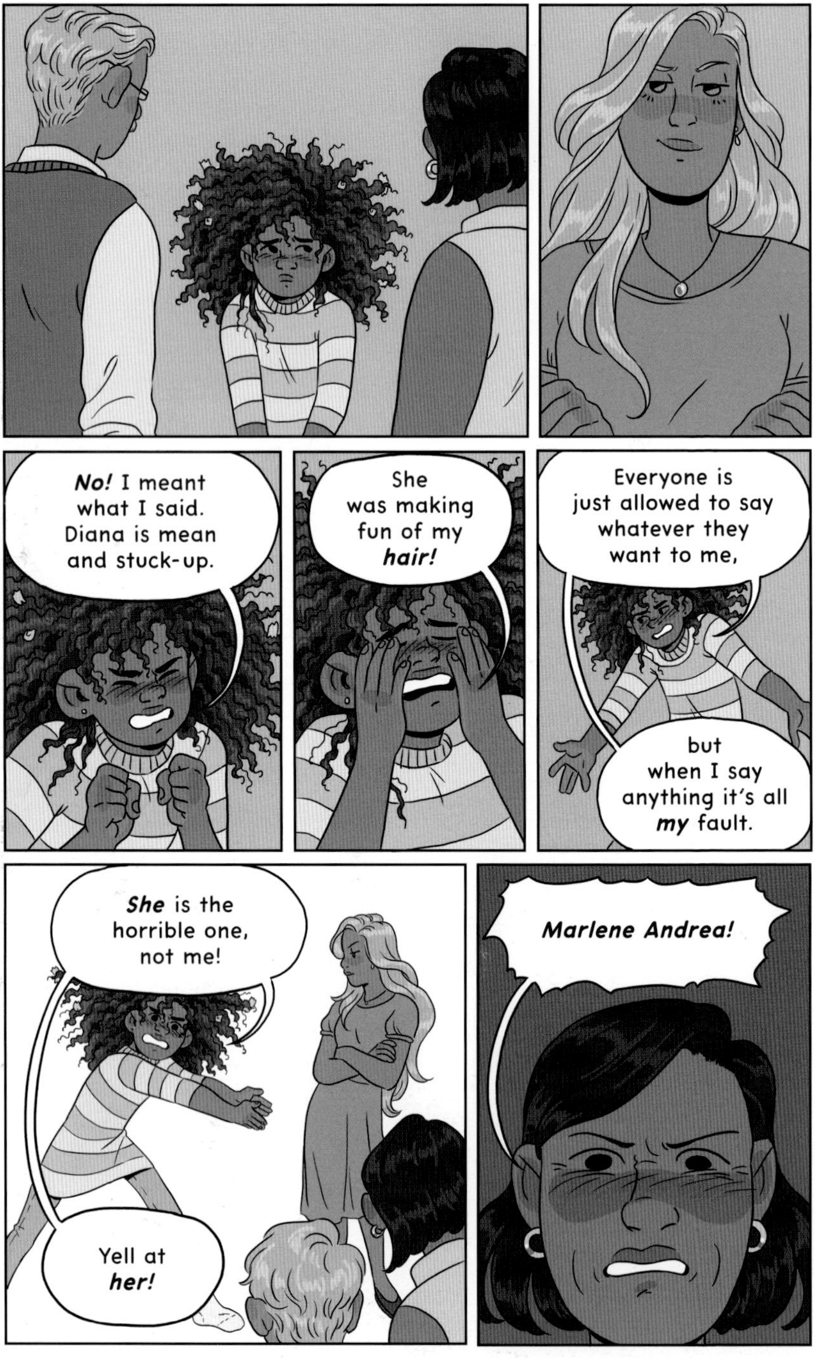

No! I meant what I said. Diana is mean and stuck-up.
She was making fun of my ***hair!***
Everyone is just allowed to say whatever they want to me,
but when I say anything it's all ***my*** fault.
She is the horrible one, not me!
Yell at ***her!***
Marlene Andrea!

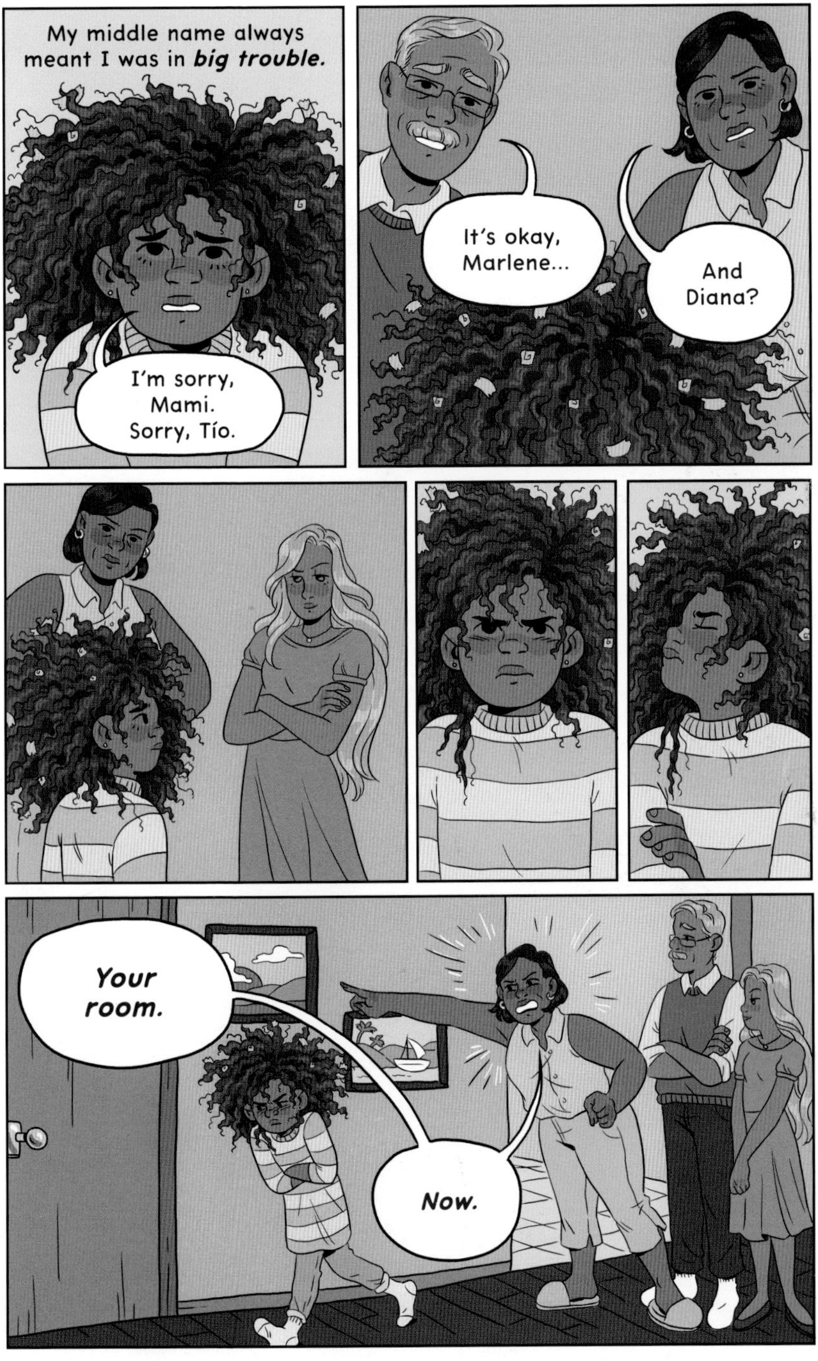
My middle name always meant I was in ***big trouble.***
I'm sorry, Mami. Sorry, Tío.
It's okay, Marlene...
And Diana?
Your room.
Now.

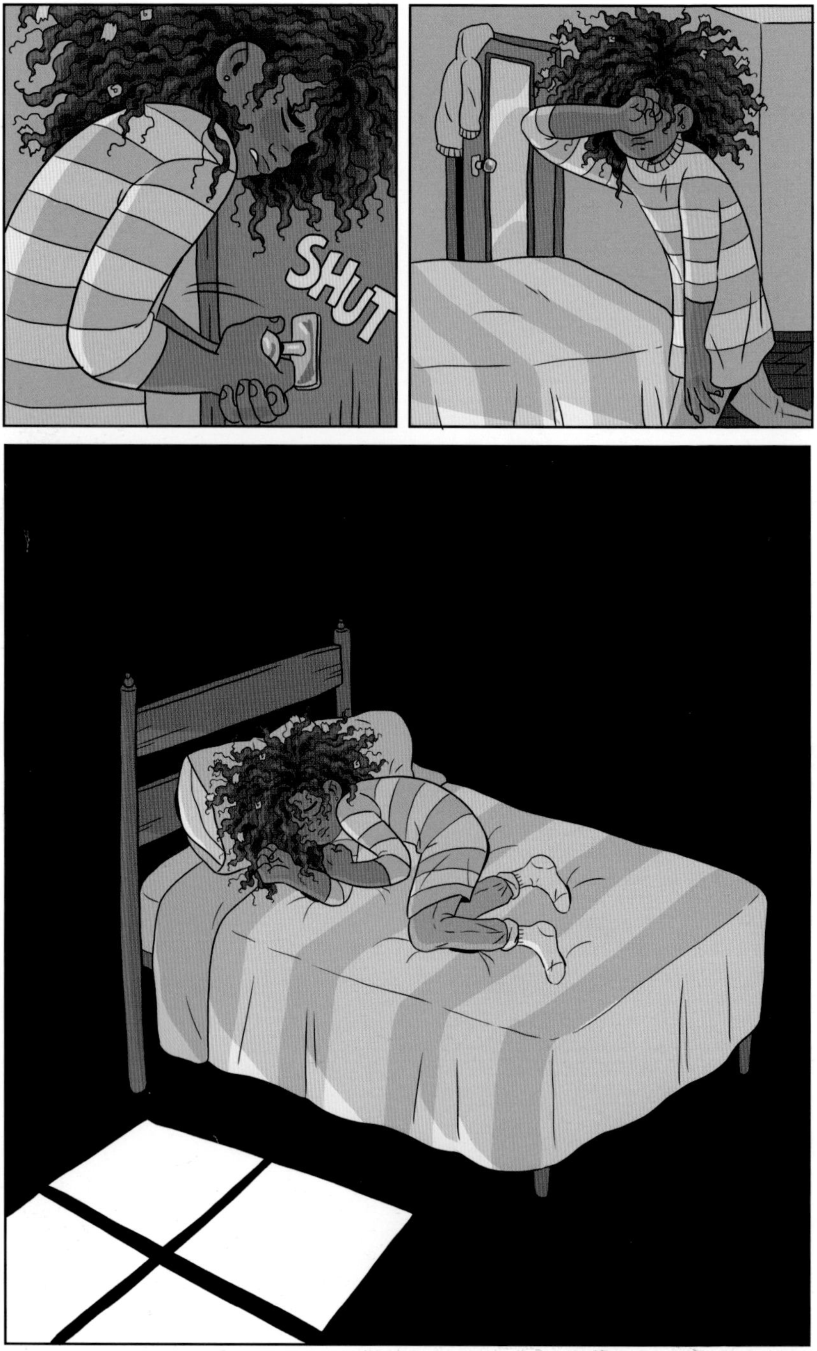
SHUT

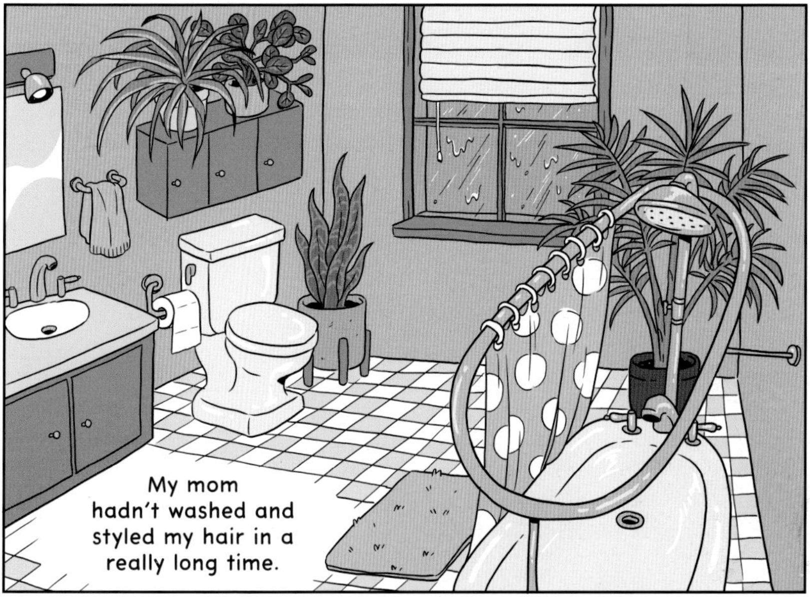
My mom hadn't washed and styled my hair in a really long time.

She used to, when I was little, and I would cry every time she detangled it.

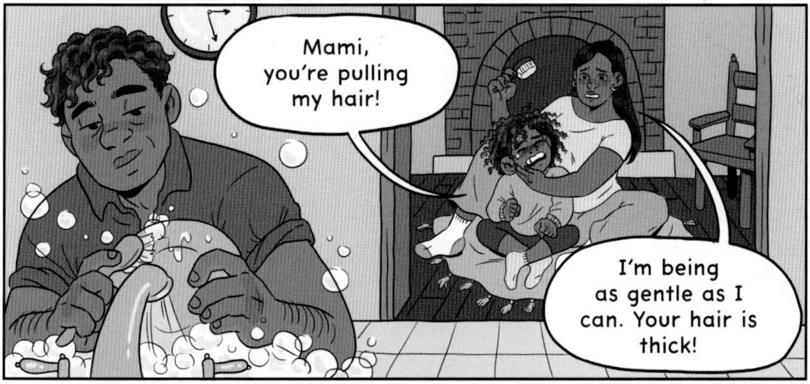
Mami, you're pulling my hair!
I'm being as gentle as I can. Your hair is thick!

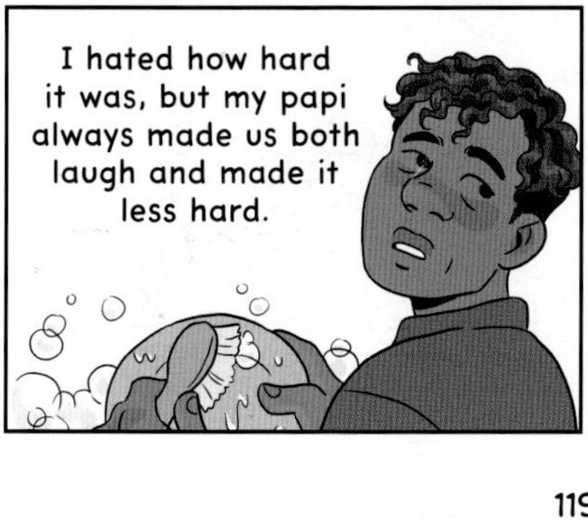
I hated how hard it was, but my papi always made us both laugh and made it less hard.

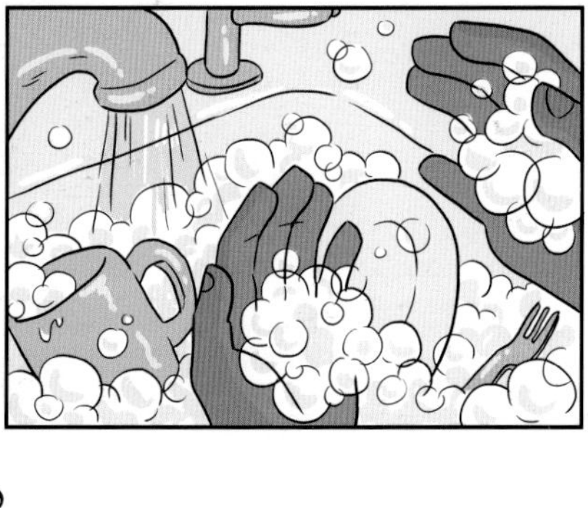

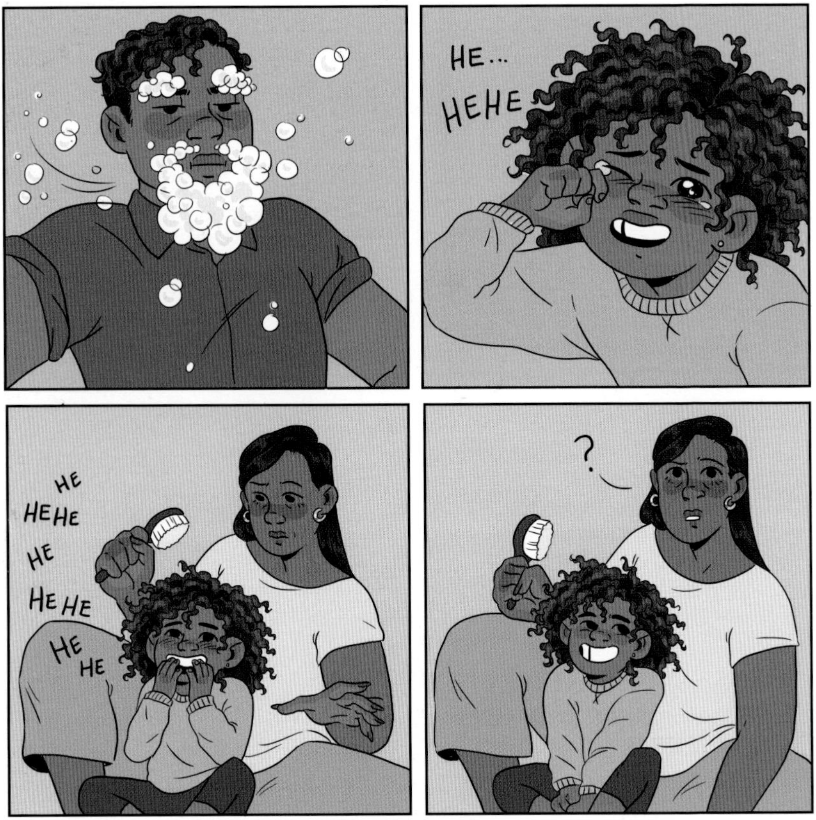
HE...
HEHE
HE
HEHE
HE
HEHE
HE
HE
?

But when I got older, after my dad passed away, we started going to the salon.

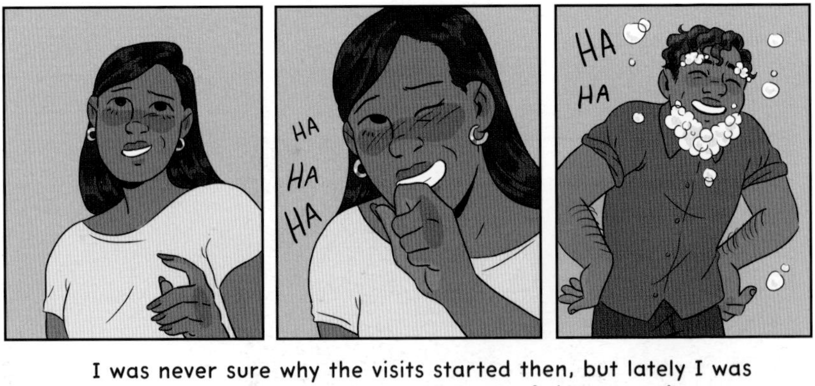
HA
HA
HA
HA
HA
HA

I was never sure why the visits started then, but lately I was beginning to think it was because of the memories.

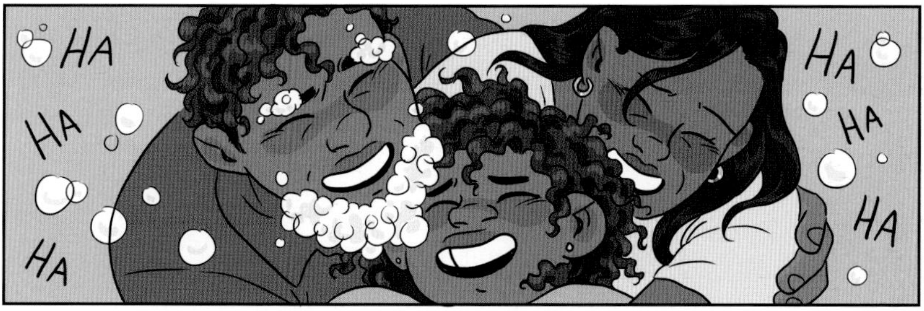
HA
HA
HA
HA
HA
HA

Maybe they just hurt my mom too much to remember.

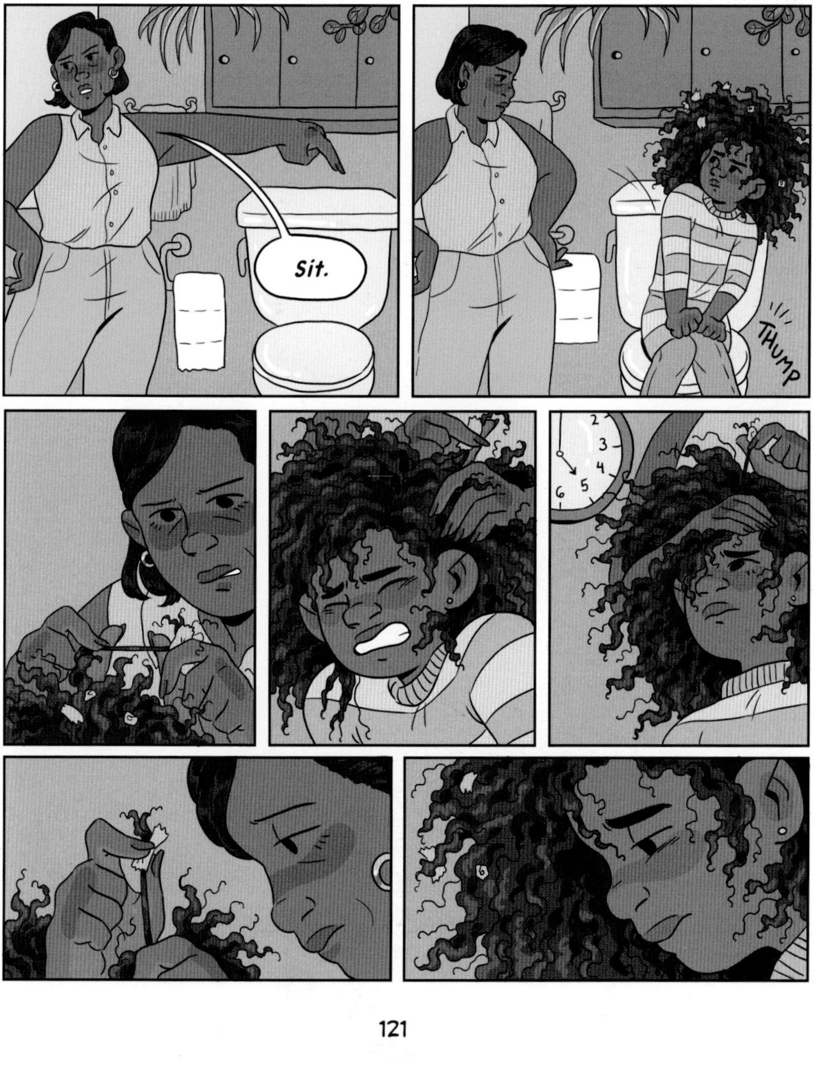
Sit.
THUMP

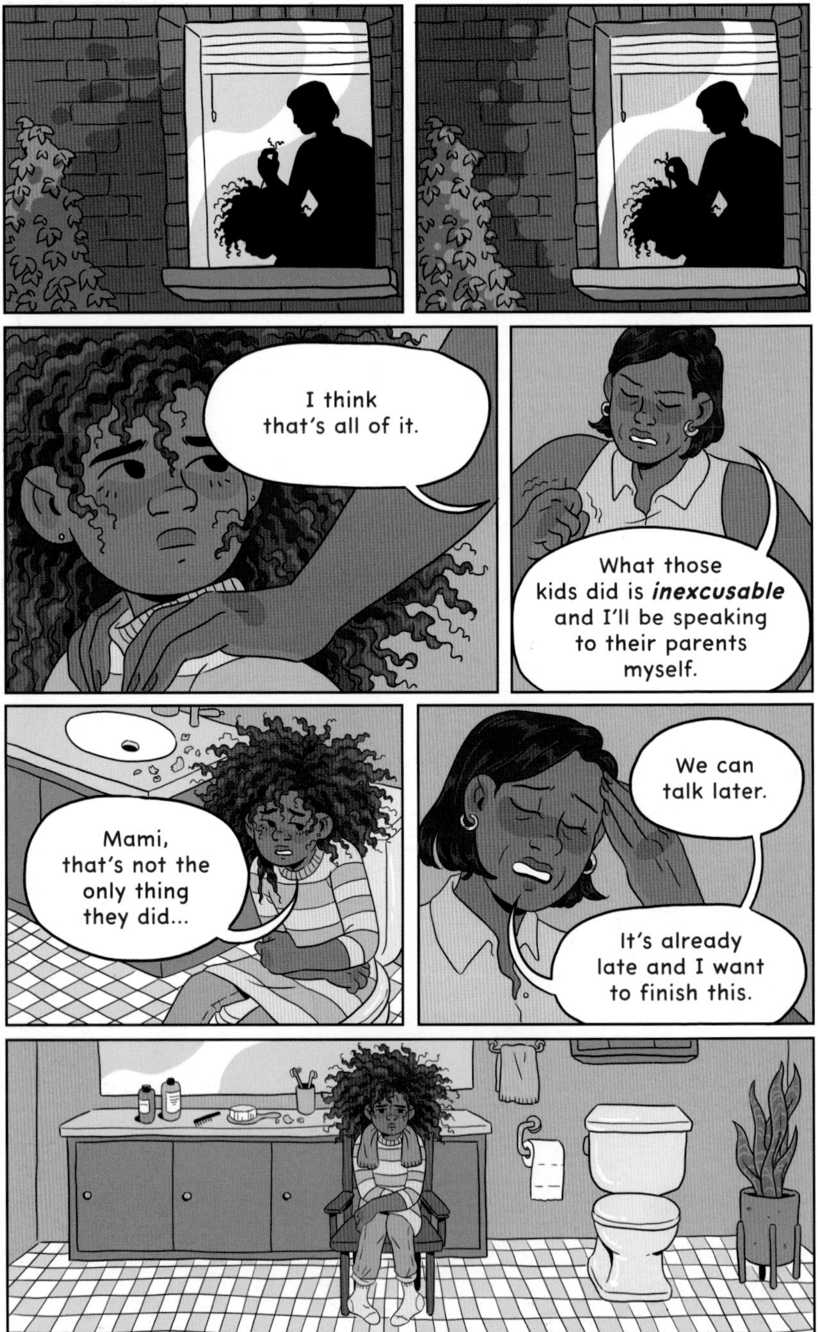
I think that's all of it.
What those kids did is ***inexcusable*** and I'll be speaking to their parents myself.
Mami, that's not the only thing they did...
We can talk later.
It's already late and I want to finish this.

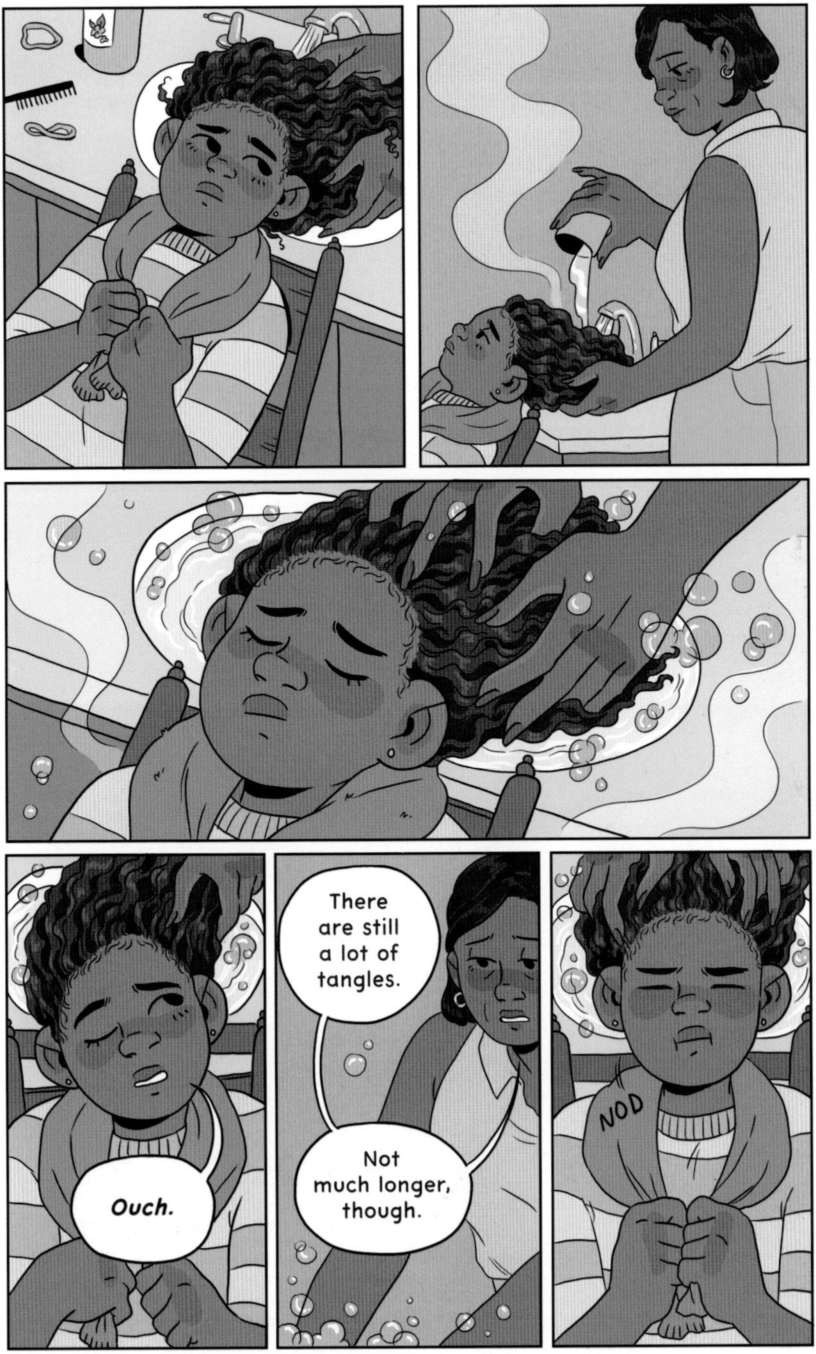
Ouch.
There are still a lot of tangles.
Not much longer, though.
NOD

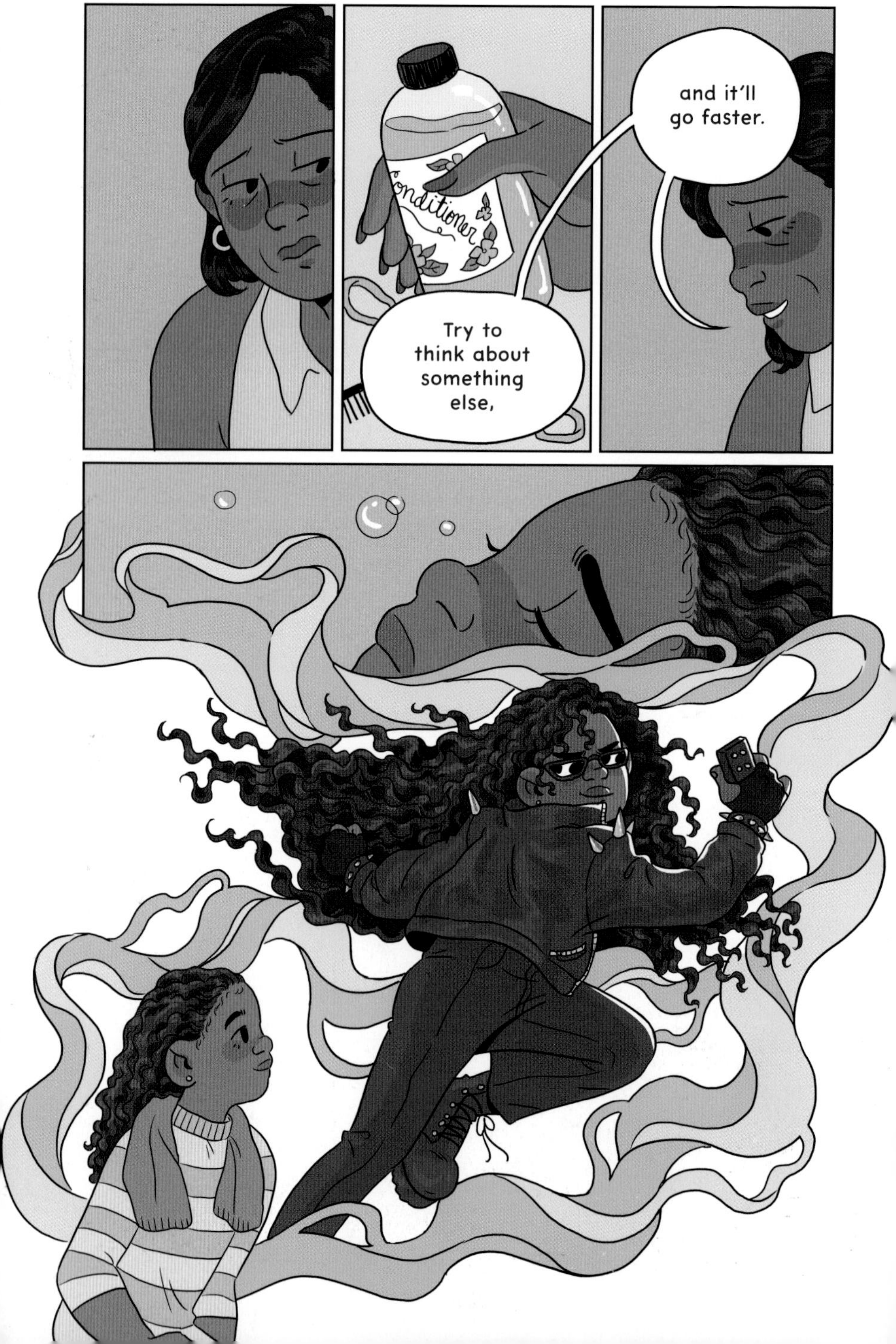
Conditioner
Try to think about something else,
and it'll go faster.

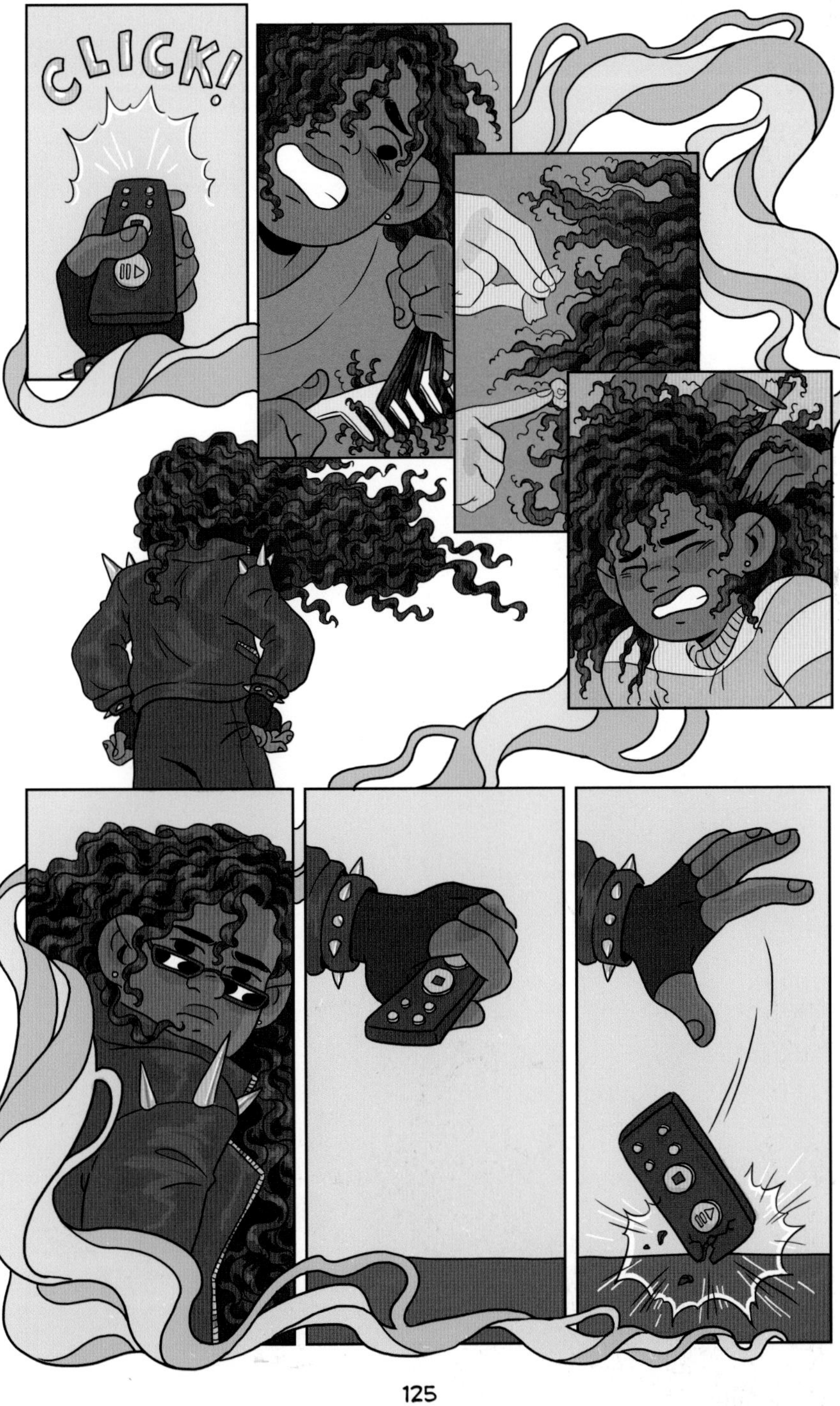
CLICK!

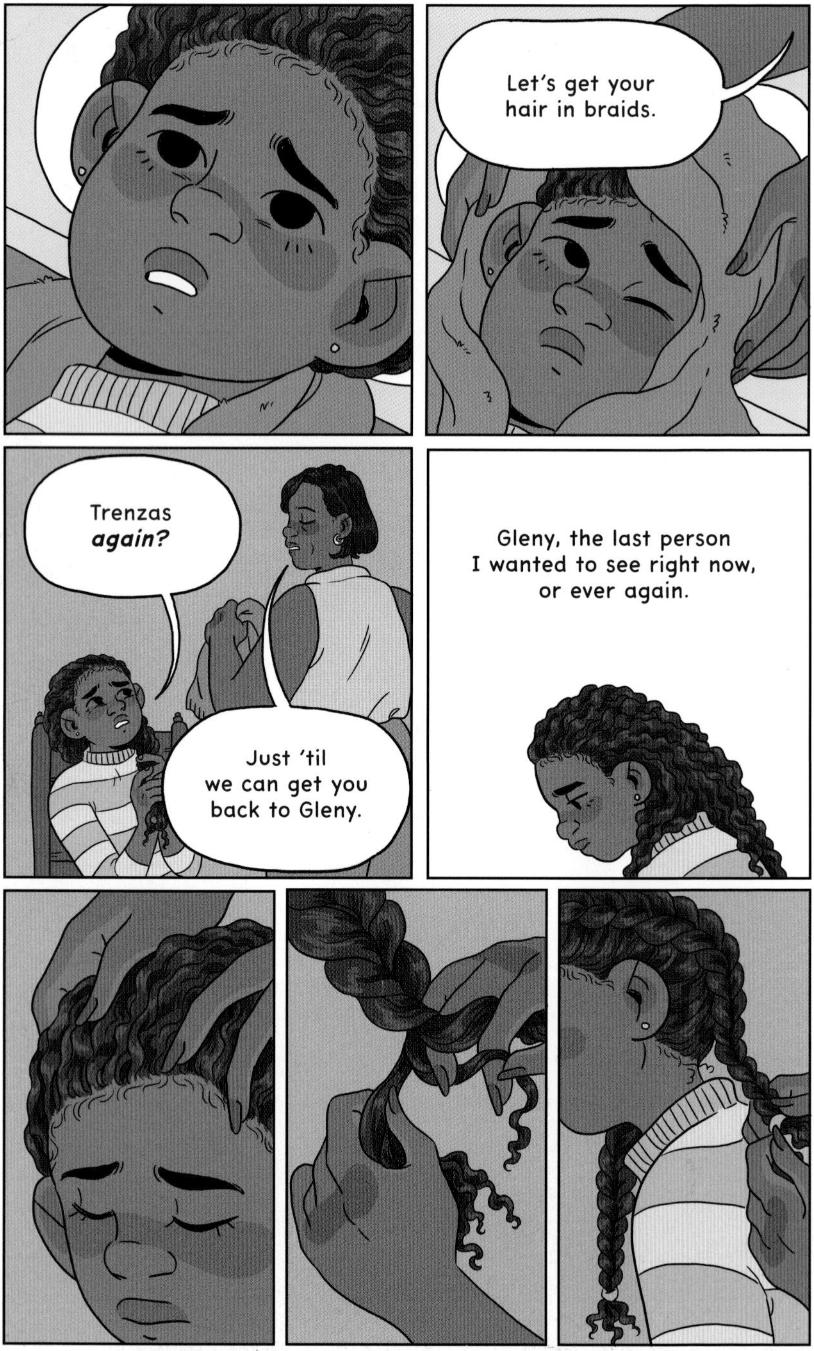
Let's get your hair in braids.
Trenzas *again?*
Just 'til we can get you back to Gleny.
Gleny, the last person I wanted to see right now, or ever again.

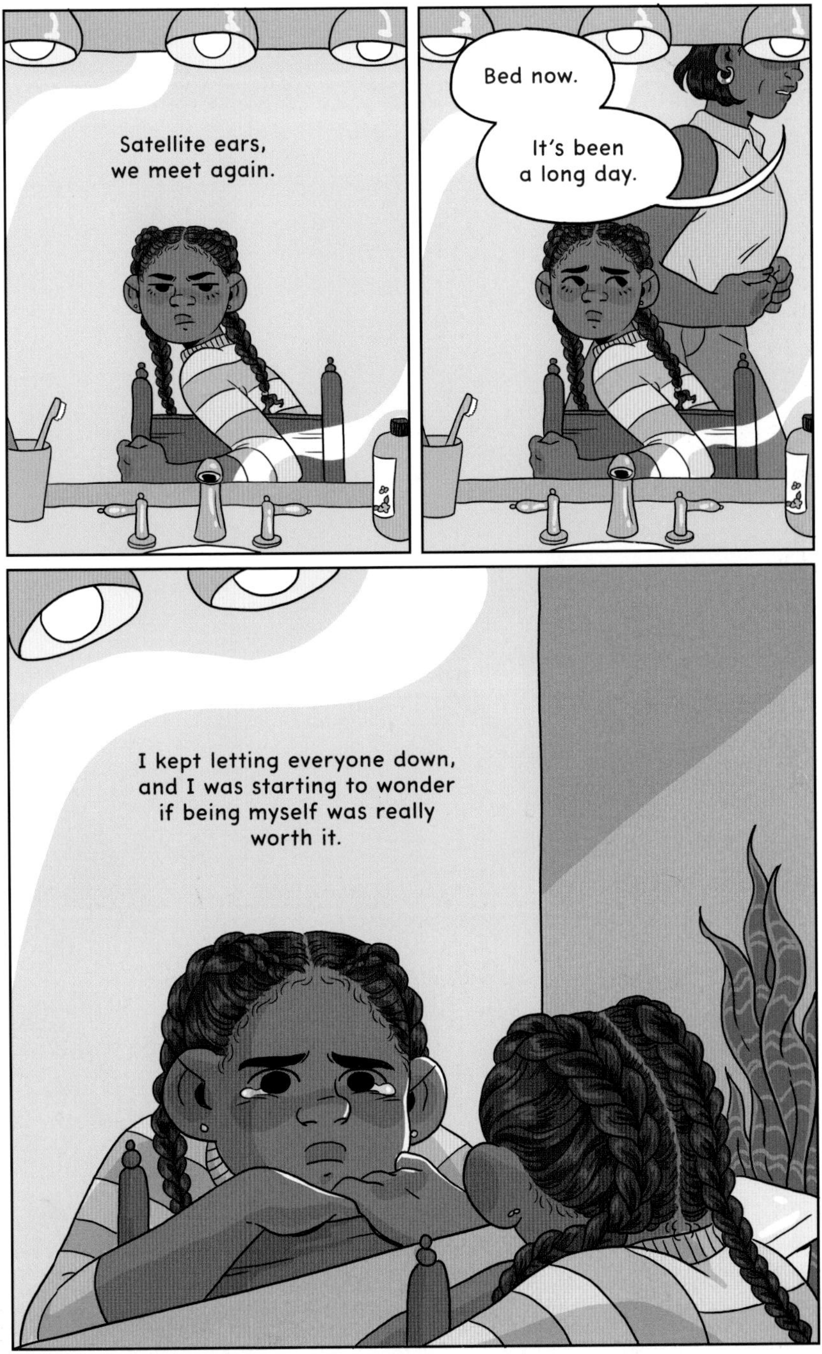
Satellite ears, we meet again.
Bed now.
It's been a long day.
I kept letting everyone down, and I was starting to wonder if being myself was really worth it.

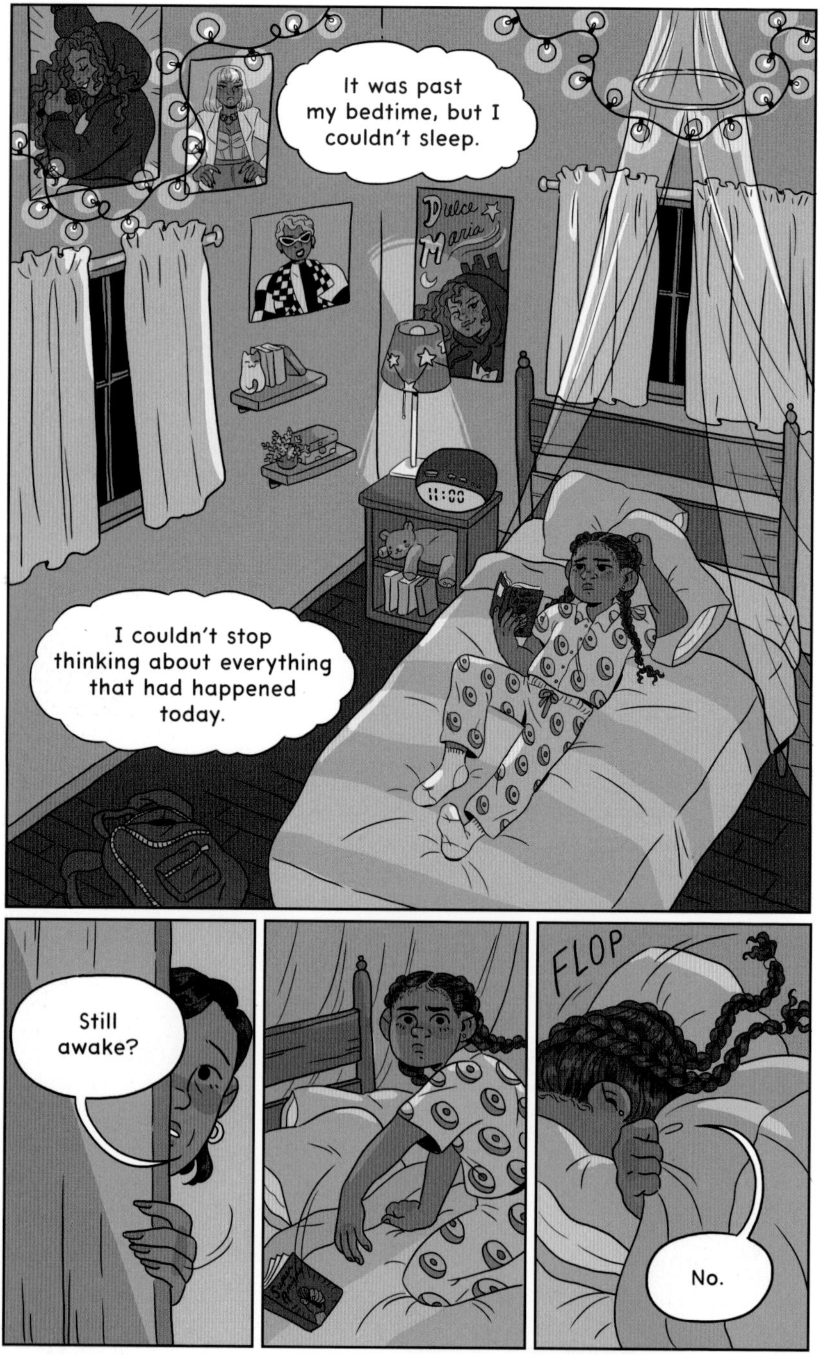
It was past my bedtime, but I couldn't sleep.
Dulce Maria
11:00
I couldn't stop thinking about everything that had happened today.
Still awake?
FLOP
No.

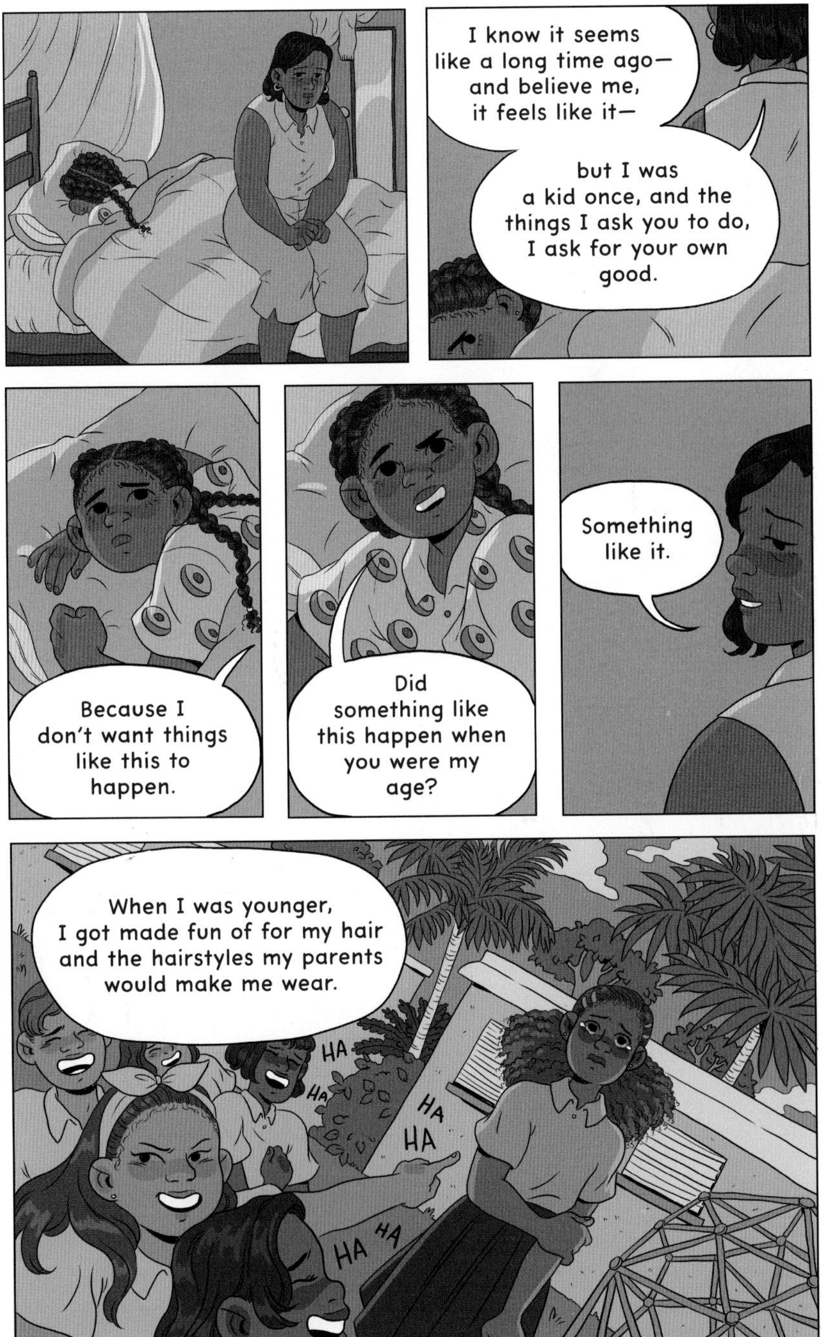
I know it seems like a long time ago— and believe me, it feels like it—
but I was a kid once, and the things I ask you to do, I ask for your own good.
Because I don't want things like this to happen.
Did something like this happen when you were my age?
Something like it.
When I was younger, I got made fun of for my hair and the hairstyles my parents would make me wear.
HA
HA
HA
HA
HA
HA

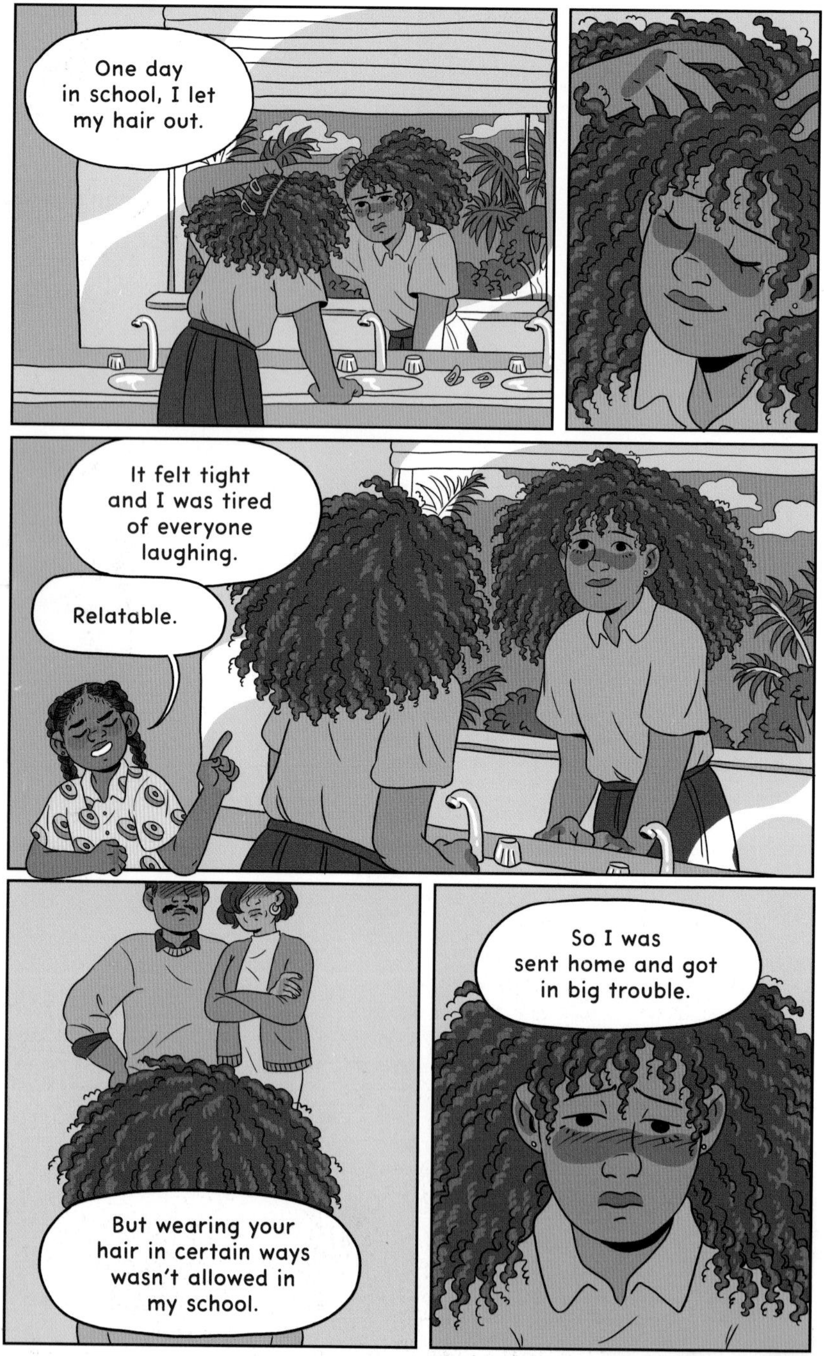
One day in school, I let my hair out.
It felt tight and I was tired of everyone laughing.
Relatable.
But wearing your hair in certain ways wasn't allowed in my school.
So I was sent home and got in big trouble.

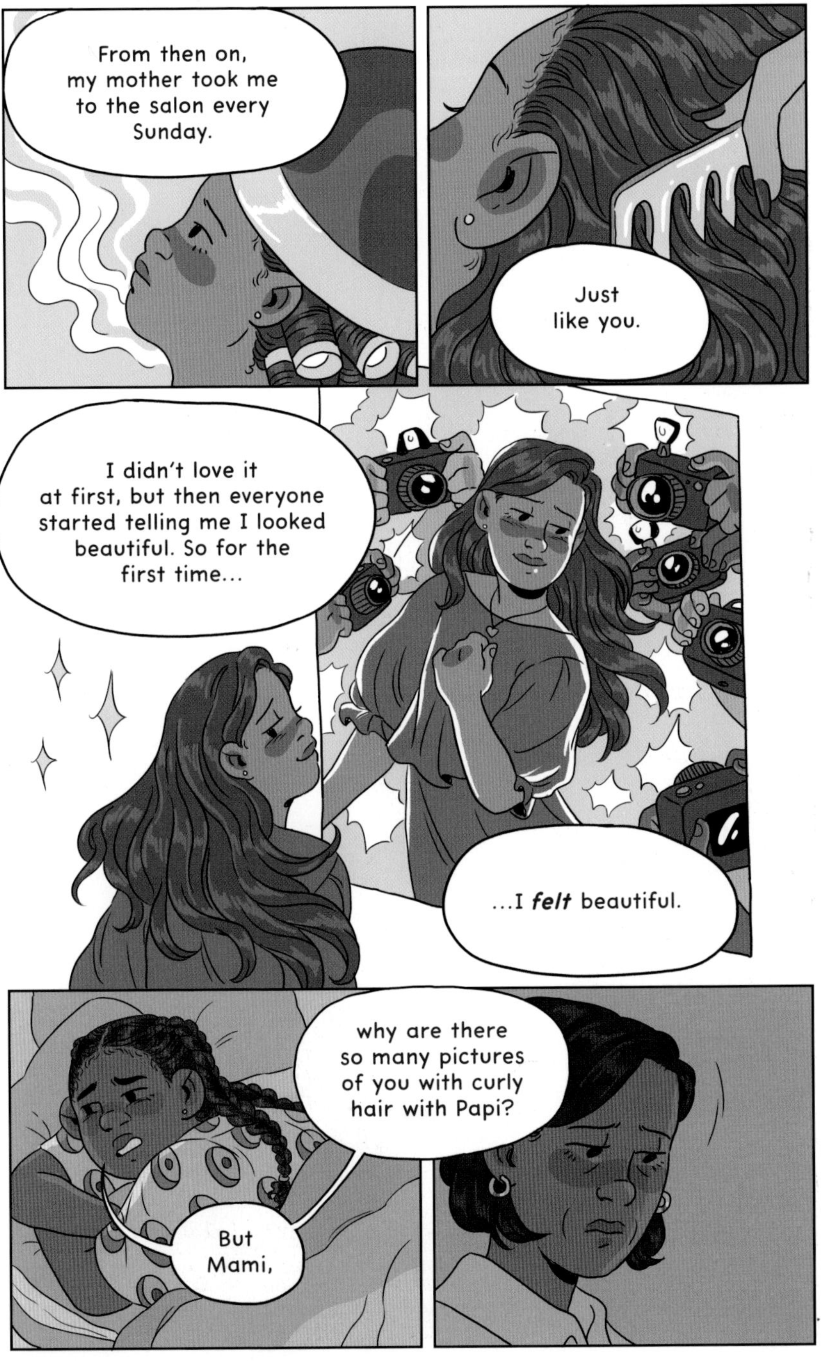
From then on, my mother took me to the salon every Sunday.
Just like you.
I didn't love it at first, but then everyone started telling me I looked beautiful. So for the first time...
...I *felt* beautiful.
But Mami,
why are there so many pictures of you with curly hair with Papi?

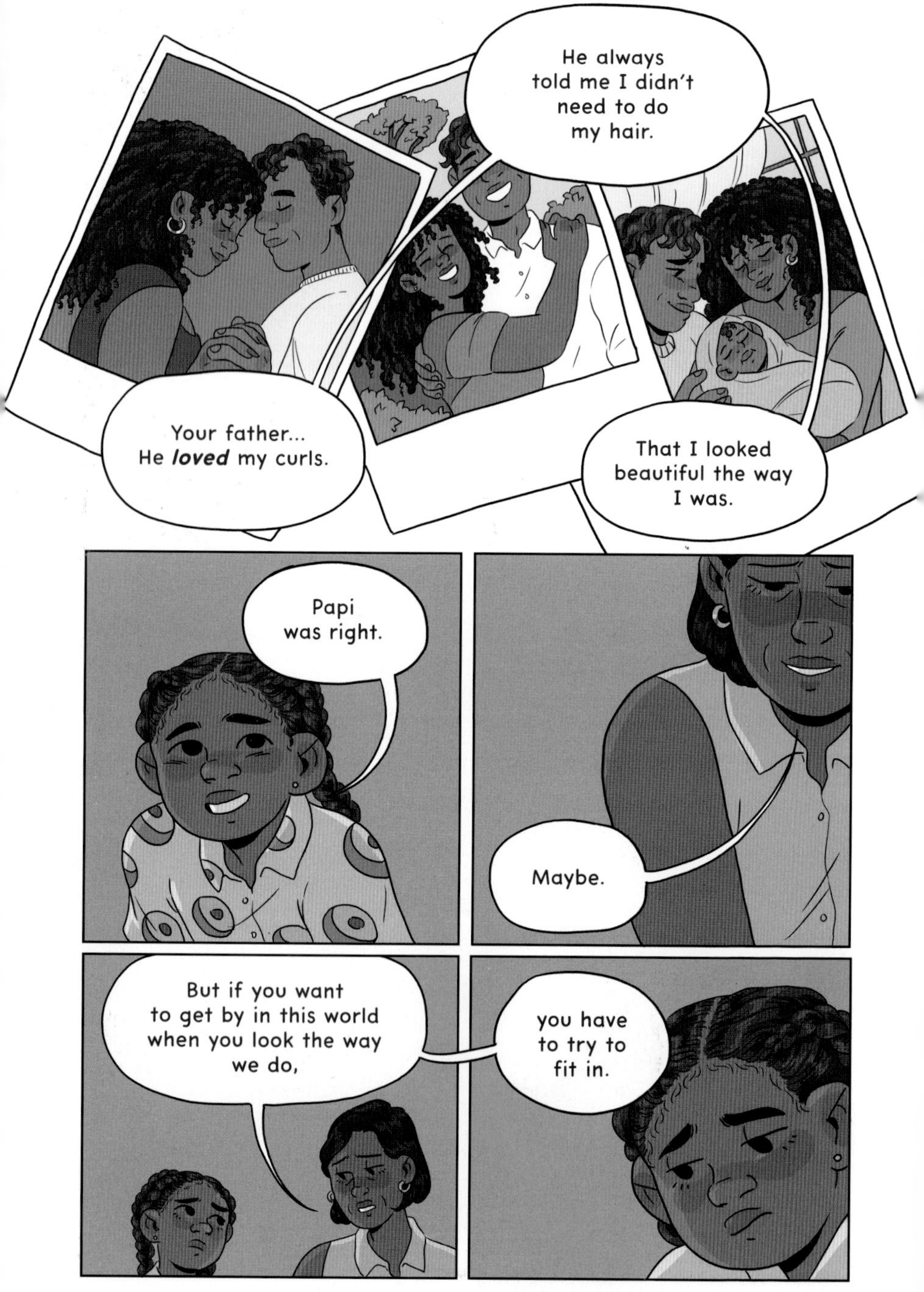
Your father...
He *loved* my curls.
He always told me I didn't need to do my hair.
That I looked beautiful the way I was.
Papi was right.
Maybe.
But if you want to get by in this world when you look the way we do,
you have to try to fit in.

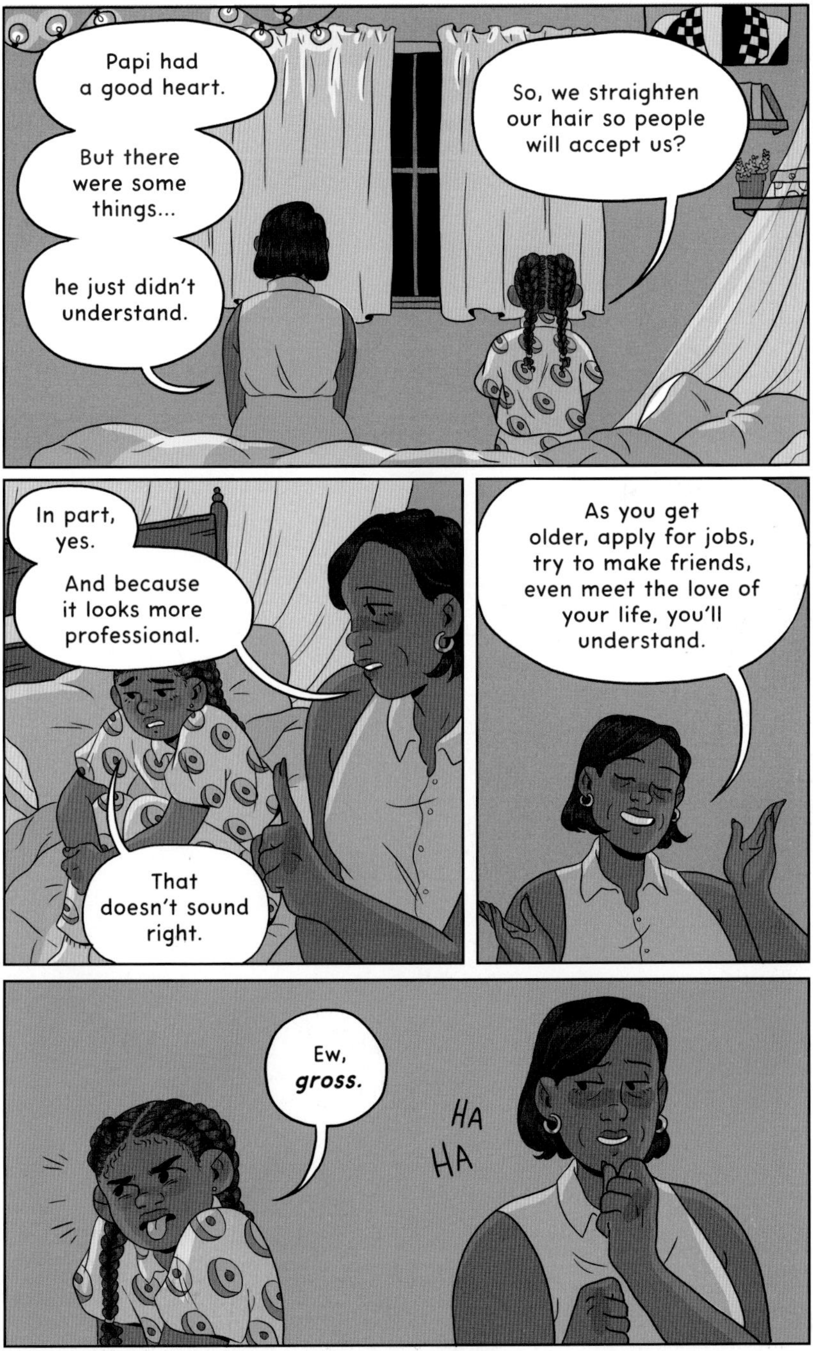
Papi had a good heart.
But there were some things...
he just didn't understand.
So, we straighten our hair so people will accept us?
In part, yes.
And because it looks more professional.
That doesn't sound right.
As you get older, apply for jobs, try to make friends, even meet the love of your life, you'll understand.
Ew, *gross.*
HA HA

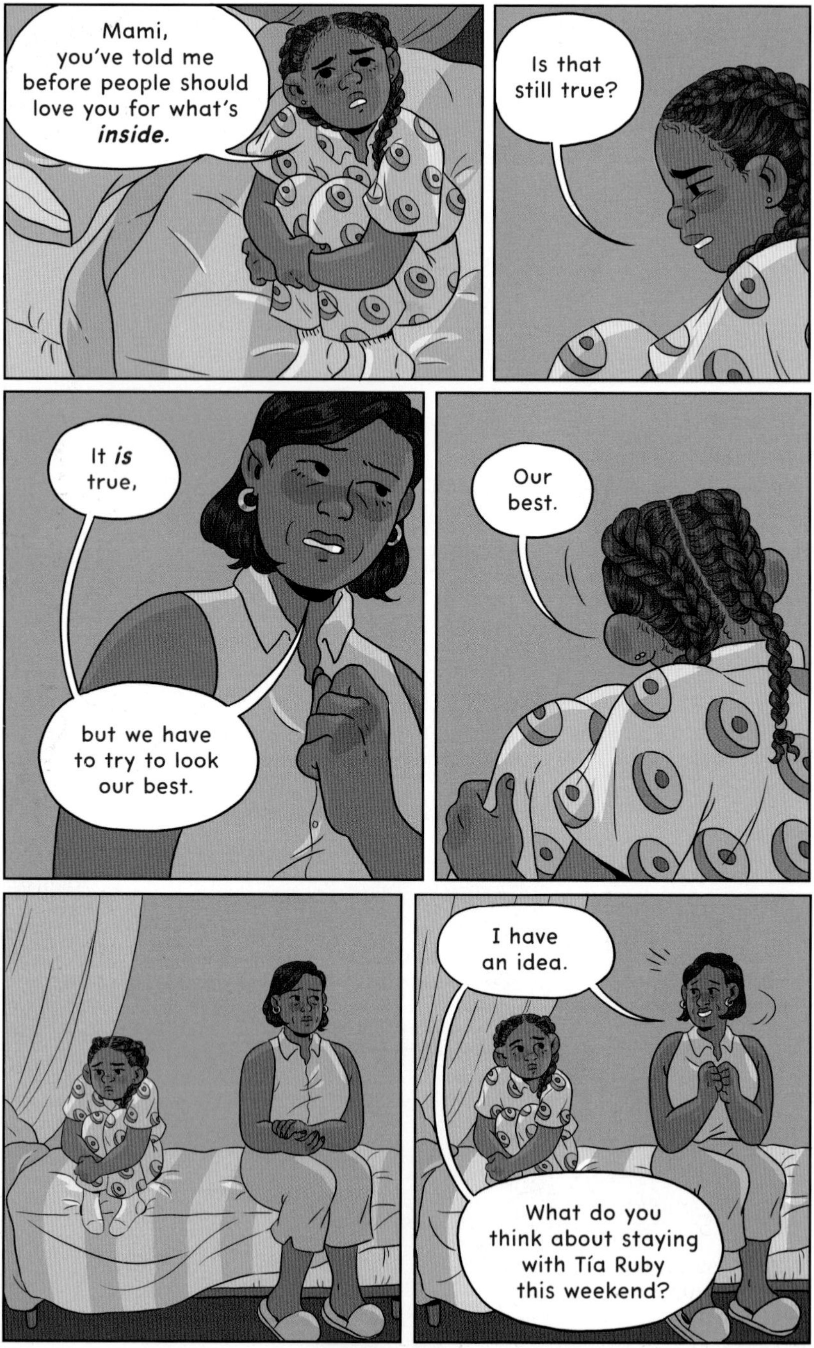
Mami, you've told me before people should love you for what's *inside.*
Is that still true?
It *is* true,
but we have to try to look our best.
Our best.
I have an idea.
What do you think about staying with Tía Ruby this weekend?

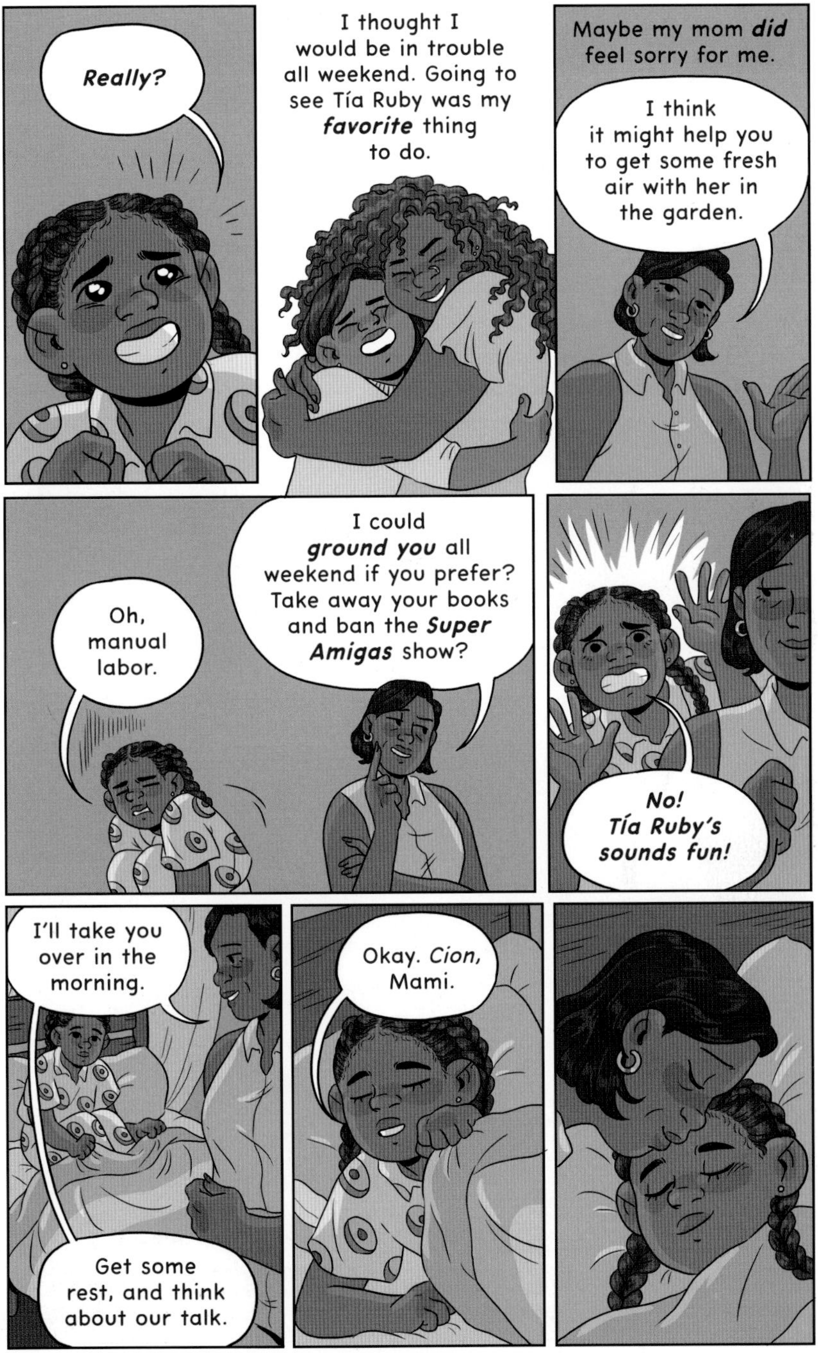

Really?
I thought I would be in trouble all weekend. Going to see Tía Ruby was my *favorite* thing to do.
Maybe my mom *did* feel sorry for me.
I think it might help you to get some fresh air with her in the garden.
Oh, manual labor.
I could *ground you* all weekend if you prefer? Take away your books and ban the *Super Amigas* show?
No! Tía Ruby's sounds fun!
I'll take you over in the morning.
Get some rest, and think about our talk.
Okay. *Cion,* Mami.

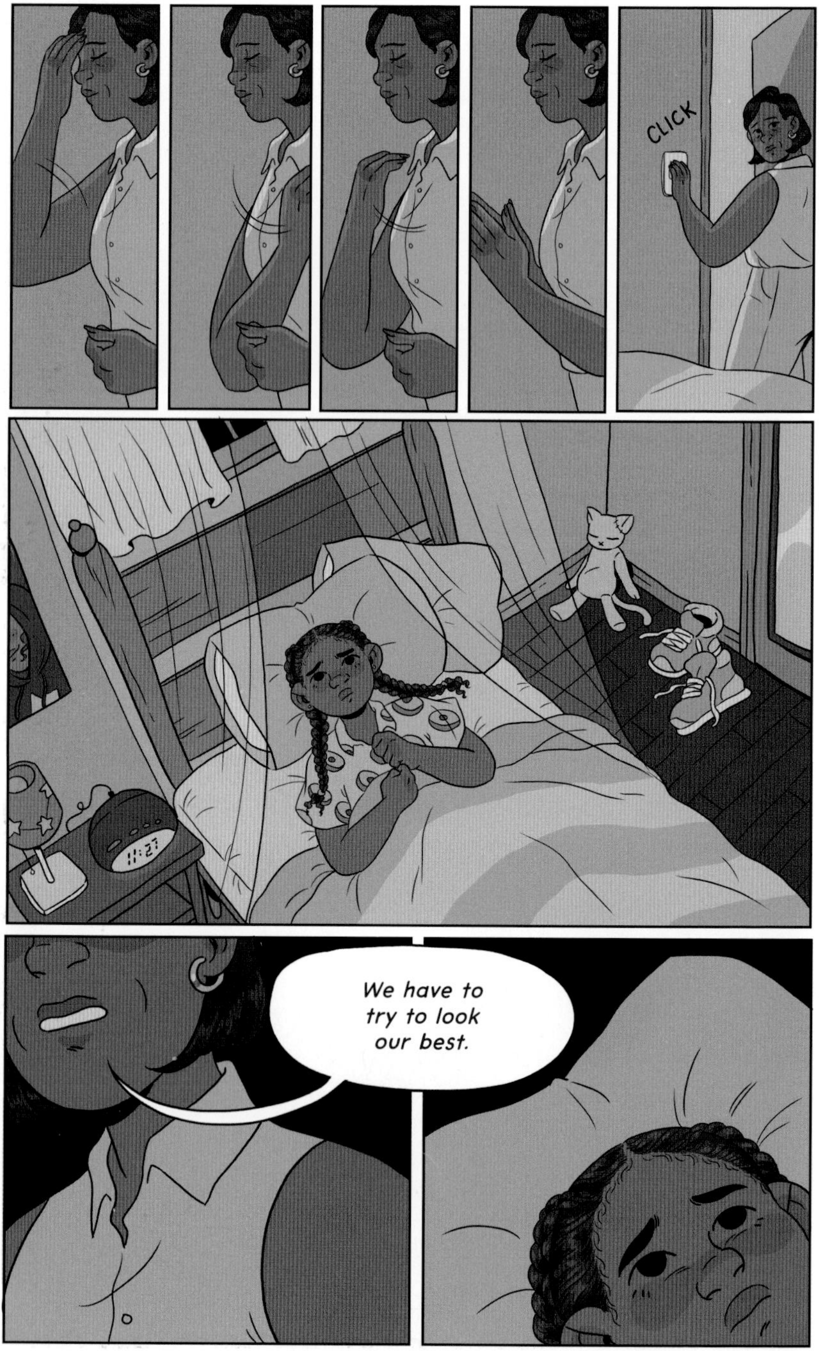
CLICK
We have to try to look our best.

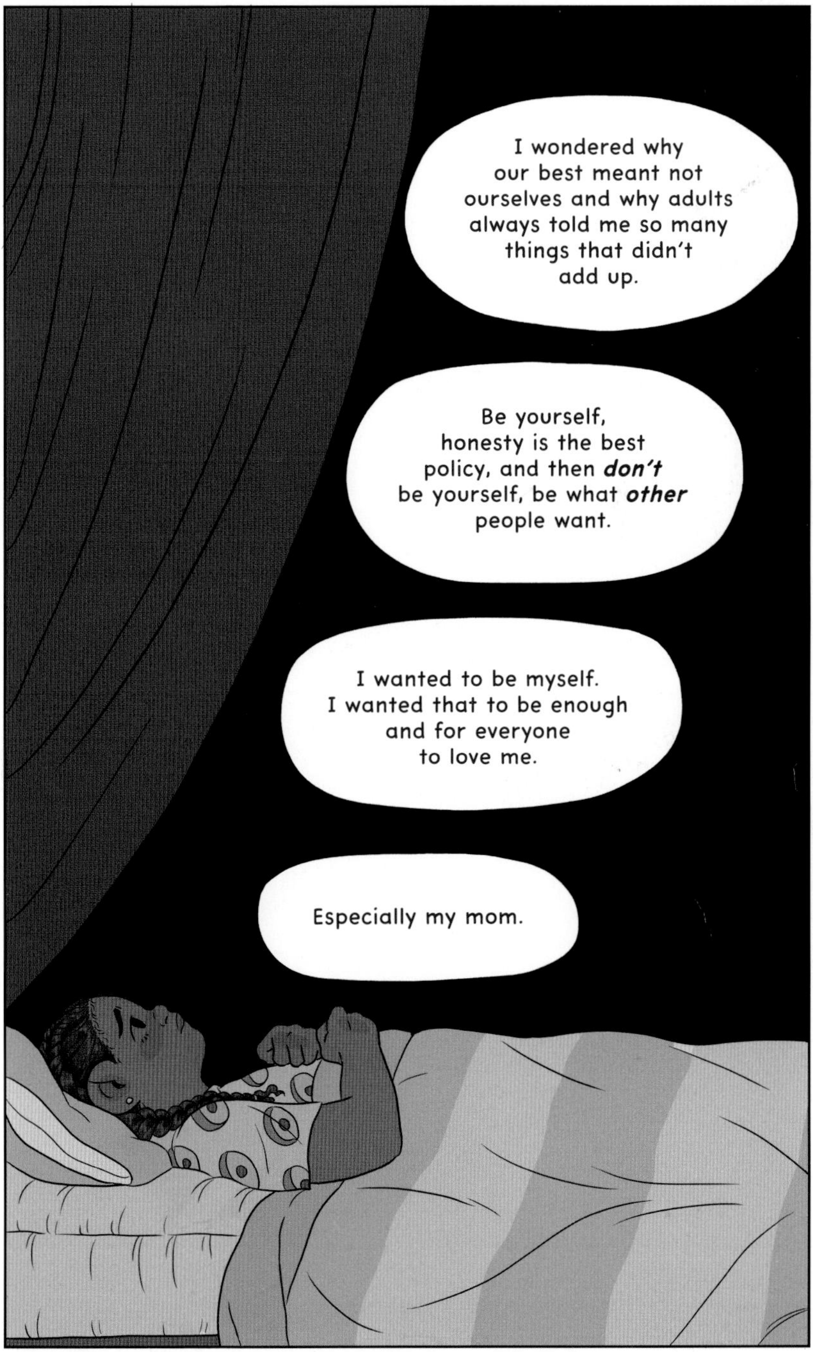
I wondered why our best meant not ourselves and why adults always told me so many things that didn't add up.
Be yourself, honesty is the best policy, and then ***don't*** be yourself, be what ***other*** people want.
I wanted to be myself. I wanted that to be enough and for everyone to love me.
Especially my mom.

A SPECIAL WASH DAY

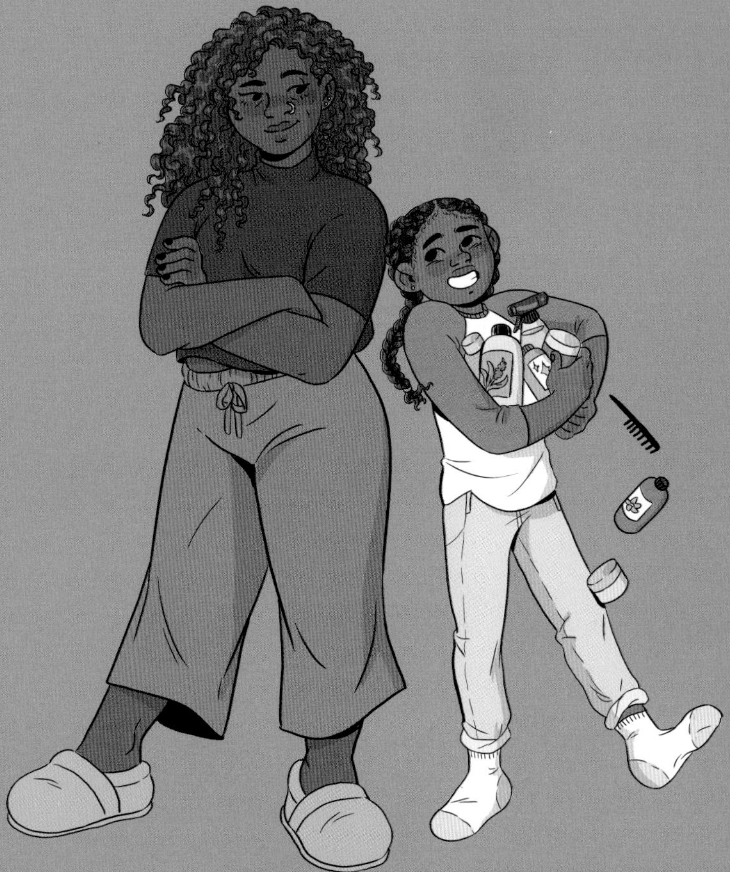

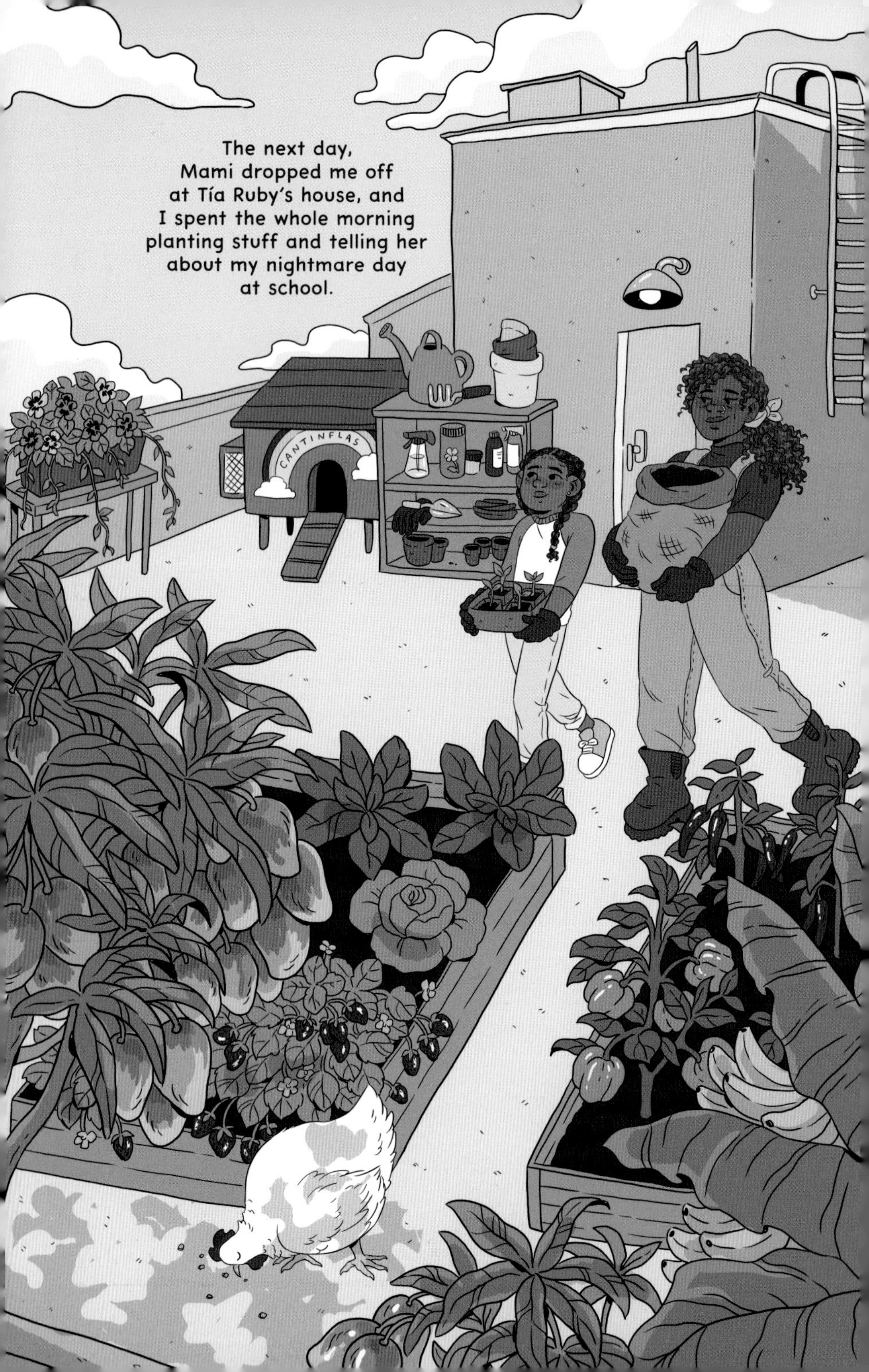
The next day, Mami dropped me off at Tía Ruby's house, and I spent the whole morning planting stuff and telling her about my nightmare day at school.
CANTINFLAS

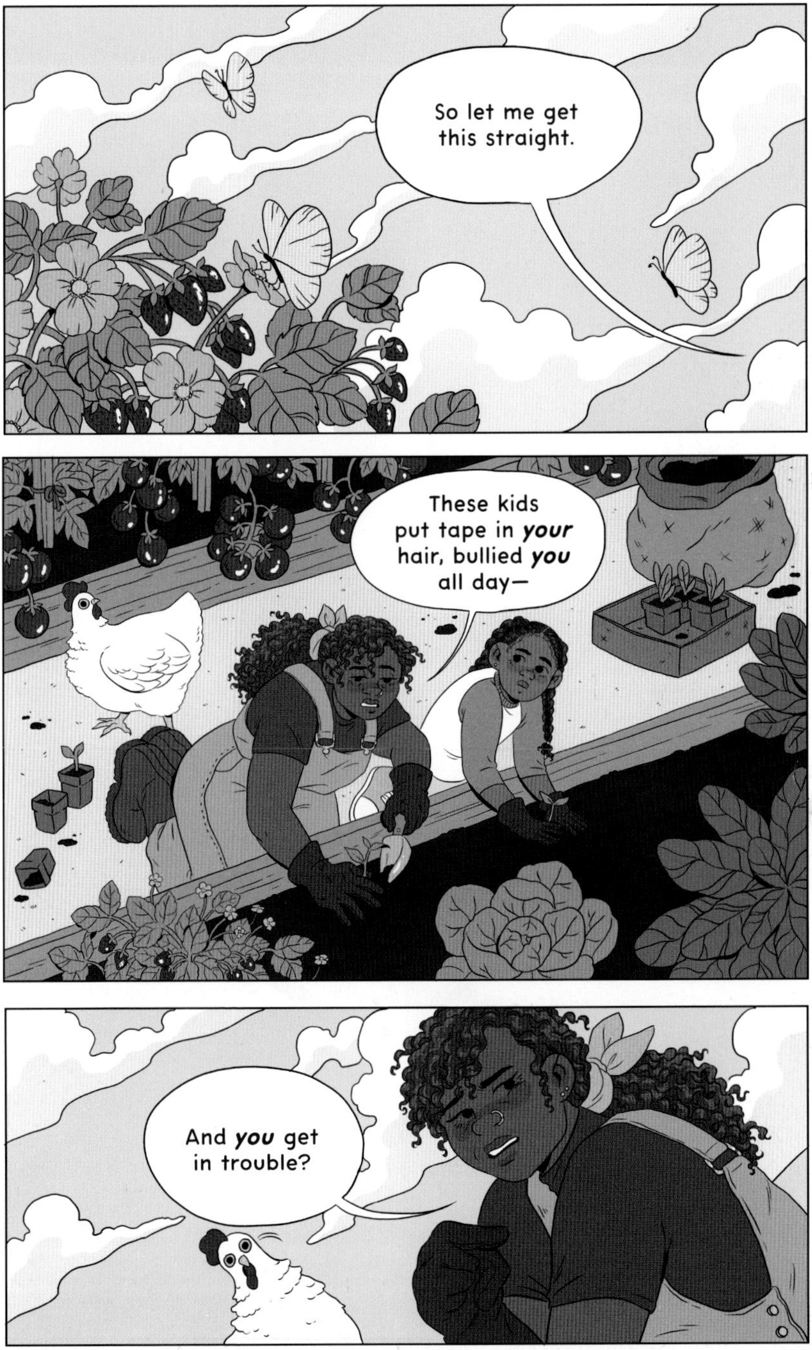
So let me get this straight.
These kids put tape in *your* hair, bullied *you* all day—
And *you* get in trouble?

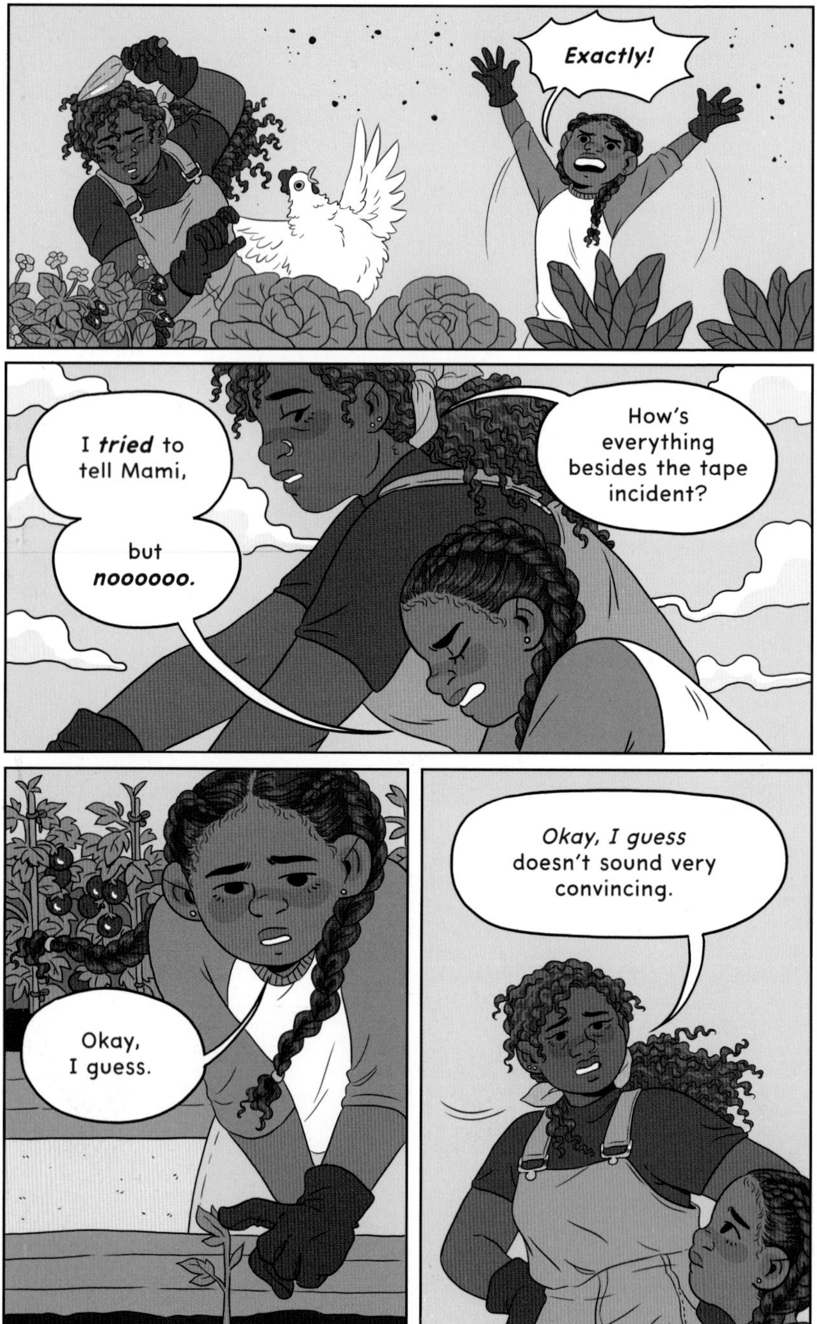
Exactly!
I *tried* to tell Mami,
but ***noooooo.***
How's everything besides the tape incident?
Okay, I guess.
Okay, I guess doesn't sound very convincing.

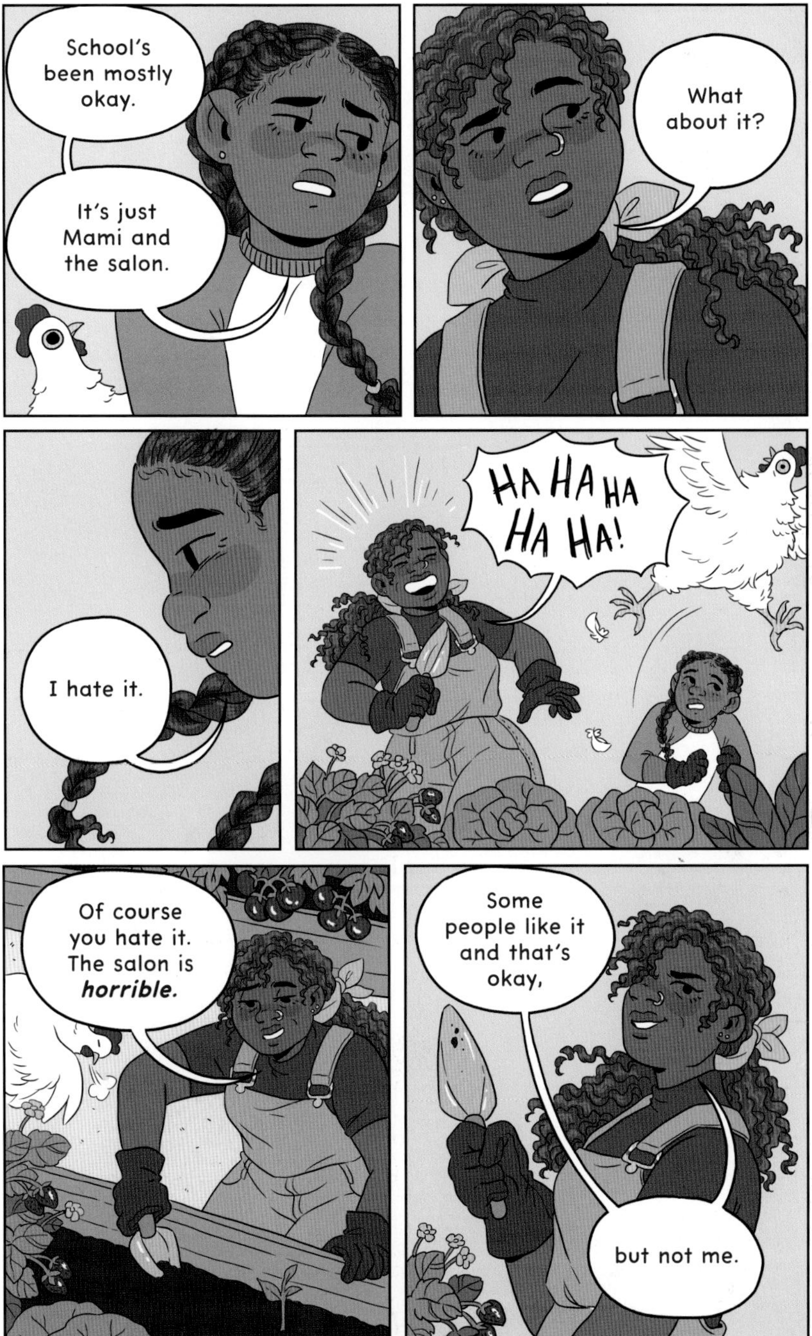
School's been mostly okay.
It's just Mami and the salon.
What about it?
I hate it.
HA HA HA HA HA HA!
Of course you hate it. The salon is ***horrible.***
Some people like it and that's okay,
but not me.

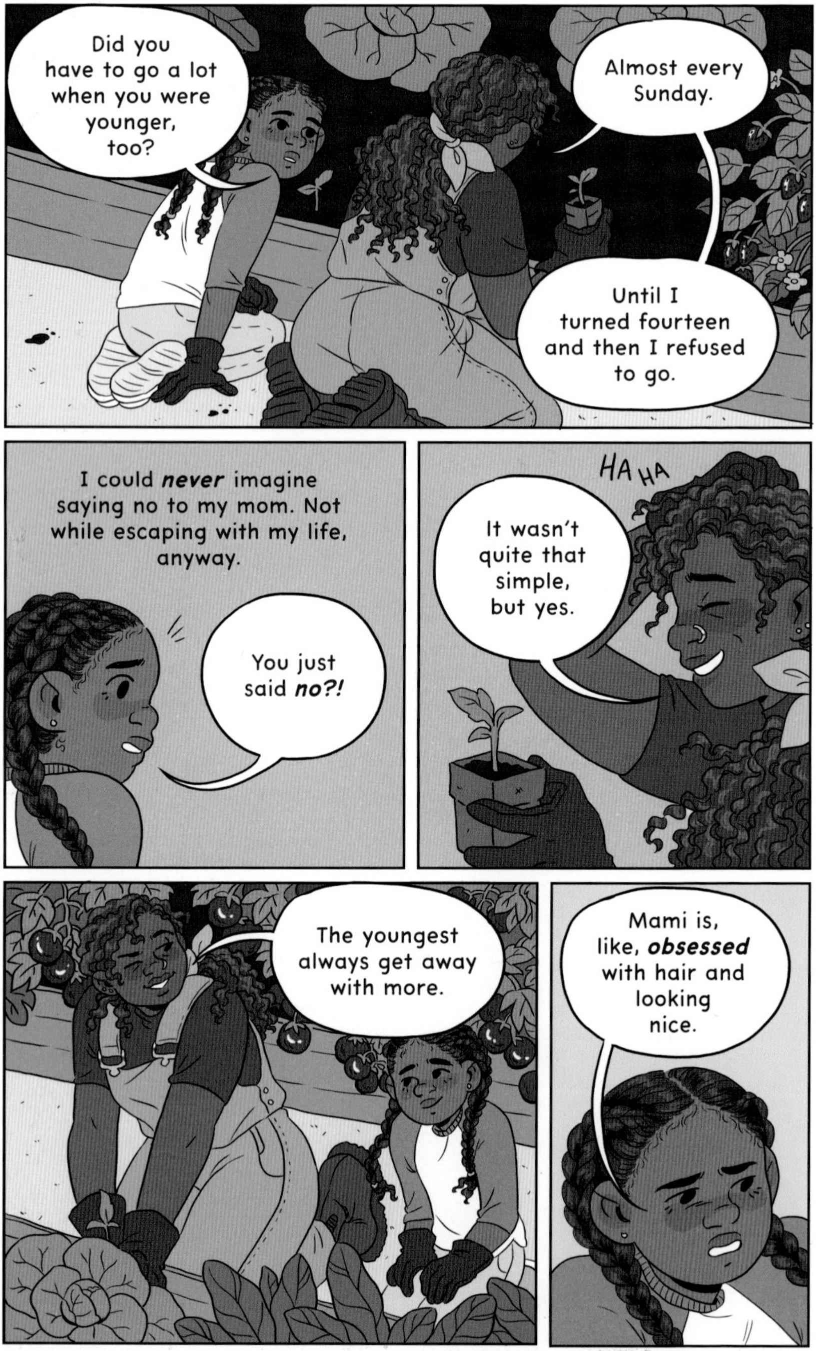
Did you have to go a lot when you were younger, too?
Almost every Sunday.
Until I turned fourteen and then I refused to go.
I could **never** imagine saying no to my mom. Not while escaping with my life, anyway.
You just said **no?!**
HA HA
It wasn't quite that simple, but yes.
The youngest always get away with more.
Mami is, like, **obsessed** with hair and looking nice.

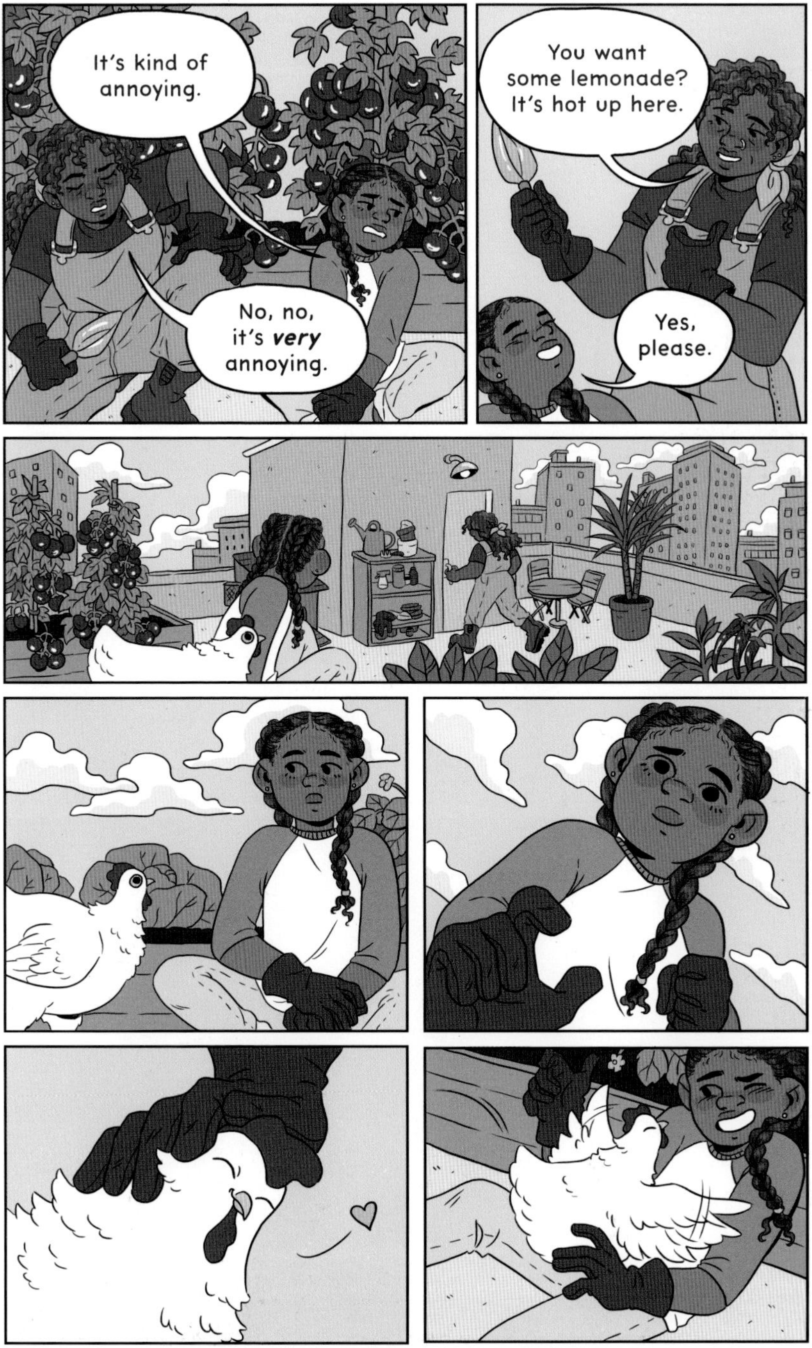
It's kind of annoying.
No, no, it's ***very*** annoying.
You want some lemonade? It's hot up here.
Yes, please.

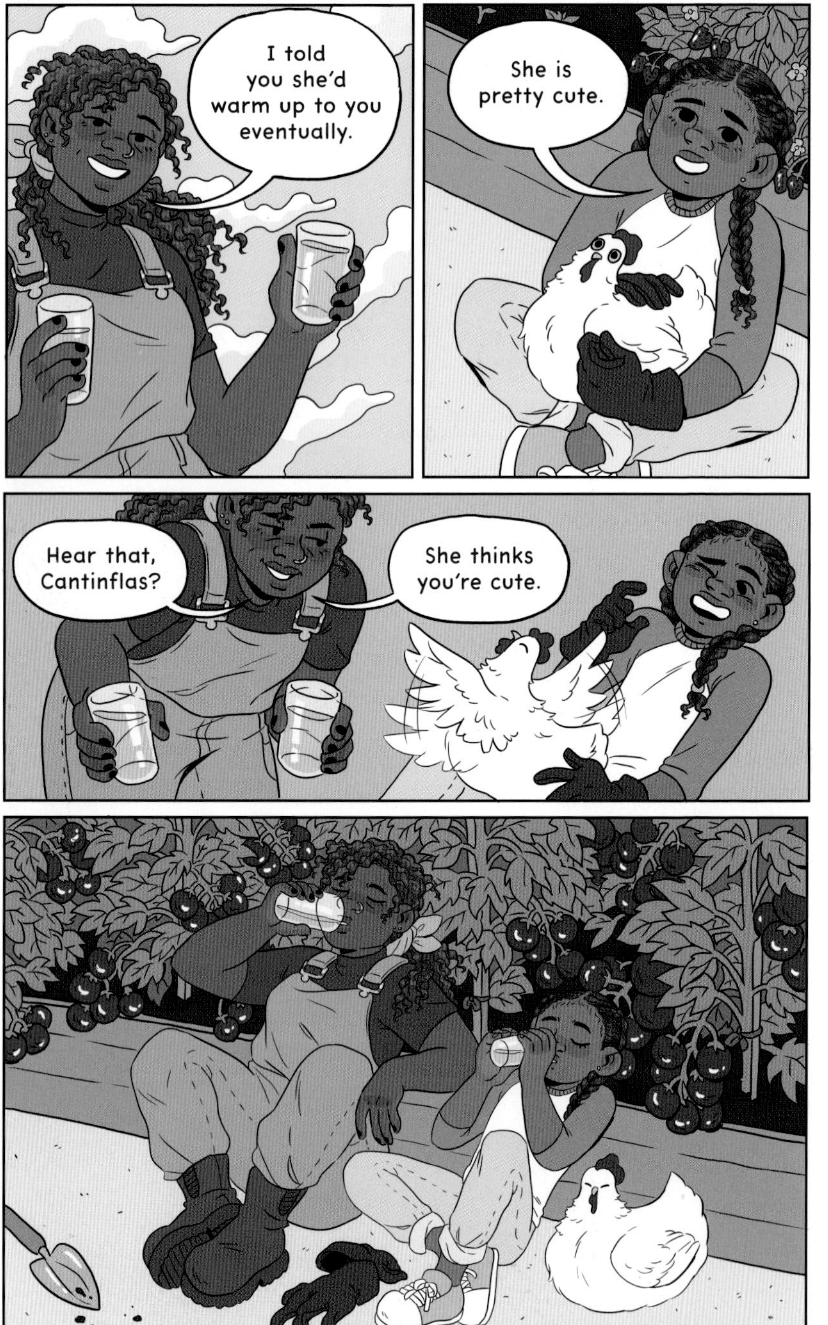
I told you she'd warm up to you eventually.
She is pretty cute.
Hear that, Cantinflas?
She thinks you're cute.

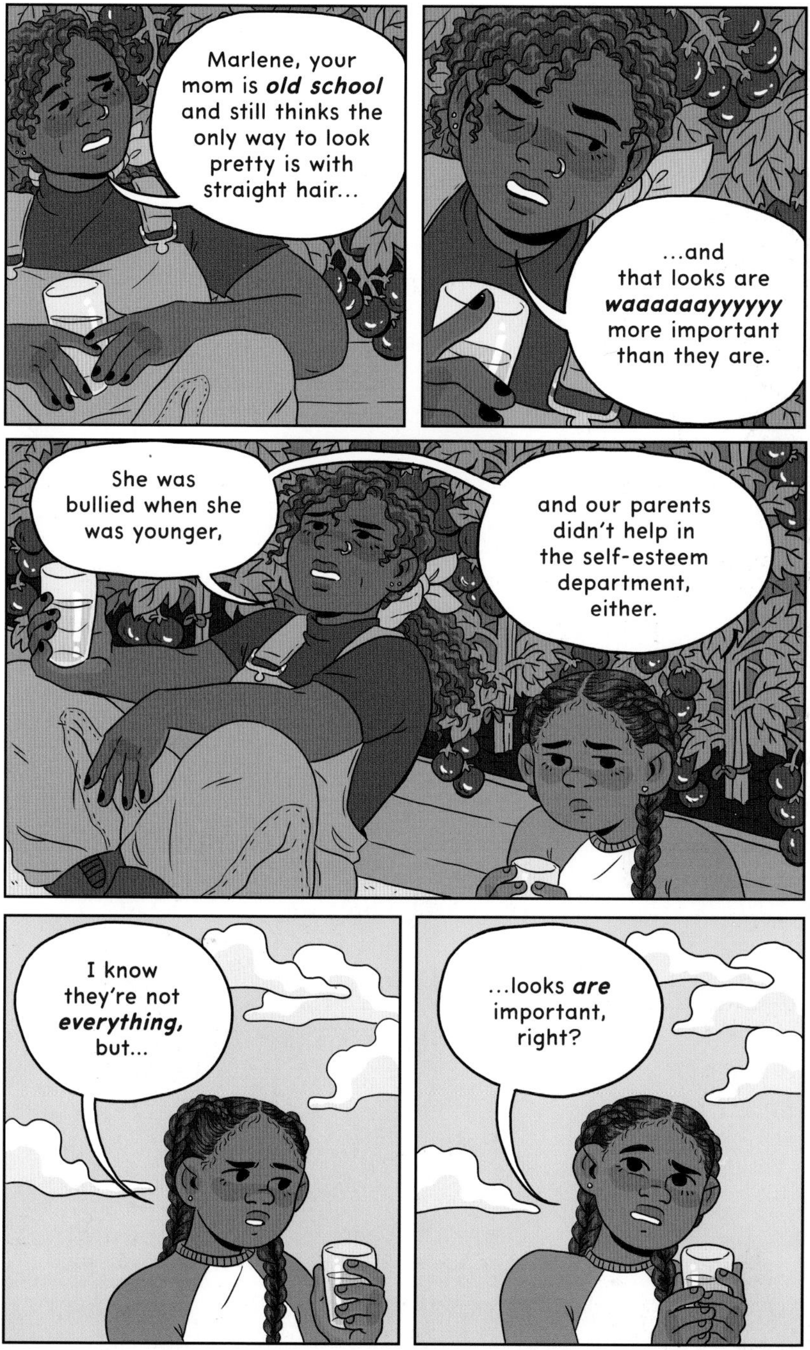
Marlene, your mom is ***old school*** and still thinks the only way to look pretty is with straight hair...
...and that looks are ***waaaaaayyyyyy*** more important than they are.
She was bullied when she was younger,
and our parents didn't help in the self-esteem department, either.
I know they're not ***everything,*** but...
...looks ***are*** important, right?

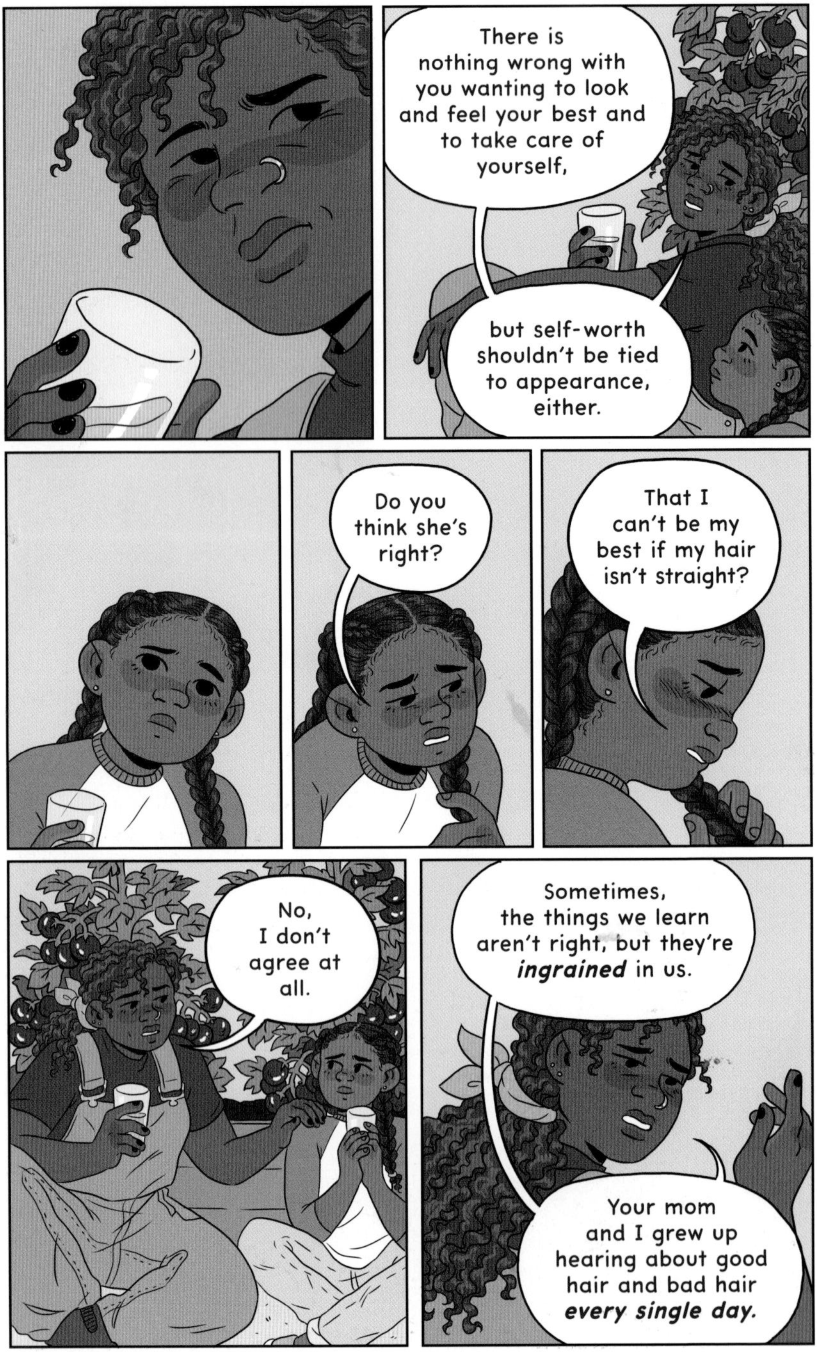
There is nothing wrong with you wanting to look and feel your best and to take care of yourself,
but self-worth shouldn't be tied to appearance, either.
Do you think she's right?
That I can't be my best if my hair isn't straight?
No, I don't agree at all.
Sometimes, the things we learn aren't right, but they're ***ingrained*** in us.
Your mom and I grew up hearing about good hair and bad hair ***every single day.***

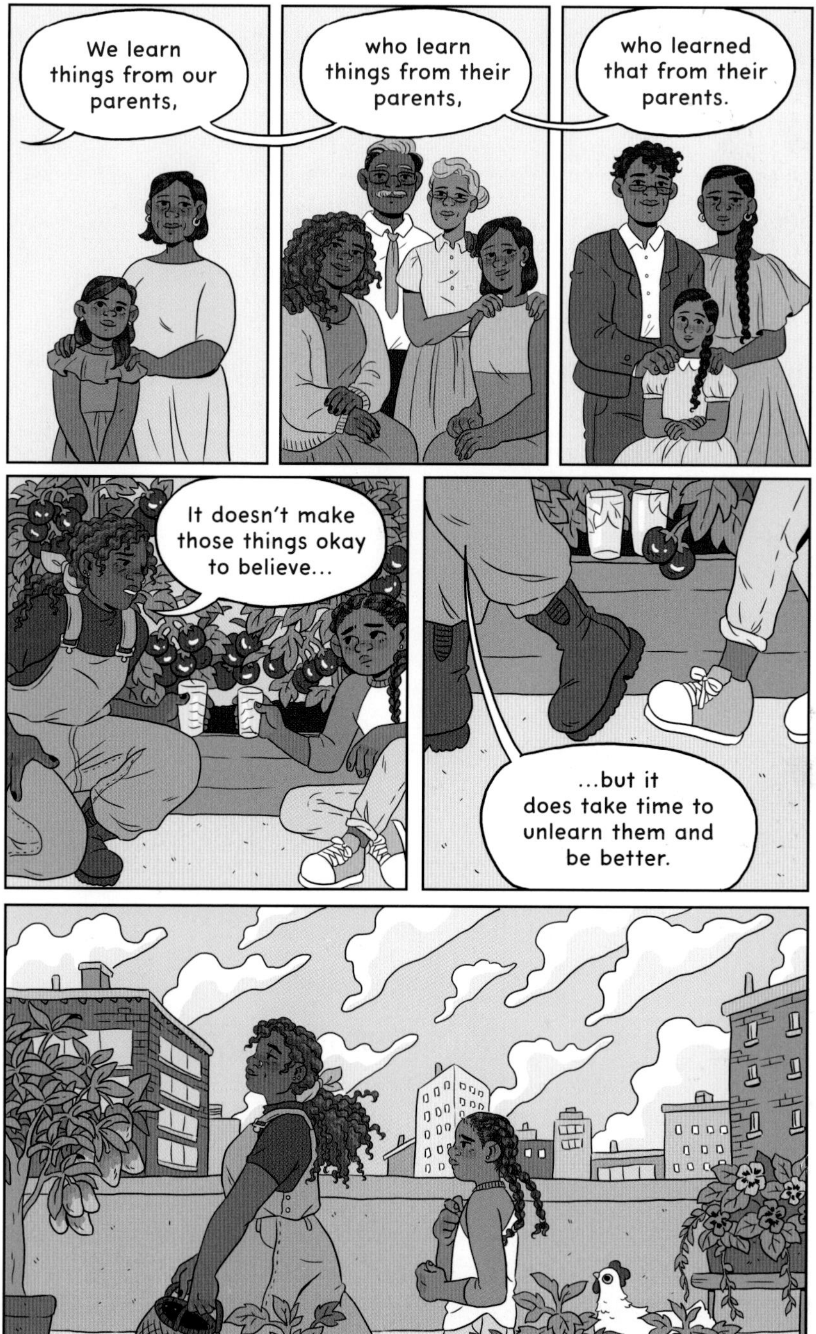
We learn things from our parents,
who learn things from their parents,
who learned that from their parents.
It doesn't make those things okay to believe...
...but it does take time to unlearn them and be better.

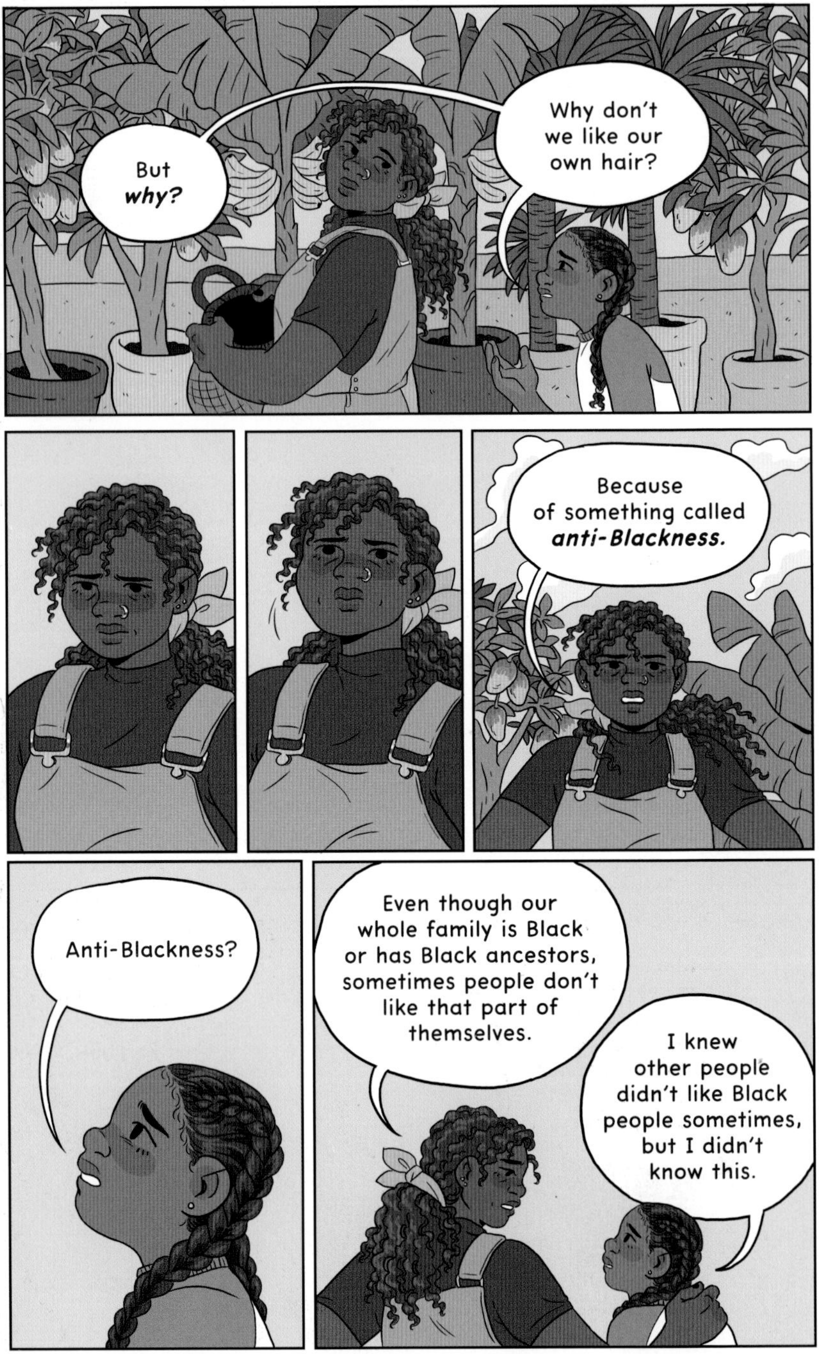
But *why?*
Why don't we like our own hair?
Because of something called ***anti-Blackness.***
Anti-Blackness?
Even though our whole family is Black or has Black ancestors, sometimes people don't like that part of themselves.
I knew other people didn't like Black people sometimes, but I didn't know this.

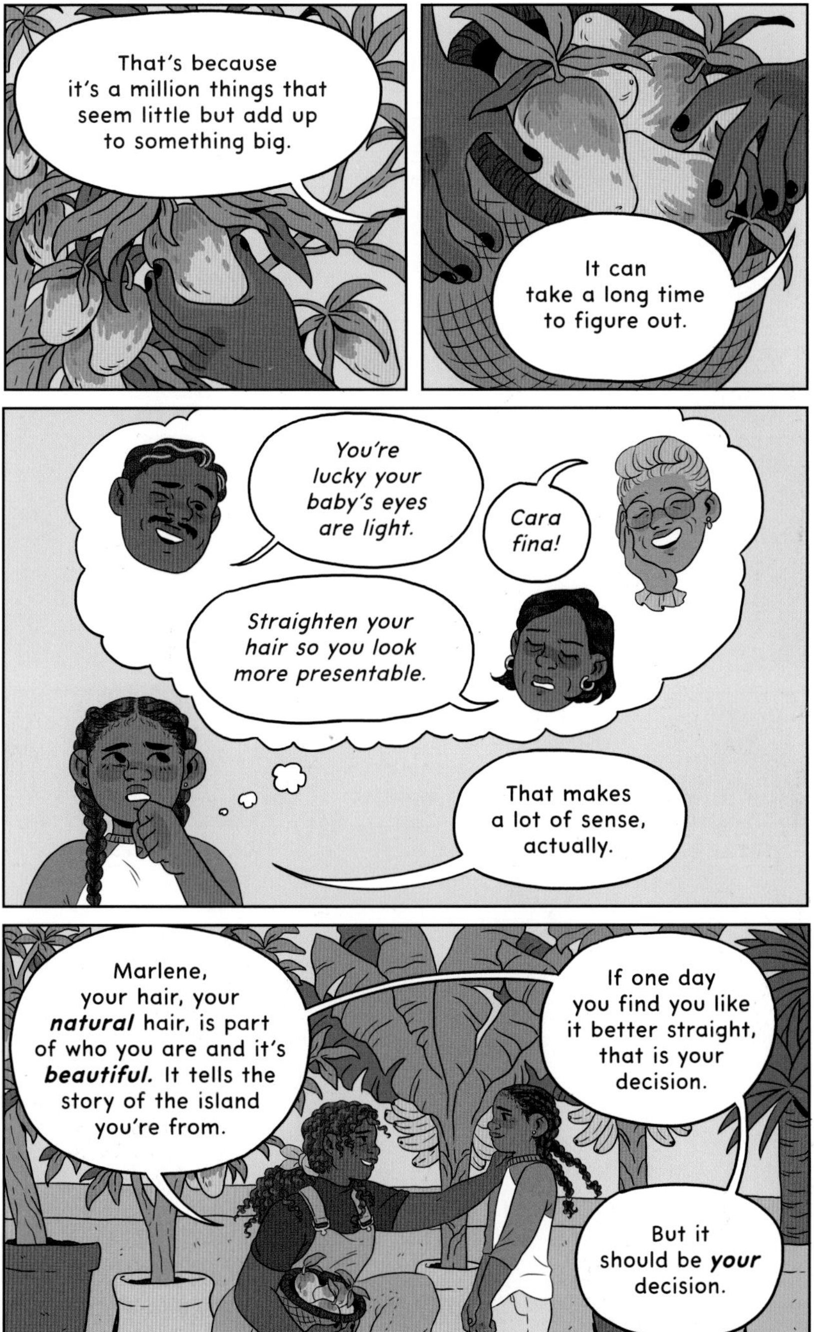
That's because it's a million things that seem little but add up to something big.
It can take a long time to figure out.
You're lucky your baby's eyes are light.
Cara fina!
Straighten your hair so you look more presentable.
That makes a lot of sense, actually.
Marlene, your hair, your ***natural*** hair, is part of who you are and it's ***beautiful.*** It tells the story of the island you're from.
If one day you find you like it better straight, that is your decision.
But it should be ***your*** decision.

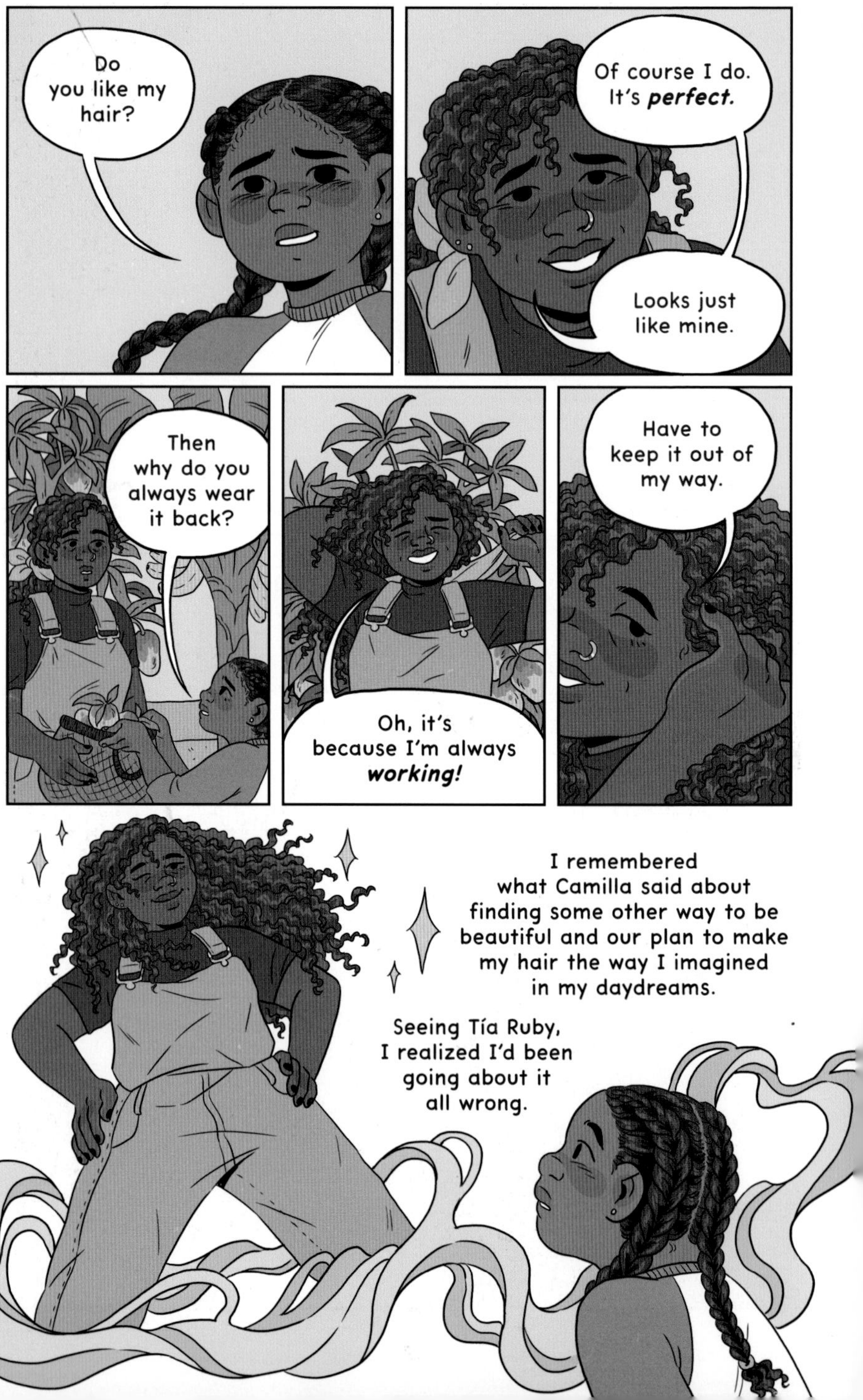
Do you like my hair?
Of course I do. It's ***perfect.***
Looks just like mine.
Then why do you always wear it back?
Oh, it's because I'm always ***working!***
Have to keep it out of my way.
I remembered what Camilla said about finding some other way to be beautiful and our plan to make my hair the way I imagined in my daydreams.
Seeing Tía Ruby, I realized I'd been going about it all wrong.

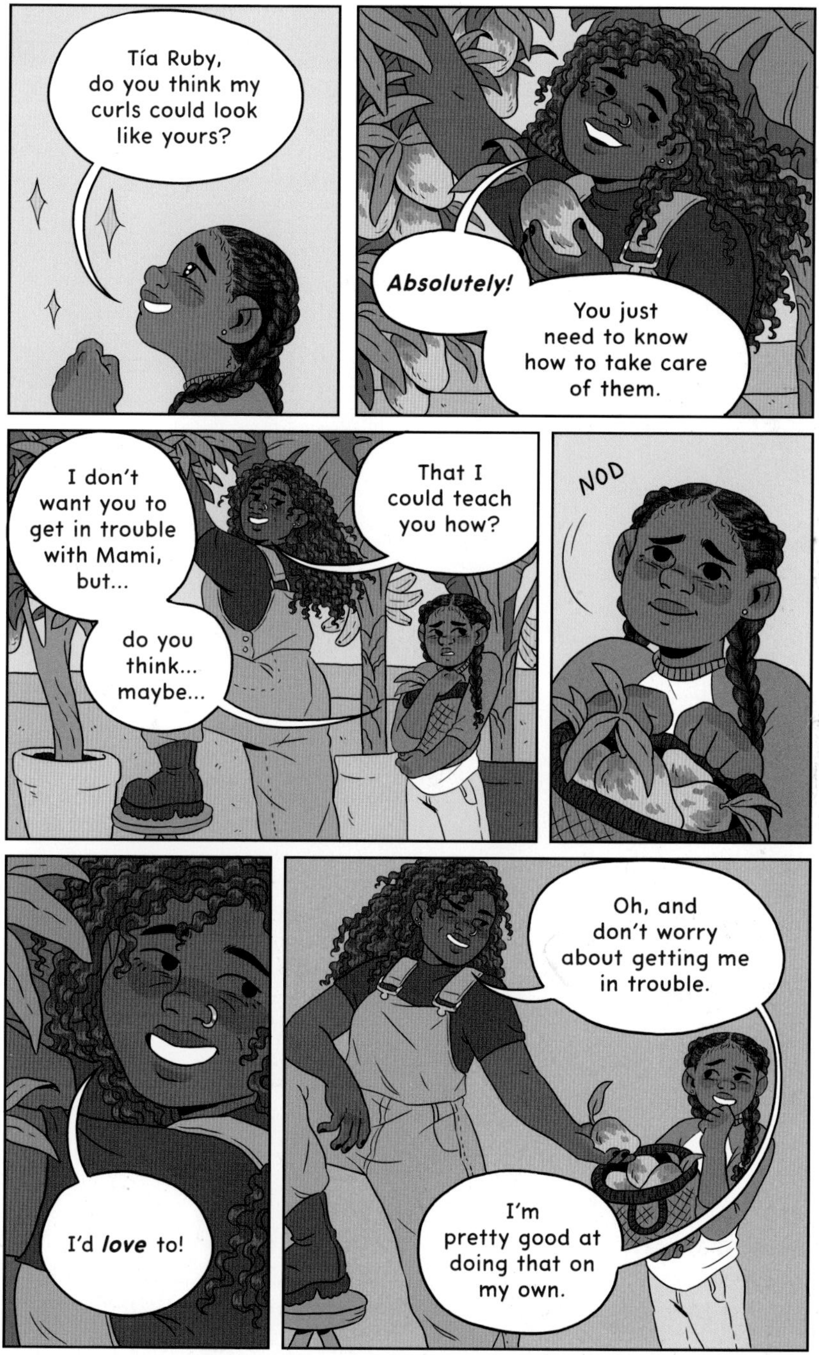
Tía Ruby, do you think my curls could look like yours?
Absolutely!
You just need to know how to take care of them.
I don't want you to get in trouble with Mami, but...
do you think... maybe...
That I could teach you how?
NOD
I'd love to!
Oh, and don't worry about getting me in trouble.
I'm pretty good at doing that on my own.

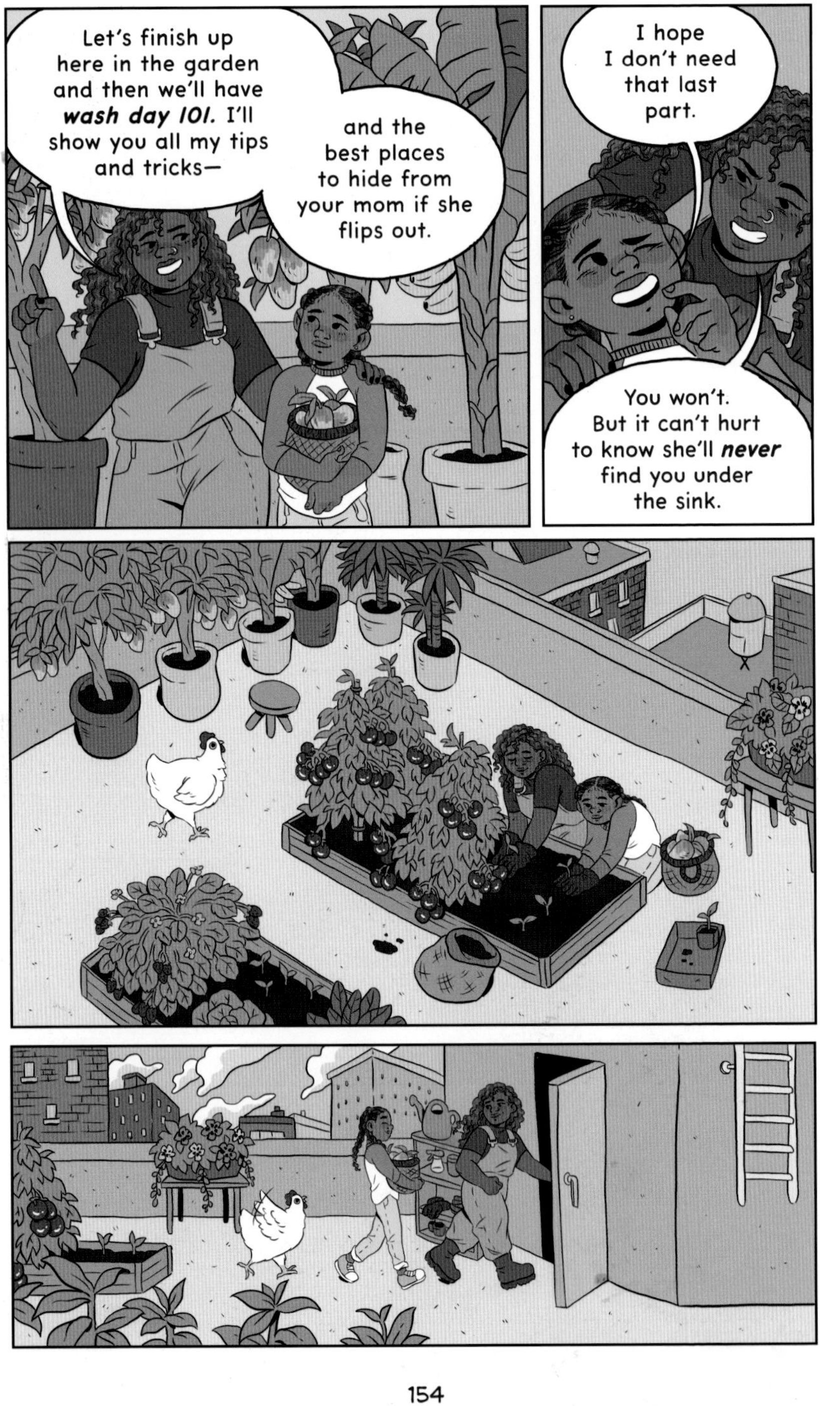
Let's finish up here in the garden and then we'll have ***wash day 101.*** I'll show you all my tips and tricks—
and the best places to hide from your mom if she flips out.
I hope I don't need that last part.
You won't. But it can't hurt to know she'll ***never*** find you under the sink.

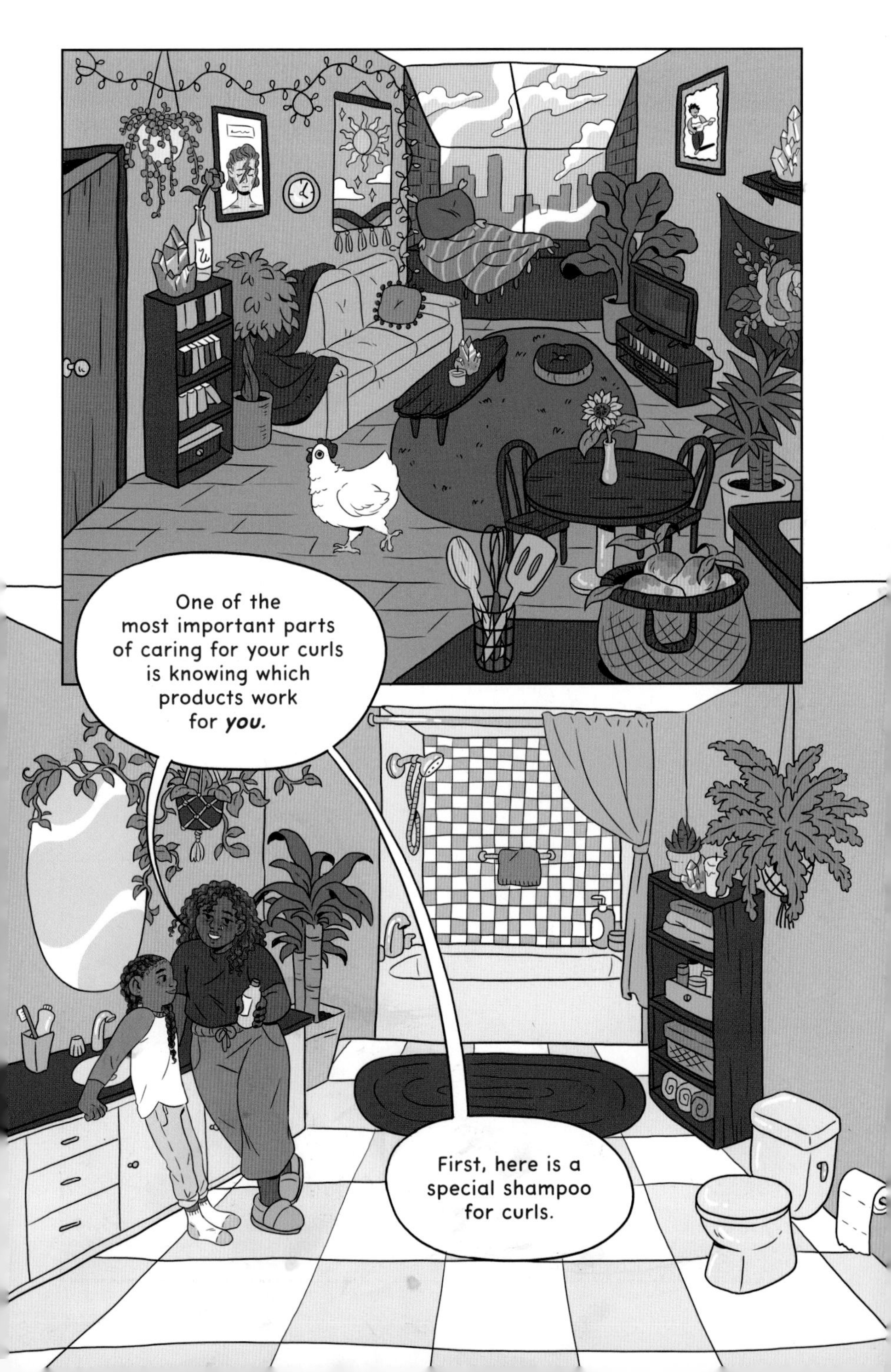
One of the most important parts of caring for your curls is knowing which products work for *you.*
First, here is a special shampoo for curls.

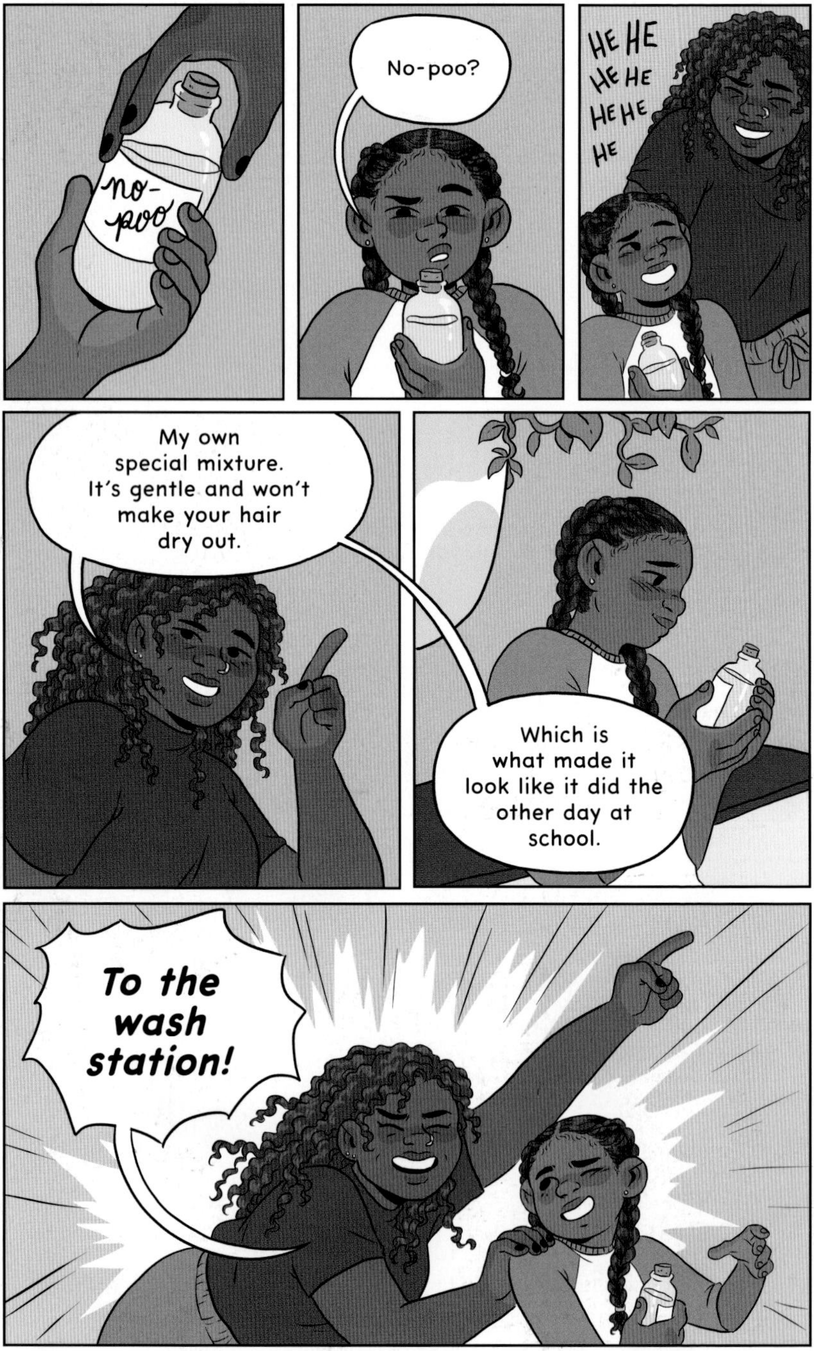
no-poo
No-poo?
HE HE HE HE HE HE HE
My own special mixture. It's gentle and won't make your hair dry out.
Which is what made it look like it did the other day at school.
To the wash station!

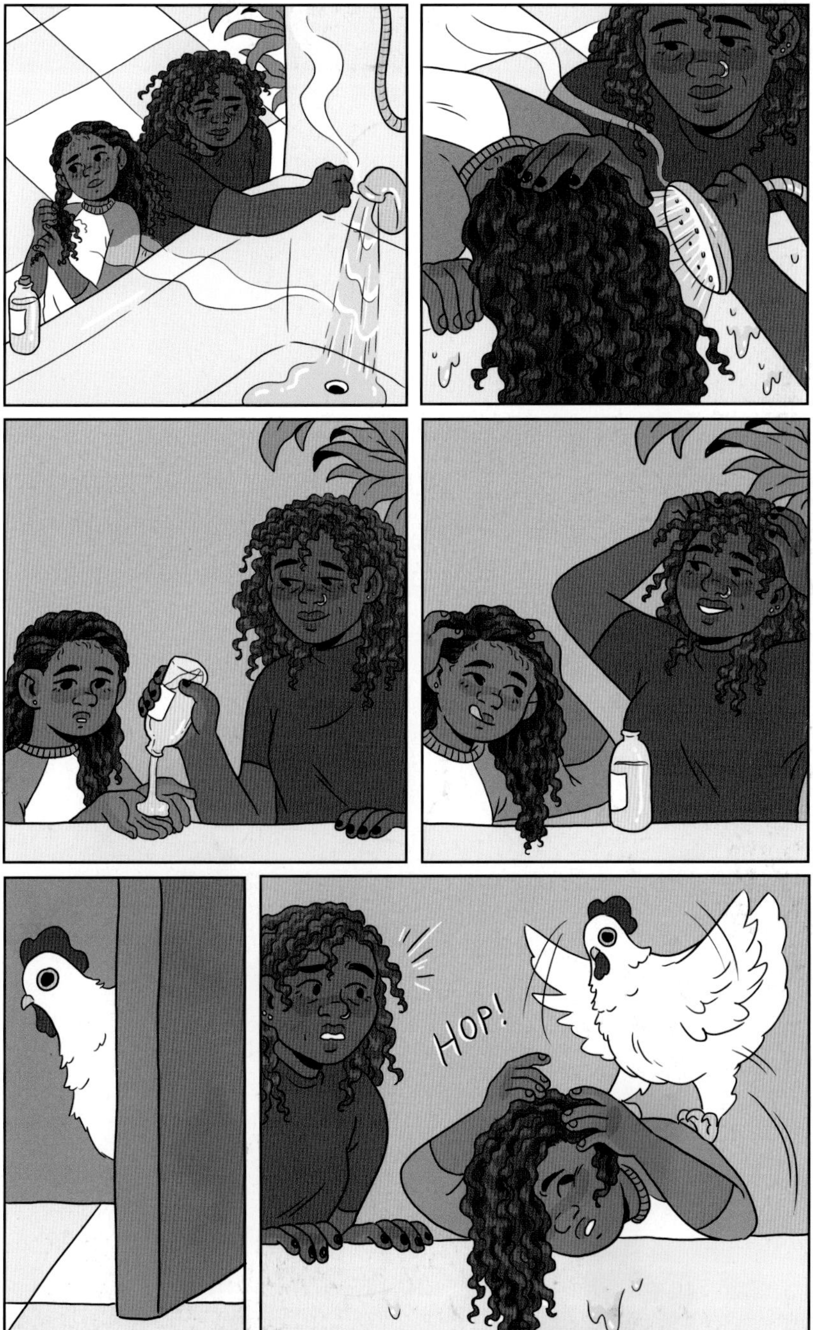
HOP!

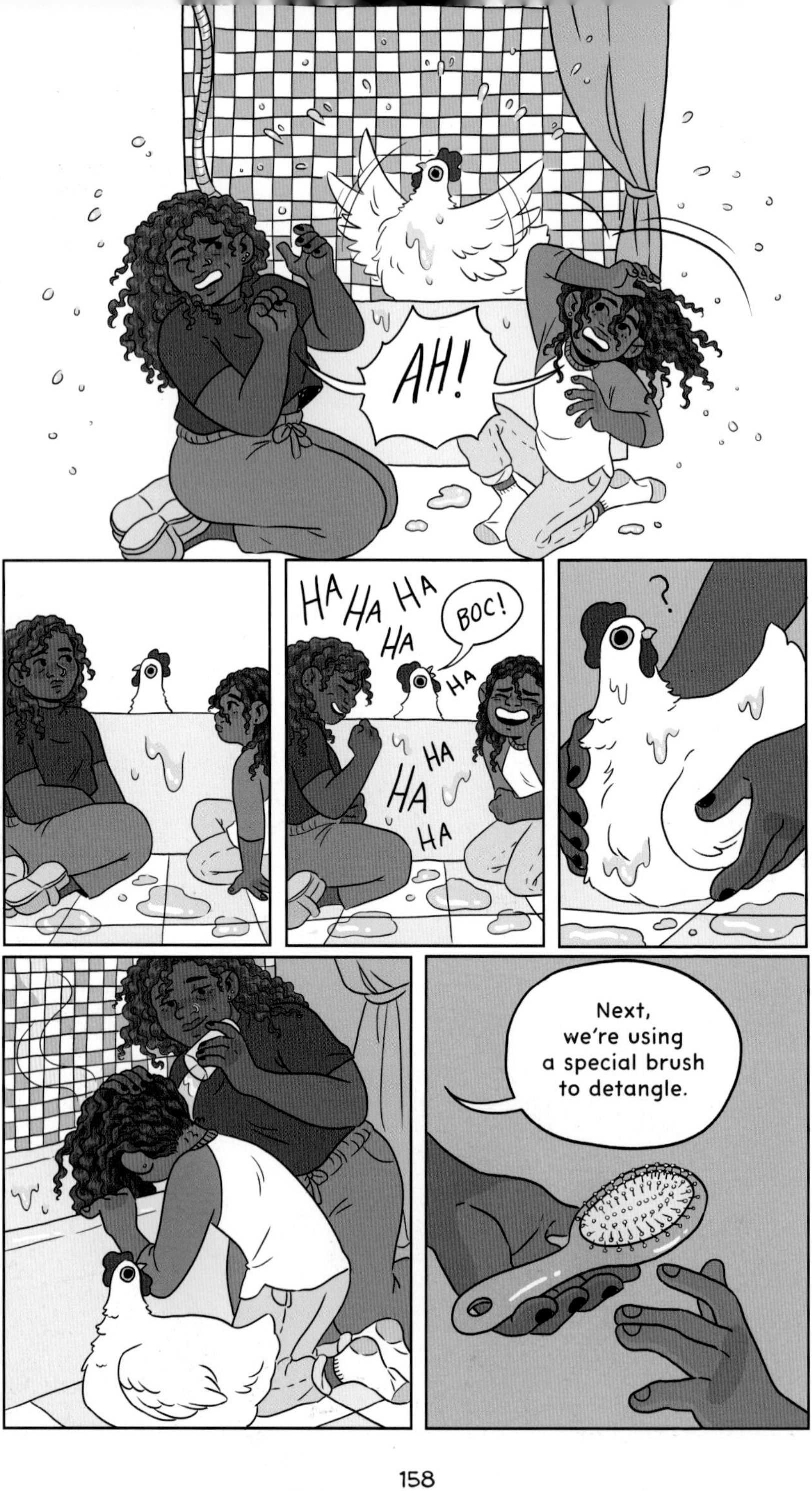
AH!
HA HA HA HA
BOC!
HA
HA HA HA HA
?
Next, we're using a special brush to detangle.

I was getting
a lot of information
at once...

...but maybe the
part that was
hardest to believe
was that it didn't
have to hurt to
do your hair.

It's made
special for your hair
texture. You can't just use
the same things as people
with straighter or
fine hair.

I've
never used a
brush like this
before.

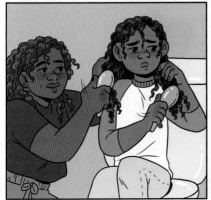

You mean
good hair.

159

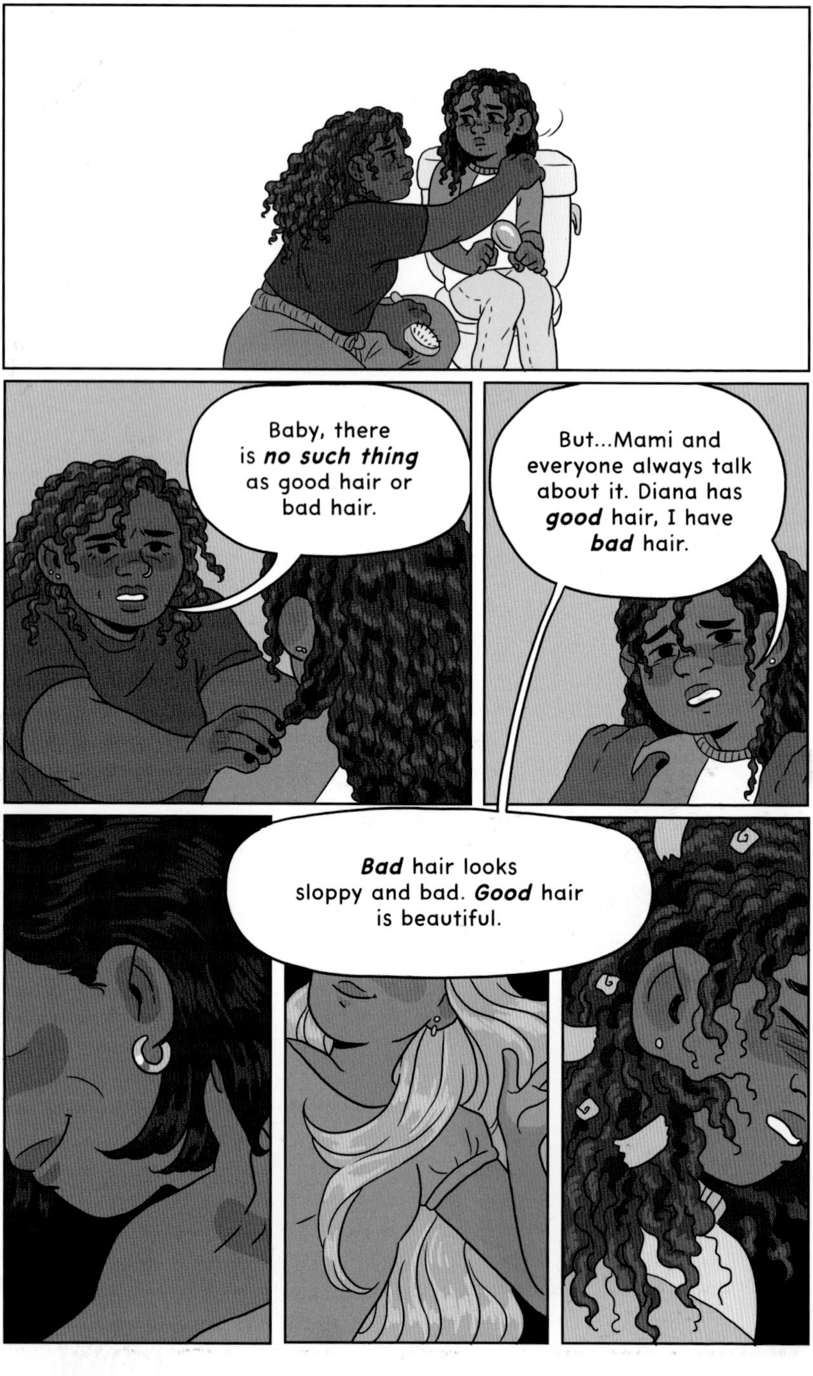
Baby, there is ***no such thing*** as good hair or bad hair.
But...Mami and everyone always talk about it. Diana has ***good*** hair, I have ***bad*** hair.
Bad hair looks sloppy and bad. ***Good*** hair is beautiful.

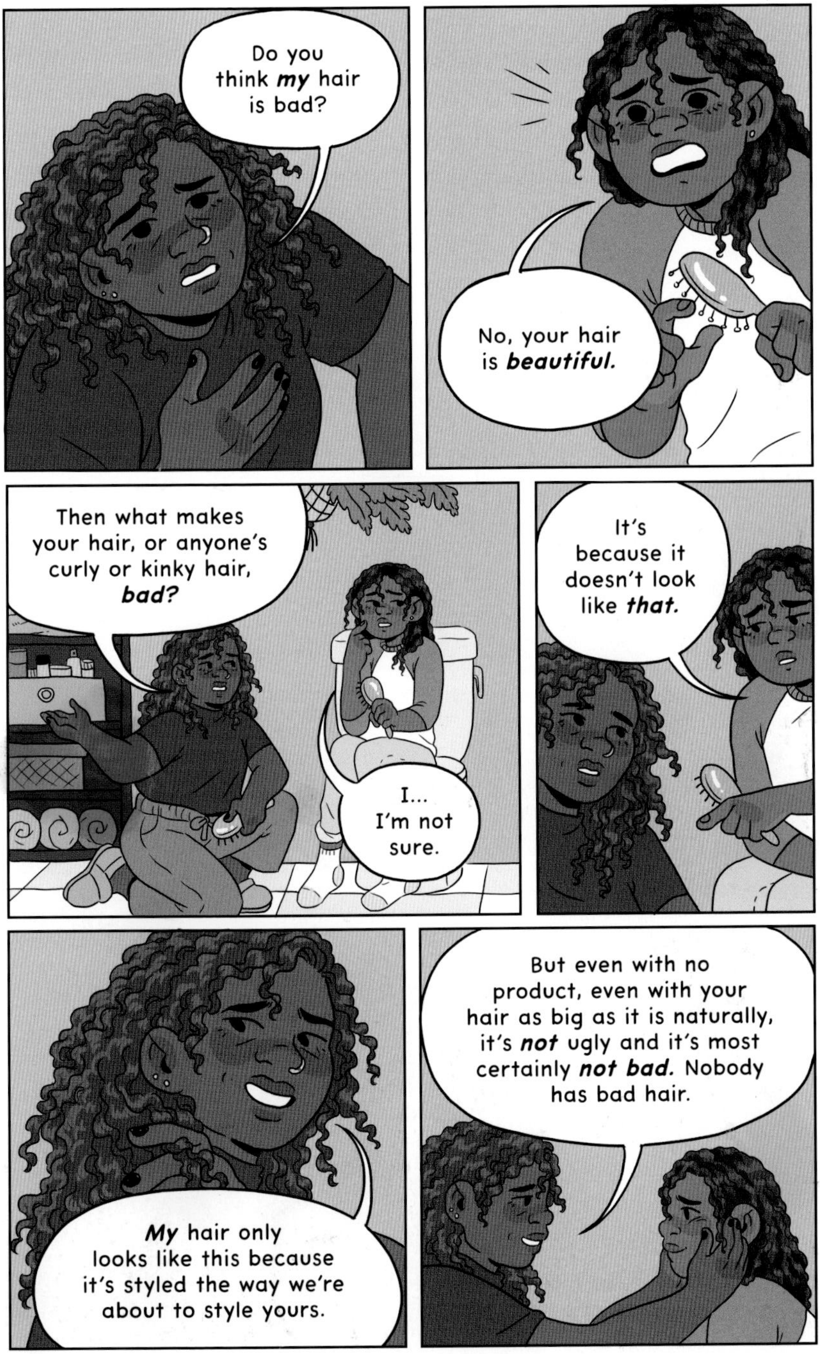
Do you think *my* hair is bad?
No, your hair is ***beautiful.***
Then what makes your hair, or anyone's curly or kinky hair, ***bad?***
I... I'm not sure.
It's because it doesn't look like ***that.***
My hair only looks like this because it's styled the way we're about to style yours.
But even with no product, even with your hair as big as it is naturally, it's ***not*** ugly and it's most certainly ***not bad.*** Nobody has bad hair.

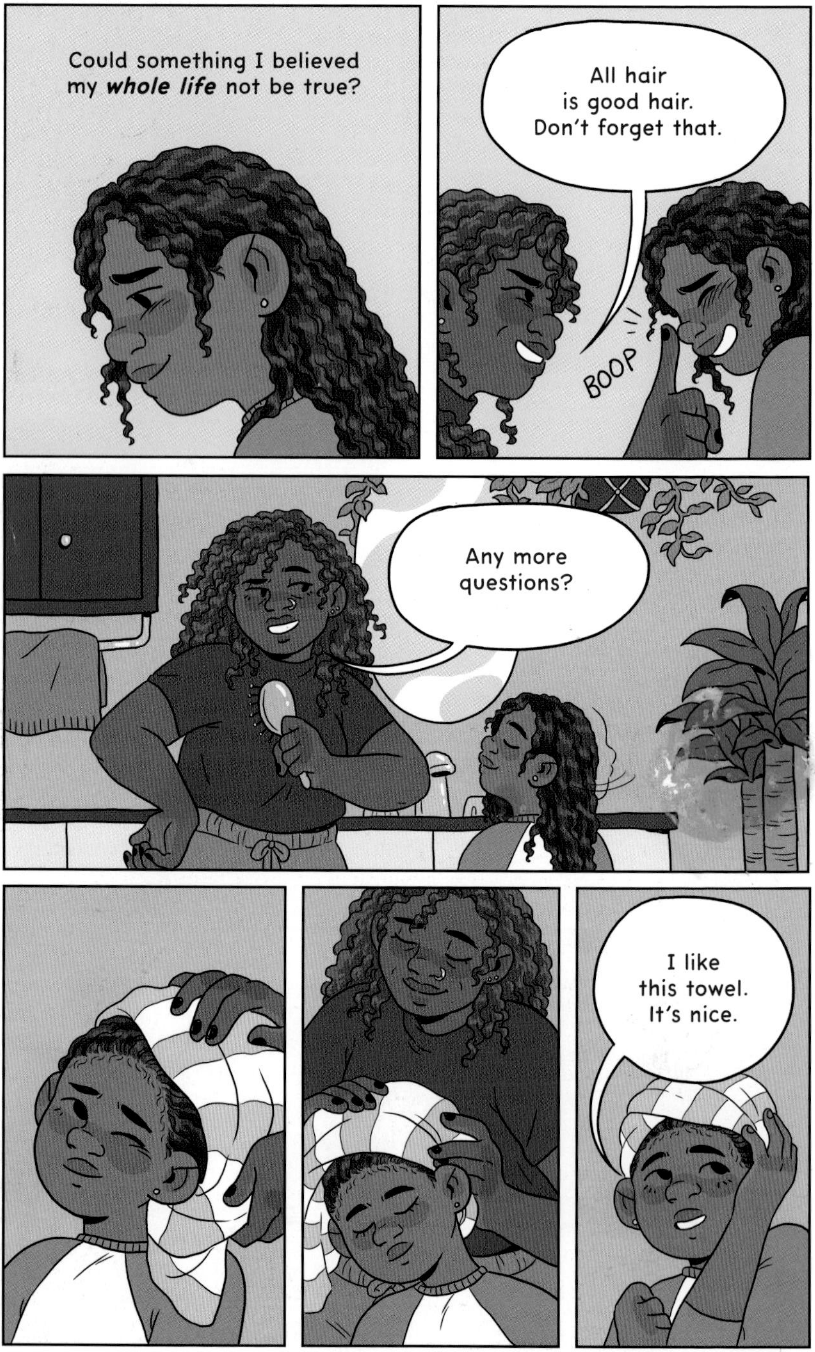
Could something I believed my ***whole life*** not be true?
All hair is good hair. Don't forget that.
BOOP
Any more questions?
I like this towel. It's nice.

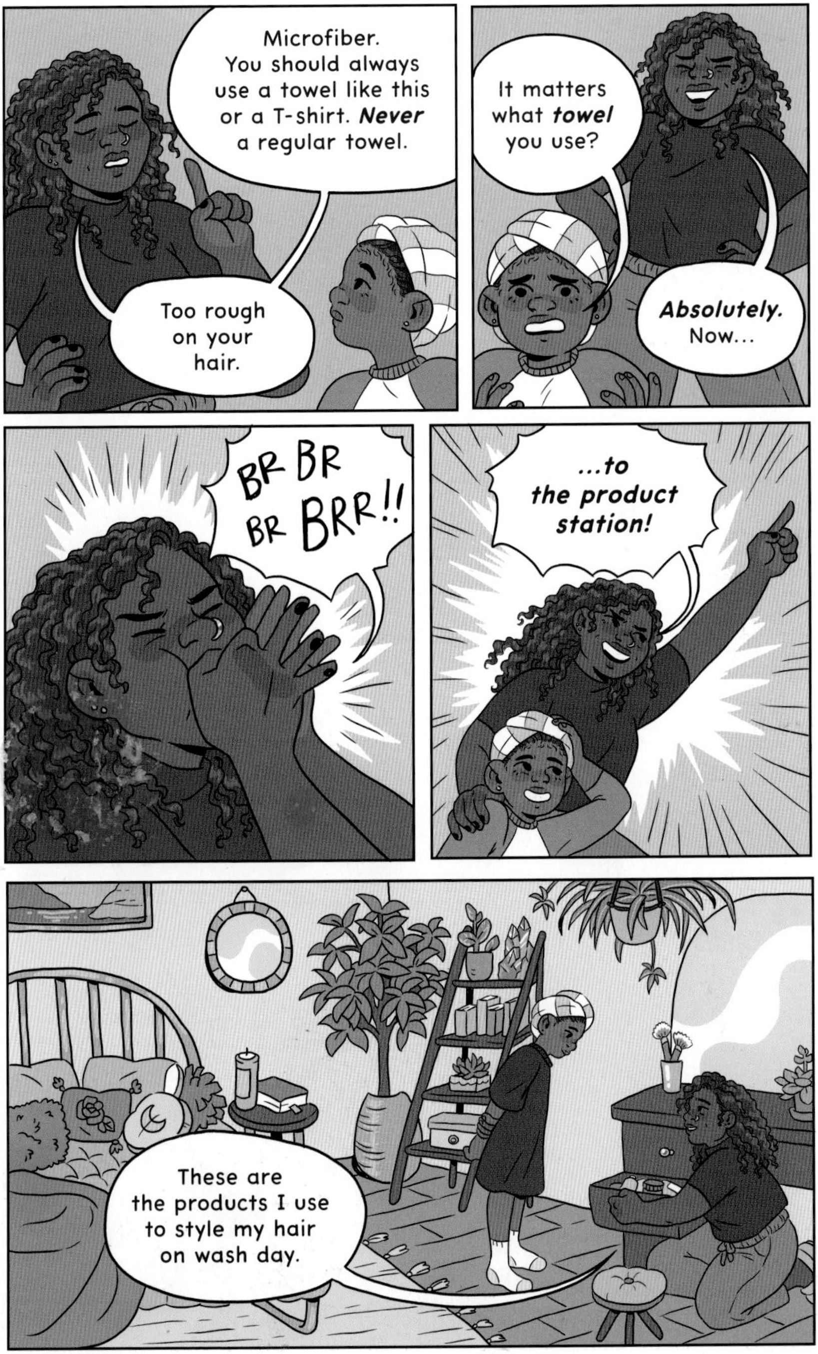

Microfiber. You should always use a towel like this or a T-shirt. ***Never*** a regular towel.
Too rough on your hair.
It matters what ***towel*** you use?
Absolutely. Now...
BR BR BR BRR!!
...to the product station!
These are the products I use to style my hair on wash day.

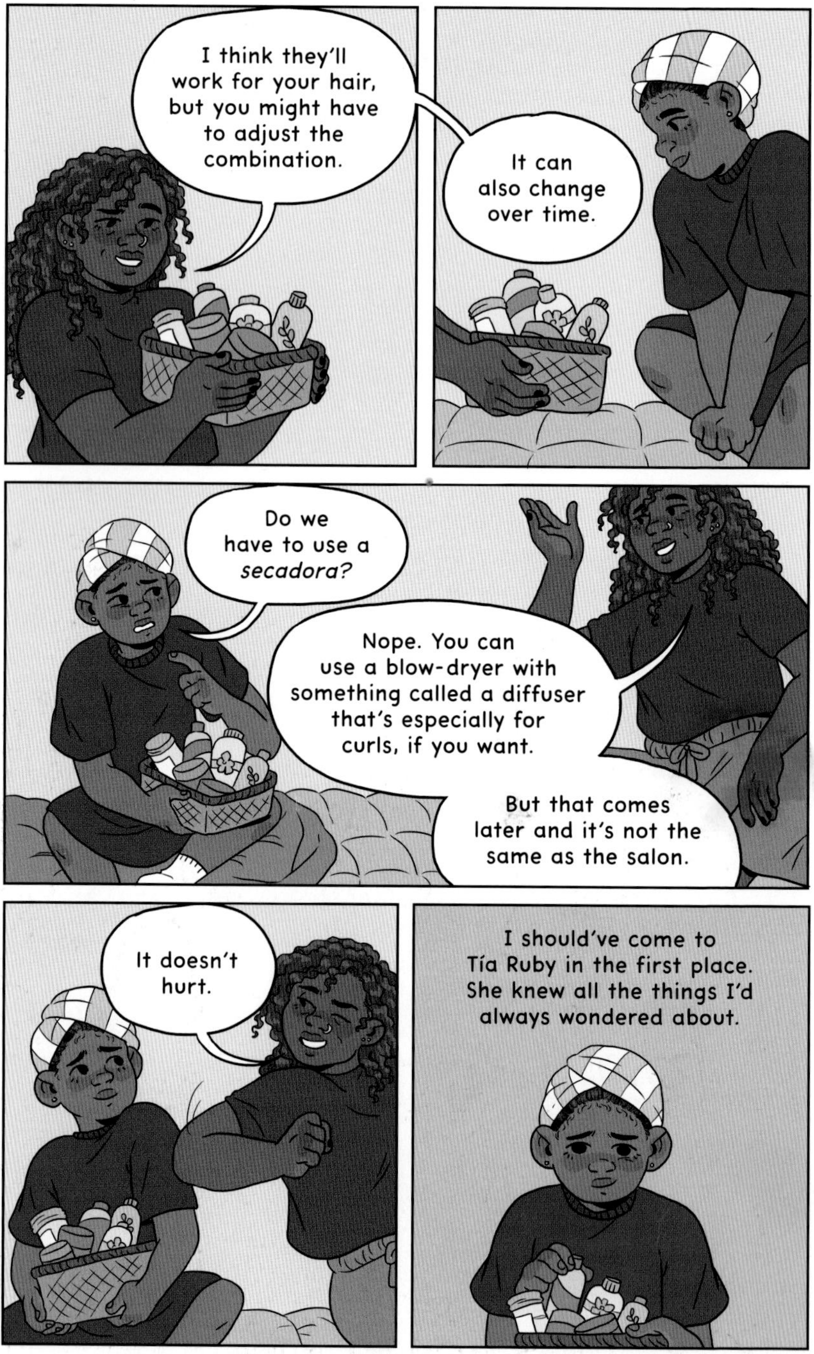
I think they'll work for your hair, but you might have to adjust the combination.
It can also change over time.
Do we have to use a *secadora?*
Nope. You can use a blow-dryer with something called a diffuser that's especially for curls, if you want.
But that comes later and it's not the same as the salon.
It doesn't hurt.
I should've come to Tía Ruby in the first place. She knew all the things I'd always wondered about.

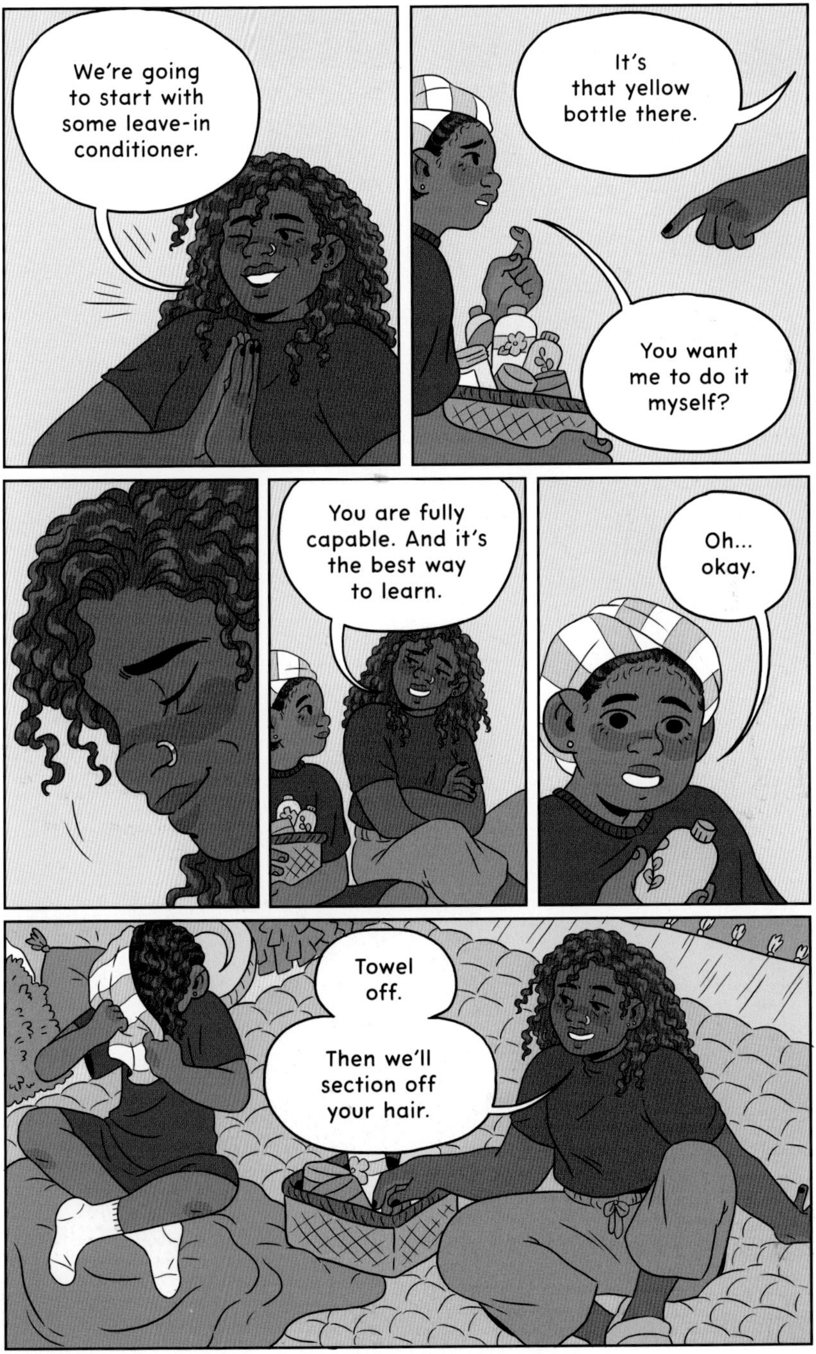
We're going to start with some leave-in conditioner.
It's that yellow bottle there.
You want me to do it myself?
You are fully capable. And it's the best way to learn.
Oh... okay.
Towel off.
Then we'll section off your hair.

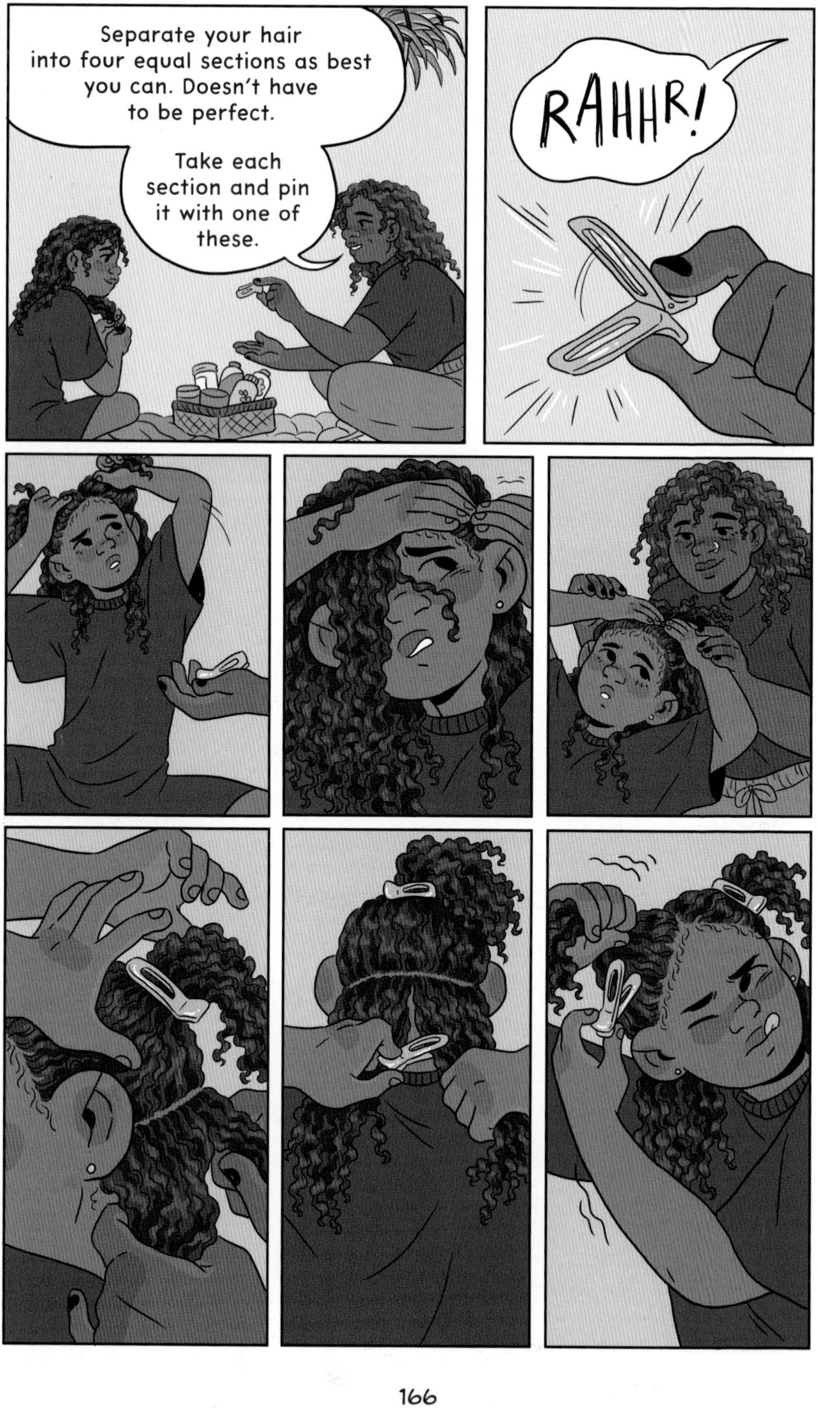
Separate your hair into four equal sections as best you can. Doesn't have to be perfect.
Take each section and pin it with one of these.
RAHHR!

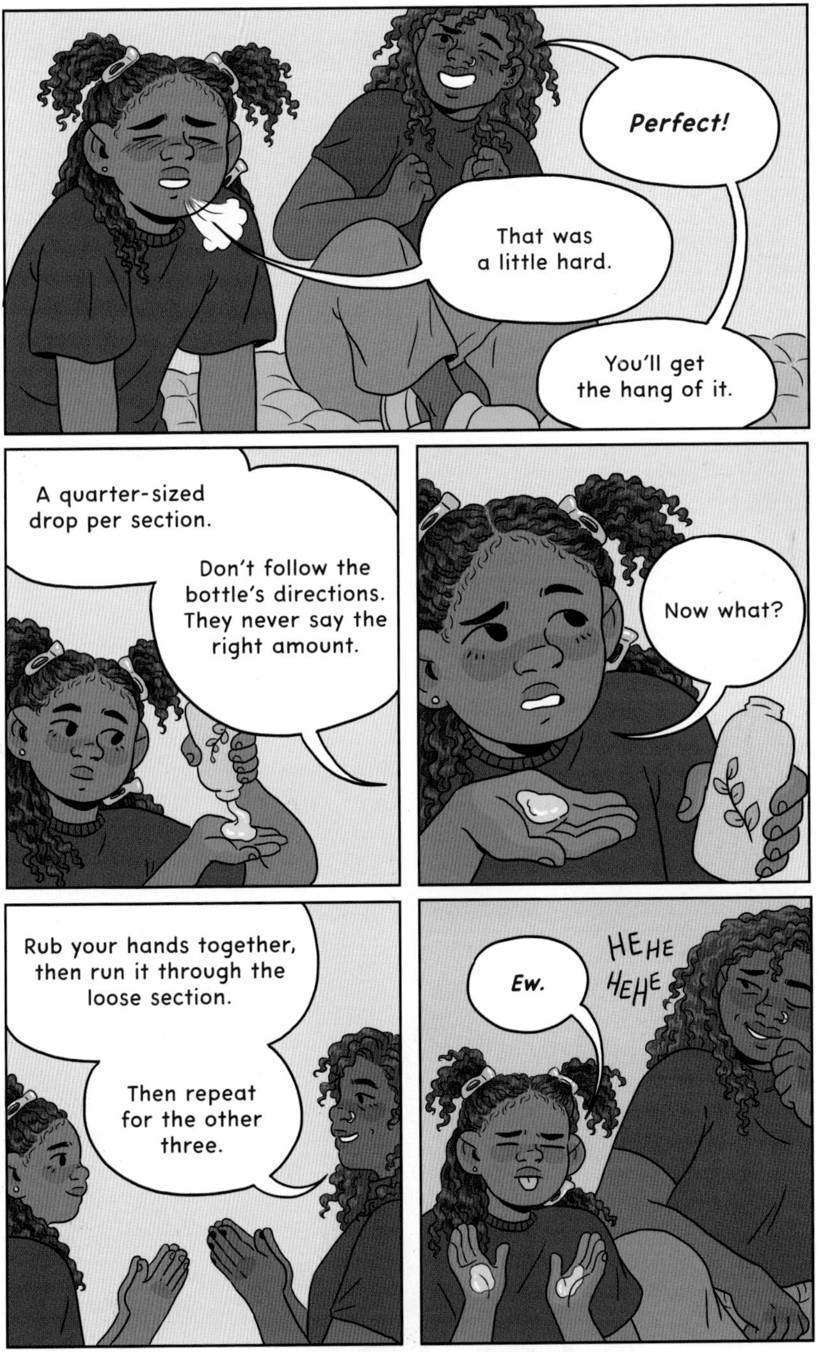
That was a little hard.
Perfect!
You'll get the hang of it.
A quarter-sized drop per section.
Don't follow the bottle's directions. They never say the right amount.
Now what?
Rub your hands together, then run it through the loose section.
Then repeat for the other three.
Ew.
HEHE HEHE

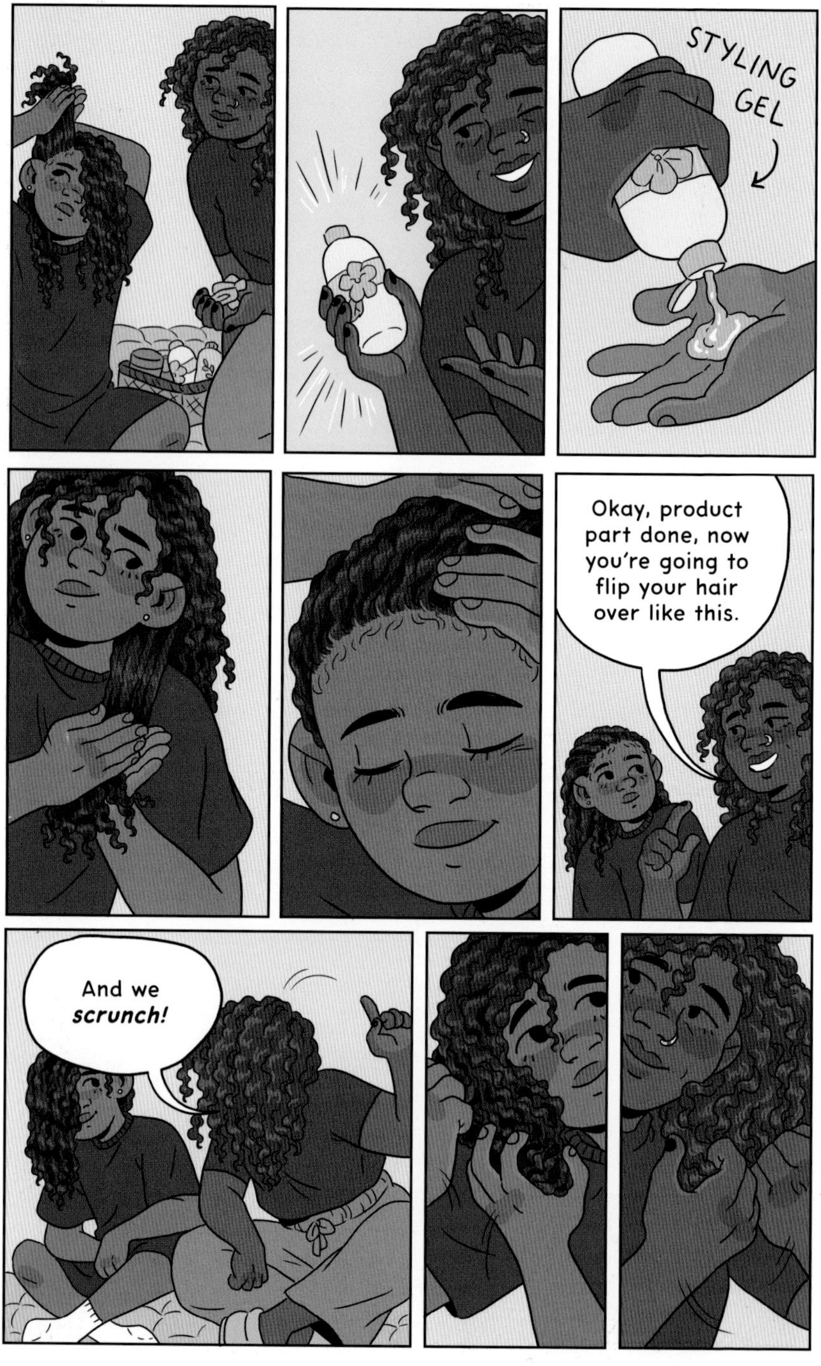
STYLING GEL
Okay, product part done, now you're going to flip your hair over like this.
And we *scrunch!*

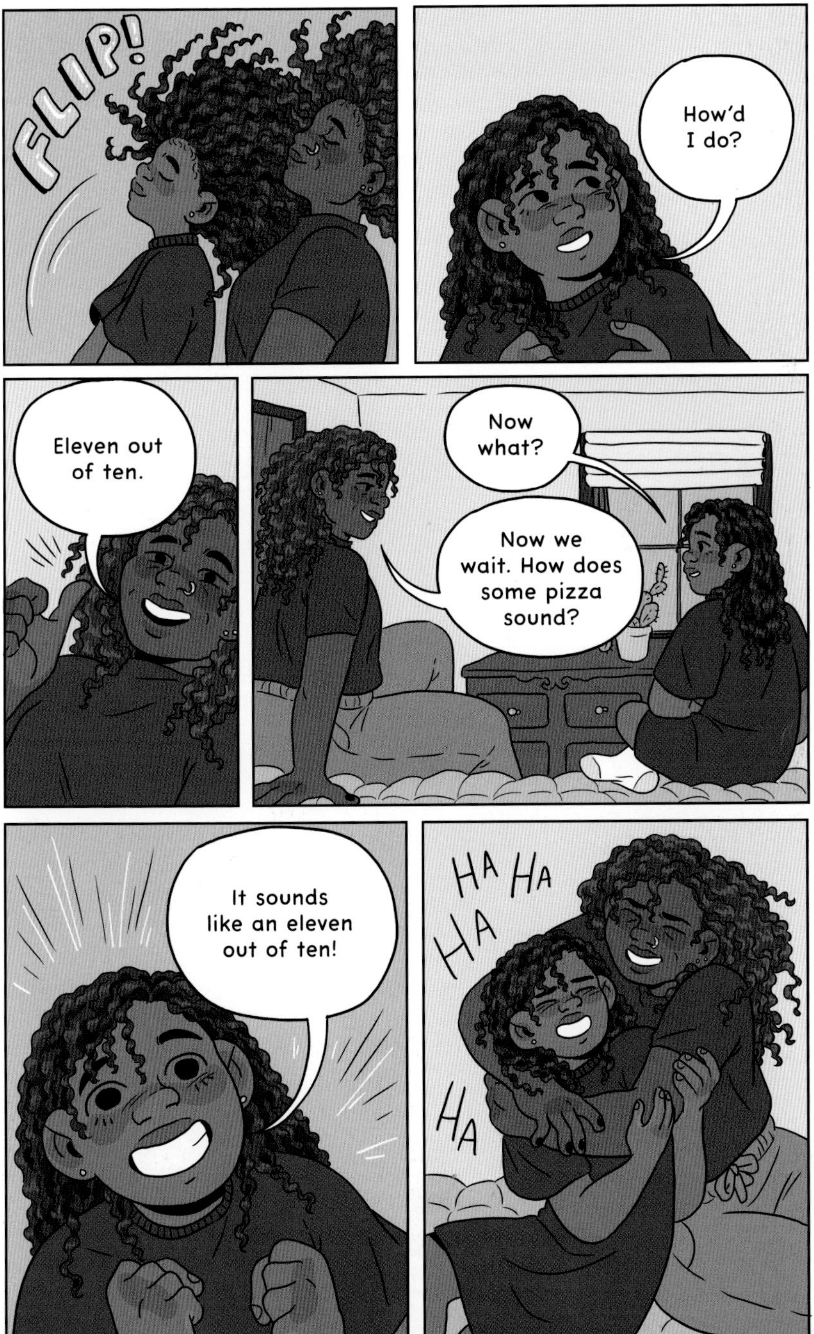
FLIP!
How'd I do?
Eleven out of ten.
Now what?
Now we wait. How does some pizza sound?
It sounds like an eleven out of ten!
HA HA HA
HA

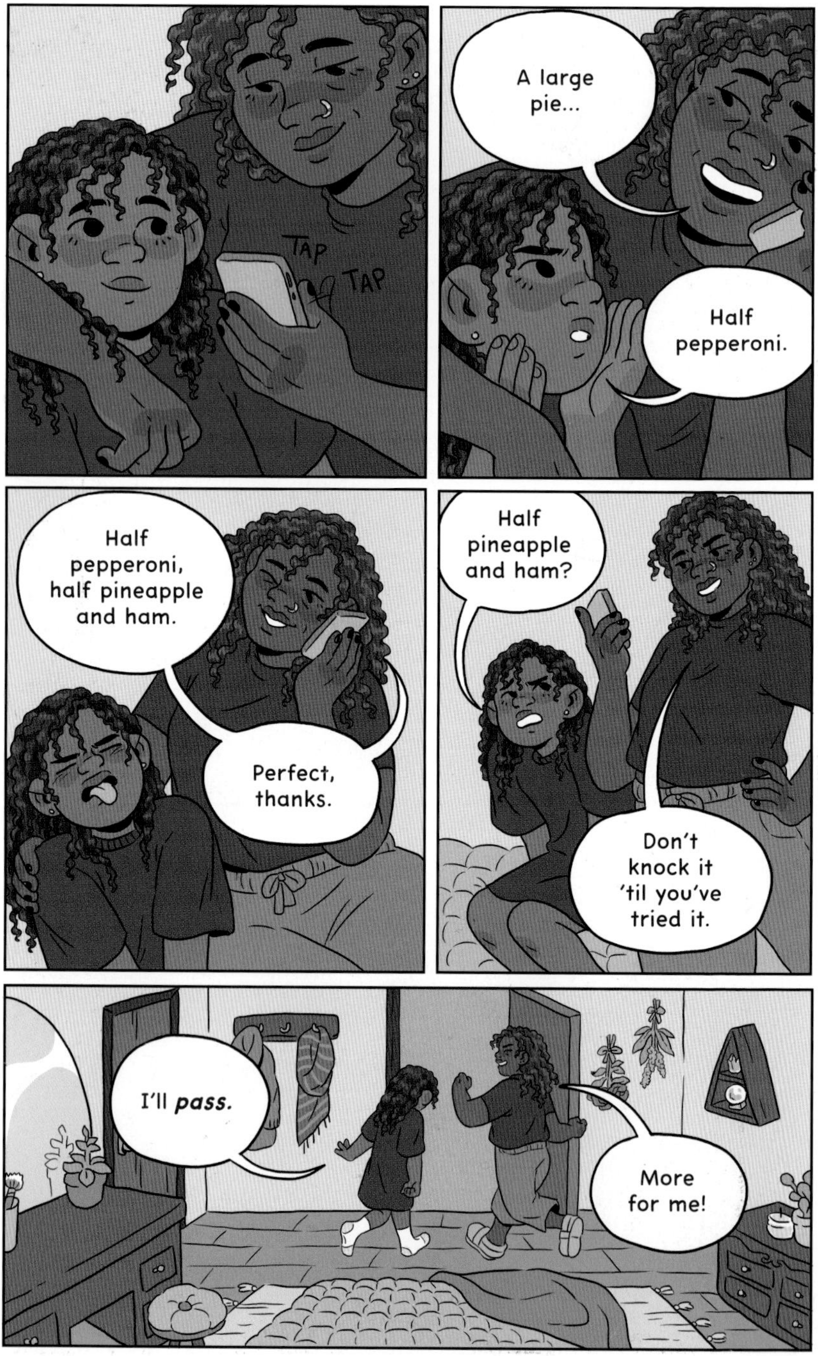
TAP
TAP
A large pie...
Half pepperoni.
Half pepperoni, half pineapple and ham.
Perfect, thanks.
Half pineapple and ham?
Don't knock it 'til you've tried it.
I'll *pass.*
More for me!

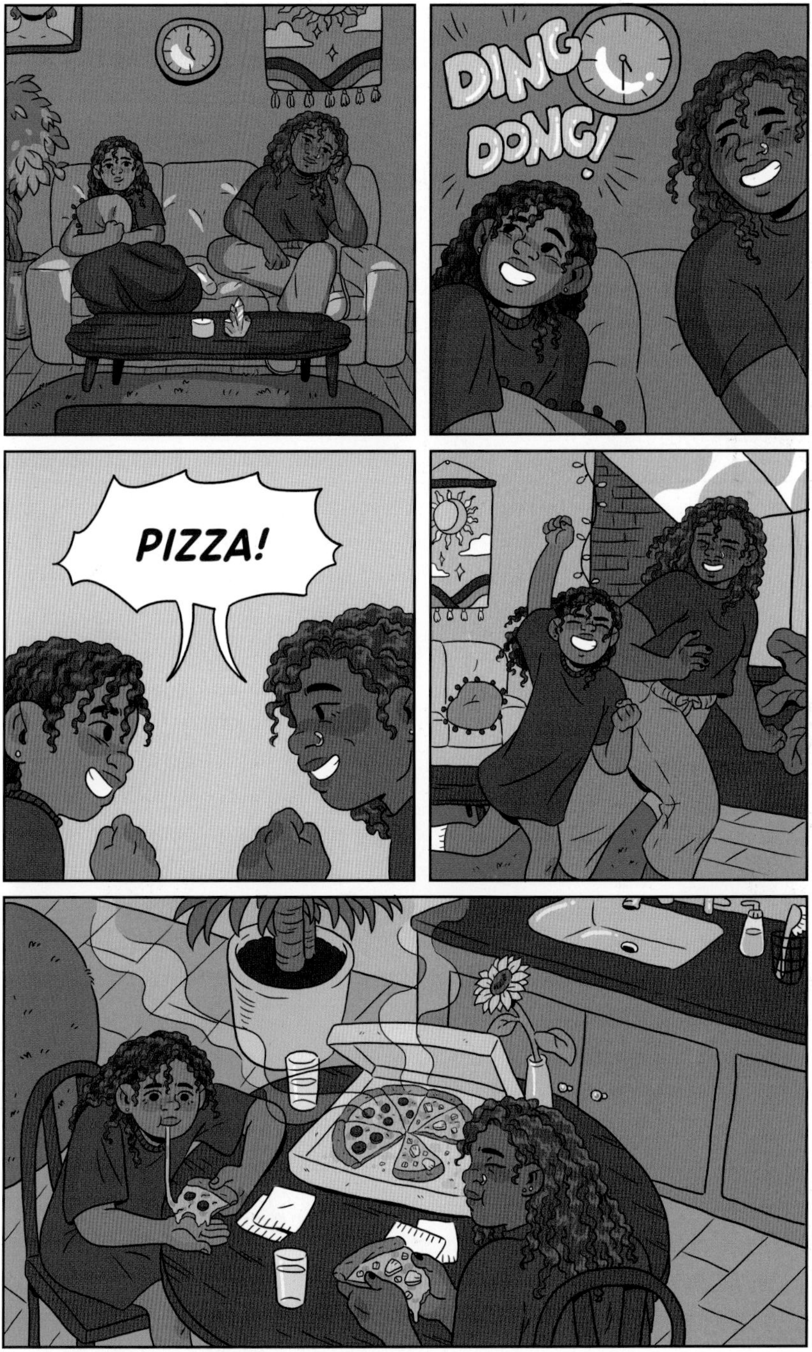
DING
DONG!
PIZZA!

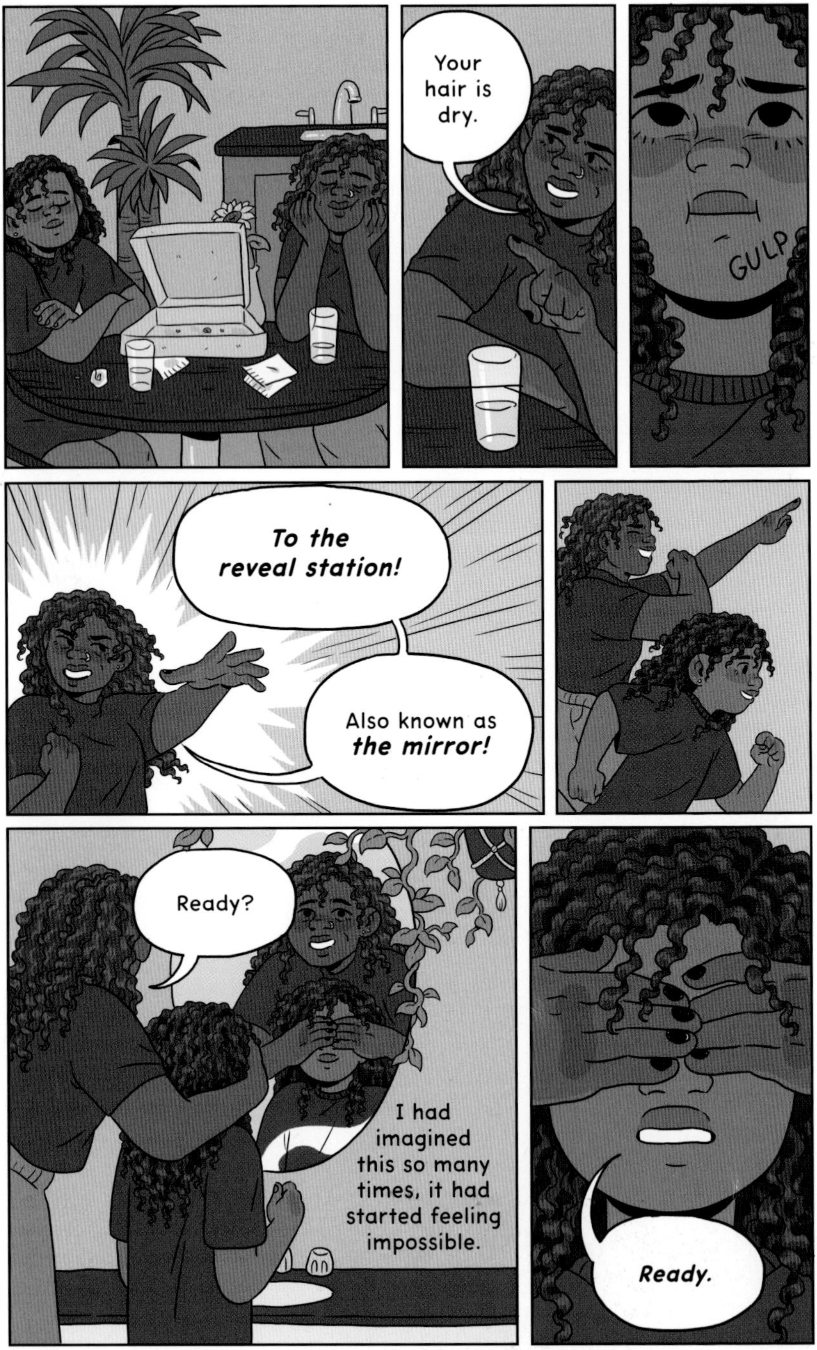
Your hair is dry.
GULP
To the reveal station!
Also known as *the mirror!*
Ready?
I had imagined this so many times, it had started feeling impossible.
Ready.

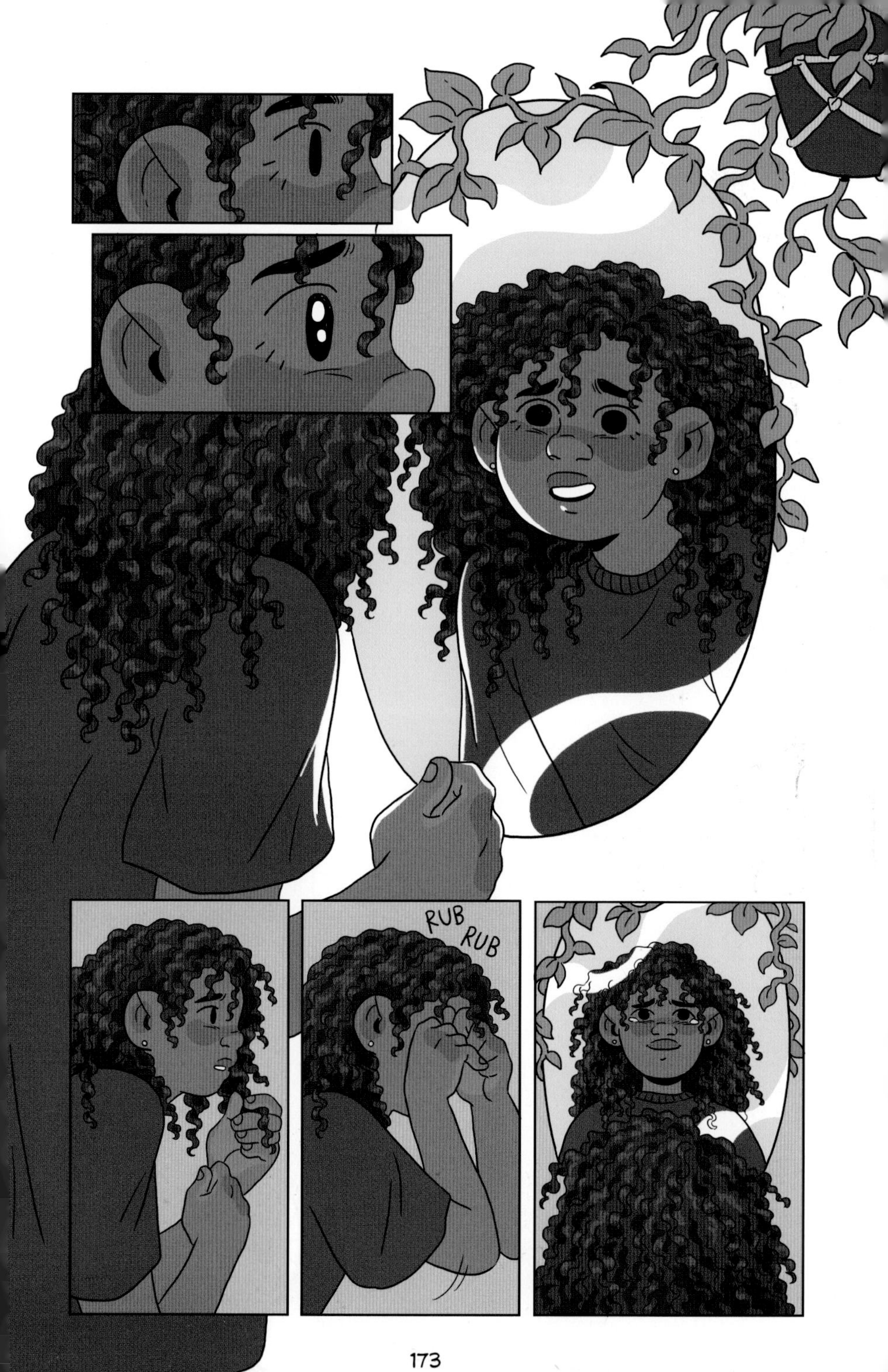
RUB
RUB

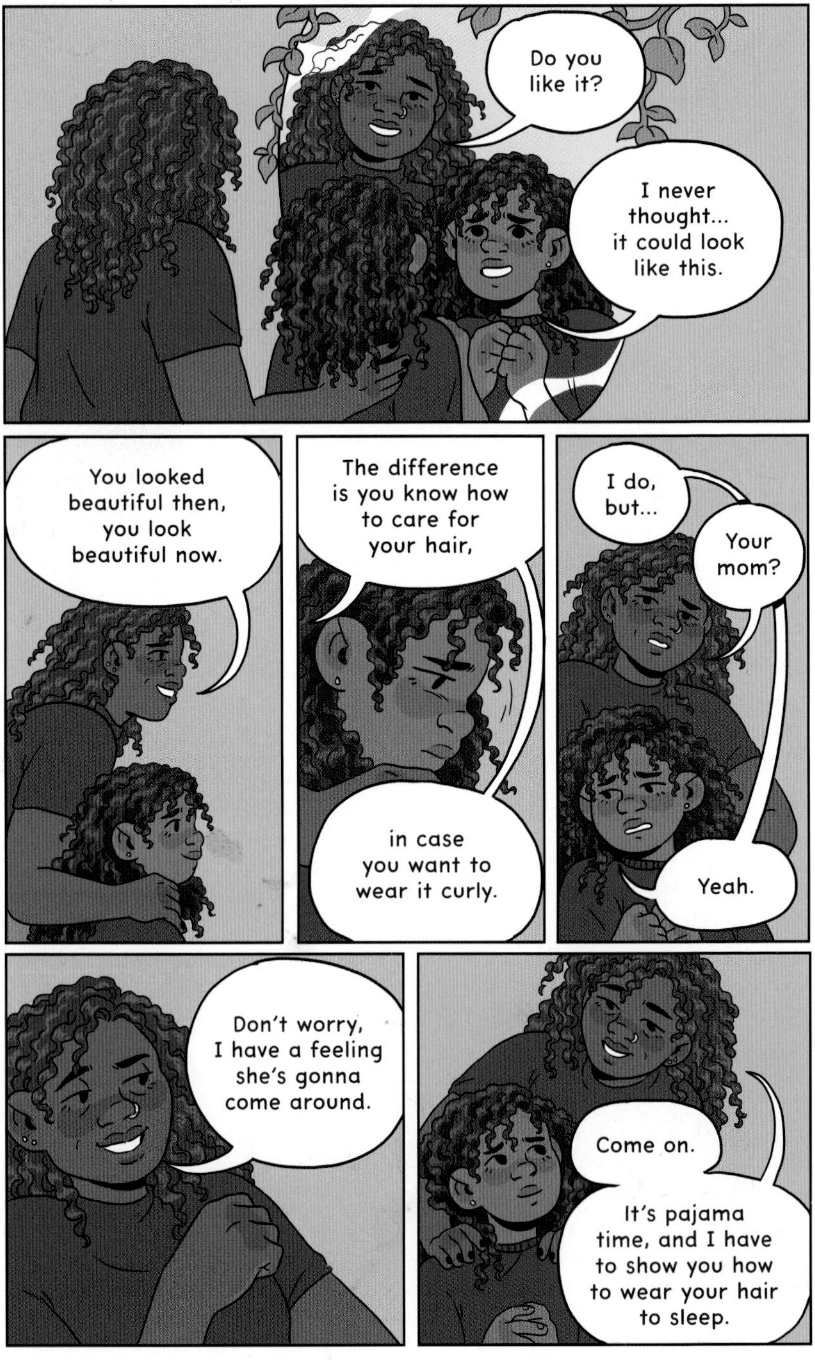
Do you like it?
I never thought... it could look like this.
You looked beautiful then, you look beautiful now.
The difference is you know how to care for your hair,
in case you want to wear it curly.
I do, but...
Your mom?
Yeah.
Don't worry, I have a feeling she's gonna come around.
Come on.
It's pajama time, and I have to show you how to wear your hair to sleep.

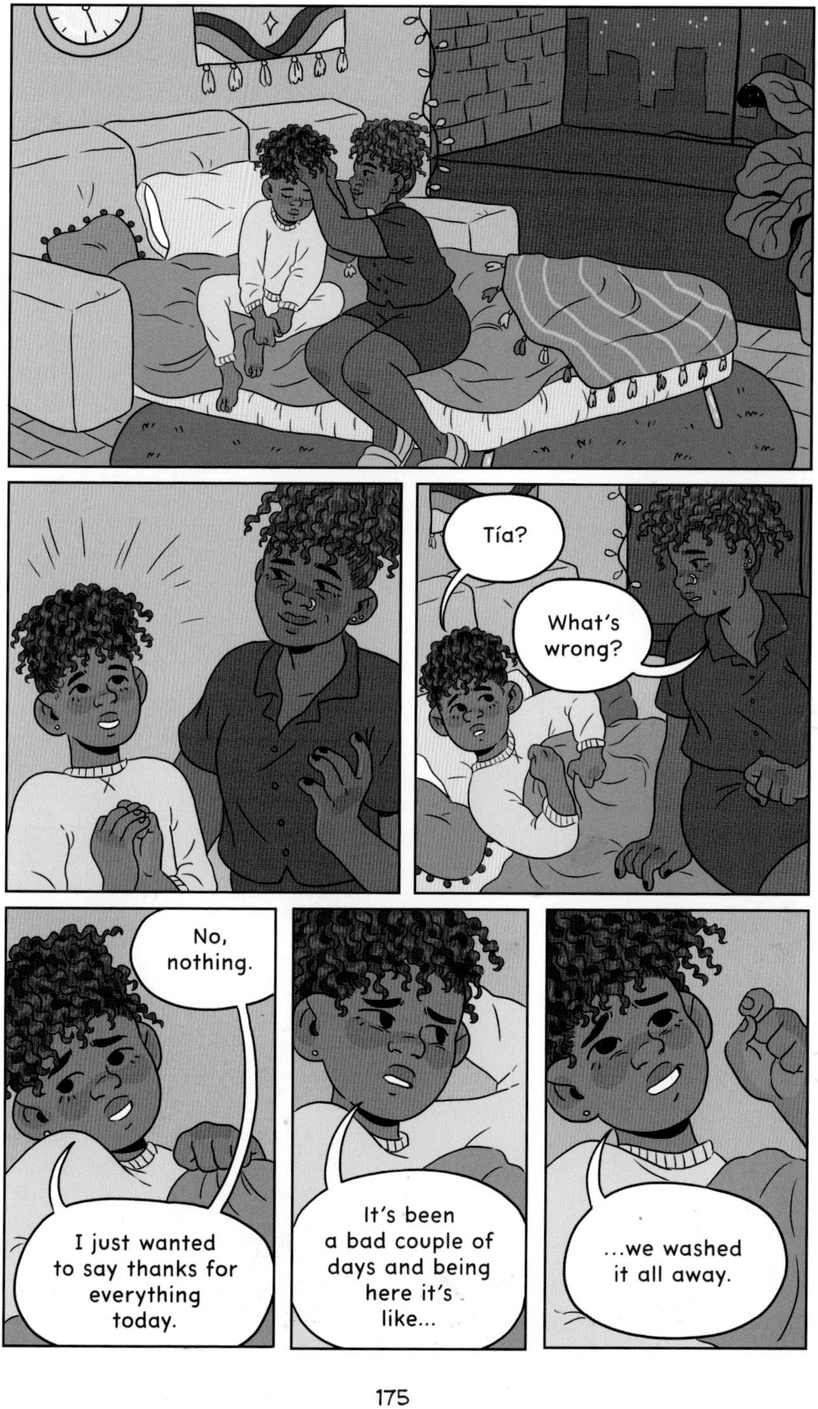
Tía?
What's wrong?
No, nothing.
I just wanted to say thanks for everything today.
It's been a bad couple of days and being here it's like...
...we washed it all away.

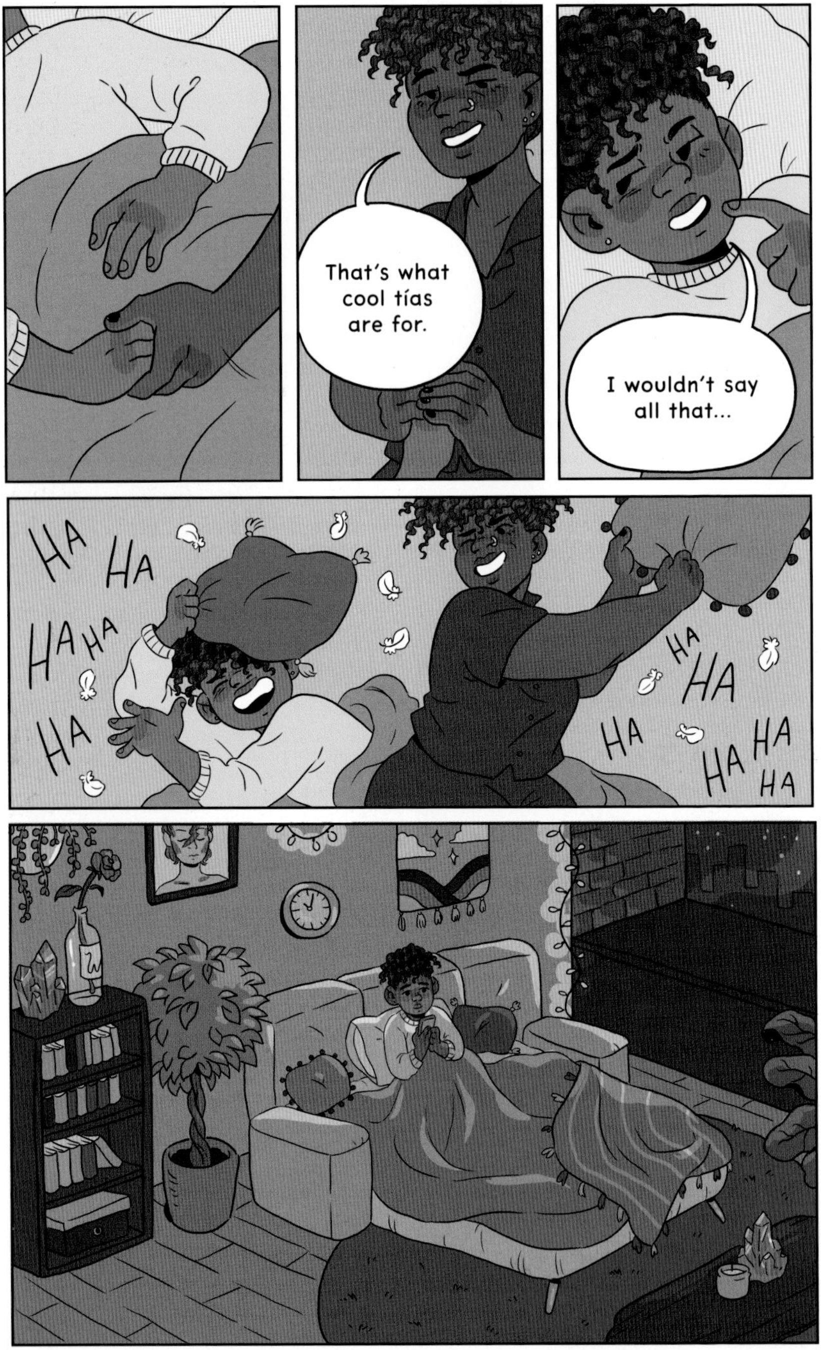
That's what cool tías are for.
I wouldn't say all that...
HA HA HAHAHA HA
HA HA HA HA HA HA HA

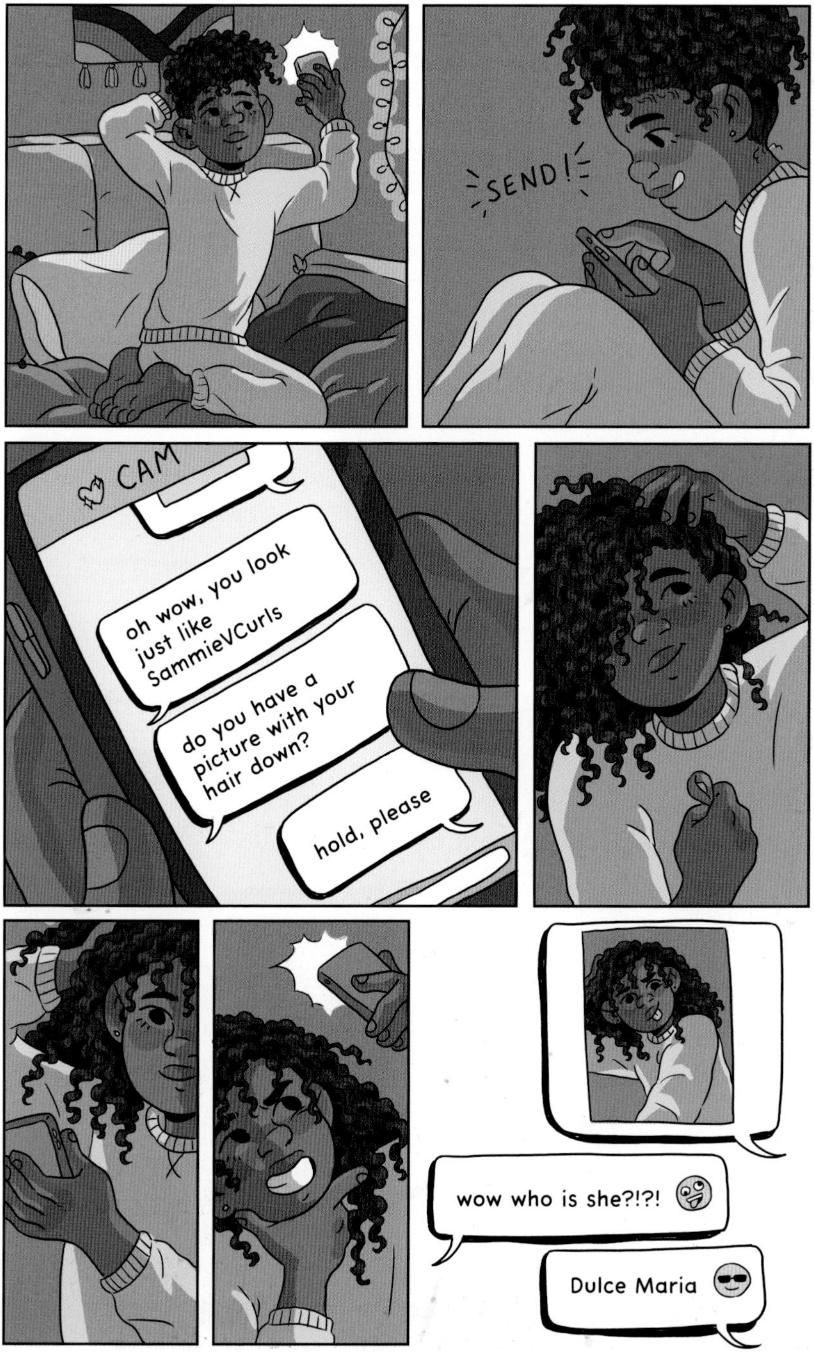
SEND!
CAM
oh wow, you look just like SammieVCurls
do you have a picture with your hair down?
hold, please
wow who is she?!?!
Dulce Maria

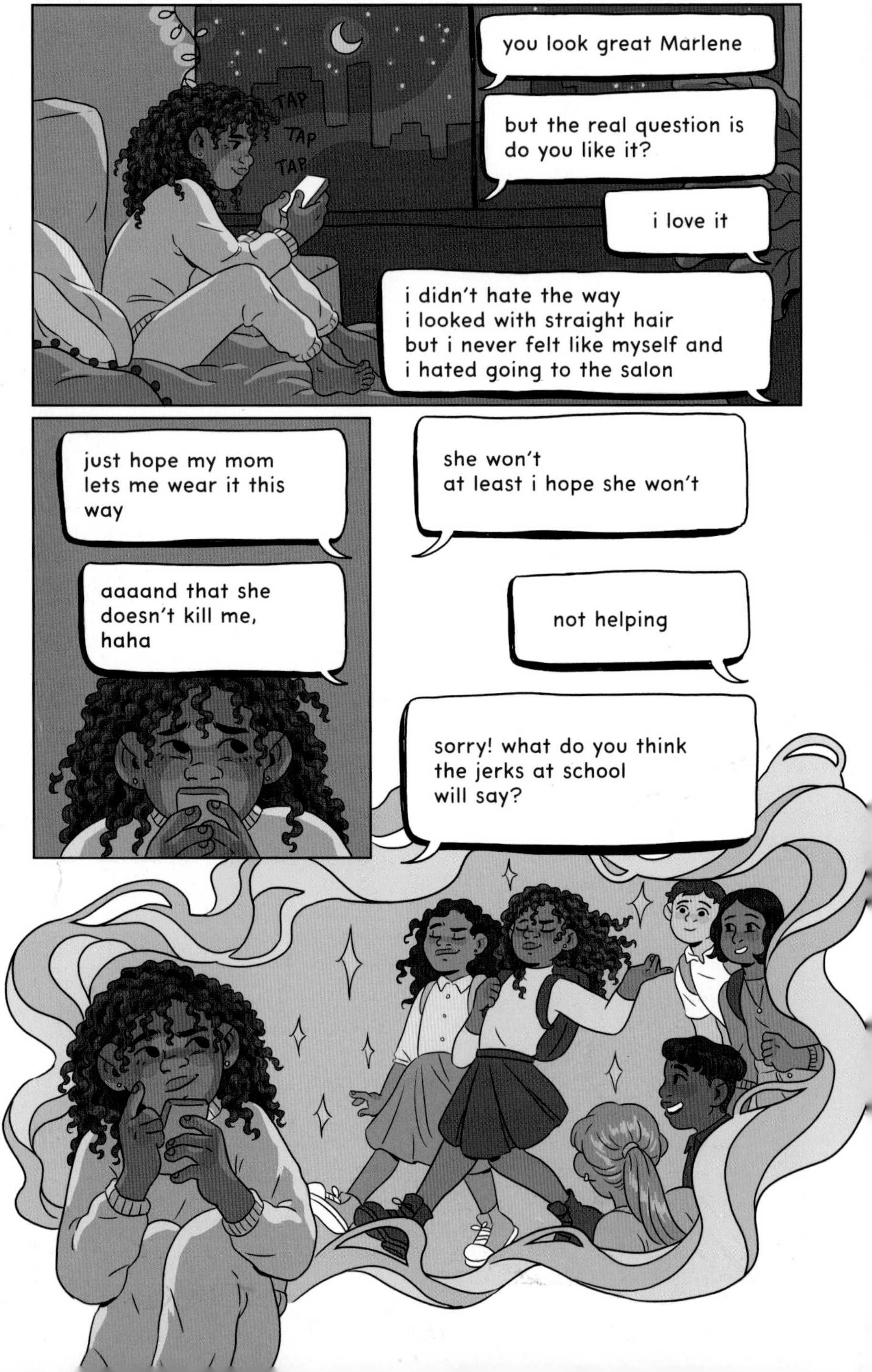
you look great Marlene
but the real question is do you like it?
i love it
i didn't hate the way i looked with straight hair but i never felt like myself and i hated going to the salon
TAP TAP TAP
just hope my mom lets me wear it this way
she won't at least i hope she won't
aaaand that she doesn't kill me, haha
not helping
sorry! what do you think the jerks at school will say?

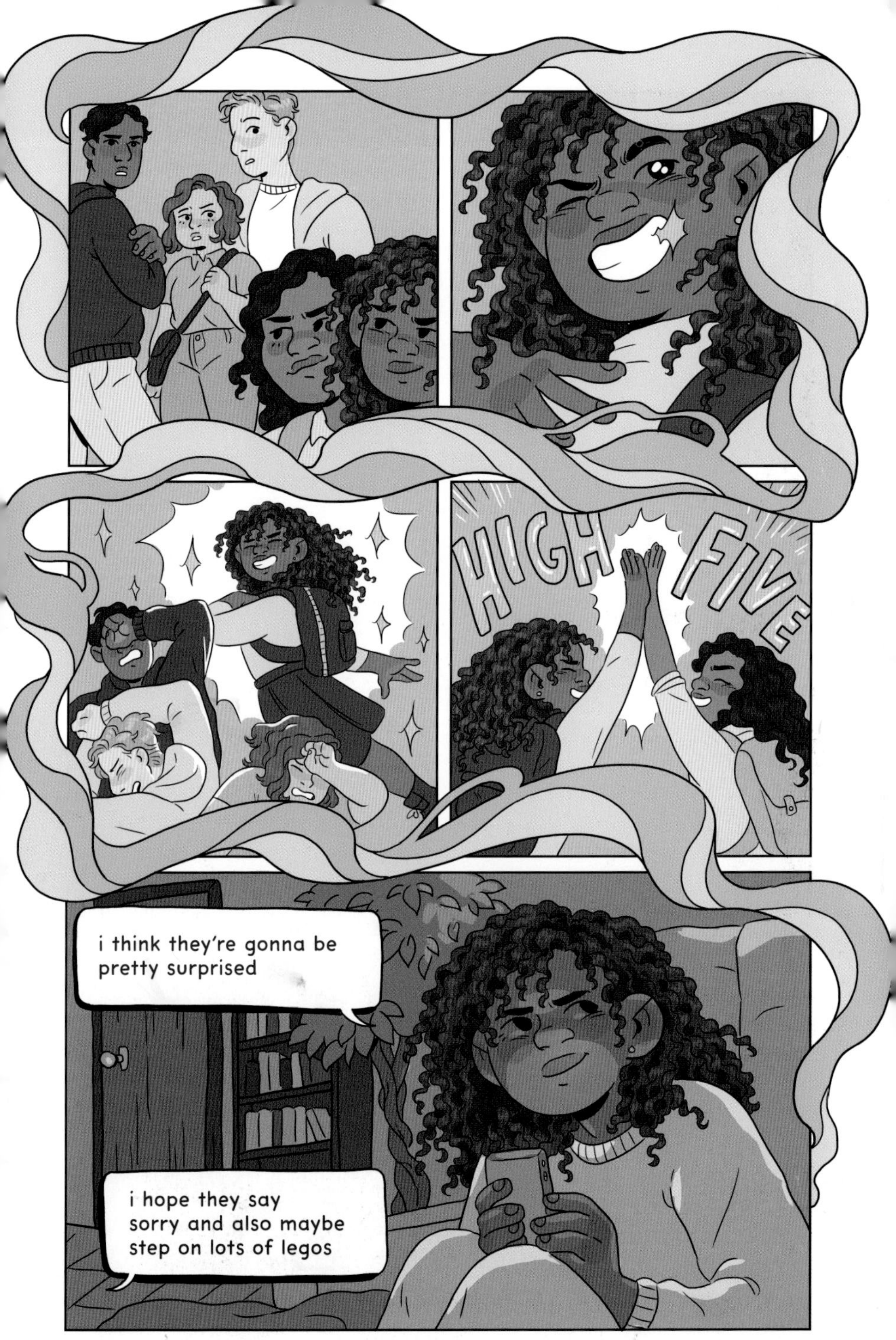
HIGH
FIVE
i think they're gonna be pretty surprised
i hope they say sorry and also maybe step on lots of legos

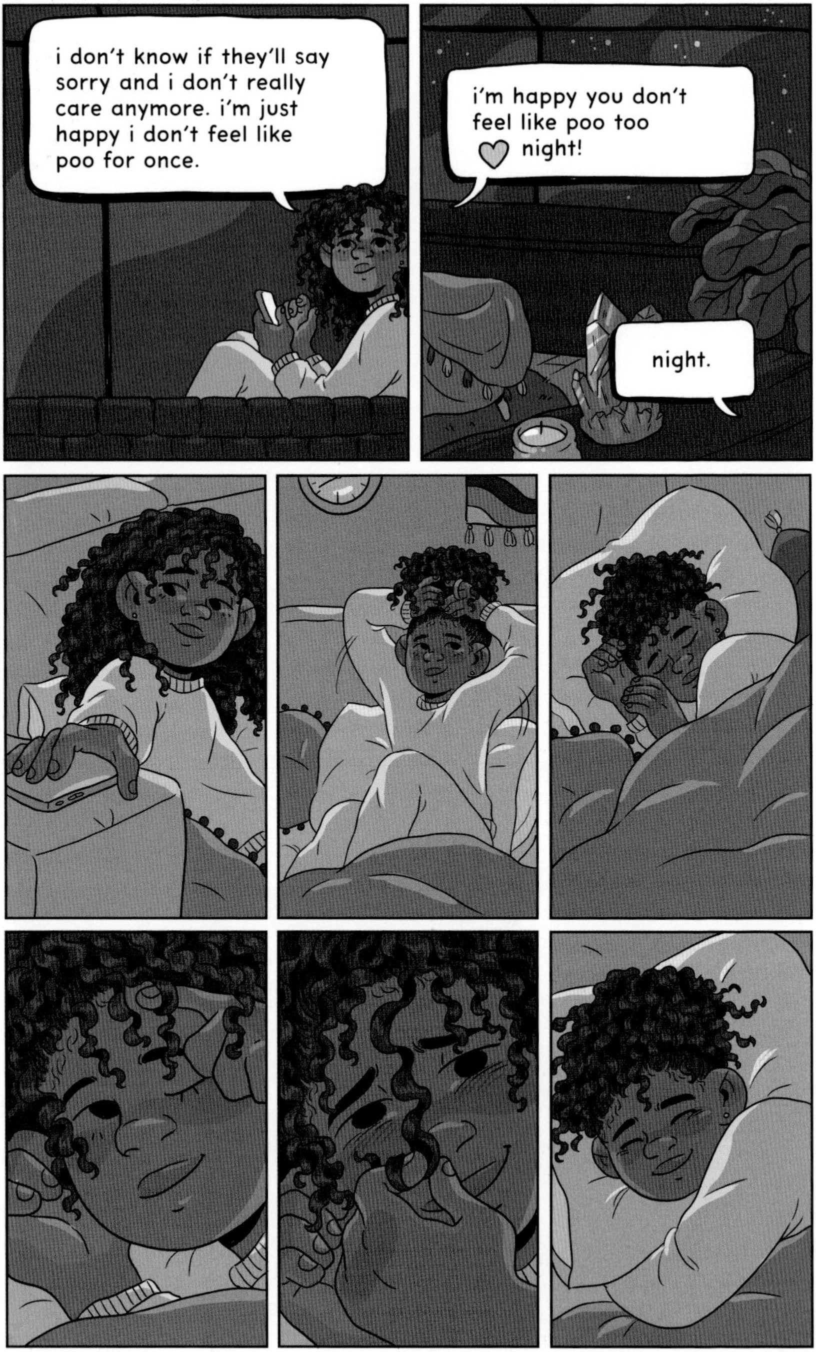
i don't know if they'll say sorry and i don't really care anymore. i'm just happy i don't feel like poo for once.
i'm happy you don't feel like poo too ♡ night!
night.

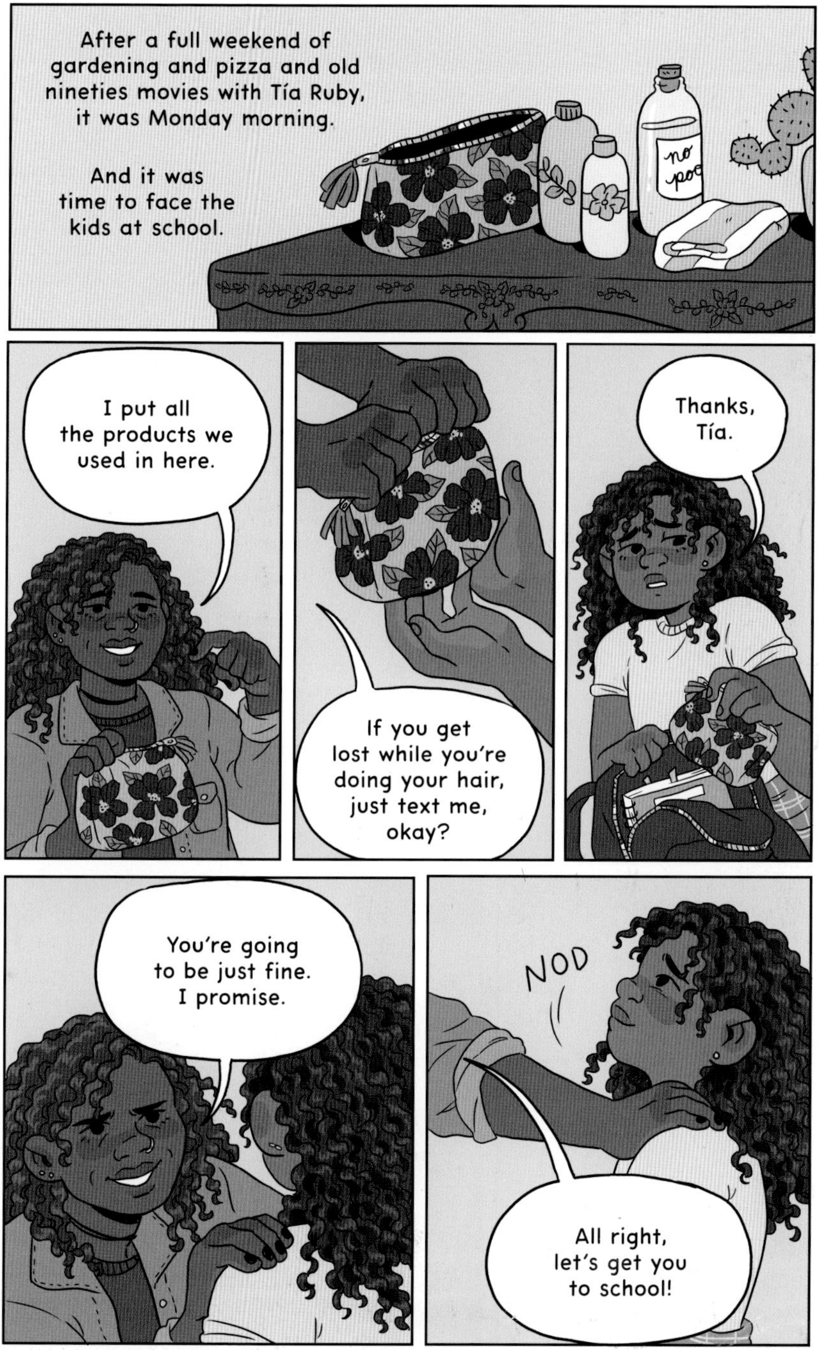
After a full weekend of gardening and pizza and old nineties movies with Tía Ruby, it was Monday morning.
And it was time to face the kids at school.
no poo
I put all the products we used in here.
If you get lost while you're doing your hair, just text me, okay?
Thanks, Tía.
You're going to be just fine. I promise.
NOD
All right, let's get you to school!

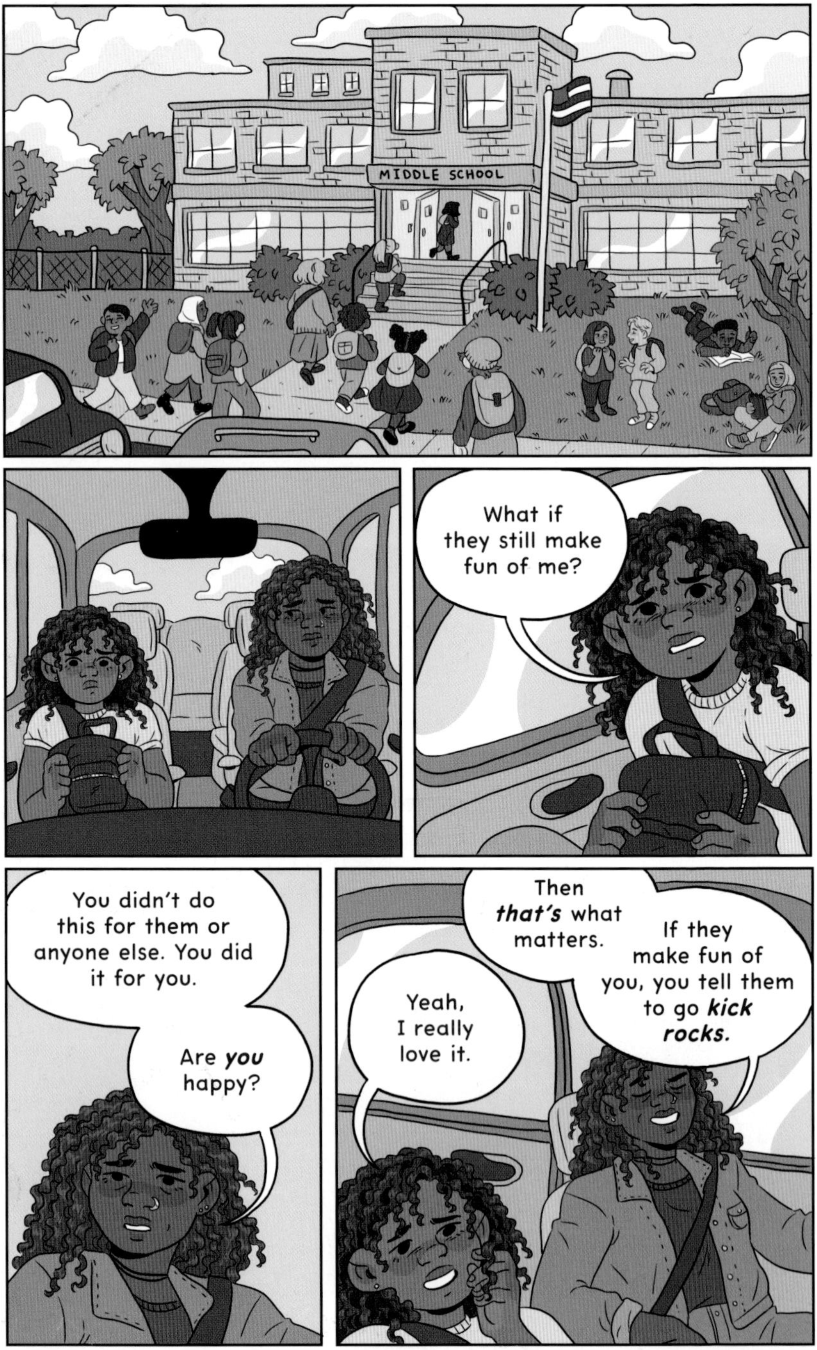
MIDDLE SCHOOL
What if they still make fun of me?
You didn't do this for them or anyone else. You did it for you.
Are *you* happy?
Yeah, I really love it.
Then ***that's*** what matters.
If they make fun of you, you tell them to go ***kick rocks.***

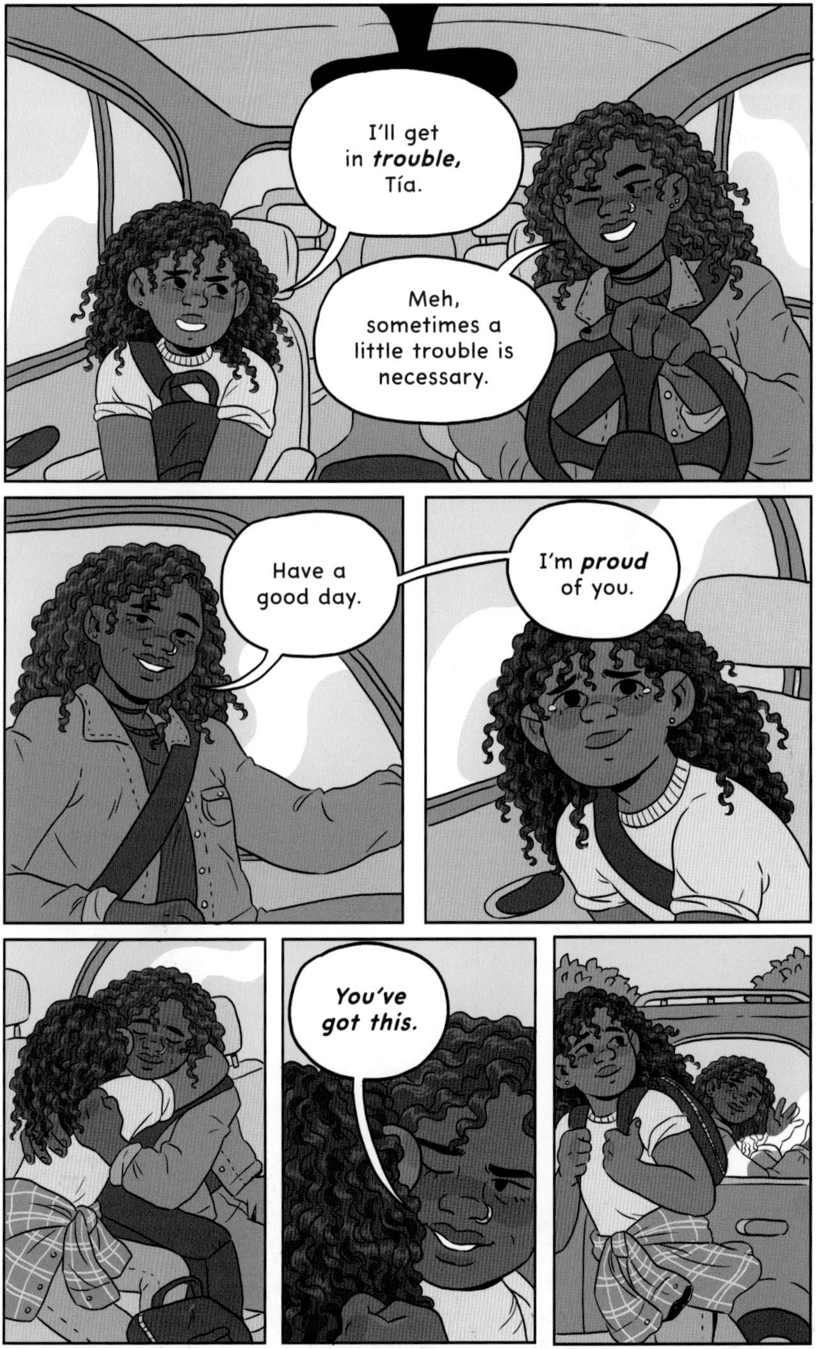
I'll get in ***trouble,*** Tía.
Meh, sometimes a little trouble is necessary.
Have a good day.
I'm ***proud*** of you.
You've got this.

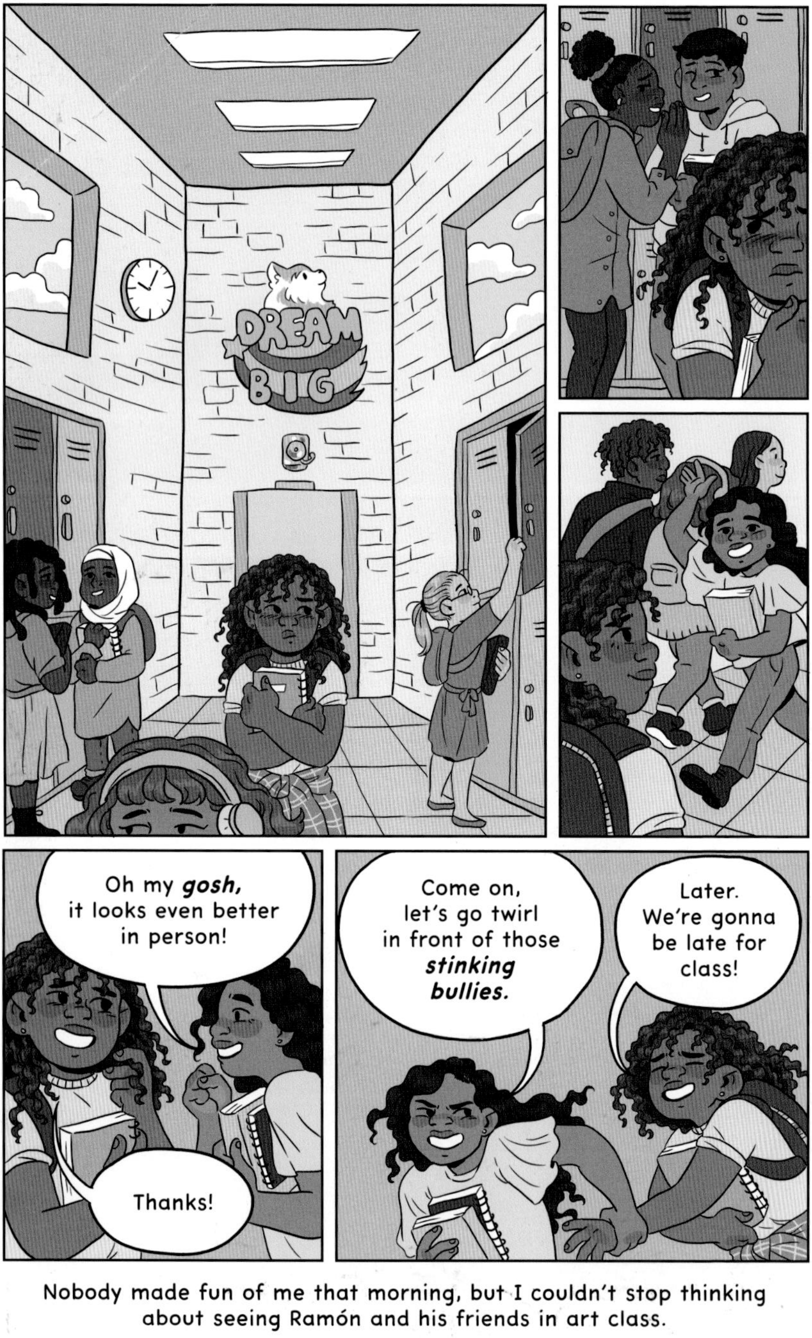
DREAM BIG
Oh my *gosh,* it looks even better in person!
Thanks!
Come on, let's go twirl in front of those ***stinking bullies.***
Later. We're gonna be late for class!

Nobody made fun of me that morning, but I couldn't stop thinking about seeing Ramón and his friends in art class.

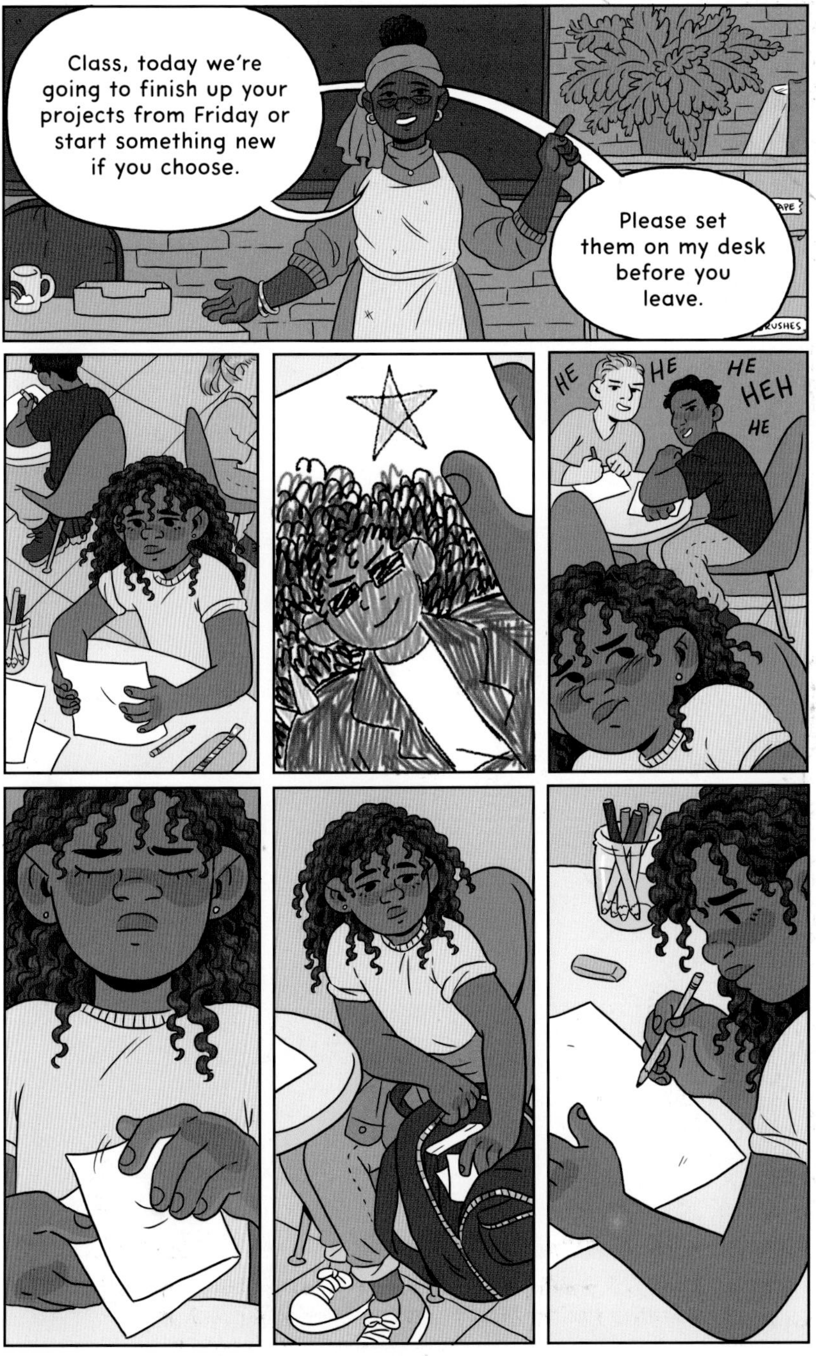
Class, today we're going to finish up your projects from Friday or start something new if you choose.
Please set them on my desk before you leave.
HE
HE
HE
HEH
HE

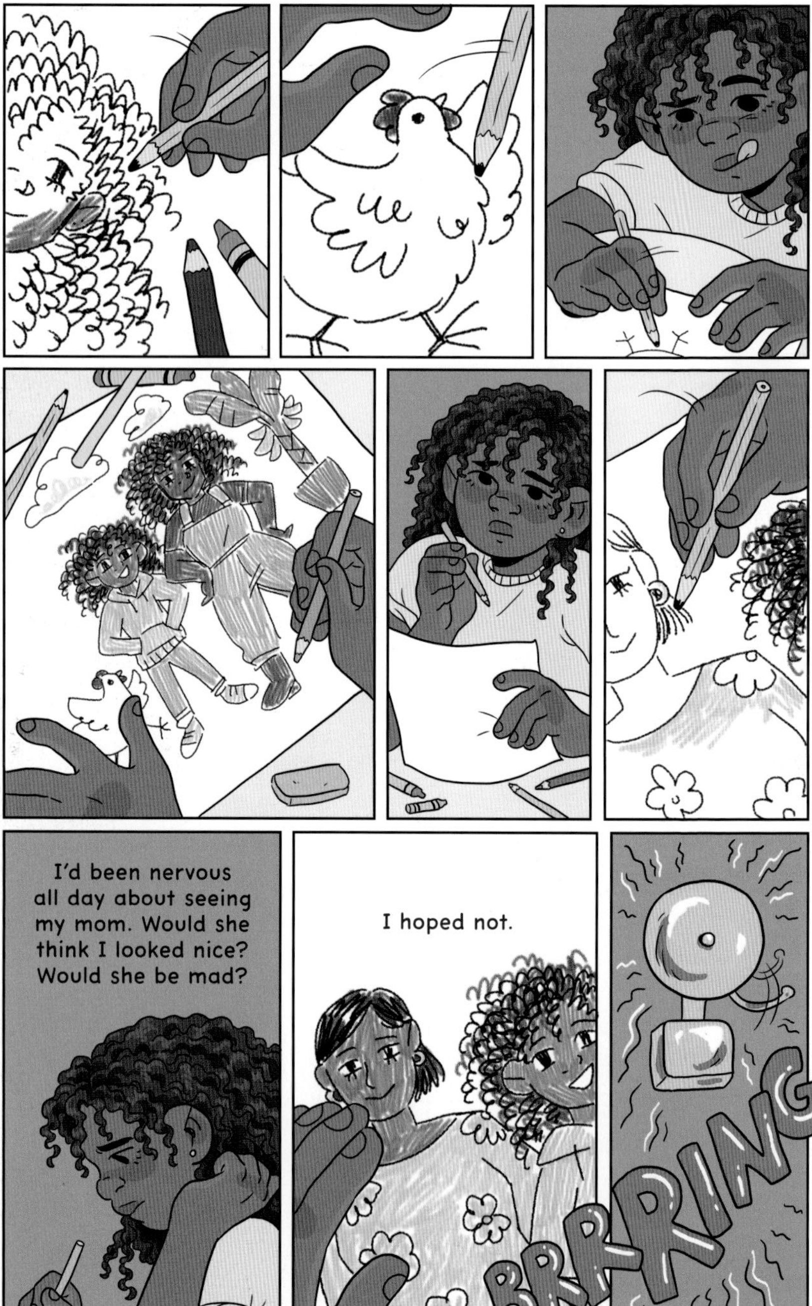
I'd been nervous all day about seeing my mom. Would she think I looked nice? Would she be mad?
I hoped not.
BRRRING

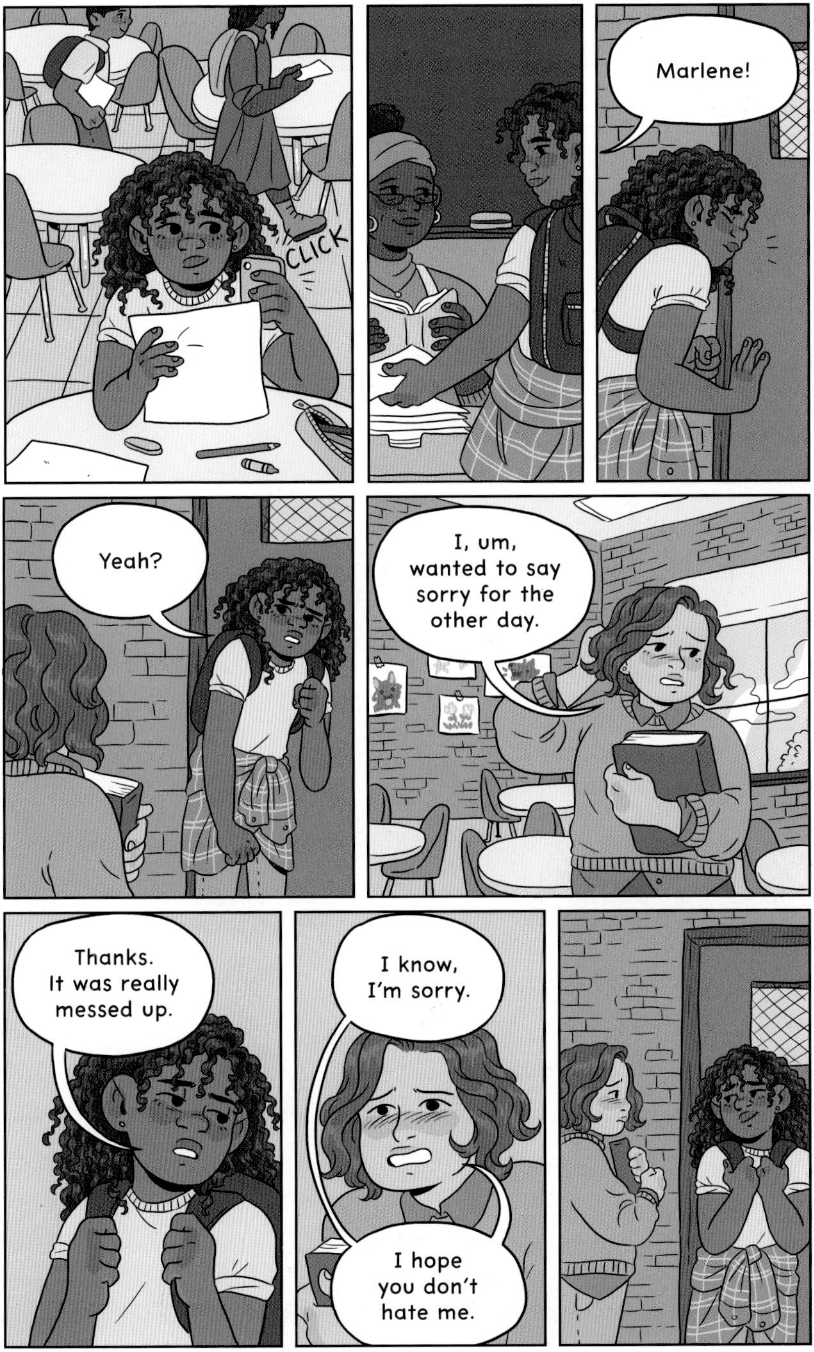
CLICK
Marlene!
Yeah?
I, um, wanted to say sorry for the other day.
Thanks. It was really messed up.
I know, I'm sorry.
I hope you don't hate me.

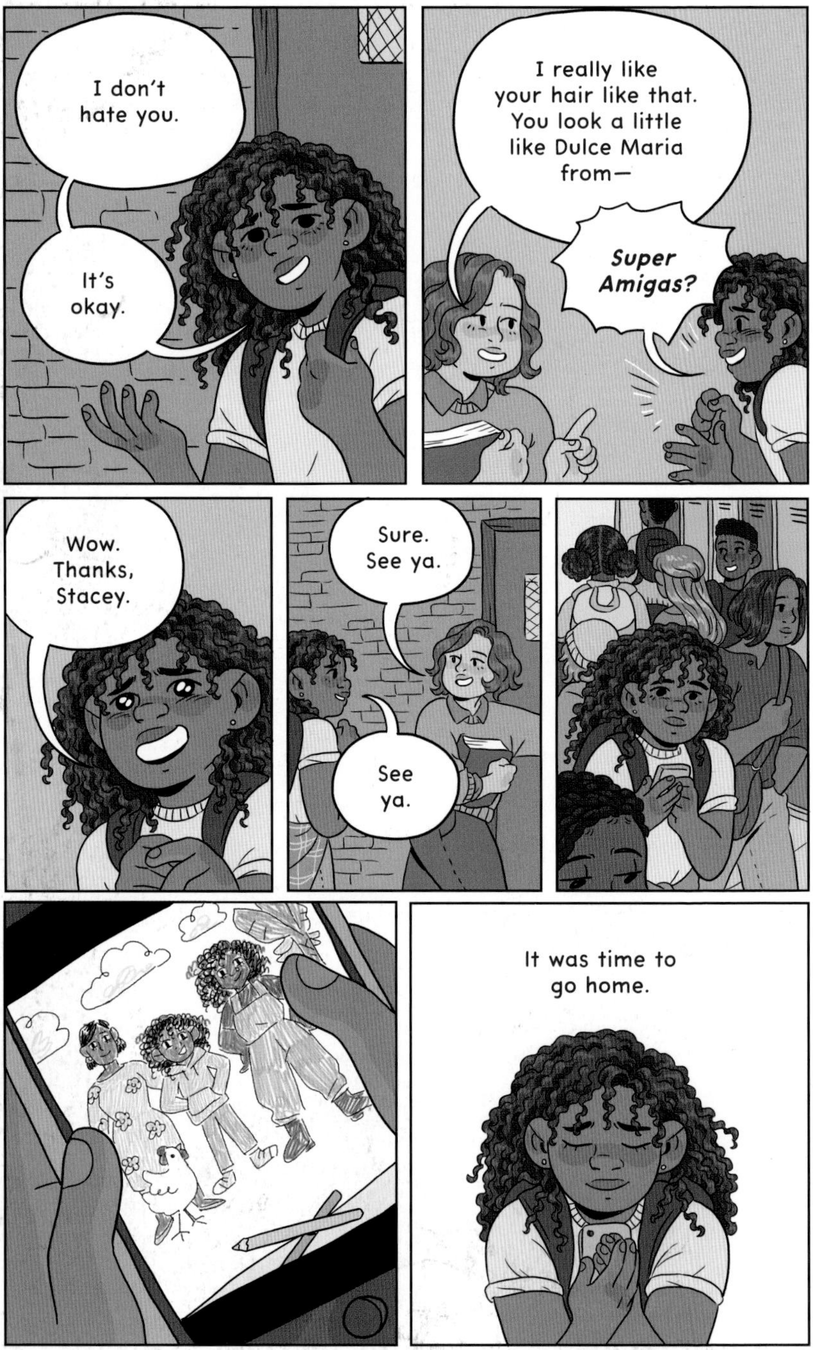
I don't hate you.
It's okay.
I really like your hair like that. You look a little like Dulce Maria from—
Super Amigas?
Wow. Thanks, Stacey.
Sure. See ya.
See ya.
It was time to go home.

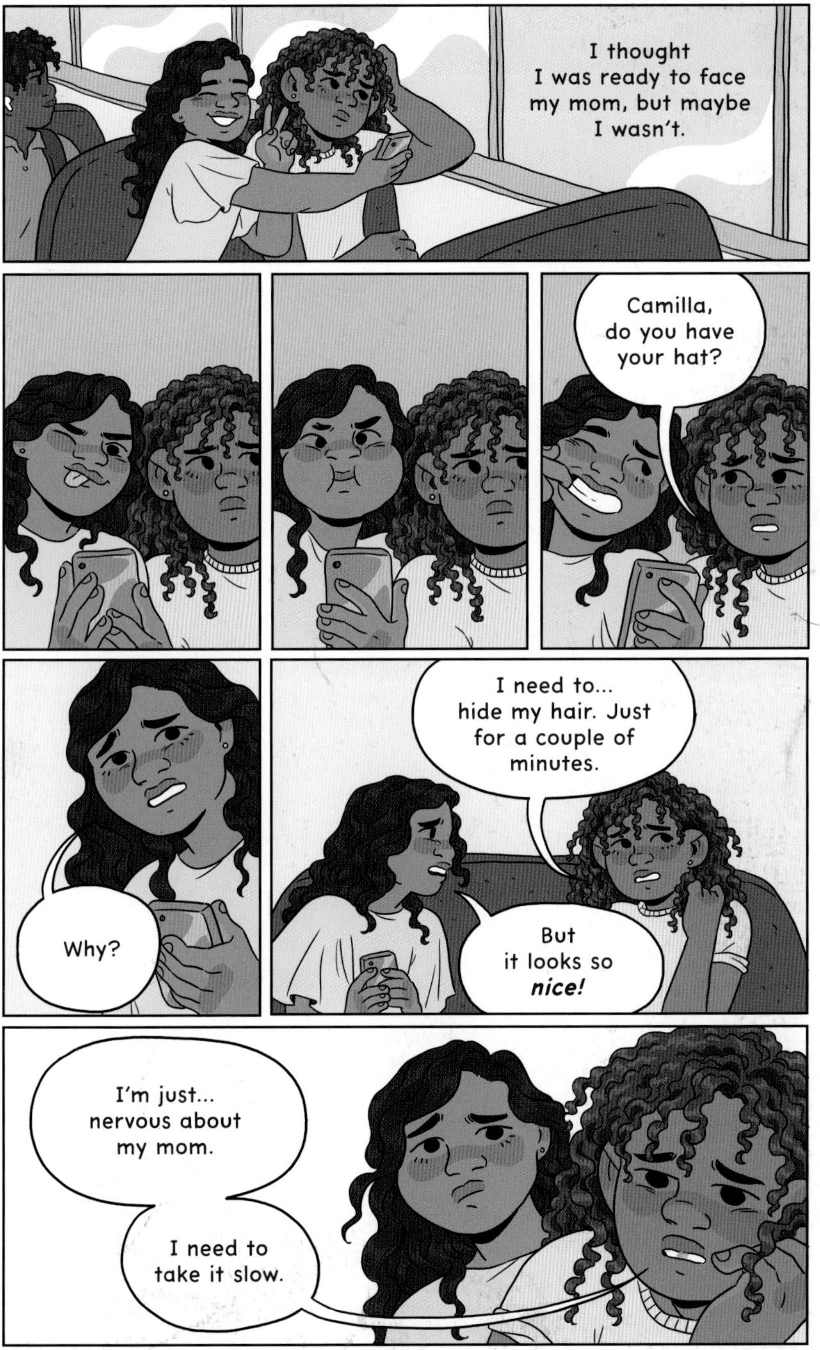
I thought I was ready to face my mom, but maybe I wasn't.
Camilla, do you have your hat?
Why?
I need to... hide my hair. Just for a couple of minutes.
But it looks so *nice!*
I'm just... nervous about my mom.
I need to take it slow.

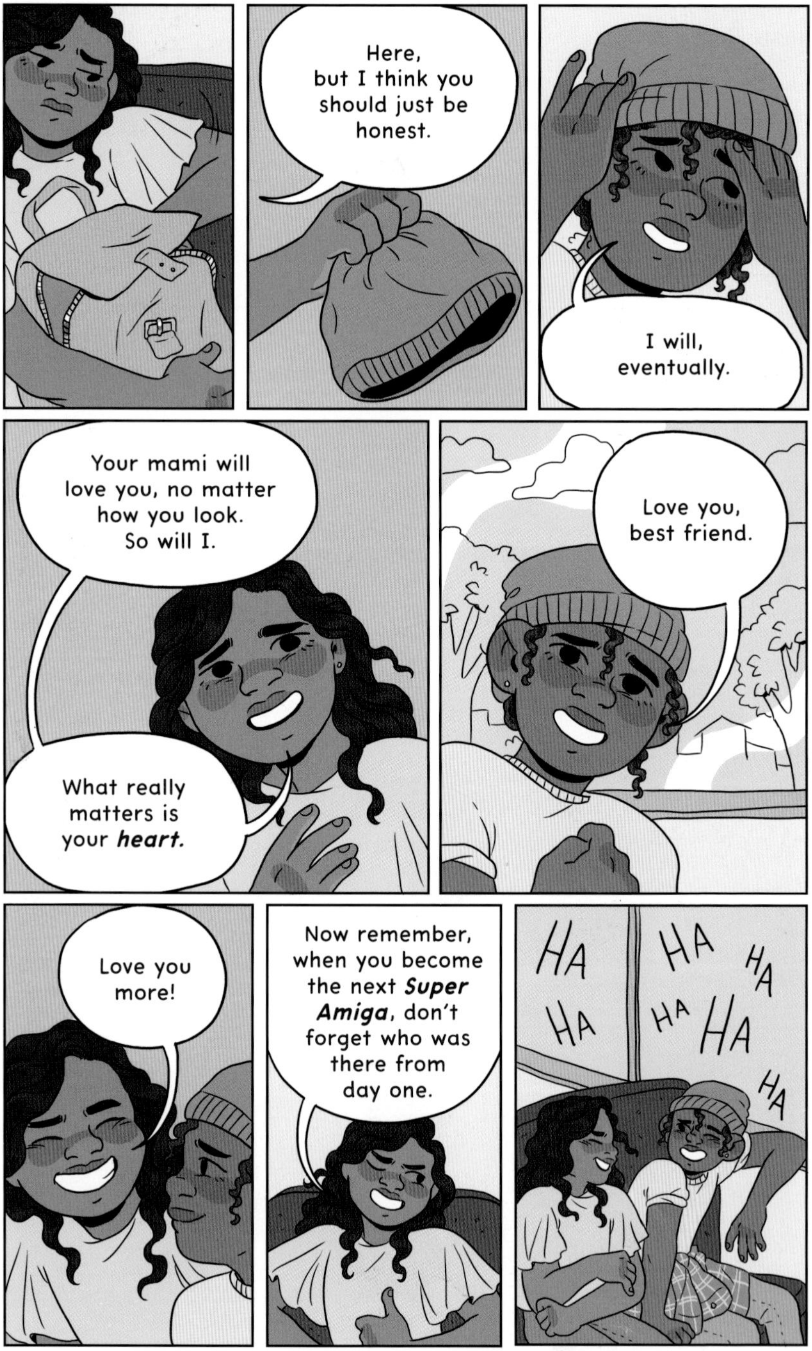
Here, but I think you should just be honest.
I will, eventually.
Your mami will love you, no matter how you look. So will I.
What really matters is your ***heart.***
Love you, best friend.
Love you more!
Now remember, when you become the next ***Super Amiga***, don't forget who was there from day one.
HA HA HA HA HA HA HA HA

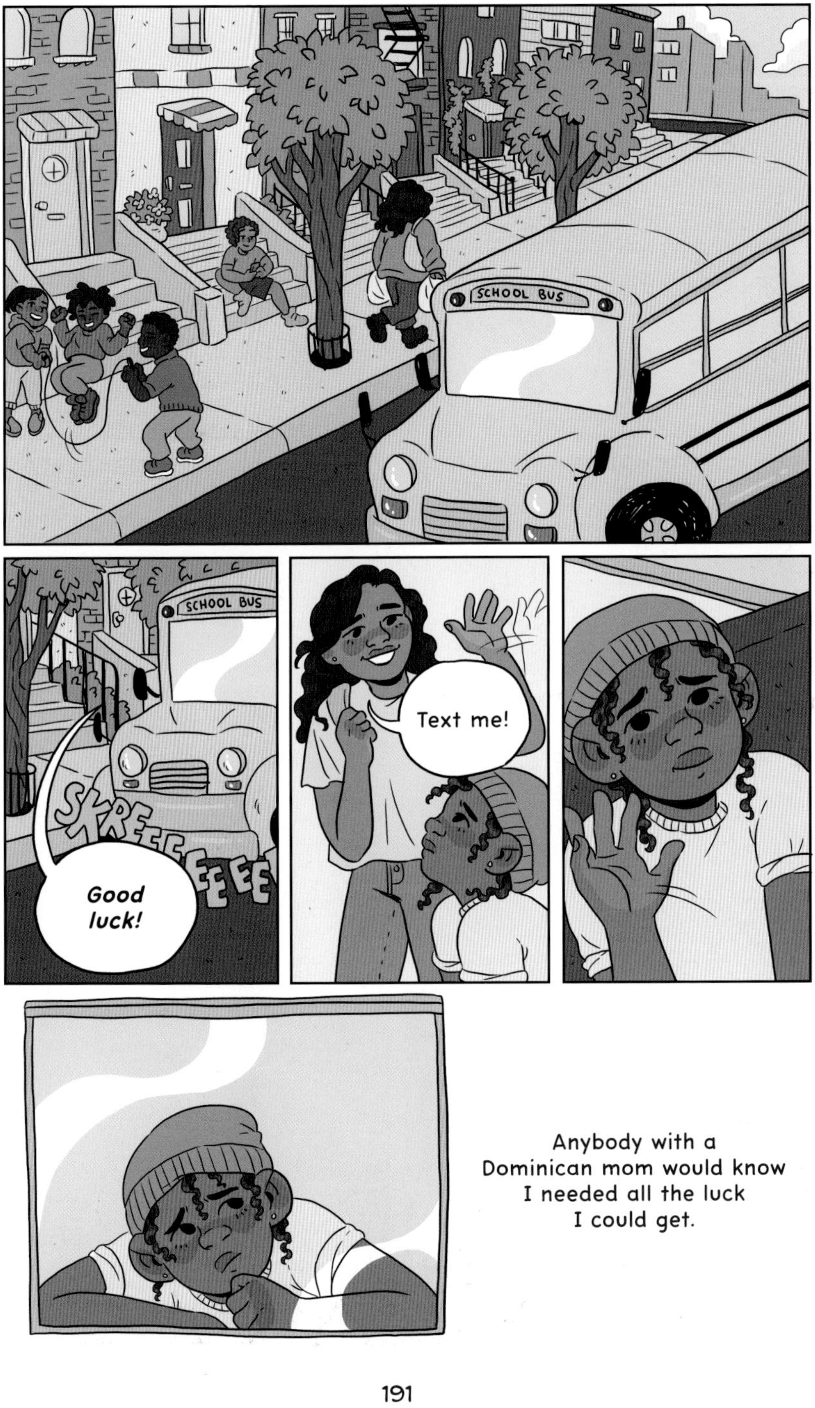
SCHOOL BUS
SKREEEEEEE
Good luck!
Text me!

Anybody with a Dominican mom would know I needed all the luck I could get.

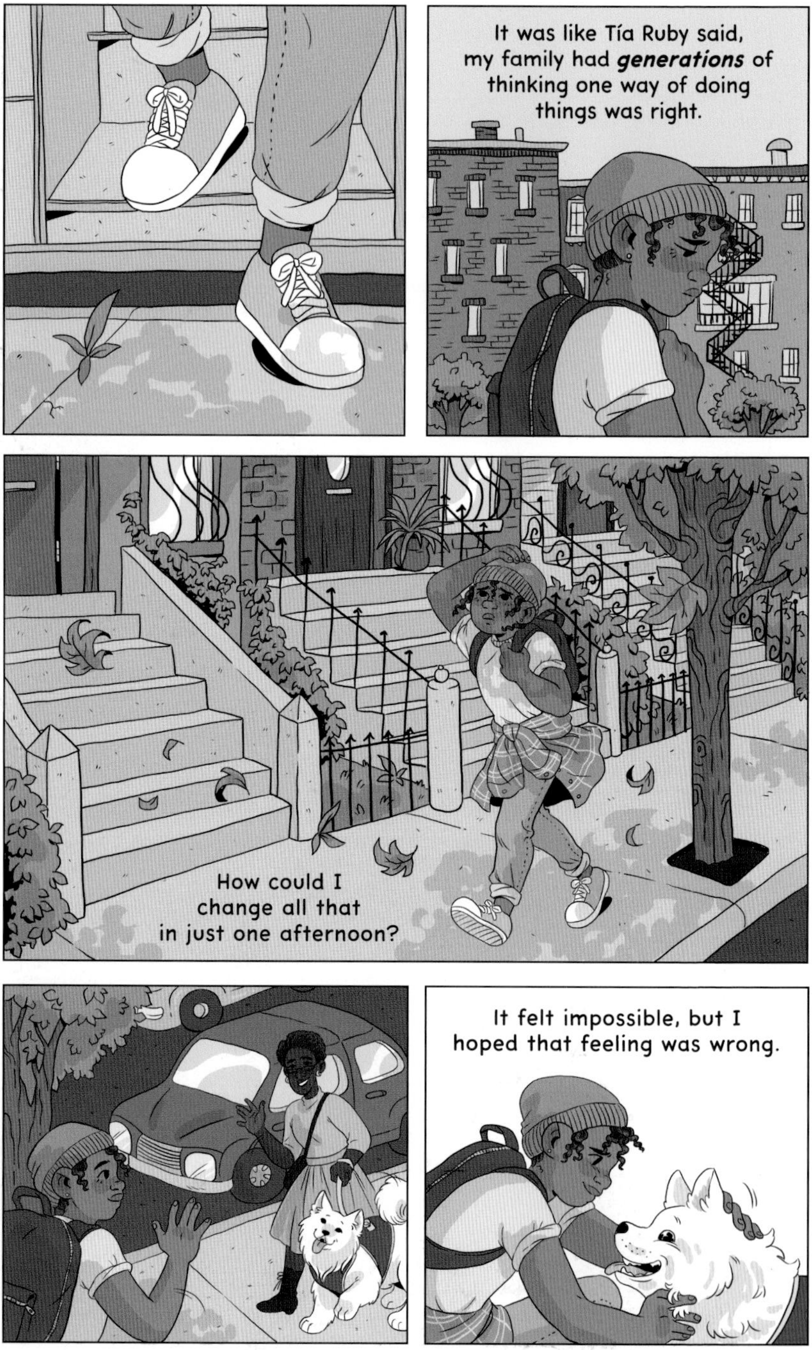
It was like Tía Ruby said, my family had *generations* of thinking one way of doing things was right.
How could I change all that in just one afternoon?
It felt impossible, but I hoped that feeling was wrong.

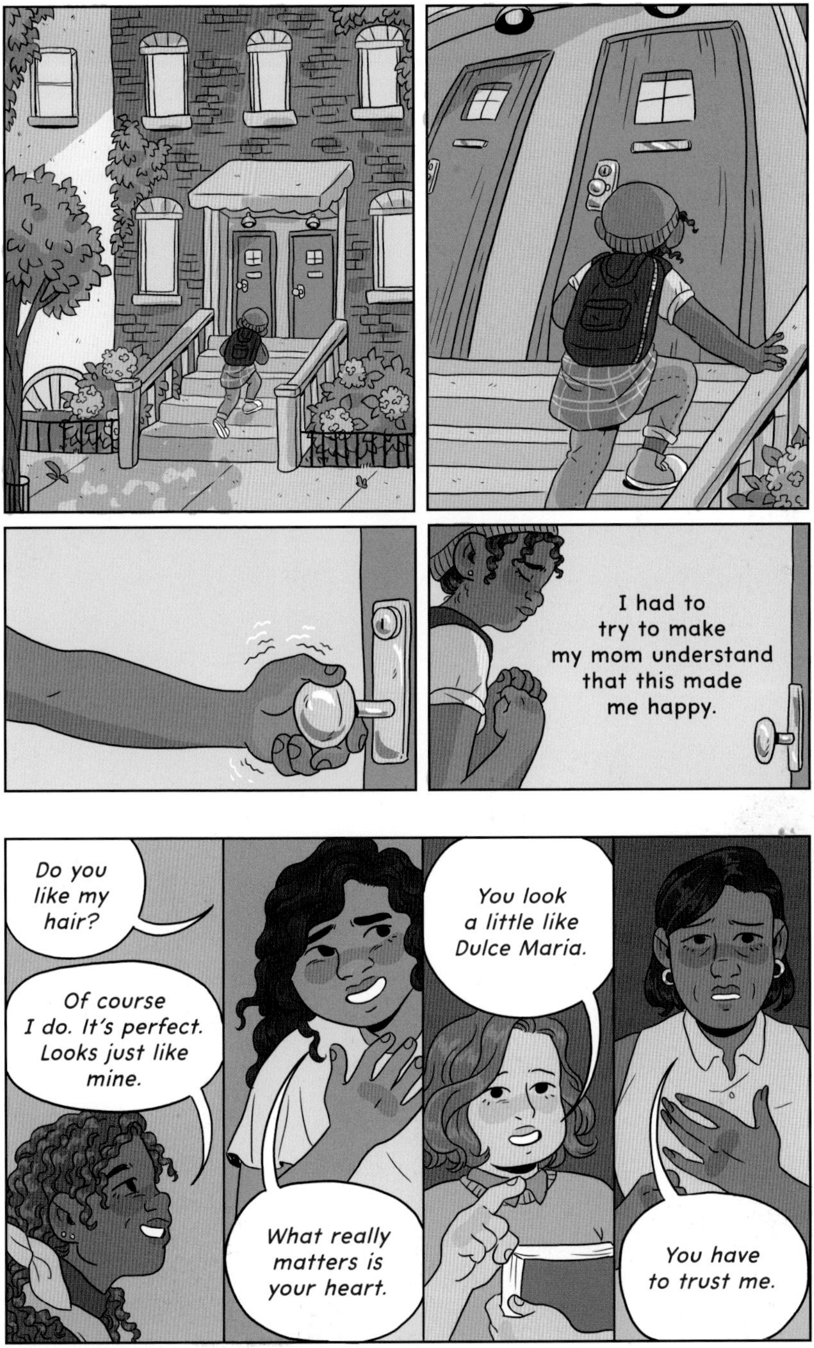
I had to try to make my mom understand that this made me happy.
Do you like my hair?
Of course I do. It's perfect. Looks just like mine.
What really matters is your heart.
You look a little like Dulce Maria.
You have to trust me.

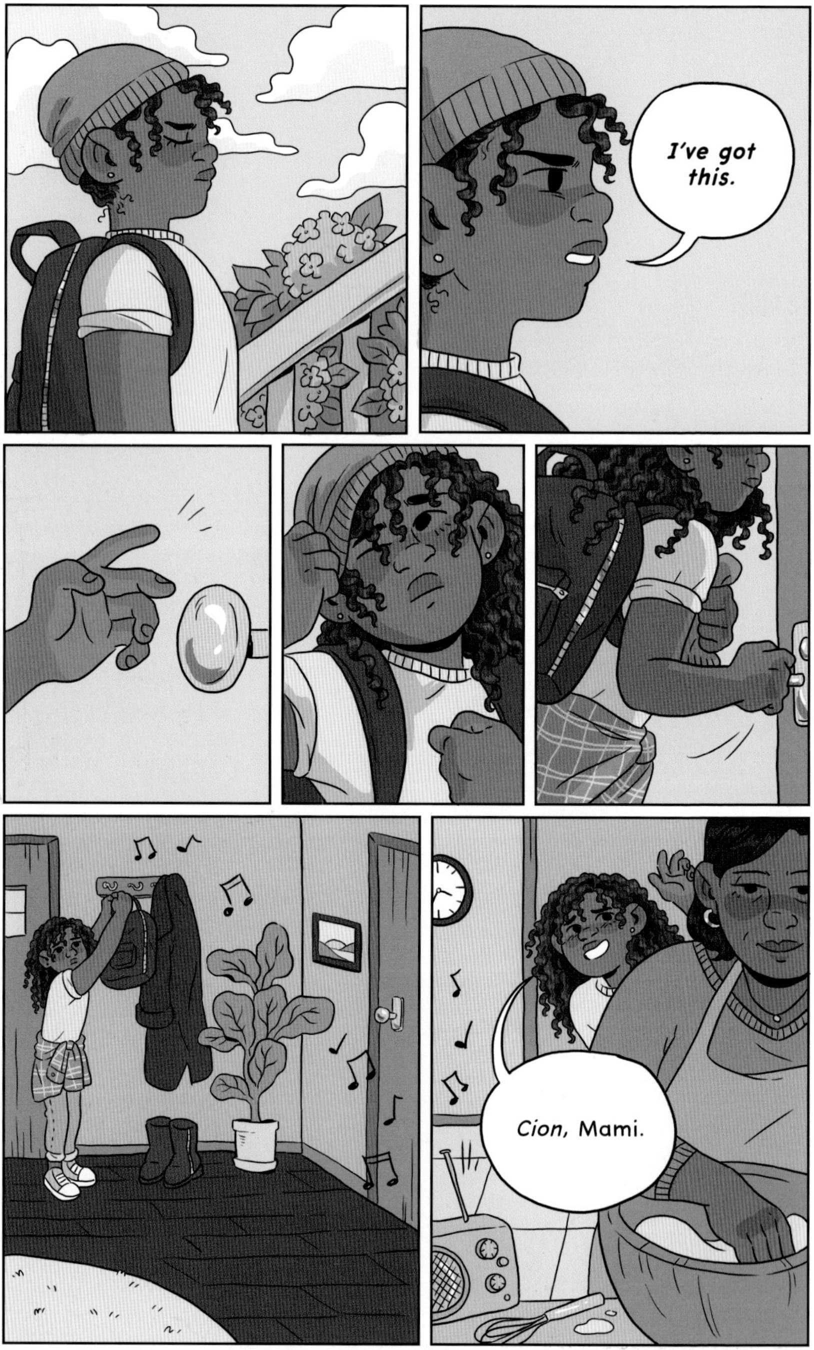
I've got this.
Cion, Mami.

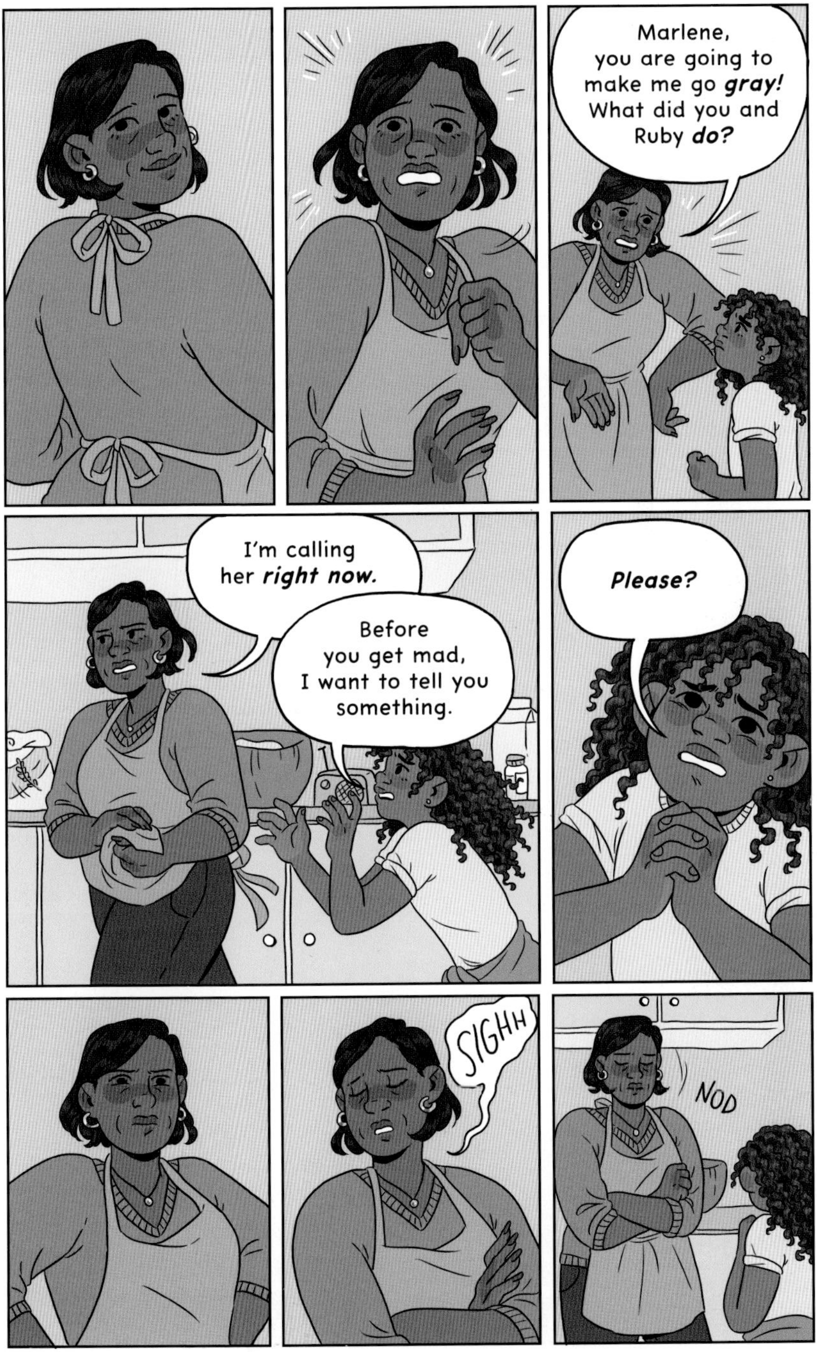
Marlene, you are going to make me go **gray!** What did you and Ruby **do?**
I'm calling her **right now.**
Before you get mad, I want to tell you something.
Please?
SIGHH
NOD

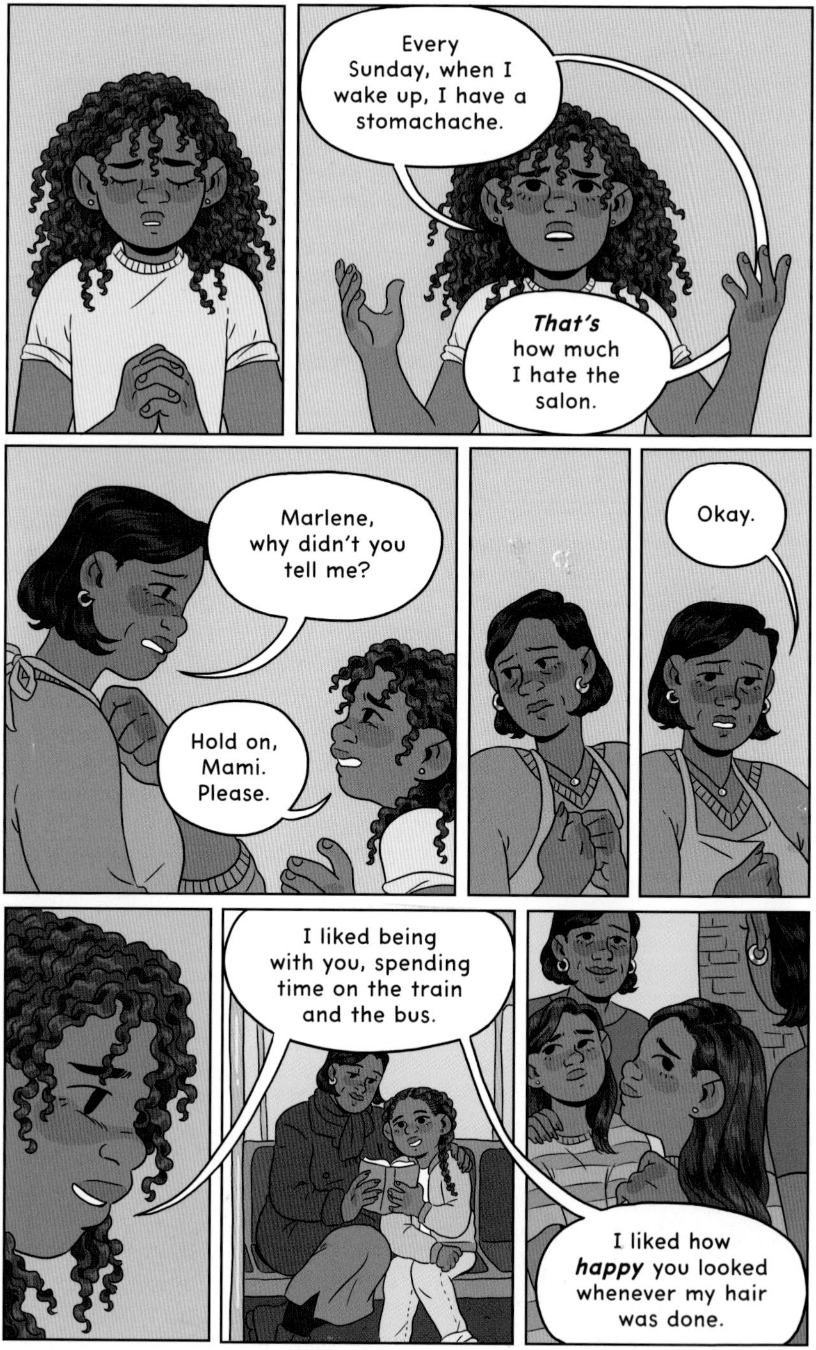
Every Sunday, when I wake up, I have a stomachache.
That's how much I hate the salon.
Marlene, why didn't you tell me?
Hold on, Mami. Please.
Okay.
I liked being with you, spending time on the train and the bus.
I liked how *happy* you looked whenever my hair was done.

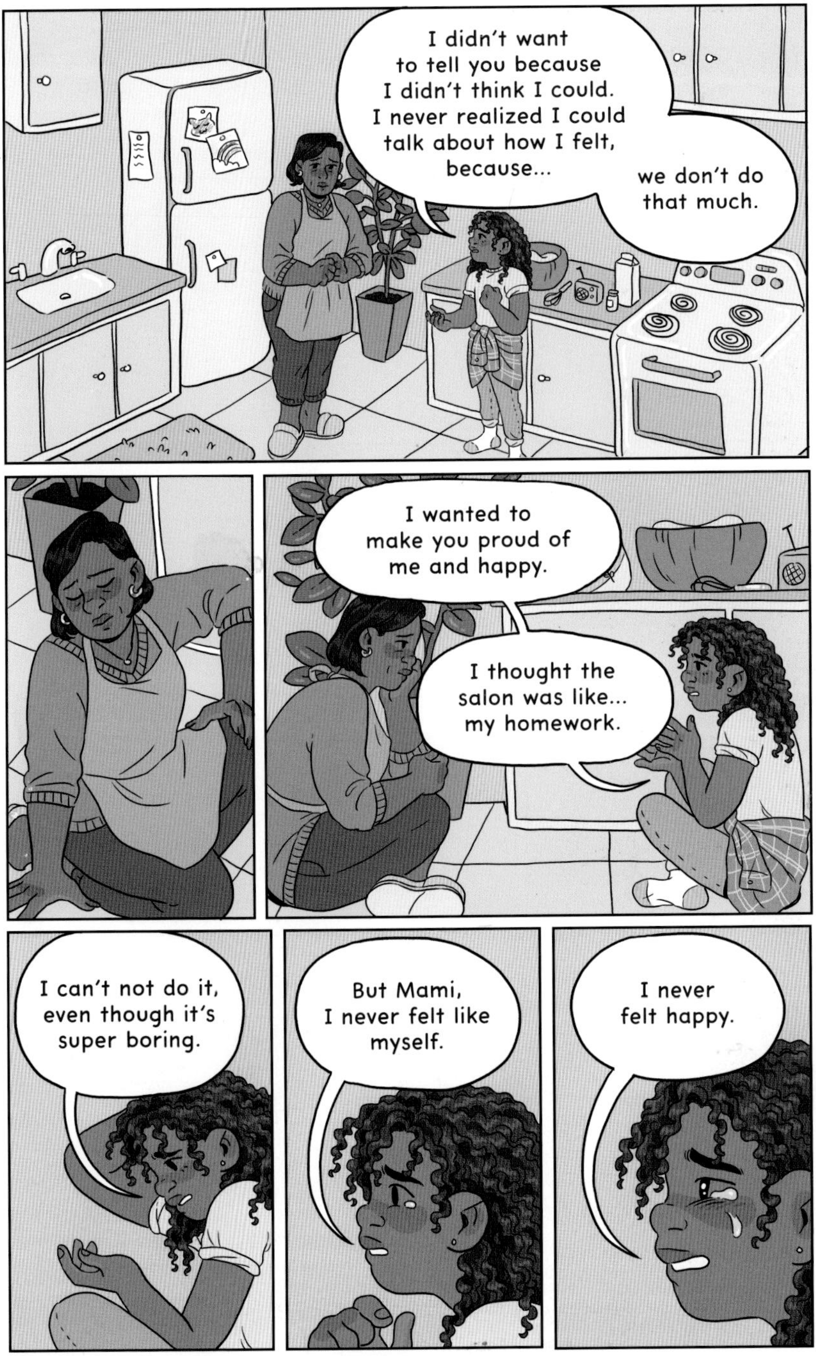
I didn't want to tell you because I didn't think I could. I never realized I could talk about how I felt, because...
we don't do that much.
I wanted to make you proud of me and happy.
I thought the salon was like... my homework.
I can't not do it, even though it's super boring.
But Mami, I never felt like myself.
I never felt happy.

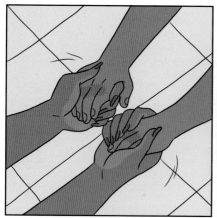

I would imagine I was someone else.

SNIFF

SNIFF

It might seem silly, but I pretended I was a Super Amiga.

It's how I kept from being too upset at the salon.

I'd imagine myself with curly hair because I thought it was the only way I could ever look that way and be the me I felt I was inside.

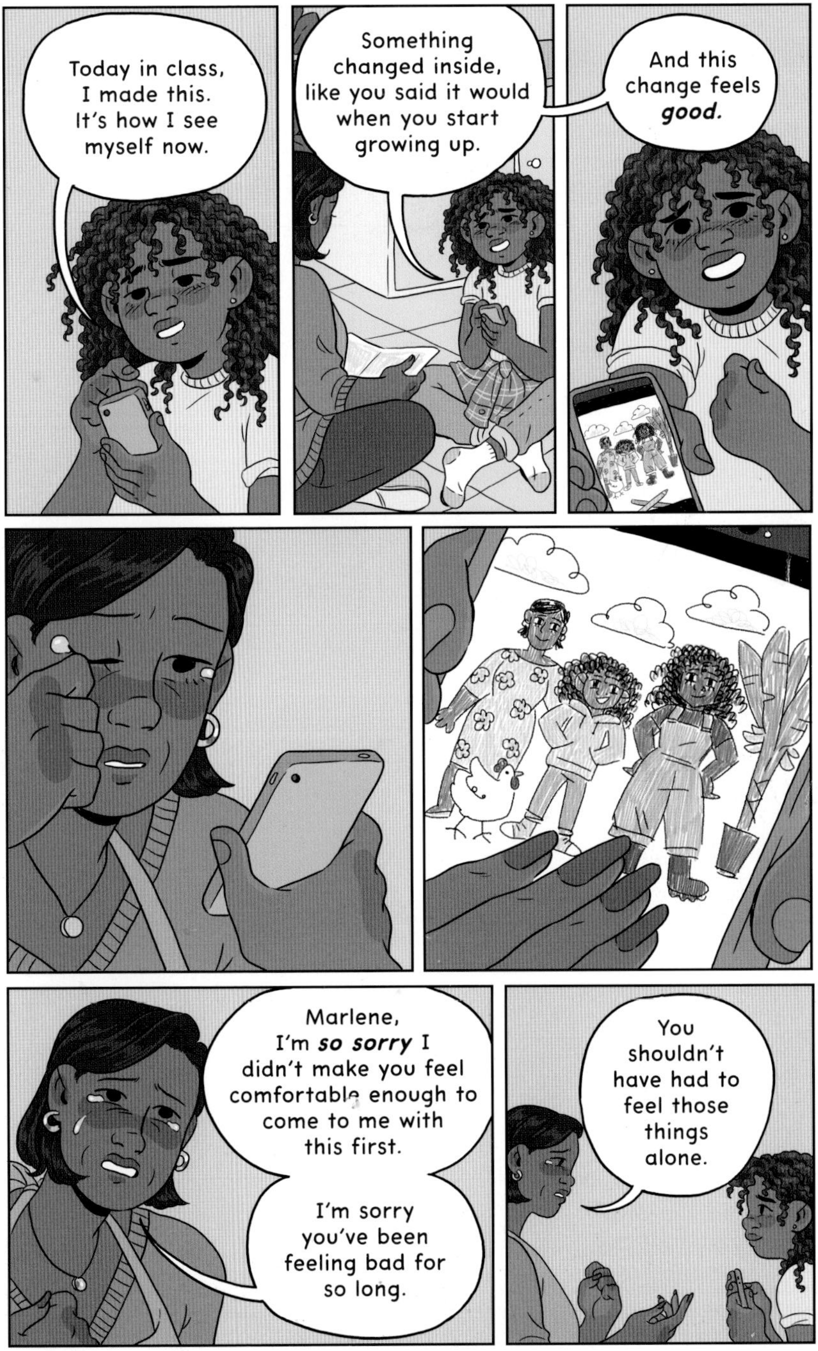

Today in class, I made this. It's how I see myself now.
Something changed inside, like you said it would when you start growing up.
And this change feels **good.**
Marlene, I'm ***so sorry*** I didn't make you feel comfortable enough to come to me with this first.
I'm sorry you've been feeling bad for so long.
You shouldn't have had to feel those things alone.

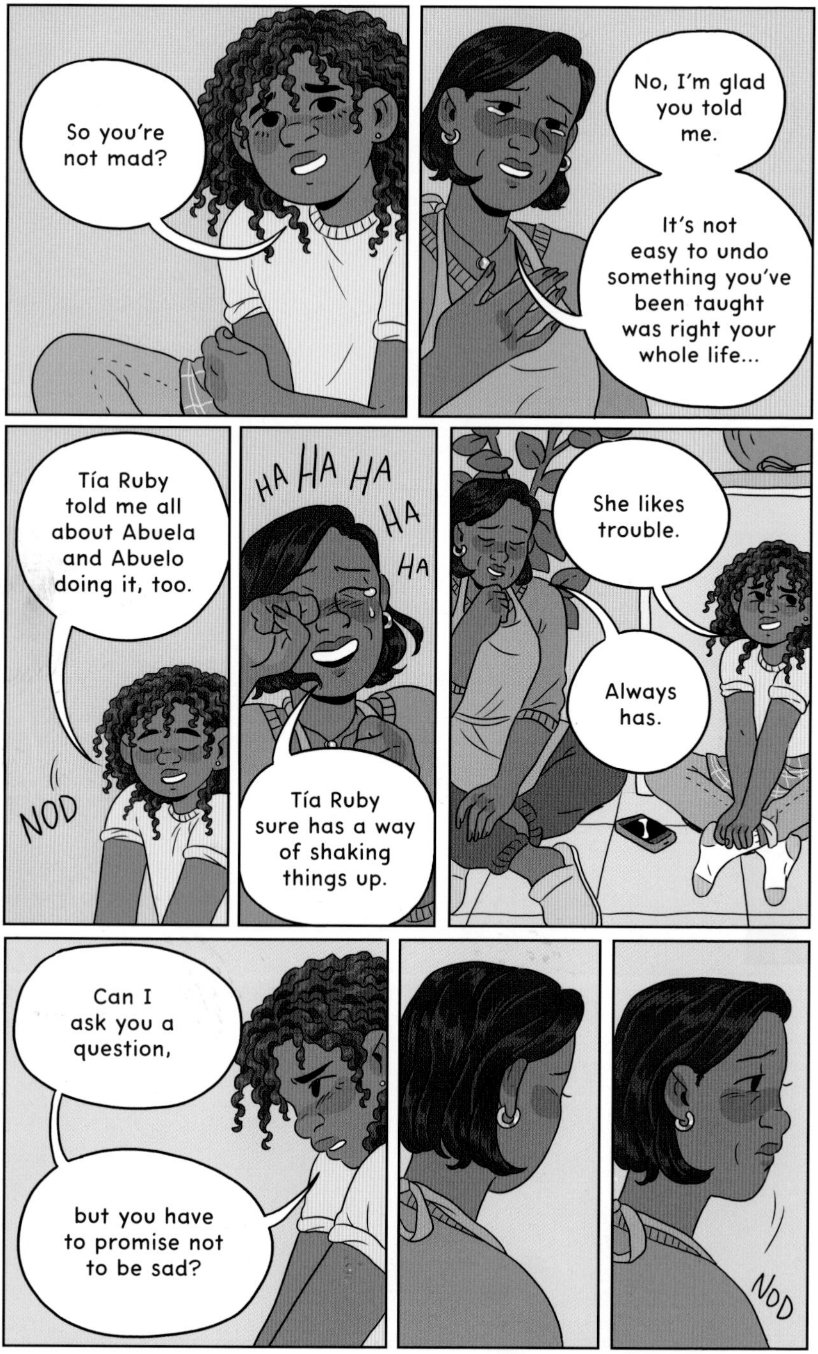
So you're not mad?
No, I'm glad you told me.
It's not easy to undo something you've been taught was right your whole life...
Tía Ruby told me all about Abuela and Abuelo doing it, too.
NOD
HA HA HA HA HA
Tía Ruby sure has a way of shaking things up.
She likes trouble.
Always has.
Can I ask you a question,
but you have to promise not to be sad?
NOD

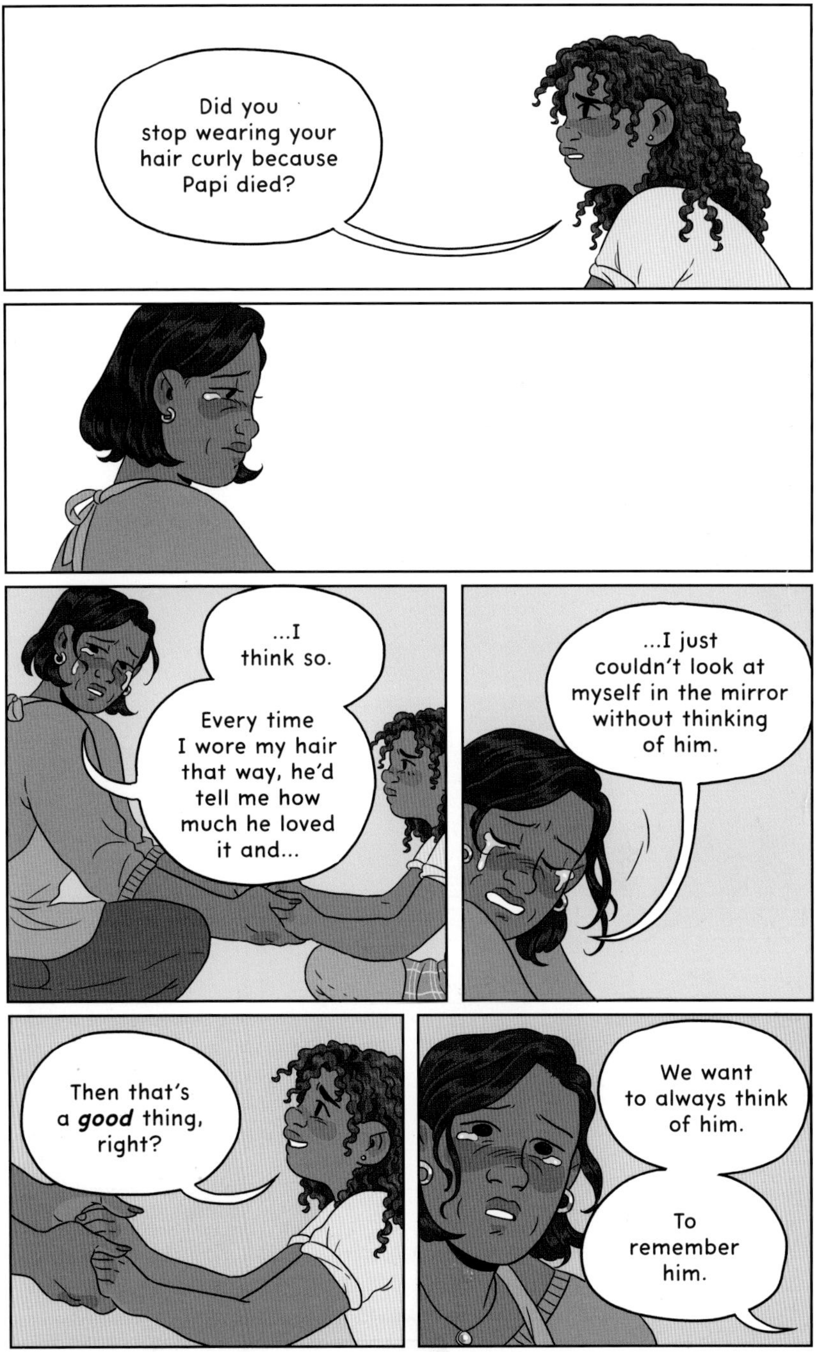
Did you stop wearing your hair curly because Papi died?
...I think so.
Every time I wore my hair that way, he'd tell me how much he loved it and...
...I just couldn't look at myself in the mirror without thinking of him.
Then that's a ***good*** thing, right?
We want to always think of him.
To remember him.

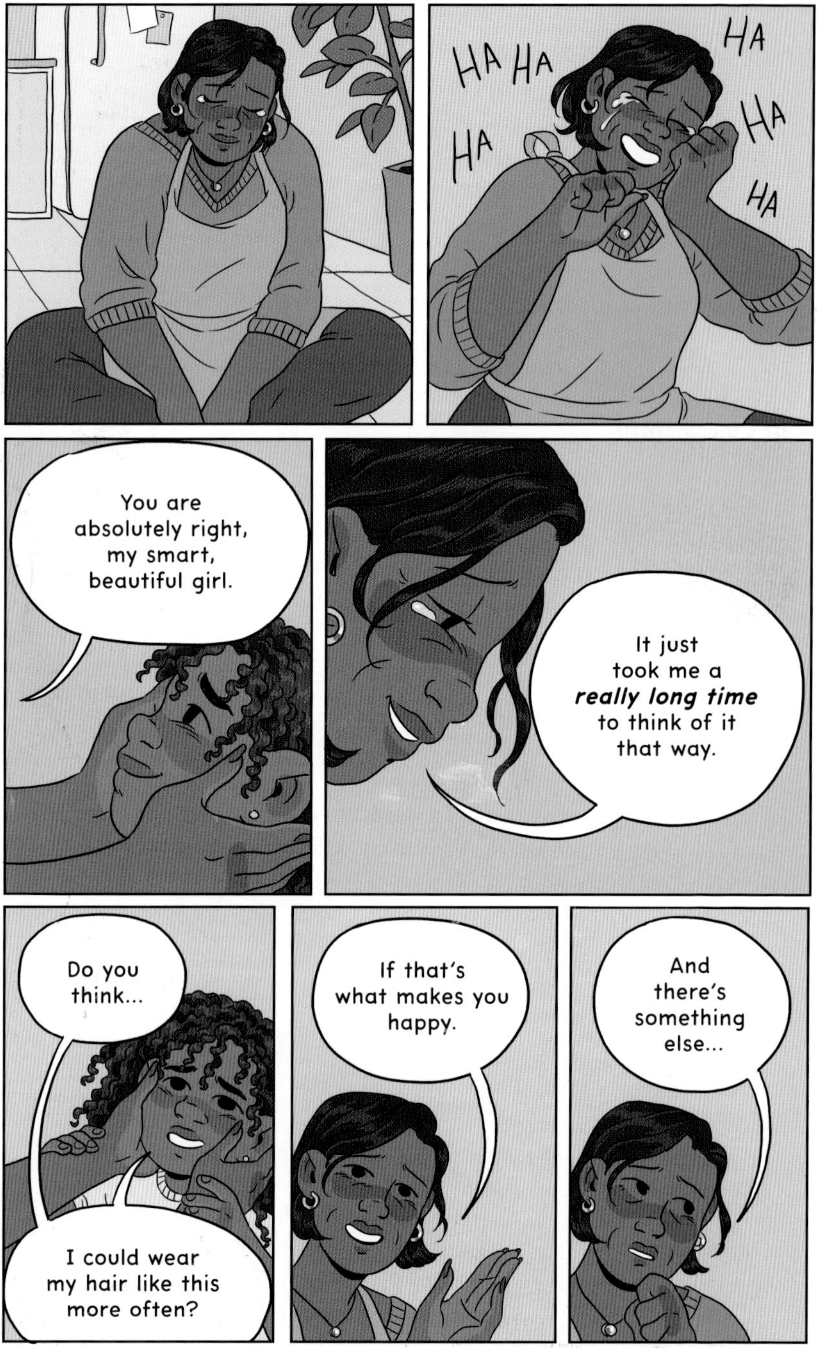
HA HA
HA
HA
HA
HA
You are absolutely right, my smart, beautiful girl.
It just took me a ***really long time*** to think of it that way.
Do you think...
I could wear my hair like this more often?
If that's what makes you happy.
And there's something else...

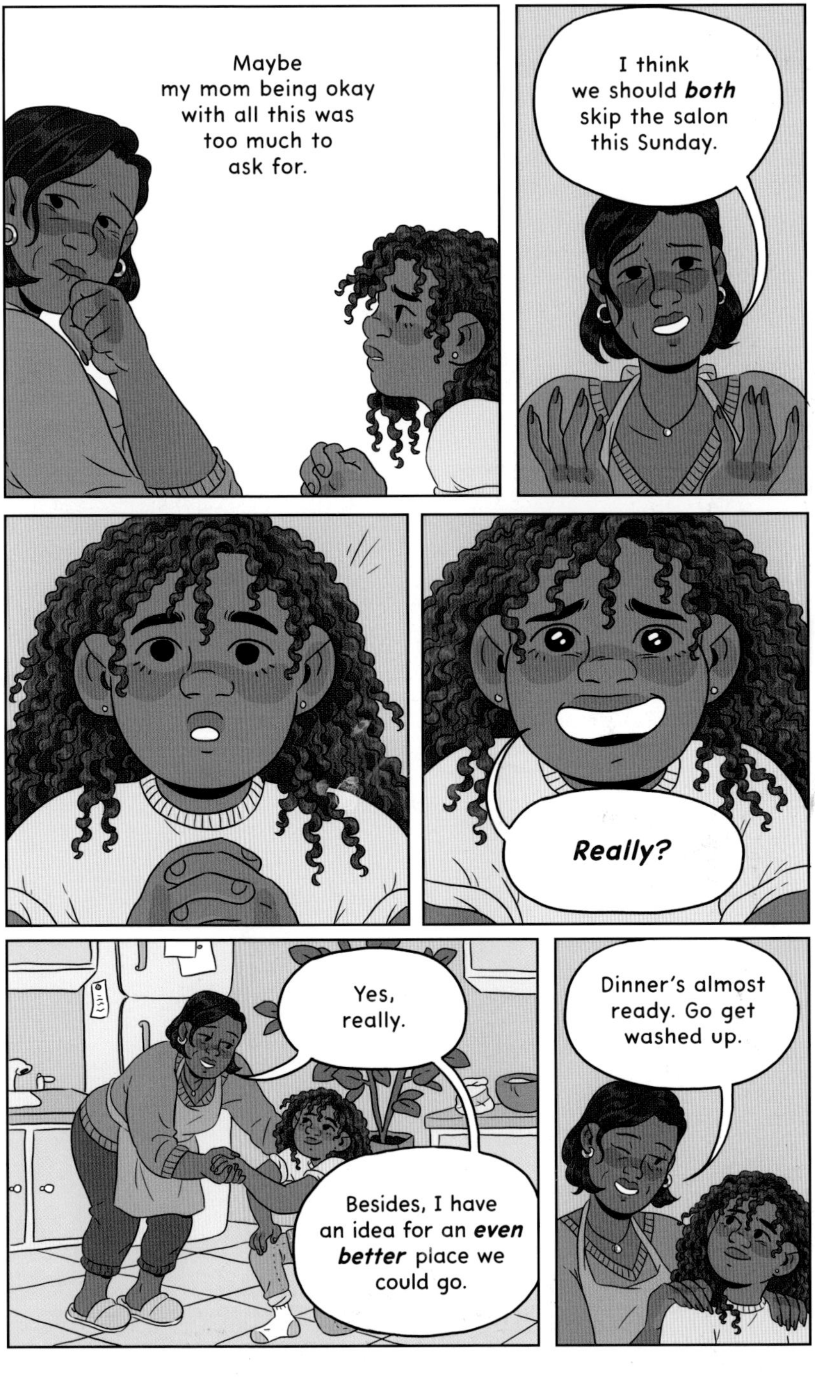
Maybe my mom being okay with all this was too much to ask for.
I think we should both skip the salon this Sunday.
Really?
Yes, really.
Besides, I have an idea for an even better place we could go.
Dinner's almost ready. Go get washed up.

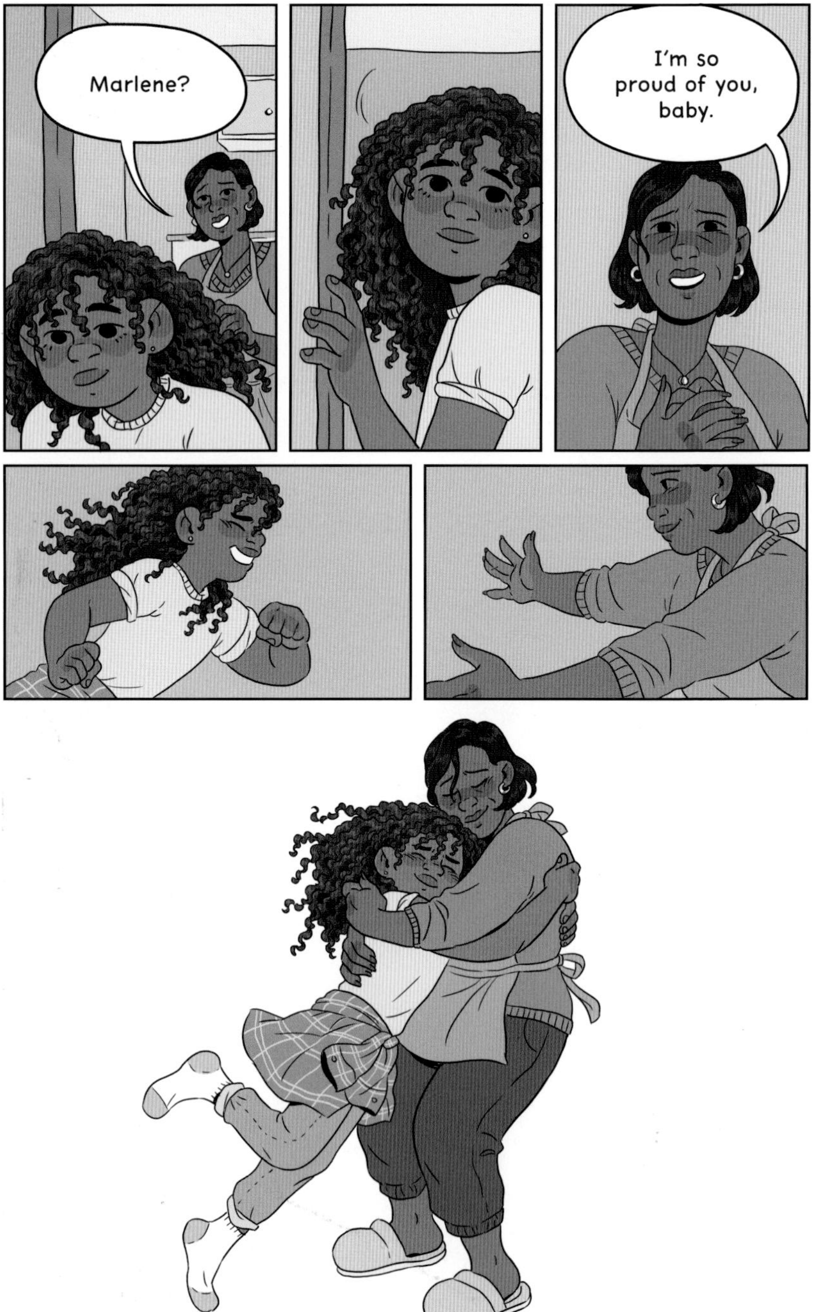
Marlene?
I'm so proud of you, baby.

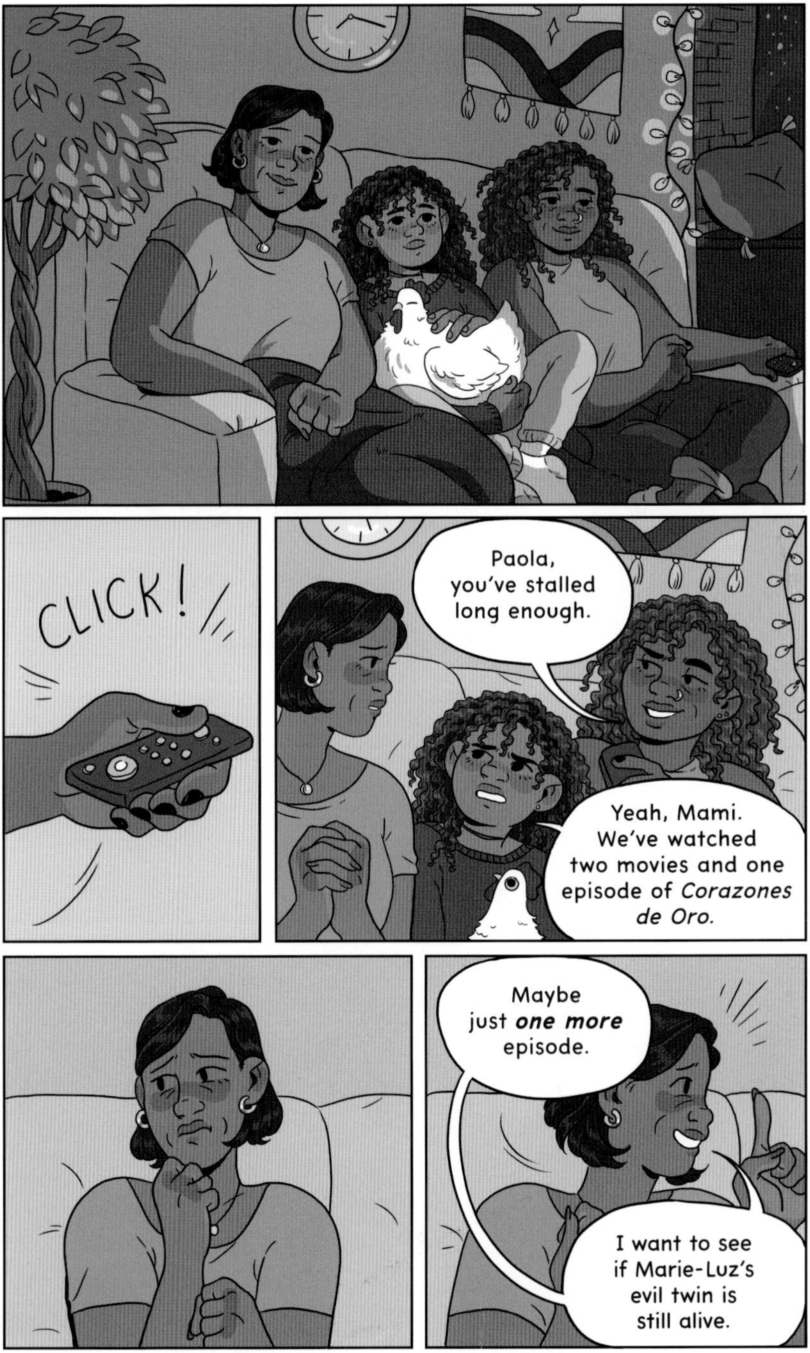
CLICK!
Paola, you've stalled long enough.
Yeah, Mami. We've watched two movies and one episode of *Corazones de Oro.*
Maybe just ***one more*** episode.
I want to see if Marie-Luz's evil twin is still alive.

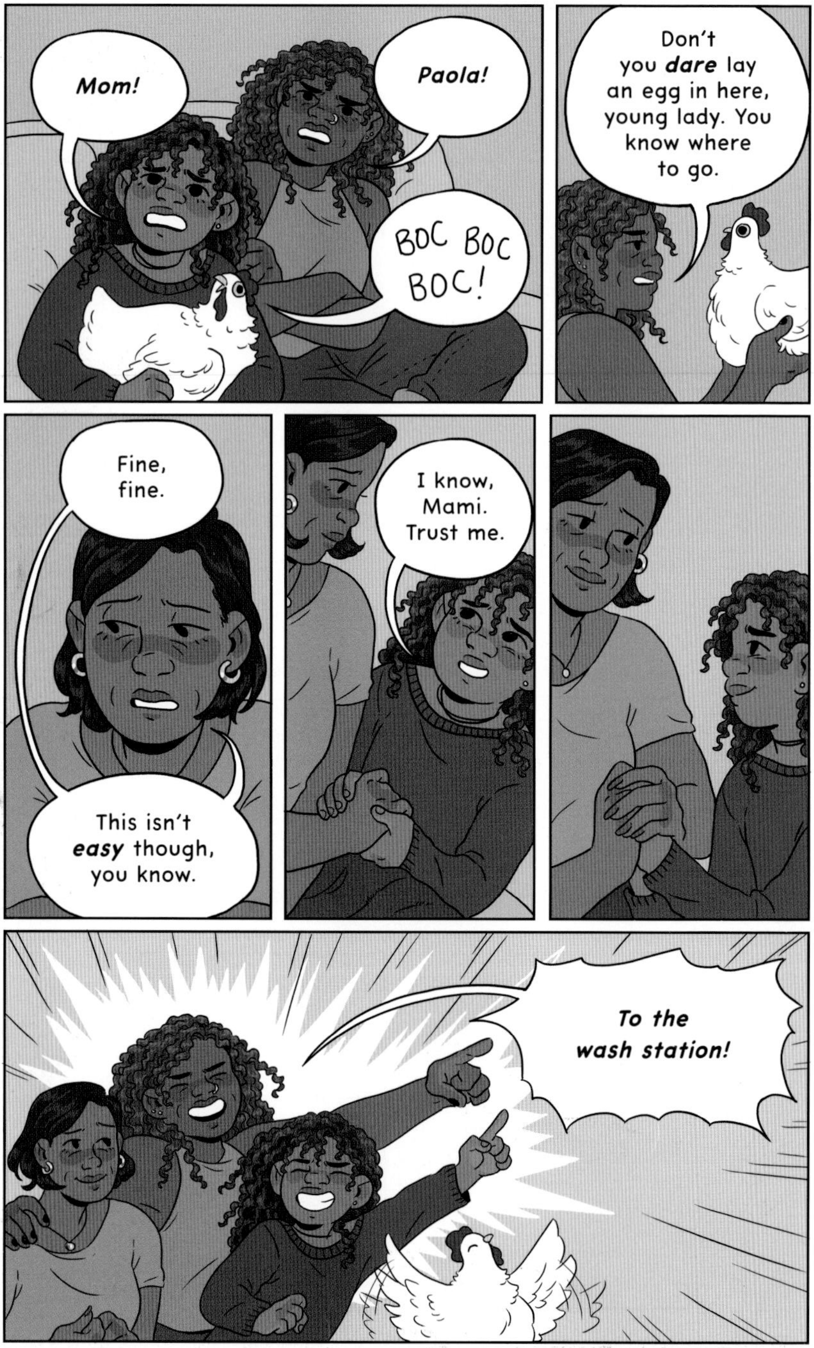
Mom!
Paola!
BOC BOC BOC!
Don't you *dare* lay an egg in here, young lady. You know where to go.
Fine, fine.
This isn't *easy* though, you know.
I know, Mami. Trust me.
To the wash station!

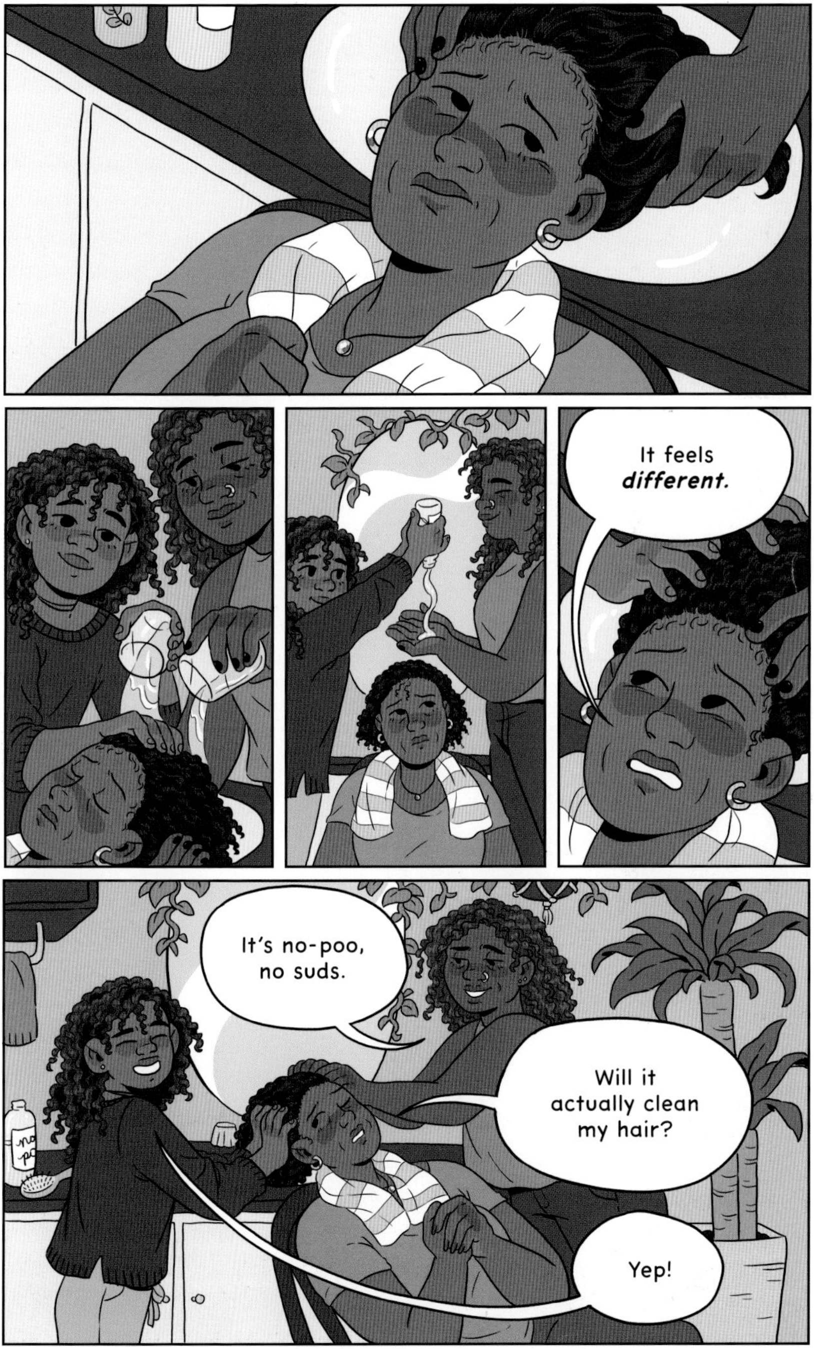
It feels ***different.***
It's no-poo, no suds.
Will it actually clean my hair?
Yep!

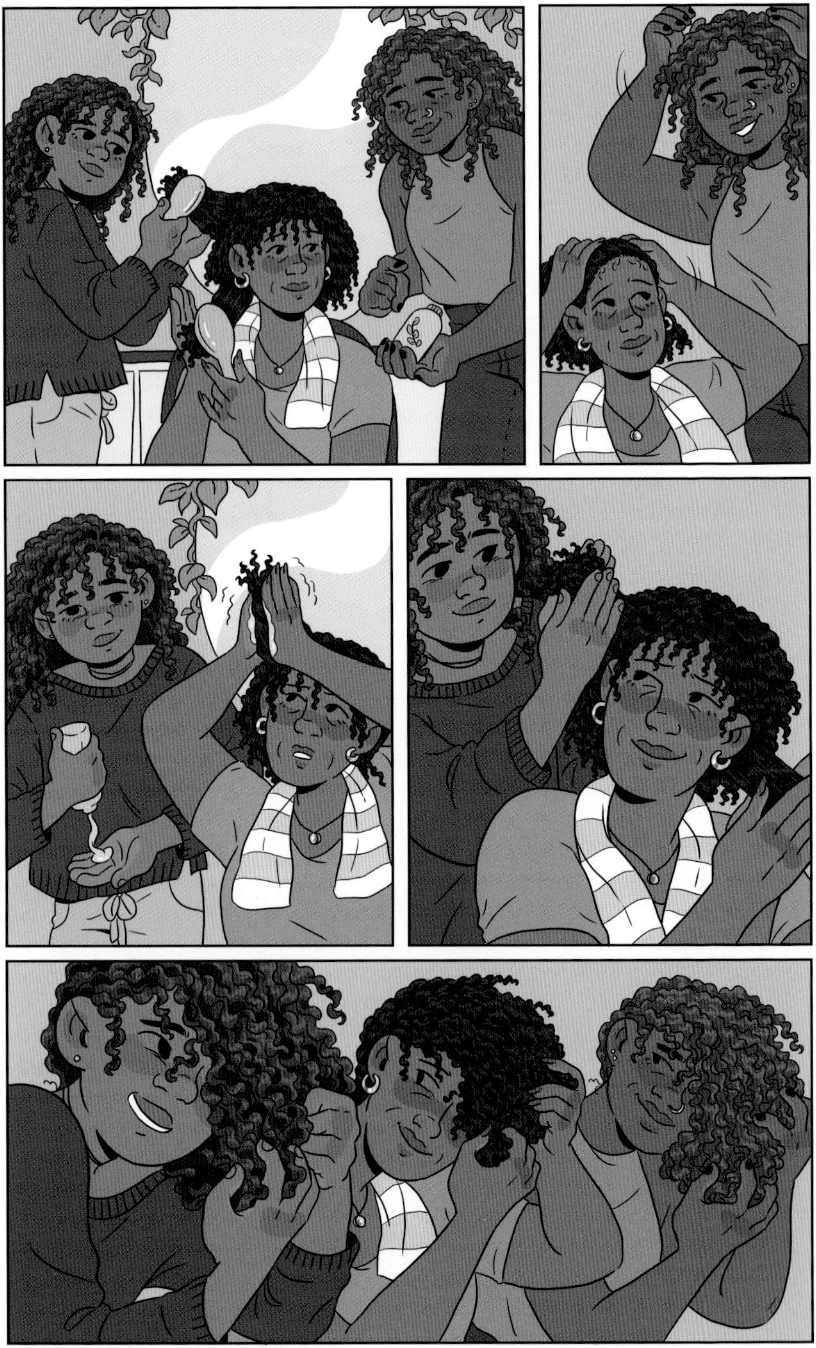

Now for the *most important* part of wash day.

PIZZA!

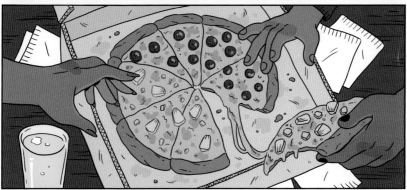

NOD NOD

I think it's time for the reveal.

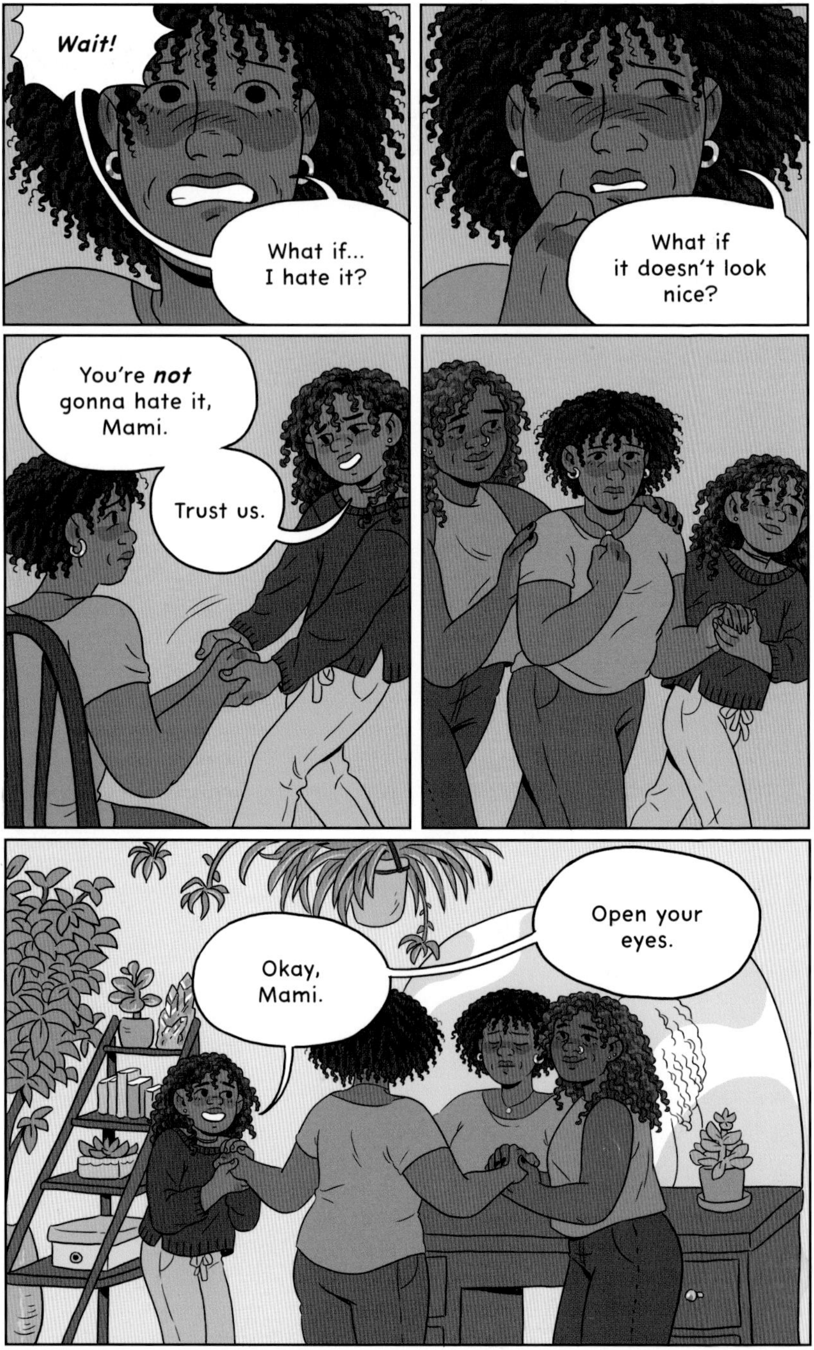
Wait!
What if...
I hate it?
What if
it doesn't look
nice?
You're *not*
gonna hate it,
Mami.
Trust us.
Okay,
Mami.
Open your
eyes.

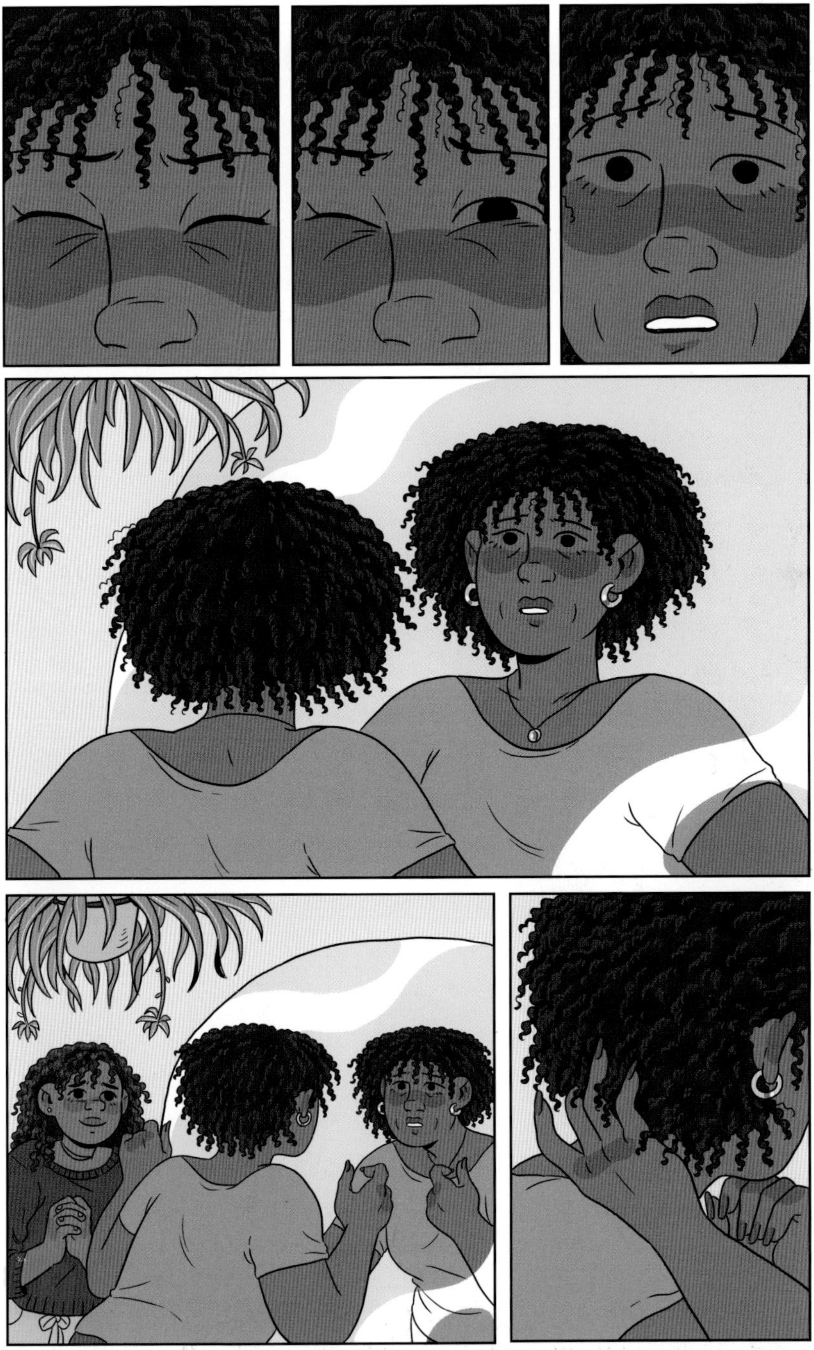

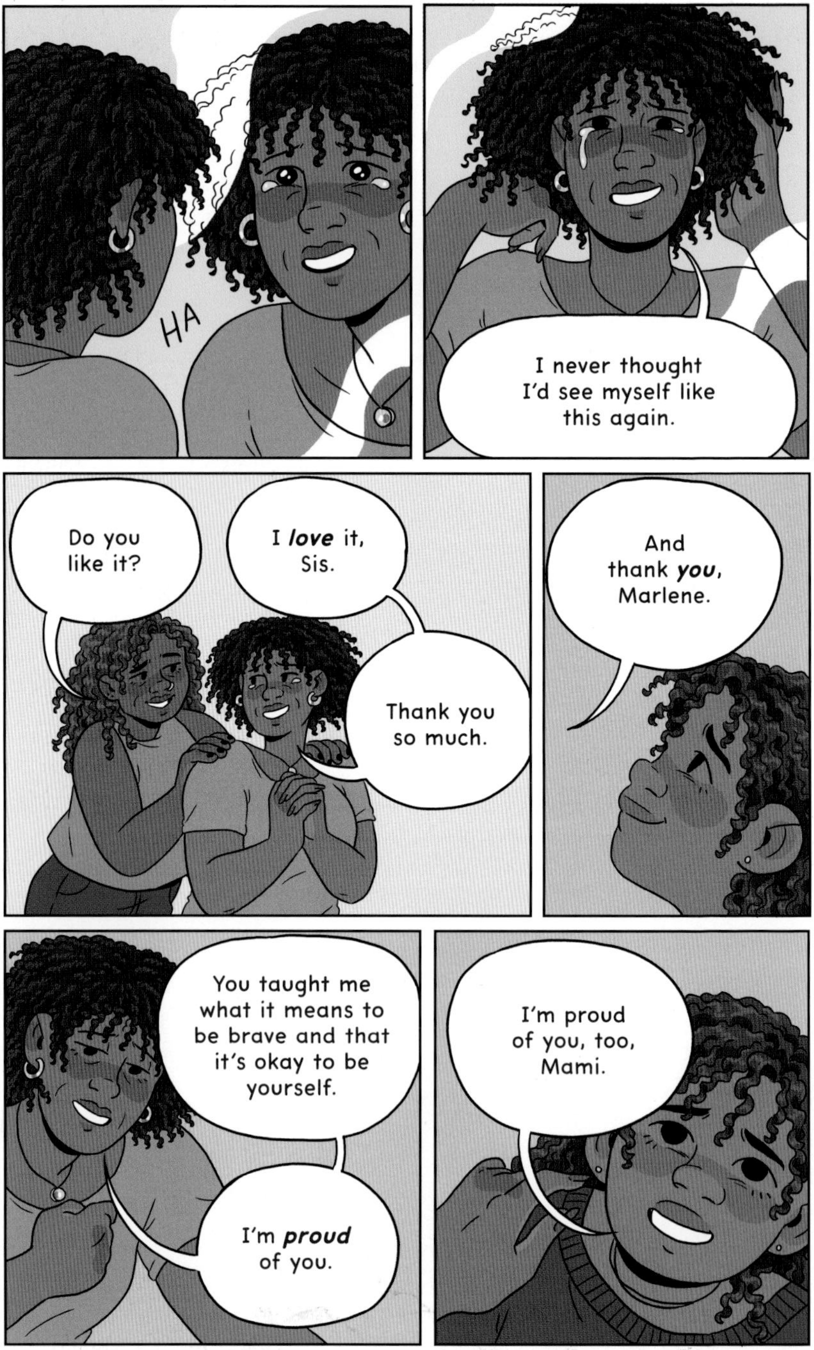
HA
I never thought I'd see myself like this again.
Do you like it?
I *love* it, Sis.
Thank you so much.
And thank *you*, Marlene.
You taught me what it means to be brave and that it's okay to be yourself.
I'm *proud* of you.
I'm proud of you, too, Mami.

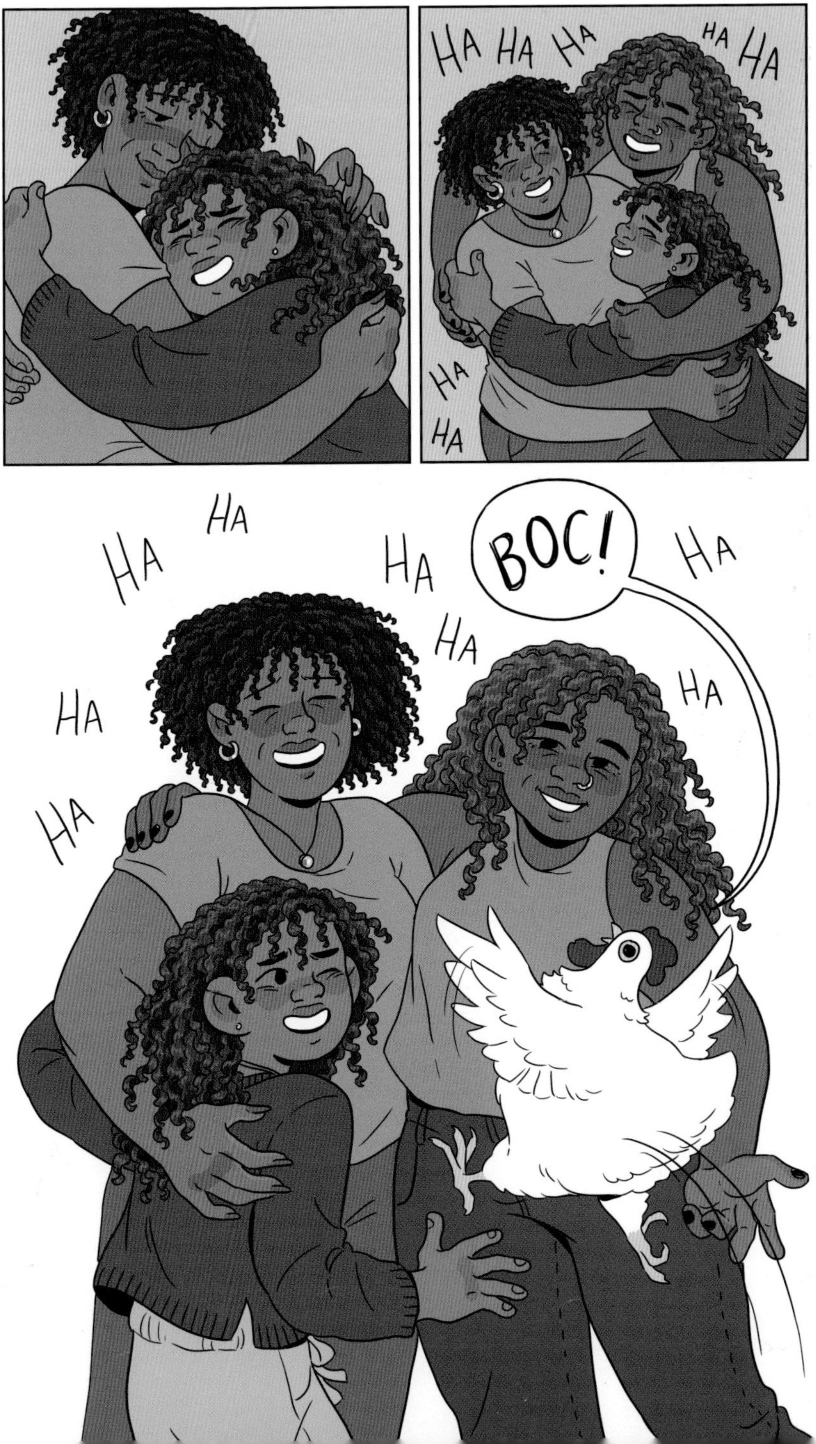
HA HA HA
HA HA
HA
HA
HA
HA
HA
BOC!
HA
HA
HA
HA
HA

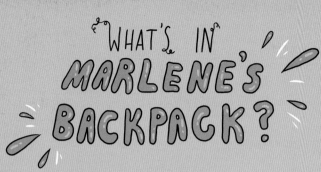

WHAT'S IN MARLENE'S BACKPACK?

Tía Ruby's homemade refreshing spray to keep my curls looking cute

History is my favorite subject aside from art!

Fave contacts: Mami, Cam, Tía Ruby

Belongs to Cam but she lets me hold it

scrunchies in my two favorite colors

ACKNOWLEDGMENTS

A giant thank-you to my editor, Kiara Valdez, for bringing this story to me and trusting me to write it. It was an amazing experience working with you, and I'm so appreciative of the thought and care you put into everything you do!

To Rose Bousamra, thank you for making my first book collab such a smooth one. You did the heavy lifting here, and I'm grateful for your work and so in awe of your talent! We make a great team <3.

To my agent, Suzie Townsend, and everyone at New Leaf, the amazing team at First Second, and the readers who have supported this book and all my writing, **thank you for everything! I wouldn't be able to do this without you.**

—Claribel

Thank you first and foremost to my incredible editor, Kiara Valdez, who reached out to me to work on this book and made my dream of illustrating a graphic novel a reality. Thank you to Claribel Ortega for trusting me with this important story, and for your wonderful storytelling that made my job feel so easy and fun. Thank you to my agent, Tamara Kawar, for cheering me on all along the way and always being there for advice and encouragement. To Kirk Benshoff, Sunny Lee, and everyone at First Second for all the hard work, guidance, and love they put in to making this book the beautiful, finished product it is today. Thank you all so much.

—Rose

FRIENDS! MUSIC! MYSTERIES!

These great graphic novels have it all!

BE PREPARED
by Vera Brosgol

Come along with Vera as she goes to summer camp for the first time ever!

STARGAZING
by Jen Wang

Meet Christine and Moon, two friends who have a lot in common but who couldn't be more different!

JUKEBOX
by Nidhi Chanani

Fly through music history with Shaheen and Tannaz in this time-traveling adventure!

CICI'S JOURNAL
by Joris Chamblain and Aurélie Neyret

Join Cici as she explores the secrets and mysteries hidden in her hometown!

Great graphic novels for every reader